VESPERS

He looked through the open rectory doorway and out into the garden where roses bloomed in medieval splendor. Such a night. On the paved garden floor, the priest lay as if dressed in mourning, wearing the black of his trade, festooned now with multiple stab and slash wounds that outrioted the roses banked against the old stone walls. A small frown creased Carella's forehead. To end this way, he thought. As rubble. On such a night. He kept looking out into the garden where the crowd of suits and blues fussed and fluttered about the corpse.

ED McBAIN

VESPERS

A NOVEL OF THE 87th PRECINCT

Mandarin

A Mandarin Paperback
VESPERS

First published in Great Britain 1990
by William Heinemann Ltd
This edition published 1991
by Mandarin Paperbacks
Michelin House, 81 Fulham Road, London SW3 6RB

Mandarin is an imprint of the Octopus Publishing Group

Copyright © 1990 by HUI Corporation

A CIP catalogue record for this title
is available from the British Library
ISBN 0 7493 0596 7

Printed and bound in Great Britain
by Cox & Wyman Ltd, Reading

This is for

ANNE EDWARDS AND STEVE CITRON

1

It was his custom to reflect upon worldly problems during evening prayers, reciting the litany by rote, the prayers a mubled counterpoint to his silent thoughts.

The Priest.

At such times, he thought of himself as The Priest. The T and the P capitalized. The Priest. As if by distancing himself in this way, by referring to himself in the third person as if he were someone not quite himself . . .

. . . a character in a novel or a movie, perhaps . . .

. . . someone outside his own body, someone exalted and remote, to be thought of with reverence as solely The Priest. By thinking of himself in this manner, by sorting out The Priest's problems as the problems of someone other than himself, Father Michael could . . .

Because, you see . . .

It was he, Father Michael, who could find comfort in the evening prayers, he who could whisper vespers for his solace as the shadows lengthened in the small, stone-paved garden behind the church rectory. But it was The *Priest* who had to cope with all the troubles that had befallen him since the middle of March, more than he quite knew how to handle, more than mere prayer could—but that was blasphemy.

Vespers was the sixth of the seven canonical hours.

At the seminary, he'd memorized the order of the prayers as a bit of rhyming doggerel:

> Matins is the morning prayer,
> At six comes Prime too soon.
> Tierce comes three hours hence
> And Sext is said at noon.

> Nones is said at three P.M.
> Nine hours past the sun.
> Vespers is the evening prayer,
> And when the day is done . . .
> Complin's said.
> And so to bed.

The Priest was thirty-two years old now.

Those soft, serene days at the seminary seemed a hundred years ago.

God, come to my assistance. Lord, make haste to help me. Glory to the Father.

The Liturgy of the Hours was as complex and as rigid as the Timetable for a space shot. Not only were there daily prayers for the seven different canonical hours, but there were special prayers as well for the Season of Advent and the Christmas Season, and for before and after Holy Week and before and after Ascension. And of course there were the Solemnities like Trinity Sunday and Corpus Christi and Sacred Heart and Christ the King, not to mention the Four-Week Psalter—just like a space shot. Deviate by a millisecond and you missed your window. The Priest wondered if such a simile was in itself blasphemy, but he heard his own voice whispering vespers into the evengloam, unperturbed.

His mind churned restlessly. He sought solutions where there seemed none. His voice said vespers by rote, but his thoughts flew helter-skelter . . . if only there were a way . . . a master plan . . . if only one could turn, for example, to the Proper of Saints, for example, to the twenty-first day of January, let's say, the Saint Day of St. Agnes, virgin and martyr, and find there the morning prayer . . . *My Lord Jesus Christ has espoused me with his ring; he has crowned me like a bride* . . . and then the directions to recite the psalms and canticle from Sunday, Week 1, on page 556, all so simple . . . *O God, you are my God, for you I long* . . . but, no, there was no such mortal scheme, you took your problems as they came, you tried to sort them out as you walked over stones laid a century and more ago in a part of the city now gone to ruin . . .

. . . the hateful threats in the rectory . . .

. . . this is blackmail, blackmail . . .

. . . the pounding at the central portal doors . . .

. . . the black boy running into the church, seeking sanctuary, Hey man, *hep* me, they goan *kill* me!

Blood running down his face.

. . . gone to ruin, all to ruin.

Graffiti on the massive stones of the church, barbarians on ponies storming the gates. Almost six weeks since all of that—today was the twenty-fourth of May, the day of Ascension—all that time, almost six weeks, and he was still on his knees to . . .

I came forth from the Father and have come into the world; now I leave the world to return to the father, alleluia!

There was the sweet scent of roses on the evening air.

The roses were his pleasure and his vice, he tended them the way he tended the Lord's flock.

Something still and silent about tonight. Well, a Thursday. The name itself. Something dusky about the name, Thursday, as soft and silken as sunset. Thursday.

God is rich in mercy; because of his great love for us . . .

. . . I'll tell, I'll tell everything . . .

The boy's blood dripping on the marble floor before the altar.

The vengeful cries echoing inside the church.

Still on his knees.

. . . by this favor are you saved. Both with and in Christ Jesus, he raised us up and gave us a place in the heavens.

Beyond the high stone walls of the garden, The Priest could see the sooted upper stories of the buildings across the street, and yet above those, beyond those, the sunset-streaked springtime sky. The aroma of the roses was overpowering. As he moved past the big maple set exactly at the center of the garden, a stone bench circling it, he felt a sudden suffusion of love . . . for the roses, for the glorious sunset, for the power of the words that soared silently in his prayers, *God our Father, make us joyful in the ascension of your Son Jesus Christ, may we follow him into the new creation, for his ascension is our glory and our hope. We ask—*

—and noticed all at once that the gate in the wall was open.

Standing wide.

The setting sun striking it so that it cast a long arched shadow that reached almost to the maple itself.

He had thought . . .

Or surely, Martha would have . . .

He moved swiftly to the gate, painted a bilious green by a taste-less long-ago priest, and yet again recently with red graffiti on the side facing the street. The gate was wooden and some four inches thick, arched at its highest point a good foot above the stone walls on either side of it, an architectural touch that further displeased The Priest's meticulous eye. The narrow golden path of sun on the ground grew narrower yet as he swung the gate closed on its old wrought-iron hinges . . . narrower . . . narrower . . . and then was gone entirely.

Alleluia, come let us worship Christ the Lord as he ascends into heaven, alleluia!

The lock on the gate was thoroughly modern.

He turned the thumb bolt.

There was a solid, satisfying click.

Give glory to the King of kings, sing praise to God, alleluia!

His head bent, he turned and was walking back toward the rectory, past the shadow-shrouded maple, when the knife . . .

He felt only searing pain at first.

Did not realize until the second slashing blow. . .

Knew then that he'd been stabbed . . .

Turned . . .

Was *starting* to turn . . .

And felt the knife entering again, lower this time, in the small of the back . . .

Oh dear God . . .

And again, and again, and again in savage fury. . .

Oh Jesus, oh Jesus Christ . . .

As complete darkness claimed the garden.

Not a day went by without Willis expecting someone to find out about her. The open house tonight was on the twelfth floor of a renovated building about to go co-op. There were a great many strangers here, and strangers were dangerous. Strangers asked questions. What do you do, Mr. Willis? And you, Miss Hollis? Willis and Hollis, they sounded like a law firm. Or perhaps a dance team. And now, ladies and gentlemen, returning from their recently completed tour of the glittering capitals of Europe, we bring you . . . *Willis* . . . and *Hollis*!

The questions about himself were merely annoying; he wondered why everyone in America had to know immediately what everyone else in America *did*. He was sometimes tempted to say he sold crack to innocent schoolchildren. He wondered what sort of response *that* would get. Tell them you're a cop, they looked at you with raised eyebrows. Oh, really? Cut the crap and tell us what you *really* do. Really, I swear to God, I'm a cop, Detective/Third Grade Harold O. Willis, that's me, I swear. Looking you over. Thinking you're too short to be a cop, a detective, no less, and ugly besides with your curly black hair and wet brown eyes, let me see your badge. Show them the potsy. My, my, I never met a real live police detective before, do you work in one of those dreadful precincts we're always reading about, are you carrying a gun, have you ever killed anyone? The questions. Annoying, but not dangerous.

The questions they asked Marilyn were dangerous.

Because there was so much to hide.

Oh, not the fact that they were living together, this was already the Nineties, man, nobody even *thought* about such things anymore. You got married by choice, and if you chose not to, then you simply lived together. Had children together, if you could, did whatever you wanted, this was the Nineties. And perhaps...in such a climate of acceptance...you could even...well, perhaps...but it was extremely unlikely. Well, who the hell knew? Maybe they could, after all, come right out and say, *Look*, people, Marilyn used to be a hooker.

The raised eyebrows again.

Oh, really? Cut the crap and tell us what she *really* did.

No, really, that's what she really did, I swear to God, she used to be a hooker. She did it for a year or so in Houston, and ended up in a Mexican prison on a dope charge, and then picked up the trade again in Buenos Aires where she worked the streets for five years, more or less. Really. That's what she used to do.

But who would believe it?

Because, you know, you looked at Marilyn, you saw this woman who'd be only twenty-six in August, slender and tall, with long blonde hair and cornflower blue eyes and a complexion as flawlessly pale as a dipper of milk, and you thought No, not a hooker. You didn't survive being a hooker. You didn't come off six years of peddling tail—not to mention the time in that Mexican hellhole—and look like this. You just didn't. Unless you were Marilyn. Then you did. Marilyn was a survivor.

She was also a murderess.

That was the thing of it.

You opened the *hooker* can of peas, and everything else came spilling out.

The cocktail party was in a twelfth-floor corner apartment, what the real estate lady kept calling the penthouse apartment, although Willis didn't think it looked luxurious enough to warrant such a lofty title. He had been in court all day long and had come up here against his better judgment, at the invitation of Bob O'Brien who said there'd be good booze and plenty to eat and besides neither of them would run the risk of getting shot, a distinct possibility if ever you were partnered with a hard-luck cop like O'Brien.

He'd called Marilyn to tell her that O'Brien's girlfriend Maizie— who turned out to be as ditsy as her name—would be coming along, and maybe the four of them could go out to dinner later, and Marilyn had said, sure, why not? So here they were with the sun just gone, listening to a real estate lady pitching renovated apartments to supposedly interested prospects like O'Brien who, Willis discovered for the first time tonight, planned to marry Maizie in the not-too-distant future, lots of luck, pal.

It was Maizie who looked like a hooker.

She wasn't. She worked as a clerk in the D.A.'s office.

But she was wearing a fuzzy pink sweater slashed in a V over recklessly endangered breasts, and a tight shiny black skirt that looked like a thin coating of crude oil, and high-heeled, ankle-strapped black patent leather pumps, a hooker altogether, except that she had a tiny little girl's voice and she kept talking about having gone to high school at Mother Mary Magdalene or some such in Calm's Point.

The real estate lady was telling Willis that the penthouse apartment, the one they were standing in this very moment, was going for only three-fifty negotiable, at a fixed eight-and-a-quarter percent mortgage with no points and no closing fees. Willis wondered if he should tell her that he was presently living in a town house uptown that had cost Marilyn seven hundred and fifty thousand dollars. He wondered if there'd be any former hookers living in this fine renovated building.

In her high, piping voice, Maizie was telling someone that a nun named Sister Letitia used to hit her on her hands with a ruler.

O'Brien was looking as if he expected to get shot at any moment.

Marilyn wondered out loud how such a reasonable mortgage rate could be offered in this day and age.

The real estate lady told her that the sponsor was a bank in Minnesota, which meant nothing at all to Willis.

Then she said, "What do *you* do, Mrs. Willis?"

"It's Hollis," Marilyn said.

"I thought . . ." She turned to Willis. "Didn't you say your name
was Willis?"

"Yes, but mine is Hollis," Marilyn said. "We're not married."

"Oh."

"The names *are* similar, though," Willis explained helpfully.

"And are you in police work, too, Miss Hollis?"

"No, I'm a student," Marilyn said.

Which was the truth.

"My education was interrupted," she said.

And did not amplify.

"What are you studying?"

All smiles, all solicitous interest; these were potential customers.

"Well, eventually, I want to be a social worker," Marilyn said.
"But right now, I'm just going for my bachelor's."

All true.

"*I* wanted to be a doctor," the real estate lady said, and looked at
Willis. "But I got married instead," she added, as if blaming him for
her misfortune.

Willis smiled apologetically. Then he turned to O'Brien and said,
"Bob, if you plan on staying a while longer, maybe me and Marilyn'll
just run along, okay?"

O'Brien seemed to be enjoying the warm white wine and cold
canapés.

"See you tomorrow," he said.

"Nice to meet you," Maizie said to Marilyn.

The church garden was crowded now with two ambulance atten-
dants, three technicians from the Mobile Crime Unit, an assistant
medical examiner, two detectives from Homicide, a woman from the
Photo Unit, and a uniformed Deputy Inspector from Headquarters.

The D.I. was here because the police department in this city was largely Irish-Catholic, and the victim was a priest.

Detective Stephen Louis Carella looked out at the assembled law enforcement officers, and tried to remember the last time he'd been inside a church. His sister's wedding, wasn't it? He was inside a church now. But not to pray. Well, not even *technically* inside a church, although the rectory was *connected* to the church via a wood-paneled corridor that led into the sacristy and then the old stone building itself.

He looked through the open rectory doorway and out into the garden where roses bloomed in medieval splendor. Such a night. On the paved garden floor, the priest lay as if dressed in mourning, wearing the black of his trade, festooned now with multiple stab and slash wounds that outrioted the roses banked against the old stone walls. A small frown creased Carella's forehead. To end this way, he thought. As rubble. On such a night. He kept looking out into the garden where the crowd of suits and blues fussed and fluttered about the corpse.

Carella gave the impression—even standing motionless with his hands in his pockets—of a trained athlete, someone whose tall, slender body could respond gracefully and effortlessly to whatever demands were placed upon it. His appearance was a lie. Everybody forgot that middle age was really thirtysomething. Ask a man in his mid-to-late thirties if he was middle-aged, and he'd say Don't be ridiculous. But then take your ten-year-old son out back to the garage and try to play one-on-one basketball with him. There was a look of pain on Carella's face now; perhaps because he had a splitting headache, or perhaps because he always reacted in something close to pain when he saw the stark results of brutal violence. The pain seemed to draw his dark, slanting eyes even further downward, giving them a squinched, exaggerated, Oriental look. Turn a group photograph upside down, and you could always pick out Carella by the slanting eyes—the exact opposite of almost anyone else in the picture.

"Steve?"

He turned from the open doorway.

Cotton Hawes was leading the housekeeper back in.

Her name was Martha Hennessy, and she'd become ill not five minutes ago. That is to say, she'd thrown up. Carella had asked one of the ambulance crew to take her outside, see what he could do for her. She was back now, the smell of her vomit still lingering in the rectory, battling for supremacy over the aroma of roses wafting in from outside. She seemed all right now. A bit pale, but Carella realized this was her natural coloration. Bright red hair, white skin, the kind of woman who would turn lobster red in the sun. Green eyes. County Roscommon all over her. Fifty-five years old or thereabouts, wearing a simple blue dress and sensible low-heeled shoes. She'd told them earlier that she'd found Father Michael in the garden as she'd come out to fetch him for dinner. That was at a little after seven tonight, fifteen minutes before she'd starting throwing up. It was now seven-forty; the police had been here for ten minutes.

"I sent one of the blues out for coffee," Hawes said. "Mrs. Hennessy said she might like some coffee."

"Actually," she said, "I asked Mr. Hawes if I could *make* some coffee. We've got a perfectly good stove . . ."

"Yes, but . . ."

"Yes," Carella said, almost simultaneously, "but the technicians will be working in there."

"That's what Mr. Hawes told me. But I don't see why I can't make my own coffee. I don't see why we have to send *out* for coffee."

Hawes looked at her.

He had explained to her, twice, that this entire *place* was a crime scene. That the killer might have been anywhere inside the church or the rectory before the murder. That the killer might even have been in the priest's small office, where one of the file cabinet drawers was open and papers presumably removed from that drawer were strewn all over the floor. Now the woman was questioning, for the *third* time, why she could not use the priest's kitchen—where, among other utensils, there were a great many knives. He knew he had adequately explained *why* she could not use the kitchen or anything *in* the kitchen. So how had he failed to communicate?

He stood in redheaded perplexity, a six-foot-two-inch, hundred-and-ninety-pound, solidly built man who dwarfed the Hennessy woman, searching for something to say that would clarify why they did not want her using the kitchen. There was an unruly white streak of hair over his left temple, a souvenir from a slashing years ago while he was investigating a burglary. It gave his haircut a somewhat fearsome Bride of Frankenstein look, which—when coupled with the consternation on his face—made it appear as if he might throttle the little housekeeper within the next several seconds, a premise entirely distant from the truth. Side by side, the two redheads stood, one huge and seemingly menacing, the other tiny and possibly confused, a blazing torch and a glowing ember.

Carella looked at both of them, not knowing Hawes had already explained the sanctity of the kitchen to her—twice—not knowing why Hawes was looking at her so peculiarly, and beginning to feel a bit stupid for not understanding what the hell was going on. Outside in the garden, the priest lay on blood-stained stones, his blood still seeping from the tattered wounds in his back. It was such a lovely night.

Getting away from the matter of the goddamn kitchen, Hawes said, "When did you last see Father Birney alive?"

"Father Michael," she said.

"Well, his name is Michael *Birney,* isn't it?" Hawes said.

"Yes," Mrs. Hennessy said, "but you can have a priest named . . . well, take Father O'Neill as used to be the pastor here. *His* name was Ralph O'Neill, but everybody called him Father O'Neill. Whereas Father Michael's name is Michael Birney, but everyone calls *him* Father *Michael.* That's the mystery of it."

"Yes, that's the great mystery of it," Hawes agreed.

"When *did* you last see him alive?" Carella asked gently. "Father Michael, that is."

Slow and easy, he told himself. If she's truly a stupid woman, getting angry isn't going to help either her *or* the situation. If she's just scared, then hold her hand. There's a dead man outside in the garden.

"When you last saw him alive," he prompted. "The time. What time was it?"

"A bit past seven," she said. "When I come to fetch him for dinner."

"Yes," Carella said, "but he was already dead by then, isn't that what you said?"

"Yes, God ha'mercy," she said, and hastily made the sign of the cross.

"When did you last see him *alive*? Before that."

"When Krissie was leaving," she said.

"Krissie?"

"Yes."

"Who's Krissie?"

"His secretary."

"And she left at what time?"

"Five. She leaves at five."

"And she left at five tonight?"

"Yes."

"And that's the last time you saw Father Michael alive?"

"Yes, when Krissie was leaving. He was saying good night to her."

"Where was this, Mrs. Hennessy?"

"In his study. I went in to clear the tea things . . . he takes tea in the afternoon, after he says his three o'clock prayers. Krissie was just going out the door, he was sayin' I'll see you in the morning."

"Krissie who?" Hawes asked.

"Krissie who's his secretary," Mrs. Hennessy said.

"Yes, but what's her full name?"

"Kristin."

"And her last name?"

"Lund. Kristin Lund."

"Does she work here full time?"

"No, only Tuesdays and Thursdays. Twice a week."

"And you? How often do . . .?"

"Who gets the coffee?" a uniformed cop asked.

"Here's your coffee, Mrs. Hennessy," Hawes said, and took the cardboard container from him.

"Thank you," she said, and then, quite suddenly, "It was the Devil who done it."

The only problem was that Willis loved her to death.

It bothered him day and night that he loved a woman who'd killed someone. A pimp, yes—a fucking *miserable* pimp, as a matter of fact—but a human being, nonetheless, if any pimp could be considered human. He had never met a pimp he'd liked, but for that matter, he'd never met a hooker with a heart of gold, either. Marilyn was no longer a hooker when he'd met her, so she didn't count.

She *had* been a hooker, however, when she'd killed Alberto Hidalgo, a Buenos Aires pimp who by then had been living off the proceeds of prostitution for almost fifty years. In addition to Marilyn, there'd been six other whores in his stable. He was hated by each and every one of them, but by none so fiercely as Marilyn herself, whom he'd casually subjected first to an abortion and next to a hysterectomy performed by one and the same back-alley butcher.

So here was Willis—a police officer sworn to protect and enforce the laws of the city, state, and nation—in love with a former hooker, a confessed murderess, and an admitted thief, not necessarily in that order. Only two other people in this entire city knew that Marilyn Hollis had once been a prostitute: Lieutenant Peter Byrnes and Detective Steve Carella. Willis knew that the secret was safe with either of them. But neither of them knew that she was also a killer and a thief. Willis alone had heard *that* little confession, he alone was the one to whom she'd . . .

"*I did. I killed him.*"

"*I don't want to hear it. Please. I don't want to hear it.*"

"*I thought you wanted the truth!*"

"*I'm a cop! If you killed a man . . .*"

"I didn't kill a man, I killed a monster! He ripped out my insides, I can't have babies, do you understand that? He stole my . . ."

"Please, please, please, Marilyn . . ."

"I'd kill him again. In a minute."

She'd used cyanide. Hardly the act of someone with a heart of gold. Cyanide. For rats.

And then . . .

"I went into his bedroom and searched for the combination to the safe because that was where my passport had to be. I found the combination. I opened the safe. My passport was in it. And close to two million dollars in Argentine money."

On the night she'd confessed all this to Willis, a night that now seemed so very long ago, she'd asked, "So what now? Do you turn me in?"

He had not known what to say.

He was a cop.

He loved her.

"Do they know you killed him?" he'd asked.

"Who? The Argentine cops? Why would they even *give* a damn about a dead pimp? But, yes, I'm the only one who split from the stable, yes, and the safe was open, and a lot of bread was gone, so yes, they probably figured I was the perpetrator, is that the word you use?"

"Is there a warrant out for your arrest?"

"I don't know."

And there had been a silence.

"So what are you going to do?" she'd asked. "Phone Argentina? Ask them if there's a warrant out on Mary Ann Hollis, a person I don't even *know* anymore? *What,* Hal? For Christ's sake, I love you, I want to live with you forever, I love you, Jesus, I *love* you, what are you going to *do?*"

"I don't know," he'd said.

He was still a cop.

And he still loved her.

But every time that telephone rang, he broke out in a cold sweat, hoping it would not be some police inspector in Buenos Aires, telling him they had traced a murder to the city here and were planning to extradite a woman named Marilyn Hollis.

It was easy to forget your fears on a night like tonight.

It was easy to forget that some problems might never go away.

At a little past ten o'clock, the city was ablaze with light. For all Willis knew, this could have been springtime in Paris: he'd never been there. But it felt like Paris, and it most certainly felt like spring, the balmiest spring he could ever remember. As he and Marilyn came out of the restaurant, a soft, fragrant breeze wafted in off Grover Park. Both of them smiled. He hailed a passing taxi and told the driver to take the park road uptown. They were still smiling. The windows were down. They held hands like teenagers.

Harborside Lane, where Marilyn owned the town house, was within the confines of the 87th Precinct, not quite as desirable as Silvermine Oval, but a very good neighborhood anyway—at least when one considered the *rest* of the precinct territory. Number 1211 was in a row of brownstones adorned with inaccessible spray-can scribblings. A wrought-iron gate to the right of the building guarded the entrance to a driveway that led to a garage set some fifty feet back from the pavement; the gate was padlocked. There were wrought-iron grilles on the ground-floor and first-floor windows, and razor wire on the roof overhanging the third floor. There were now two names in the directory set beside the bell button: M. Hollis and H. Willis.

Willis paid the driver and tipped him extravagantly; it was that kind of night. Marilyn was unlocking the front door as the taxi pulled away from the curb. It turned the corner and vanished from sight, the sound of its engine fading, fading, and then disappearing entirely. For an instant, the street, the small park across the way, were utterly still. Willis took a deep breath and looked up at the sky. Stars blinked overhead. A *Pinocchio* night. He expected Jiminy Cricket to come hopping up the sidewalk.

"Hal?"

He turned.

"Aren't you coming in?"

"It's so beautiful," he said.

He would later remember that these were the last words he'd said before the telephone rang. The last words before the terror started.

He went into the house and closed and locked the door behind him. The entry foyer and the living room beyond were paneled in mahogany. Old thick wooden beams crossed the ceiling. Marilyn began unbuttoning her blouse as she climbed the walnut-banistered staircase to the second story. Willis was crossing the living room, yanking down his tie and unbuttoning the top button of his shirt, when the telephone rang.

He looked automatically at his watch, walked to the phone on the dropleaf desk, and picked up the receiver.

"Hello?" he said.

There was a slight hesitation.

Then a man's voice said, *"Perdóneme, señor."*

And then there was an empty click.

The altar was naked.

The altar was a twenty-seven-year-old woman who lay on her back on an elevated platform shaped as a trapezoid and covered with black velvet. Her head was at the narrow end of the trapezoid, her long blonde hair cushioned on a pillow covered with black silk. White against black, she lay with her legs widespread and dangling over the wide end of the platform, her arms at her sides, her eyes closed.

Lying between her naked breasts was a thick silver disc on a heavy silver chain, sculpted in relief with the Sacred Sign of Baphomet, the Black Goat, whose image hung on the wall behind her as well, its horns, ears, face and beard contained within the center and five points of an inverted pentagram:

Smoke from the torches illuminating this infernal symbol swirled upward toward the arched ceiling of the abandoned church. Smoke from the candles clutched in the hands of the woman who was the altar drifted up toward old wooden beams that long ago had crossed over an altar made not of flesh but of marble.

The mass had started at the stroke of midnight.

Now, at a little past one A.M., the priest stood between the spread legs of the altar, facing the celebrants, his back to the woman. He was wearing a black cotton robe embroidered in richer black silk with pine cones that formed a phallic pattern. The robe was slit to the waist on either side, revealing the priest's muscular legs and thighs.

The celebrants were here to mark the day of the Expulsion. Some twenty minutes earlier, during the Canon segment, they had each and separately partaken of the contents of a silver chalice offered by the priest. The chalice had tonight contained not the usual dark red wine symbolic of the blood of Christ, but something called Ecstasy, a hallucinogenic drug that was a potent mix of mescaline and speed. A capsule of Ecstasy sold for twenty dollars. There were at least two hundred people here tonight, most of them young, and each and every one of them had swallowed a cap of X immediately after the conclusion of the third segment of the mass.

Kissing the altar/woman full on her genitals, the priest had recited the timeless words, "Satan is Lord of the Temple, Lord of the World, he bringeth to me joyous youth, all praise Satan, all hail Satan!" and the celebrants had responded "All hail Satan!" and the girl acolyte had come to the altar and raised her garments to the priest, revealing herself naked beneath them. The boy acolyte had held a silver container to catch her urine, and the priest had dipped a phallus-shaped aspergill into the container and sprinkled the celebrants with the little girl's urine, *If thou hast thirst, then let thee come to the Lord Satan. If thou wouldst partake of the water of life, the Infernal Lord doth offer it.* And then he had passed among them with the chalice containing the Ecstasy capsules, and they had washed the caps down with thick red wine offered by the deacon and one of the subdeacons, sixty-one people times twenty bucks a pop came to twelve hundred and change.

The girl acolyte stood to the right of the altar now.

She was a darling little blonde girl, all of eight years old, whose mother was tonight serving as the altar. She was dressed entirely in black, as was her father who was sitting among the other stoned celebrants and feeling enormously proud of the separate important roles his wife and daughter were playing in tonight's ritual. The boy acolyte was only seven. He was standing to the left of the altar/ woman, staring a bit wide-eyed at the tufted blonde patch above the joining of her legs. The priest was about to embark upon the fifth and final segment of the mass, called the Repudiation, especially significant tonight in that this twenty-fourth day of May was what the Christians had named the Ascension, upon which day the body of Jesus Christ was supposed to have risen to Heaven, but which here within these walls was being celebrated as the *expulsion* of Jesus from Hell.

The priest had been supplied with a host consecrated at a church in another part of the city, stolen this morning at mass by a woman worshipper whose mouth had first been coated with alum to protect the wafer from her own saliva. He held the wafer between the thumb and forefinger of his left hand now, made a deep, mocking bow over it, and said, "I show you the body of Jesus Christ, the Forgotten One, pretender to the throne of Satan, monarch to slaves, confounder of minions stumbling to perdition."

He turned to face the altar/woman, his back to the celebrants now, his right hand raised in the sign of the horns, his left hand holding the wafer aloft to the goat symbol on the wall.

"All hail Satan!" he said.

"Hail, Satan!" the celebrants responded.

"All praise these splendid breasts that gave suck to the body of Jesus," he said mockingly, and touched the wafer first to the woman's right nipple and then to her left nipple. Kneeling between her legs, he rested the hand with the wafer on her mons veneris, and said, again mockingly, "Blessed be the generous womb that begat the body of Jesus," and passed the host over the lips of her vagina.

Now began the Repudiation in earnest.

Lifting the hems of his robe, fastening them into the black silken cord at his waist, he wet the fingers of his right hand and then touched them to the head of his now-erect penis. "Jesus Christ, messenger of doom, I offer you to worm and maggot..." he said, touching the wafer to the moistened head of his penis where it clung in desecration, moving closer to the widespread legs of the altar, the boy acolyte watching excited and amazed, "thrust you down with scorpion and snake..." approaching the altar where she waited open and spread for him, "show you storm and savage strife, curse you with famine and filth, burn you in eternal fire, cause you everlasting death to the end of time unending, and reward you with the enduring fury of our Lord, Satan!"

"Hail, Satan!" the celebrants chanted. "All hail Satan!"

Hurling himself onto the altar, thrusting himself into the woman, wafer and penis entering her, the priest said, "I descend anew, and ascend forever, saith the Infernal Lord. My flesh is your flesh..."

"My flesh is thy flesh," the woman murmured.

"My flesh is our flesh..."

"Thy flesh is our flesh," the celebrants intoned.

"In flesh, let us find the glory of Satan!"

"In flesh, find the glory of Satan!"

"In lust, let us know the goodness of Satan!"

"In lust, know the goodness of Satan!"

"In flesh and in lust, let us all praise Satan!"

"In flesh and in lust, we praise Satan's name!"

"Blessed be Satan!"

"Blessed be Satan!"

"All hail Satan!"

"Hail, Satan!"

This was four blocks away from where the police had chalked Father Michael's outline onto the blood-stained stones in the small church garden.

2

The two men were speaking entirely in Spanish.

One of them was exceedingly handsome. Tall and slender, with black hair combed straight back from a pronounced widow's peak, he looked a lot like Rudolph Valentino. He did not know who Rudolph Valentino *was,* and so he wasn't flattered when people told him he looked like Rudolph Valentino. But he guessed that Rudolph Valentino had to be *some* handsome *hombre* because if there was one thing Ramon Castaneda knew for certain it was that he himself was handsome as sin.

The man sitting with him was named Carlos Ortega and he was exceptionally ugly. He had crooked teeth and a nose that had been broken often in street fights hither and yon, and a scar that ran through his right eyebrow and partially closed his right eye, and moreover he was bald and hulking and he resembled an escaped inmate from a hospital for the criminally insane, which he was not. But such was the vanity of men that he, too, thought he was handsome. In fact, many women had told him he was handsome. He believed them, even if all of them were hookers.

On this twenty-fifth day of May, another beautiful spring morning, the two men sat in a coffee shop close to their hotel, discussing why they were here in the city. It was still early in the morning, a little past seven; the place was full of people catching quick breakfasts before going to work. The two men were in no hurry. The handsome one, Ramon, had ordered steak and eggs for breakfast. Carlos, the ugly one who only thought he was handsome, had ordered pancakes and sausage. They sat sipping their coffee, waiting for the food to come, chatting idly.

Ramon said in Spanish that he thought it was a pity a man had answered the telephone last night. A man might complicate matters.

Carlos said in Spanish that he could break every fucking bone in the man's body, whoever he was, so what difference did it make if she was living with a man, a woman, or a chihuahua?

"*If* she's the right woman," Ramon said.

"Well, yes, we have to make sure she's the right woman," Carlos said.

"Which won't be easy without a photograph."

"But we have her description from the German whore."

The German whore was a buxom blonde who claimed she'd been openly abducted in Munich. Her name was Constantia. While they waited for their food, the two men discussed whether or not she was reliable. Ramon mentioned that she'd been a drug addict for many years. Carlos said he knew many people who were drug addicts who nonetheless made very reliable witnesses. They got sidetracked wondering if she was a good lay. When their food came, they fell silent for a while, Ramon eating with the exquisite table manners of a man who knew he was devastatingly handsome, Carlos eating like a brute who believed that handsome men like himself could eat any fucking way they *wanted* to.

"You think she could be so stupid?" Ramon asked.

"How do you mean?"

"To put her name in the book?"

"It says only M. Hollis," Carlos said. "Also, there are twenty-eight Hollises in the book."

"But only one M. Hollis."

"True. How's the steak?"

"Ours are better."

He was referring to Argentine beef; a bit of national pride there. But Carlos noticed that he was enjoying it. The pancakes he himself had ordered were only so-so. He wondered why he'd ordered pancakes, anyway; he didn't even *like* pancakes.

"So what we have to do," Ramon said, "is go up there and take a look."

"She could have changed what she looks like, you know," Carlos said.

"Yes, women can do that," Ramon said wearily, an observation a handsome man familiar with the strange and wonderful ways of women could make in utter boredom.

"She could be a redhead by now," Carlos said. "Or a brunette. Never mind the blonde. The blonde could be history by now."

"We can always look under her skirt," Ramon said, and smiled confidently.

"She could have changed it there, too. Or shaved it like a baby's. She could be an entirely different woman by now."

"The blue eyes, she can't change," Ramon said.

"She can wear contacts to make them green or brown or purple. A woman can change everything about herself. We could go up there, it could be the same woman, and we wouldn't recognize her."

"So what are you saying?" Ramon asked. "We *shouldn't* go up there?"

"We should go, we should go. But we shouldn't be disappointed if we look at her, and she doesn't fit the German whore's description. Who, by the way, may have been lying, anyway."

"Why would she have lied?"

"For the money. We gave her money."

"With the promise of more."

"*If* we locate the Hollis woman. If that's even her name."

"The German whore says that was her name. Mary Ann Hollis."

"So then why is there only an 'M' in the phone book?"

"Because if a woman puts an 'M.A.' in the phone book, a man immediately knows it's a woman," Ramon said.

"So if you put J. F. Kennedy in the phone book, it means it's a woman, correct?" Carlos said.

"Well, I don't *know* why she put only an 'M' in the phone book," Ramon admitted. "Maybe in this country it's cheaper than using two initials."

Carlos looked at him.

"Why do *you* think she put only an 'M'?" Ramon asked.

"Because, one, it could be the wrong woman . . ."

"Well, of course, but . . ."

"Or, two, it could be that the *man* who answered the phone is the one who's listed in the book, it's a *Mr.* M. Hollis . . ."

"No, it's only women who use initials," Ramon said.

"Or, three, she could have changed her name," Carlos said.

"That's true. But then why use an 'M'? Why not change it completely?"

"Even with an 'M,' it could be changed completely," Carlos said. "From Mary Ann, she could have changed it completely to Magdalena or Mercedes or Marta or . . ."

He was an Argentine, and so all these names were Spanish, naturally.

". . . Matilda or Maurita or Mirabella or Miranda or Modesta or . . ."

"I think I get the point," Ramon said.

"What I'm saying," Carlos said, "is we get uptown, we find a curly-haired redhead with big tits and a fat ass and brown eyes and her name is Margarita and we think we have the wrong number, but instead it's really Mary Ann Hollis who once upon a time was tall and thin and had blue eyes and straight blonde hair, is what I'm saying."

"So we have to be careful, is what you're saying."

"No, I'm saying we may have to beat the shit out of her," Carlos said.

"Well, of course," Ramon said, as if it went without saying that *all* women had to have the shit beat out of them every now and then.

"If she tells us she's not who we *think* she is," Carlos said.

"Yes," Ramon said.

"To find out who she *really* is, is what I'm saying," Carlos said.

"I agree with you entirely."

"So when do you want to go?"

"Let me finish my steak," Ramon said.

"You eat more slowly than any person I know."

"Because I was born rich," Ramon said. "Only the poor eat quickly. For fear someone will snatch the food away before they're finished."

"You were born rich, ha!" Carlos said.

"Yes, I was born rich, ha!" Ramon mimicked.

"What I want to do," Carlos said, "I want to be waiting when she comes out of the building. We take it slow and easy. Follow her, see where she goes, what she does. We make our move when we're *ready* to make it. And not near a house where a man answers the phone." He looked at the remaining bit of steak on Ramon's plate. "Now hurry up and finish, rich man," he said. "Because you'll be even richer once she gives us the money."

"*Sin duda,*" Ramon said.

Kristin Lund looked exactly like her name. Blonde hair and blue eyes, a full tempestuous mouth, and a figure that reminded Hawes of the gently sloping hills of Sweden, where he'd never been. Kristin Lund. Krissie sounded closer to home and just as beautiful. Krissie Lund. It rolled off the tongue like a balalaika riff. On this fine spring morning, she was wearing a pastel blue skirt, high-heeled pumps of the same subtle shade, and lemon-colored pantyhose that matched her lemon-colored sweater. Krissie. She looked very much like spring. She smelled a lot like spring, too. If Hawes was not mistaken, she was wearing *Poison*.

She was not surprised to find two detectives on her doorstep so early in the morning; she had heard about Father Michael's murder late last night, on television. In fact, she had called 911 at once, to ask how she could get in touch with whoever would be investigating the case. The woman who'd answered the phone said, "What is the emergency, Miss?" When Krissie told her there *was* no emergency, the woman asked, "Do you wish to report a crime?" Krissie told her No, she didn't wish to report a crime, but she worked for the man whose murder she'd just heard reported on television and she wanted to know who'd be handling the case so she could contact them. The woman on the other end said, "One moment, please, I'll give you my supervisor." The supervisor came on and immediately said, "I understand you witnessed a murder," whereupon Krissie hung up, even if she was not a native of this city.

"But I *did* try to contact you," she said, and smiled so dazzlingly that Hawes almost swooned.

"When was this?" Carella asked.

"When?"

"When you tried to contact us."

"Oh. Right after the Eleven O'Clock News. I was going to call the church, but I called 911 instead. And then, after I spoke to that supervisor, I didn't know what to do. So I went to sleep. I figured you'd get to me sooner or later."

"Yes," Hawes said.

"So here you are," she said, and smiled again.

"Miss Lund," Carella said, "Father Michael's housekeeper..."

"Yes, Martha Hennessy."

"Yes, told us that the last time she saw him alive was when he was saying good night to you."

"That's the last time *I* saw him, too."

"At about five o'clock yesterday."

"Yes."

"Where did you go after that?"

"I came straight here."

They were in the kitchen of her small apartment on the fourth floor of a building downtown in The Quarter, far from the precinct territory. Coffee was brewing in a pot plugged into an outlet above a butcher block counter. Krissie leaned against the counter, her arms folded, waiting for the coffee to perk. She had set out three cups and saucers near the coffeepot. The detectives stood by the open window.

A mild breeze fluttered the sheer white curtains on the window. Sunshine danced on the counter top, setting the bone white cups and saucers aglitter. Krissie lifted the pot and poured the three cups full. She carried them one at a time to a small round table near the window. The table was already set with teaspoons, paper napkins, a creamer, and a small bowl containing pink packets of a sugar substitute.

"Did you see anyone suspicious-looking outside the church?" Carella asked. "When you left last night?"

"Well, what do you mean by suspicious-looking? I mean . . . I guess you know that's a pretty rotten neighborhood. I mean, no offense, I know you guys do a good job. But to me, *everyone* up there looks suspicious."

"I was referring to anyone lurking about . . ."

Those words always made him feel foolish.

". . . anyone who seemed out of place . . ."

Those words, too.

". . . anyone who just didn't *belong* there," he said.

"Just the usual," Krissie said, and shrugged. Hawes loved the way she shrugged. "Milk?" she asked. "It's skim."

"By the usual . . . ?" Hawes asked.

"The usual," she said, and shrugged again. "I'm sure you know what's up there. The usual street mix. Crack dealers and buyers, hookers, hoodlums, the mix." She lifted her cup, sipped at the coffee.

"And last night, when you left . . . nothing but the mix."

"Just the mix."

"How about inside the church?" Carella asked. "See anything strange there? Anything out of the normal?"

"No."

"When you left the office . . . this was at five, you say?"

"Five, a little bit after."

"Were any of the file cabinets open?"

"They're never locked. We have keys, but . . ."

"No, I mean, were any of the drawers standing open?"

"No. Open? Why would they be?"

"Any papers on the floor?"

"No. Of course not."

"Everything neat and orderly."

"Yes."

"Miss Lund," Hawes said, "Father Michael's housekeeper mentioned that in recent weeks he'd been taking a strong church stand against..."

"Well, you don't think *that* had anything to do with his murder, do you?"

"What are you referring to?"

"The tithe."

"The tide?" Carella asked, puzzled.

"Tithe," she said, "tithe. The congregation is supposed to contribute ten percent of its earnings to the church. As a tithe. Aren't you familiar with that word? Tithe."

"Well, yes, it's just..."

He was thinking the word sounded medieval. He was thinking it did not sound like a word that should be lurking about in the here and now, a word that seemed out of place, a word that just didn't belong in this day and age. Tithe. Altogether archaic. Like a chastity belt. But he did not say this.

"What about this... tithe?" he asked.

"Well, she probably meant the sermons."

"What sermons?"

"Some pretty stiff sermons about shortchanging the church."

"Shortchanging?"

"Not dropping enough in the basket."

"I see. How many of these sermons were there?"

"Three. I know because I'm the one who typed them. All hellfire and brimstone. Unusual for Father Michael. He was normally..."

She hesitated.

"A very gentle man," she said at last.

"But not in these sermons," Hawes said.

"No. I suppose... well, the church really *is* in need of repair, hardly anything's been done to it in years. And, you know, the neighborhood *around* the church may be falling apart, but a lot of the parishioners come from five, six blocks away, where things are much better. Well, you know this city; you'll have a slum right next door to buildings with doormen. So he really *was* within his rights to ask for the proper tithe. Because, honestly, I think the neighborhood would be even *worse* by now if it wasn't for the work Father Michael does there. *Did* there," she said, correcting herself.

"What sort of work?" Carella asked.

"Well, trying to promote harmony," she said, "especially among the kids. The neighborhood up there is a mix of Italian, Irish, Hispanic and black—well, what am I telling you? Father Michael worked wonders with those kids. I'm sure you know what happened there on Easter Sunday . . ."

Carella shook his head.

So did Hawes.

"Well, it's *your* precinct," Krissie said, "I mean, don't you know what *happened* there? On Easter Sunday?"

"No, what happened there?" Carella asked, and tried to remember whether he'd had the duty on Easter Sunday.

"This was late in the afternoon," Krissie said, "this black kid came running into the church with his head all bloody. Half a dozen white kids were chasing him with stickball bats and garbage can covers, chased him right into the church, right up the center aisle to the altar. Father Michael stood his ground. Told them to get out of his church. Walked them right up the aisle to the door, escorted them out, told them not to come back until they knew how to behave in the house of God. I don't know who the kids were, neighborhood kids, I'm sure the incident is in your records, just look up Easter Sunday. Anyway, that's the kind of thing I mean. Father Michael was a meaningful force in that neighborhood. His congregation should have realized that. Instead of getting so offended. By the sermons, I mean."

"The money sermons," Carella said.

"The tithe sermons, yes," Krissie said.

"Some of his parishioners were offended by them?"

"Yes. By him calling the congregation . . . well, cheapskates, in effect."

"I see."

"From the pulpit."

"I see."

"One of the parishioners, I forget his name, distributed a letter that said Jesus had driven the money-changers from the temple and here they were back again . . . he was referring to Father Michael, you know. And the tithe sermons."

"They must have been pretty strong sermons," Hawes said.

"Well, no stronger than the *cult* sermons. I typed those, too."

"What cult sermons?" Carella asked.

"About the Church of the Bornless One."

"What's the Church of the Bornless One?"

"You mean you don't . . . come on, you're kidding me. It's right in the precinct. Only four blocks from St. Catherine's."

Hawes was wondering if Krissie Lund had ever thought of becoming a cop.

"I take it that the Church of the Bornless One is some kind of cult," he said.

"Devil worship," Krissie said.

"And you're saying that Father Michael wrote some sermons about . . ."

"About Satan being worshipped within a stone's throw of St. Catherine's, yes."

"Then that's what she was talking about," Hawes said, to Carella. "The housekeeper."

Carella nodded.

He reached into his jacket, took out his notebook, and removed a photograph from the front-cover flap.

"Ever see this before?" he asked, and handed the picture to Krissie.

The picture had been taken last night, by a police photographer using a Polaroid with a flash. Her exposure had been a bit off, and so the red wasn't as true as the actual red of the paint the graffiti artist had used, nor was the green of the gate quite as bilious. But it was a good picture nonetheless.

Krissie studied it carefully:

"What's it supposed to be?" she asked.

"Ever go around to the Tenth Street side of the church?"

"Yes?"

"Past the garden gate?"

"Yes?"

"This is what's painted on that gate."

"I'm sorry, I never noticed it," she said, and handed the photo back. "Does it mean something?"

Carella was thinking it meant that Satan was being worshipped within a stone's throw of St. Catherine's church, where a black kid had sought sanctuary from an angry white gang on Easter Sunday, and where an offended parishioner had circulated a letter about money-changers in the temple. He was thinking that in the world of the 87th Precinct, far uptown, any one of these things could be considered a reasonable cause for murder.

"Excuse me, Miss Lund," Hawes asked, "but is that *Poison*?"

"No," Krissie said, apparently knowing exactly what he was talking about. "It's *Opium*."

* * *

She had trained herself never to respond to the name Mary Ann.

So when she heard the voice behind her now, speaking Spanish, using the name she'd discarded the moment she'd come to this city, she kept right on walking, paying no attention to it. She was *not* Mary Ann. She was *certainly* not Marianna to anyone speaking Spanish.

And then the voice said, "Ai, Mariucha," which was the Spanish diminutive for Mary. She had been called Mariucha in the Mexican prison. The nickname had followed her to Buenos Aires. And apparently here to this city as well. She kept walking. Her heart was pounding.

"Mariucha, *despacio*," the voice said, and two men fell into step beside her, one on either side of her.

"Get away from me," she said at once, "or I'll yell for a cop."

"Oh, dear," the handsome one said in Spanish.

"We don't want to hurt you," the ugly one said in Spanish.

Which meant he *did* want to hurt her, and *would* hurt her.

There was a switchblade knife in her handbag. She was prepared to use it if she had to.

They were coming up Concord, walking away from the cluster of buildings that in a city this size passed for a campus. The school was familiarly known as The Thousand Window Bakery, a reference too historically remote for Marilyn to understand, but accurate enough in that the university complex seemed to be fashioned entirely of glass. This was almost smack in the center of the island that was Isola, equidistant from the rivers bordering it north and south, only slightly closer to the old Seawall downtown than to the Riverhead bridges all the way uptown. The neighborhood was still a good one. Plenty of shops and restaurants, movie theaters, apartment buildings with doormen and—there ahead on the corner—a pair of uniformed cops basking in the spring sunshine.

"Don't do anything foolish," the handsome one said in Spanish.

She walked directly to the policemen.

"These men are bothering me," she said.

The cops looked at the two men.

The handsome one smiled.

The ugly one shrugged.

Neither of them said a word. They seemed to recognize that if they opened their mouths in this city and either Spanish or broken English came tumbling out, they'd be in serious trouble.

Marilyn kept waiting for the cops to do something.

The cops kept looking at the two men.

They were both well-dressed. Dark suits. White shirts. A red tie on one of them, a blue tie on the other. Both wearing pearl grey fedoras. Very neat. Very elegant-looking. Two legitimate business-men enjoying a fine spring day.

"Guys," one of the cops said, "the lady doesn't wish to be both-ered."

He said this in the fraternal tone that men adopt when they are suggesting to other men that this is a nice piece of ass here and we could all handily take our pleasure of her were we of a mind to, but out of the goodness and generosity of our masculine hearts, let's not bother the lady if she does not wish to be bothered, hmmhh? Marilyn almost expected him to wink at the handsome one and nudge the ugly one in the ribs.

The handsome one shrugged, as if to say We are all men of the world who understand the vagaries of women.

The ugly one sighed heavily, as if to say We are all occasionally burdened by these beautiful, unpredictable creatures, especially at certain times of the month. Then he took the handsome one's arm, and led him away quickly and silently.

"Okay?" the cop asked Marilyn.

She said nothing.

The ugly one was looking back at her.

There was a chilling promise in his eyes.

All of the windows in the station house were open. The barred windows on the ground-floor level, the grilled windows on the upper stories. It suddenly occurred to Carella that a police station looked like a prison. Even with the windows open, it looked like a prison.

Grey, soot-covered granite blocks, a green-tiled roof stained with a century's worth of pigeon shit, green globes flanking the entrance steps and announcing in faded white numerals that here was the Eight-Seven, take it or leave it. Carella had been taking it for a good many years now.

The priest's papers were waiting on his desk.

Not eighteen hours after the discovery of Father Michael's body, his various papers—those strewn on his office floor, those still in his file cabinets or on his desk—had already been examined by the lab and sent back uptown again by messenger. This was very fast work. But the Commissioner himself—who happened to be black and who attended a Baptist church in the Diamondback section of the city where he'd been born and raised—had this morning made a television appearance on *The Today Show,* announcing by network to the nation at large that this city *could* not, and *would* not tolerate the wanton murder of a gentle man of God of whatever persuasion. Not too many day-watch cops caught the show because they were already out on the beat asking discreet questions in an attempt to aid and abet the investigating cops of the Eight-Seven while simultaneously mollifying the irate Commissioner himself. Up in the Eight-Seven, life went on as usual; priest or not, this was just another garden-variety murder, no pun intended, in a part of the city choked with weeds.

It was lunchtime in the squadroom.

The detectives sat around in shirt sleeves and pistols. Sandwiches and coffee, pizza and Cokes were spread on the desks before them. Only Meyer waved to Carella as he came in. The others were too busy listening to Parker.

"There is not going to be no mystery in these Dallas murders, I promise you," Parker said.

"There's *never* any mystery," Brown said.

"That I know. But what I'm saying, this is going to be even *less* of a mystery than there usually is. Especially since it's Texas."

"Love or money," Meyer said. "Those are the only two reasons for murder."

"That's why there are no mysteries, is what I'm saying," Brown said.

"Tell me all about it," Parker said. "But what *I'm* saying is the only mystery here is *who* the guy *is*. *What* he is, is a crazy."

"That's the third reason," Kling said. "Lunacy."

"There's nothing mysterious about any lunatic in the world," Parker said. "This thing in Dallas is gonna turn out to be just what the newspapers and the TV are saying it is, I'll bet you a hundred bucks. It's a crazy running around killing blondes. That's *all* it is. When they catch this guy, he'll be nuttier than a Hershey bar, you wait and see."

Carella wasn't particularly eager to tackle the priest's papers. Hawes had gone downtown directly after they'd left the Lund apartment, heading for Ballistics where he was trying to pry loose a report on a gun used in an armed robbery. This meant that Carella now had to wade through all this stuff by himself. The papers were in several large manila envelopes marked EVIDENCE. The papers themselves, however, were not *evidence* per se, in that the prints lifted from them had already been marked and filed downtown. Without the prints, the papers were merely *papers*, which might or might not contain information.

But the Police Department had a lot of manila envelopes of various sizes, all of them printed with the word EVIDENCE, and a cop was likely as not to grab one of these envelopes whenever he wanted to send or take something someplace, even if the something was a ham sandwich he planned to have for lunch. So whoever had examined these papers at the lab had later stuffed them into seven large EVIDENCE envelopes, and then had stamped the envelopes RUSH, and further stamped them BY MESSENGER because a priest had been killed in this city with an Irish-Catholic police department, and then had wrapped the little red strings around the little red buttons, and here they were on Carella's desk alongside another EVIDENCE envelope that did in fact contain a ham sandwich he planned to eat for lunch.

He hated paperwork.

This was a whole hell of a lot of paperwork on his desk.

The clock on the wall read ten minutes to one.

"What this is," Brown said, "is a guy whose mother was a blonde, she used to lock him in the closet every day 'cause he wet the bed. So now he's got a thing about blondes. He thinks all blondes are his mother. So he's got to kill every blonde in the world before one of them locks him in the closet again."

"Like I said," Parker said.

"My mother is blonde," Kling said.

"Did she lock you in the closet every day?"

"She chained me in the basement."

"Because you wet the bed?"

"I still wet the bed."

"He thinks he's kidding," Parker said.

"What this thing in Texas is," Kling said, "is a guy who has a blonde wife he hates. So first he kills the two blondes he already did, then the next one'll be his wife, and he'll kill two more blondes after that, and everybody'll think it's a crazy blonde-hater doing the murders. When instead it's just this little guy, he's an accountant or something, his wife is a big fat blonde he's been married to for forty years, he can't stand her, he has to get rid of her."

"No, I don't think this is no smoke screen," Parker said.

Carella figured he'd sooner or later have to dig into this mound of stuff here on his desk. It was just that it looked so *formidable*. All those envelopes full of papers. Stalling, he picked up the phone and dialed the lieutenant's extension.

"How do you feel?" Byrnes asked.

"What do you mean?"

"Your headache."

"All gone."

"The P.C. was on television this morning," Byrnes said.

"Yes, I know."

"A speech for every occasion, right? So what do you think? Any leads yet?"

"Not yet. I just got the priest's papers, there's a lot of stuff to look at here."

"What kind of papers?"

"Correspondence, sermons, bills, like that."

"Any diary?"

"Not according to the lab inventory."

"Too bad," Byrnes said, and then hesitated and said, "Steve . . ." and hesitated again and finally said, "I'd like to be able to tell the Commissioner something soon."

"I understand."

"So let me know the minute anything looks good."

"I will."

"It was probably some kind of bug," Byrnes said, "the headache." And hung up.

Carella put his own phone back on the cradle, and looked at all those unopened evidence envelopes again. The pile hadn't diminished one damn bit. He decided to go to the Clerical Office for a cup of coffee. When he got back to his own desk, they were still talking about the murders in Dallas.

"You want to know what *I* think it is?" Genero said.

"What is it, Genero?"

"It's the full moon, is what it is."

"Yes, Genero, thank you," Parker said. "Go down the hall and take a pee, okay?"

"It's a known fact that when there's a full moon . . ."

"What has the full moon got to do with blondes?"

"Nothing. But . . ."

"Then what the fucka you talkin' about?"

"I'm saying in the same week there's two dead blondes is what I'm saying. And there happens to be a full moon this week."

"There is no such thing as a full moon that lasts a whole *week*," Parker said. "And also, what makes you think a full moon here in this city means there's also a full moon in Dallas, Texas, where this fuckin' *lunatic* is killin' these blondes?"

"It's a known fact," Genero said, "that there was a full moon on Monday when the first blonde turned up. And the moon was *still* pretty full *last* night when the *second* blonde turned up."

"Go take your pee, willya?"

Carella looked at all the evidence bags and wondered which one he should open first. He looked up at the clock. Almost a quarter past one. He could not think of a single other thing that might keep him from starting the paperwork. So he opened the bag with the ham sandwich in it.

Alternately chewing on his sandwich and sipping at his coffee, he began browsing—no sense jumping into icy-cold water all at once—through the papers in the first envelope. From the handwritten list on the outside of the envelope—written by someone at the lab whose initials were R.L.—and through his own corroboration of the list, the first envelope contained only bills, canceled checks, and check stubs. The checks were printed with the heading *St. Catherine's Roman Catholic Church Corporation*, and beneath that *Michael Birney, PSCCA*. All of the bills were for expenses Father Birney had incurred as parish priest. There were bills and consequent checks for electricity...

...and fuel oil...

...and snow plowing...

...and food...

...and postage...

...and salaries...

Martha Hennessy, for example, got a check every week for $224.98 after deductions of $21.02 for FICA and $34.00 for Federal Withholding Tax. Kristin Lund got a check every other week for $241.37 after deductions of $21.63 for FICA and $25.00 for Federal Withholding Tax...

"You want to know what this is?" Meyer said. "This is a guy who went out with this blonde, Mary, Marie, whatever her name was..."

"Matilda," Parker said. "The first one."

"Matilda, and it was a first date, and he tried to score but she turned him down. So he got so pissed off, he killed her. Then last night . . ."

"Where'd you get Mary or Marie?" Brown asked. "When the woman's name was Matilda?"

"What difference does it make what her name was? She's dead. The point is . . ."

"I'm just curious how you got Mary from Matilda?"

"I made it up, okay?"

"You musta."

. . . and telephone bills, and bills from a photocopying service and a local garage, and bills for the church's missalettes, and mortgage bills, and bills for maintenance of the church grounds, and medical insurance bills, and newspaper delivery bills, and bills for flowers for the altar, and dozens of other bills, all of which Father Michael paid like clockwork on the first and the fifteenth of every month. There were very few bills for personal clothing, and these for relatively small amounts. The biggest such item was for a new down parka at two hundred and twenty-seven dollars; it had been a severe winter.

"What I'm saying," Meyer said, "is that last night, this guy is *still* pissed off just *thinking* about it. So he goes out and finds himself another blonde to kill."

"How long's he gonna stay pissed off, this guy?"

"I'll bet you the one last night was the end of it."

"Until there's another full moon," Genero said.

"Will you fuck off with your full moon?" Parker said.

"One thing I'm glad of," Brown said.

"Tomorrow's your day off," Parker said.

"That, too. But I'm also glad this lunatic ain't doing it *here*."

"Amen," Parker said.

The priest sent quarterly checks to the archdiocese—the last one had been written on the thirty-first of March—for something he listed as "cathedraticum" on the stub; Carella had no idea what this might be. Six checks had been written on the day of Father Michael's death:

A check to Bruce Macauley Tree Care, Inc. for "Spraying done on 5/19" in the amount of $37.50.

A check to US Sprint for "Service thru 5/17" in the amount of $176.80.

A check to Isola Bank and Trust for "June mortgage" in the amount of $1480.75.

A check to Alfred Hart Insurance Company for "Honda Accord LX, Policy £# HR 9872724" in the amount of $580.

A check to Orkin Exterminating Co. Inc. for "May services" in the amount of $36.50.

And a check to The Wanderers for "Band deposit" in the amount of $100.00.

That was it.

Each month, the balance in the St. Catherine's Roman Catholic Church Corporation checkbook leveled off at about a thousand dollars. There seemed to be nothing irregular about Father Michael's accounts.

The next evidence envelope contained his correspondence.

The first letter Carella took out of the package was written on blue stationery, addressed in a woman's hand to Father Michael Birney at St. Catherine's Church Rectory. He looked at the return address. Mrs. Irene Brogan. The postmark on the envelope was from San Diego, California, and it was dated May 19. He opened the envelope and took the letter from it:

> *My dearest brother,*
> *I am now in receipt of yours of May 12th, and I cannot tell you with what a saddened heart I hasten to . . .*

"I'm back," Hawes said from the gate in the slatted rail divider. "Did you solve it yet?"

3

"What's this case you're working, anyway?" Parker said, turning to Carella.

Carella told him they had a D.O.A. priest, stab-and-slash, weapon unknown, housekeeper and secretary last ones to see him alive, wild prints all over the church and the rectory, random latents lifted from the papers here, but they were most likely the secretary's. He also told Parker that the housekeeper thought the Devil had dusted the priest and that in addition to the Devil the priest had also pissed off some local youngsters as well as his own congregation.

Parker thought this was very comical. He began laughing. So did Genero.

"This is his correspondence here," Carella told Hawes. "Just dig in."

"You're gonna have a lot of fun there," Parker said, "reading a priest's mail," and burst out laughing again. Genero started laughing again, too. Both men sat there giggling like teenagers. Hawes figured it was spring fever.

At his own desk, Carella went back to the letter from Father Michael's sister:

My dearest brother,

I am now in receipt of yours of May 12th, and I cannot tell you with what a saddened heart I hasten to respond. Michael, how have you managed to construct such a tower of doubt for yourself? And don't you feel you should relate your fears to the bishop of your diocese? I just don't know how to counsel or advise you.

I wish I could be closer to you during this difficult time. What makes matters worse is that Roger and I are leaving for Japan this Saturday, and we won't be back till the tenth of June. I'll try to call you before we leave, so we can have a good long telephone visit. Perhaps, by then, the skies above will look a bit clearer.

Meanwhile, let me say only this: I know that you are a devout and loyal servant of God and that however troubled you may now be, you will find through prayer the way to enlightenment and salvation.

Your loving sister,
Irene

Carella turned over the envelope again.

He pulled the phone to him, lifted the receiver, asked the operator for the San Diego area code, dialed 1-619-555-1212 for information, and got a listing for a Roger Brogan at the address on the back of the envelope. He dialed the number and let the phone ring twenty times before hanging up.

"Here's something," Hawes said.

She did not think they were policemen. If they were policemen, they'd have identified themselves at once to the street-corner cops she'd approached. Flash the tin, reveal themselves as part of the great fraternal order of law enforcement officers. So no, they weren't cops.

They were Spanish-speaking. This frightened her. They had known the name Mary Ann and had further known the nickname Mariucha. This frightened her even more. They could have got the Mary Ann from Houston, but not the Mariucha. This had to have come from either *La Fortaleza* or Buenos Aires. So either they'd been asking questions at the prison, or else they'd been snooping around B.A. Either way, they were here. Moreover, they had tracked her to the school. Which meant they probably knew where she lived as well.

She knew she should tell Willis, but she was so afraid of losing him. Afraid, too, that the trouble these men represented might somehow rub off on him, cause problems for him on the job. She loved him too dearly for that. So no, she couldn't tell him. She'd brought this trouble upon herself, whatever it turned out to be, and she had to handle it herself. Which was why she had to get a gun; the switchblade knife seemed suddenly inadequate for defense, especially against the big, ugly one. But how? And where?

The gun laws were tough in this state. You needed a permit before you could walk into a shop and pick one off the shelf. And you needed a damn good reason for *wanting* that permit. So how far would she have to travel to buy a gun? Even in the immediately adjoining states, didn't shopowners have to file police applications well before letting you walk out with a gun? So where did the gun laws get easy? How far across the river and into the trees? How far north, east, south or west? Where in these surrounding United States could a person legally buy a gun to kill her husband or her mother or, better yet, two Spanish-speaking goons who'd called her by her prison name, her Buenos Aires street name?

Where?

She was living with a cop and personally knew at least three dozen cops in this city, had gone out to dinner with them, been in their homes, but there wasn't a single one of them she could ask about getting a—well, maybe...yes, that was a possibility. Eileen Burke. Call her up, ask her out to lunch. Eileen was a cop, casually swing the conversation around to how and where a person might acquire a hot gun in this—no, she was too smart, she'd tip in a minute, know immediately that it was Marilyn herself who was looking for the gun. Besides, she wasn't sure Eileen even *liked* her. Wasn't sure, for that matter, that *any* of Willis's friends liked her. A hooker. A former hooker.

Hookers knew people who knew where to get guns.

In Houston, she'd have known where to get a gun.

In Buenos Aires, she'd have known where to get a gun.

But this was here and this was now, and she'd been out of the life too long.

Or had she?

"If you're looking for a motive, this could be a motive," Hawes said, and handed a sheet of paper across the desk. It was the sort of newsletter that years ago would have been typed first and then mimeographed. Today, it had started as a computer printout and had later been photocopied, several copier streaks across the page being the only clues to duplication. Carella wondered how many of them had been distributed. He also wondered how anyone had got along before Xeroxing was invented. Xeroxing? That was already the Stone Age. The Clerical Office's new fax machine was the *true* miracle.

My Fellow Parishioners:

For the past several weeks now, Father Michael Birney, the pastor assigned to guide the flock of St. Catherine's Church, has on more than one occasion seen fit to use the pulpit as a scolding board for our . . .

"What's a 'scolding board'?" Carella asked.
"Just keep reading," Hawes said, "it's self-explanatory."

. . . scolding board for our congregation. On
these occasions, he has taken it upon himself
to rail, nag, upbraid, revile, and berate . . .

"See what I mean?" Hawes said.
"Mmm," Carella said.

. . . the good and decent people of this parish for failing to meet their financial obligations by way of the weekly tithe to the Lord
Our God. He has pointed out that there are no
less than forty-eight references to the tithe
in scriptures. He has seen fit to quote many of
these Old Testament passages, the most recent
of which he included in last Sunday's sermon at
a time of the year better suited to more spiritual matters. I quote it again now:

"From the days of your fathers you have
turned aside from my statutes and have not
kept them. Return to me, and I will return
to you, says the Lord of hosts.
But you say, 'How shall we return?'
Will man rob God? Yet you are robbing me.
But you say, 'How are we robbing thee?'
In your tithes and offerings! You are
cursed with a curse, for you are robbing
me!
Bring the full tithes into the storehouse, that there may be food in my house!"

This from a spiritual leader, who has known nothing but kindness and generosity from the good people of this parish. My fellow parishioners, I would like to offer my own quote from the Holy Bible. This is from the Gospel According to John, Chapter 2, verses 14 to 16:

"In the temple he found those who were selling oxen and sheep and pigeons, and the money-changers at their business. And making a whip of cords, he drove them all, with the sheep and oxen, out of the temple; and he poured out the coins of the money-changers and overturned their tables. And he told those who sold the pigeons, 'Take these things away; you shall not make my Father's house a house of trade!'"

Father Michael Birney is making our Father's house a house of trade!

We are all well aware of our obligation to the Lord, we know full well that five percent of our annual income is expected by way of a weekly offering to the church. But we refuse to be turned into a congregation of bookkeepers. Let Father Michael count the offerings again and yet another time, and then let him count his blessings as well. A noble man of God might then do well to apologize from the pulpit for accusing his parishioners of robbing from . . .

"Catch the last line," Hawes said.

. . . robbing from the Lord! Pride goeth be-

fore destruction, and a haughty spirit before
a fall.

Yours in Christ,
Arthur L. Farnes

"Well . . ." Carella said, and handed the letter back.

"I know. You dismiss a loony right off because you think nobody mails such a letter to the whole congregation and then actually goes out to *kill* somebody. But suppose . . ."

"Uh-huh."

". . . suppose this guy really *was* mad enough to go juke this priest? I mean, he sounds pretty damn angry, doesn't he? I'm not a Catholic, so I don't . . ."

"Me neither," Carella said. He considered himself a lapsed Catholic; his mother said, "Shame on you."

"Okay, so I don't know how far you can go with yelling at the priest assigned to your church, *if* in fact he *is* assigned, that's something I don't know."

"Me neither."

"But let's *say* he's assigned and let's say you're unhappy with the way he's bugging you about paying your dues . . ."

"Your tithe."

"Same thing, so you write a letter . . . for what purpose? To get him recalled? Do they do that in the Catholic Church? Recall a priest who isn't getting along with his congregation?"

"I really don't know."

"Neither do I."

"Or do you write to warn him that if he doesn't cut it out you're going to overturn his tables? I mean, really, Steve, a lot of the stuff in this letter sounds like a warning."

"Where does it sound like a warning?"

"You don't think this whole money-changer-in-the-*temple* stuff sounds like a warning?"

"No."

"You *don't*?"

"I really don't. Where else do you see a warning?"

"Where *else*? Okay, where else? How about here, for example? Dit-dah, dit-dah, dit-dah, di . . . *here*. 'Let him count his blessings.' Doesn't that sound like a warning?"

"No."

"Let the man count his *blessings*? That doesn't sound like a warning to you?"

"No, it doesn't."

"Let him count his blessings before it's too *late*!"

"Where does it say that?"

"Say what?"

" 'Before it's too late.' "

"It doesn't. I'm extrapolating."

"What does that mean, extrapolating?"

"It means to infer from what you already know."

"How do you know that?"

"I just happen to know it."

"I still don't think if you ask a man to count his blessings it's necessarily a warning."

"You don't."

"No, I don't."

"Okay, how about here? 'A noble man of God might then do well to apologize from the pulpit for accusing his parishioners of robbing from the Lord!' Or *else*, right?"

"Where does it say 'Or else'?"

"Right here. 'Pride goeth before destruction, and a haughty spirit before a fall.' "

"That doesn't say 'Or else.' "

"That's the *code* for 'Or else.' Look, you don't want to go talk to this guy, we won't go talk to him, forget it. I just thought . . ."

"He sounds like a very religious man, that's all," Carella said. "There are people like that in the world."

Like my father, Hawes thought, but didn't say. Who named me Cotton. After the Puritan Priest.

"You want to know something?" he said. "In this world, there are a lot of very religious people who are out of their minds, did you know that? And some of them have been known to stick knives in other people. Now I'm not saying this Arthur L. Farnes—which is the name of a lunatic to *begin* with—is the dude who done the priest, but I *am* saying you get a letter like this one, it could be a death threat is what I'm saying, and we'd be very dumb cops if we didn't go knocking on this guy's door right this minute, is what we should do."

"I agree with you," Carella said.

Schuyler Lutherson wanted to know who among his disciples had sprayed the inverted pentagram on St. Catherine's churchyard gate.

"Because, see," he said, "I don't want policemen coming here."

Schuyler Lutherson was not his real name. His real name was Samuel Leeds, a nice enough name except that the Samuel sounded like a prophet in the Old Testament (which was the last thing on earth he wanted to sound like) and the Leeds sounded like a manufacturing town in the north of England. Actually, his great-great-great-grandfather *had* been an ironmonger in Leeds before coming to America, but that was ancient history and Schuyler chose to trace his heritage more fancifully.

He had picked the given name Schuyler not because it meant a "scholar" or a "wise man" in Dutch (actually, he was quite unfamiliar with the Dutch language) but because it sounded like "sky," as in the skies above, or the heavens above, or the kingdom of God above, from which an angel once had fallen. For was it not Satan himself who'd been unceremoniously expelled from Heaven, hurled from the upper stratosphere to the fiery lower depths? And was not Satan simultaneously known as Lucifer, whose name Samuel Leeds could not appropriate out of worshipful humility, but whose name he could at least echo alliteratively...Lucifer, Luther...and then rhyme

slantingly . . . Lucifer, Lutherson . . . the surname achieving grandeur
in retrospect, Lutherson, the son of Luther, the son of Lucifer, leader
of the Church of the Bornless One, all hail Satan!

Not bad for a kid of nineteen, which was how old Schuyler had
been when he originated his church in Los Angeles. He was now
thirty-nine years old, that had been twenty years ago, away back in
the days of the flower children, remember, Maude? When everyone
was preaching love? Except Schuyler Lutherson on the pulpit of the
Church of the Bornless One, where between the spread legs of a
different voluntary "altar" each week, he preached the opposite of
love, he preached hate, scorching pussy after pussy with the white-hot
scorn of his seed. Everything in the worship of Satan was a study in
opposites, an exercise in reversal or obversion. Through hate, love.
Through denial, acceptance. Through darkness, light. Through evil,
good.

Even Schuyler's carefully cultivated appearance supported the
tenets of his creed. Not for him the sham look of a bearded devil with
arched eyebrows, nor for him the silken crimson robes and peaked
hood. Was he a true and sacred priest of a church dedicated to the
Infernal One, or merely a Halloween caricature? Would the Devil on
earth appear before man *as* the Devil, or would he in his infinite evil
and guile assume the shape of some lesser form? And likewise, and
even so, would the *son* of Satan—Lucifer's Son, *Lutherson!*—lift the
cuff of an earthly trouser to expose a furry ankle and a cloven hoof?
Would he advertise his yellow eyes like beacons to unbelievers?
Would he blow the foul breath of brimstone and piss from his nostrils,
regurgitate purple vomit into the faces of fools, would this be the
proper behavior and appearance of Lord Satan's son and servant?

Schuyler Lutherson was blond.

He had blue eyes.

He had begun lifting weights during a short stretch he'd served in
a juvenile detention facility in California, back before he'd changed
his name, and he still worked out at a gym near the church three times
a week. As a result, he had the slim, lithe, sinewy body of a long-
distance runner.

His nose would have been Grecian perfection, had it not once been broken at that selfsame detention facility, where the fair-haired, fuzzy-cheeked as-yet-unborn Schuyler Lutherson was forced to protect his ass from an older, huskier boy determined to have a taste of it at all costs. The "all costs" he'd had in mind did not include the ruptured spleen he'd suffered after he'd broken the nascent Schuyler's nose and declared his intention of making him his "private and personal pussy." The Schuyler-Lutherson-to-be used a two-by-four by way of discouragement, picking it up from a pile of lumber in the carpentry shop and wielding it like a baseball bat. The older boy never bothered him again. Neither did anyone else.

Schuyler had a wide androgynous mouth, with the full lower lip of a pouting screen siren, and the rather thin upper lip of a politician. He had even white teeth, the better to eat you with, my dear. That they were capped was a matter of small import or note. When he smiled, the gates to the infernal chambers opened wide and eternal midnight beckoned.

He was smiling now, wanting to know who—exactly—had painted the pentagram on the church gate.

He spoke deliberately and precisely.

"Who, exactly, painted the pentagram on the fucking gate?" he asked.

Through obscenity, purity.

The three looked at him.

Two women and a man. Each of the women had served as altars many times. Through Satan, Schuyler knew them intimately. The man knew them intimately as well, through the public rites of Satanic fornication that followed each ritual renunciation. One of the women was named Laramie. The other was named Coral. These were not their real names. The man was named Stanley. This *was* his real name; who on earth would want to change his name *to* Stanley unless he planned on becoming a dentist? Stanley was a salary-drawing church deacon. Laramie and Coral were disciples, and did not draw salaries per se, but money somehow stuck to their fingers. Laramie was black and Coral was white and Stanley was Hispanic; this was a regular United Nations here. Together they pondered who might have been foolish enough to decorate the church gate with a pentagram.

"Because now, see," Schuyler said, "the priest is dead."

Stanley shook his head, not in sorrow, but in dismay: the priest was now indeed dead, and someone had painted a pentagram on St. Catherine's gate. Stanley's head was massive and covered with long tawny, tangled hair that gave him the look of a middle-aged lion; when he shook his head, the gesture was monumental.

"We have nothing to hide here, that's true," Schuyler said.

Both women nodded, a symphony in black and white togetherness. Coral was wearing a paisley patterned skirt and a white peasant blouse, no bra. She had long blonde hair, eyes as blue as Schuyler's, and a button nose dusted with freckles. Laramie was wearing skin-tight jeans, boots, and a sweater. She was tall and strikingly good-looking, a Masai woman miraculously transported to the big bad city. By comparison, Coral looked like a prairie housewife—which incidentally she'd been before coming east to join Schuyler's church. The women were thinking hard. Who could have been dumb enough to paint a pentagram on the churchyard gate? This was the burning question of the day.

"But, see," Schuyler said, "suppose the police start raising some of the same questions that asshole priest raised? Suppose they come here and want to know this or that, see, as for example, are we popping X during the mass, which is a controlled substance, see? We can always tell the Man we are *not* doing Ecstasy nor anything *else* at our services, which by the way are private services, see, and not open to the public except by invitation, is what we could tell the Man. But then we'll have police shit, see, we'll have them coming around with search warrants and whatnot, looking for this or that, breaking our balls merely on principle, which is what cops know how to do very well. Because what they are going to figure, see, in their limited way, is that if somebody painted a pentagram on the fucking gate, then maybe that same person did the priest. And they're going to be all over us like locusts."

"Excuse me, Sky," Coral said.

"Yes, Coral."

Gently. His eyes caressing her. He would ask her to serve as altar again this Saturday night, May twenty-sixth, a night of no particular significance in the church calendar except that it followed immediately after the high holy solemnity of the Feast of the Expulsion. The two most important religious holidays, of course, were Walpurgisnacht and All Hallows' Eve. But these were nights of wild abandon, and the Feast of the Expulsion was traditionally more sedate. This was why the mass on the Saturday following was generally anticipated as a time of greater release and realization. Coral would make a perfect altar. Lying on the draped trapezoid each time, her legs spread, her hands clutching those candelabra, she was a woman in constant motion, twitching in expectation. Even standing here before him now, she shifted from foot to foot, her right hand twisting her skirt like a little girl, twisting it.

"I feel we should open this to the entire congregation, Sky, put to them that someone in our midst—perhaps through overzealousness, or perhaps through just sheer stupidity—has placed the church in a precarious position, Sky. And we should ask whoever it was that painted the pentagram on the gate to come forward and admit it, and then perhaps go to the police voluntarily, himself or herself, and say what it was they done. So the investigation would end right there, with whoever actually put that symbol on the gate. Is what I think, Sky."

Flat midwestern voice, little gap between her two upper front teeth. Twisting her skirt like a little girl called on to recite. Like to do a mass over her right this fucking minute, he thought.

"I think Coral's right," Stanley said, nodding his massive leonine head. "Throw it open to the congregation . . ."

Throw it open *wide* to the congregation, Schuyler thought.

". . . this Saturday night, before the mass actually starts, before you do the Introit. Explain to them we're in jeopardy here because of some dumb thing somebody did in all innocence . . ."

"Un*less*," Laramie said.

Woman of few words.

Said her piece, did her little Masai dance, and then got off the stage.

"Unless whoever painted the star *also* killed the priest."

Schuyler looked at her.

"Do you think that's really a possibility?" he asked.

"After what the priest said?"

She shrugged.

The shrug made it abundantly clear that whatever the priest had said could, in the proper mind, have taken seed as a motive for murder.

"A total asshole," Schuyler said. "If he'd kept his mouth shut . . ."

"But he didn't."

This from Laramie again, who made an art of keeping her mouth shut most of the time.

"No, that's true," Schuyler said, "he didn't. Which is why we now find ourselves in a situation that is potentially, see, dangerous. I can tell you I don't want policemen coming here. I don't want them looking into this or that, discovering that little girls perform certain parts of the ritual, discovering that on occasion we've used harmless though controlled substances in support of the mass, discovering that on occasion we've even sacrificed small animals during the mass, though I can't imagine *that's* against the fucking law, is it? The point is, see, the priest made enough of a fuss from the pulpit, brought enough attention to us, calling us—what was it, Stanley?—a neighborhood thorn in the side of Christ, can you believe it? Which, of course, illustrates what a threat our church actually *is*, illustrates clearly, see, how desperately the Christ-lovers would love to drive us into non-existence, murder the infant church in its cradle, see. But . . ."

"Sky."

From Coral. Softly.

"I think we ought to contact the police our ownselves," she said, "*before* the mass tomorrow night—right *away,* in fact—to tell them we're aware of what's painted on that gate and to let them know we're doing our own internal examination . . ."

The *words* she used.

". . . in an effort to determine who put the star on there, so he or she herself can come forward and reveal who they are, Sky. This way we're immediately letting the police know we're doing everything in our power to cooperate. So they won't think some kind of *cabal* connected with our church put the sacred sign on the priest's gate and then killed him."

"Un*less*," Laramie said.

They all turned to look at her.

"Unless that's exactly what *did* happen," she said.

Arthur Llewellyn Farnes was a tall, rangy white man with the speech of a born and bred city-dweller, and the look of a weather-hardened New England farmer. His men's clothing store was on The Stem between Carson and Coles, and he had just come back from lunch when the detectives walked in at two o'clock that afternoon. Most of his lunch seemed to have spilled onto his tie and his vest. Carella guessed he was the only man outside of Homicide Division who still wore a vest. He was willing to bet he also wore a fedora.

The detectives identified themselves and told him they were investigating the murder of Father Michael Birney. Farnes went into a long and apparently heartfelt eulogy on the priest he had only recently challenged in his open letter, now calling him a dedicated man of God, a true servant of the Lord, a kind and gentle shepherd to the church's flock, and a wonderful human being whose absence would be sorely felt.

All this with a straight face.

"Mr. Farnes," Hawes said, "we were looking through Father Michael's correspondence, and we came across this letter you sent to the congregation . . ."

"Yes," Farnes said, and smiled, and shook his head.

"You know the letter I mean, right?"

"Yes. The one I wrote in response to his sermons about the tithe."

"Yes," Hawes said.

"Yes," Farnes said.

He was still smiling. But now he was nodding. Yes, his head went. Yes, I sent that letter. Yes. In response to him chastening us about our church obligations. Yes, I'm the one who voiced resentment. Yes. Me. Nodding, nodding.

"What about that letter, Mr. Farnes?"

"What about it?" Farnes said.

"Well, I'd say it was a pretty angry letter, wouldn't you?"

"Only *pretty* angry? I'd say it was *monumentally* angry."

The detectives looked at him.

"In fact, Mr. Farnes," Hawes said, "you wrote some things in that letter..."

"Yes, I was furious."

"Uh-huh."

"Demanding money that way! As if we weren't *already* giving our fair share! All the man had to do was trust us! But, no! Runs his mouth off at the pulpit instead, week after week of fire-and-brimstone sermons better suited to Salem Village than to this parish! Never once trusting us! Excuse me," he said, and walked immediately to where a man was taking a pair of trousers from the rack. "May I help you, sir?" he asked.

"Just looking," the man said. "Are these all the forty-two longs you have?"

"Yes, from here to the end of the rack."

"Thank you," the man said.

"Let me know if I can be of any assistance," Farnes said, and walked back to the detectives. Lowering his voice, he said, "That man is a shoplifter. He walked out of here at Christmastime with an entire suit under the suit he was already wearing. I realized it after he was gone. Forgive me for watching him, but I'd like to catch the son of a bitch."

"So would we," Carella said.

"You were saying something about trust," Hawes said.

"Yes," Farnes said, his eyes following the man as he moved along the rack. "In many respects, the church is a business—and I mean no blasphemy. This is why a tithe is specified in the Bible, so there won't be any misunderstanding about the *business* the church is forced to conduct. In order to survive, do you understand? Ten percent, spelled out in black and white. Five in the basket every week, the other five as gifts to worthwhile charities. Do you follow me so far?"

"Yes, we follow you," Carella said.

"Okay. How do you know whether you're getting five percent in the basket? Instead of two percent or three and a half percent? The answer is you don't. You trust the congregation. By trusting them, you'll inspire their trust in turn, and you'll find that instead of getting a short count every week, you'll be generating even more revenue for the church. Any fool should . . ."

"Excuse me, but is this the dressing room?"

"Yes," Farnes said, "through the curtains there. Let me roll those trouser cuffs back for you, sir."

"That's all right, I can . . ."

"No problem at all, sir," Farnes said, and took the three pairs of trousers that were draped over the man's arm, and rolled back the cuffs, and said, "There you are, sir."

"Thank you," the man said.

"Let me know if you need any help," Farnes said, and came back to the detectives. Lowering his voice again, he said, "He's going in there with three pairs of pants. Let's see how many he walks out with."

"You were talking about trust," Hawes said.

"Yes," Farnes said. "I was saying that any fool should know you can't get anywhere in business—even if it's the business of saving souls for Jesus Christ—by not trusting the people you're doing business with. That's what I tried to explain to Father Michael, may God rest his soul, in my letter."

"It didn't sound as if your letter was about trust," Hawes said.

"It didn't? I thought it did."

"Well, for example, Mr. Farnes," Hawes said, having already gone over this with Carella and now considering himself an expert, "you don't think these words, do you, are about trust, here, this passage here," he said, unfolding the letter and finding what he was looking for, "here, Mr. Farnes, 'and he poured out the coins of the money-changers and overturned their tables.' Is that about trust, Mr. Farnes?"

"It's about not turning a place of worship into a place of commerce."

"Or how about this," Hawes said, gathering steam, "right here, Mr. Farnes, 'Let Father Birney count the offerings again and yet another time, and then let him count his blessings as well.' What did you mean by 'let him count his blessings as well'?"

"Let him realize that he is blessed with a good and generous congregation."

"And this? What does this mean? 'Pride goeth before destruction, and a haughty spirit before a fall.' Is that about trust?"

"It's about trusting the Lord to show the path that leads away from pride and haughtiness."

"Well, you certainly have an odd way of interpreting your own words," Hawes said. "Did you discuss any of this *personally* with Father Michael?"

"Yes. In fact, we had a good laugh over it."

"A good *what?*"

"A good laugh. Me and Father Michael."

"Had a laugh over this letter you wrote?"

"Oh, yes. Because I was so *incensed*, you see."

"And he found that funny, did he? That you were incensed enough . . ."

"Yes."

". . . by the sermons he'd given . . ."

"Yes."

". . . to have written a letter you yourself just described as 'monumentally angry.' He found that . . ."

"Yes, we both did."

". . . hilarious."

"Well . . ."

"Side-splittingly funny."

"No, but we *did* find it humorous. That I'd got so angry. That I'd written this righteous, indignant letter to the congregation when all I had to do, really, was go see Father Michael personally—as I finally did do—and have a pleasant chat with him, and straighten the whole thing out."

"So you straightened the whole thing out."

"Yes."

"When?"

"On Easter Sunday. I stopped by in the afternoon sometime, went back to the rectory with him. We had a good long talk."

"How'd you finally settle it?"

"Father Michael said he would ask each member of the congregation to confide in him the amount he or she could comfortably afford to contribute each Sunday, and then he would trust them to contribute that amount faithfully. It was all a matter of trust, you see. That's what I was able to explain to him when we talked. That he should just have a little trust." He glanced toward the curtains. The man who'd gone back with the three pairs of pants was just coming through into the store again. There were now only two pairs of pants slung over his arm.

"Just a minute, sir!" Farnes called.

"Ah, there you are," the man said. "I'll take the ones I'm wearing. Can I get them measured, please?"

"Why . . . why, yes, sir, certainly, sir," Farnes said, "please step right this way, the tailor's at the other end of the store."

"I left my own pants in the dressing room," the man said. "Will they be safe there?"

"Just have a little trust, sir," Hawes said.

Carella placed the call to the archdiocese at four-fifteen that afternoon. The man who answered the phone identified himself as Archbishop Quentin's secretary and told him that His Eminence was out at the moment but perhaps he could be of assistance. Carella told him this had to do with a murder he was investigating . . .

"Oh, dear."

"Yes, the murder of the priest up here . . ."

"Ah, yes."

"Father Michael Birney."

"Yes."

"And I'm calling because I'm trying to locate his sister, but there's no answer at the number I . . ."

"His Eminence has already taken care of that," the secretary said.

"Taken care of what?"

"Notifying Father Michael's sister."

"In Japan? How'd he . . . ?"

"Her husband's office number was in our files here. His Eminence was able to get the name of their hotel from Mr. Brogan's secretary, and he called Mrs. Brogan there. She'll be here Sunday in time for the funeral."

"Well, good," Carella said. "Would you happen to know if there are any other relatives? I'd like to . . ."

"I believe there was only the sister."

"And you say she'll be here Sunday?"

"She's already on the way, sir."

"Well, thank you very much."

"Not at all."

Carella put the phone back on the hook.

Already on her way, he thought.

Which meant that whatever had been troubling the good priest would have to wait till Sunday, after all.

The man sitting opposite Marilyn was a white man in his early fifties. His name was Shad Russell, and he knew why she was here, but he was making his pitch anyway because he figured it never hurt to take a chance. Shad used to be a gambler in Las Vegas before he came East and got himself settled in various other little enterprises. He had a pockmarked face from when he was a little kid, and he had a mustache that looked as if it could use some fertilizer, and he was as thin and as tall as Abraham Lincoln and he thought he had a devastating smile. Actually, he looked like a crocodile when he smiled. He was smiling now.

"So old Joe give you my number, huh?" he said.

"Yes," Marilyn said.

"Old Joe Seward," he said, and shook his head.

They were in his room on the second floor of the old Raleigh Hotel on St. Sebastian Avenue, near where the Warringer Theater used to be. Marilyn had come up here to Diamondback by taxi. She was wearing jeans and a leather jacket over a tan sweater. Her hair was pinned up under a woolen cap. It was one thing for a white woman to go alone into an exclusively black neighborhood to talk to someone a Texas pimp had recommended. It was another to go flashing long blonde hair.

"How is he?" Shad asked.

"I haven't seen him in years," she said.

"How come you know him?"

"He said you could help me find a gun."

"But that don't answer my question, does it?" Shad said, and smiled his crocodile smile. Marilyn had the sudden feeling that this was going to be harder than she'd thought.

"If you think I'm a cop or something . . ." she said.

"No, I . . ."

". . . you can call Joe on my credit card, and ask him to . . ."

"I already did."

The crocodile smile.

"Though not on your credit card."

The smile widening.

"On my own nickel. Right after you hung up. To ask him who this Mary Ann Hollis was that needed a gun so bad."

"And what'd he tell you?"

"He told me you used to work for him it musta been eight, nine years ago. When you were still in diapers. He said you used to have a piano-man pimp down there in Houston, but he got himself stabbed in a bar, which was when Joe come into your life. He also told me you got busted at the ripe old age of seventeen, and that he paid the five-bill fine and let you walk away from his stable 'cause you asked him nice and he happens to be a gent. So no, I'm not worried you're fuzz."

"Then why are you asking me things you already know?"

"I wanted to see if you'd lie."

"I would've."

"I figured. Why you need this piece?"

"Some people are bothering me."

"You going to shoot these people?"

"If I have to."

"And then what?"

"Then what what?"

"Who do you tell where you got the piece?"

"Not even my priest," Marilyn said.

"Yeah, I'll just bet you got a priest," Shad said, and smiled the crocodile smile again. "You still in the same line of work?"

"No."

"Too bad. 'Cause I could maybe find some major situations for somebody like you."

"Thanks, I'm not looking for any major..."

"Some *really* major..."

"...or even *minor* ones. I need a gun. Can you sell me one? If not, *adiós*."

"Think about the other for a minute."

"Not even for a second."

"Think about it," he said, and smiled. "Is there any harm thinking about it?"

"Yes, there is."

"Who you gonna shoot with this gun?"

"That's none of your business."

"If the gun comes back to me, then it *becomes* my business."

"It won't come back to you, don't worry."

"Are these people pimps? Does this involve prostitution?"

"No. I already told you, I'm not..."

"'Cause I don't want some angry pimp comin' here yellin' one of his cunts tried to . . ."

"Goodbye, Mr. Russell," Marilyn said, and stood up, and slung her shoulder bag, and started for the door.

"What'd I do?" Shad asked. "Insult you? Too fuckin' bad. I got my own ass to protect here. I don't want no gun of mine involved in a family argument. You got a quarrel with your old man, go settle it with him quiet, you don't need no gun of mine."

"Thanks, I understand your position. It was nice meeting you."

"Look at her. All insulted on her fuckin' high horse. I hit it right on the head, didn't I? You want this gun to dust your pimp."

"Yep, right on the head. Goodbye, Mr. Russell. I'll be sure to tell Joe how helpful you were."

"Sit down, what's your fuckin' hurry? If this ain't a pimp, then what is it? Dope?"

"No."

"You say some people are bothering you, what are they bothering you for? Did you forget to pay them for their cocaine?"

"Do you have a gun for me, or don't you? I don't need this bull-shit, I really don't."

"A gun will cost you," he said.

"How much?"

"It's a shame you ain't in the trade these days," he said, and smiled the crocodile smile. "'Cause I have this very major Colombian merchant who'll be here in the city this weekend, I'm sure we could work out some kind of barter arrange—"

And suddenly he saw what was in Marilyn's eyes.

"All right, all right, all right," he said, "forget it, all right?"

And just as suddenly turned all business.

"What kind of gun did you have in mind?" he asked.

4

The three who came into the squadroom on Saturday morning at the crack of dawn—well, at three minutes to eight, actually—looked either like a wandering band of twelfth-century minstrels or a gypsy troupe out of *Carmen*, depending on your perspective. The perspective from Cotton Hawes's desk was sunwashed and somewhat hazy, the light slanting in through open windows to create an almost prismatic effect of golden air afloat with dancing dust motes. Out of this refracting mass, there appeared the tentative trio, causing Hawes to blink as if he were witnessing either a mirage or a religious miracle.

There were two women and a man.

The man was between and slightly forward of the women, the point of a flying wedge, so to speak, for such it resembled as the three came through the gate in the slatted-rail divider and immediately homed in on the closest desk, which happened to be Hawes's. Perhaps his red hair had served as a beacon. Or perhaps he'd emanated a sense of authority that naturally attracted anyone seeking assistance. Or perhaps they gravitated toward him because he was the only person in the squadroom at this ungodly hour of the morning.

The man was wearing bright blue polyester trousers and a rugby shirt with a white collar and alternating red-and-blue stripes of different widths. He was a hairy giant of a man, with long tawny tresses and a solid, muscular build. One of the women flanking him was tall and black and the other was blonde and not quite as tall, and both women were dressed as if to complement the synthetic glitz of the hirsute giant.

The blonde was wearing a wide, flaring red skirt and a turtleneck shirt (no bra, Hawes noticed) that was the same color as the man's polyester trousers. She was also wearing sandals, although it wasn't yet summertime. The black woman was wearing an equally wide, flaring skirt (hers was green) and a turtleneck shirt (again, no bra, Hawes noticed) that was the color of the blonde's hair. She, too, was wearing sandals.

"There's a sign," Hawes said.

All three looked around.

Hawes pointed.

The hand-lettered sign just to the right of the gate in the railing read:

STATE YOUR BUSINESS
BEFORE ENTERING
SQUADROOM

"Oh, sorry," the man said. "We didn't notice it."

Slight Hispanic accent.

"The desk sergeant said we should come up," the blonde said. Little tiny voice. Almost a whisper. But it compelled attention. Eyes as blue as the sky that stretched beyond the squadroom windows. Voice as flat as the plains of Kansas. Hawes visualized cornfields. "My name is Coral Anderson," she said.

Hawes nodded.

"I'm Stanley Garcia," the man said.

"Laramie Forbes," the black woman said.

"Is it all right to come in?" Coral asked.

"You're in already," Hawes said. "Please sit down."

Stanley took the chair alongside the desk. Quite the gent, Hawes thought. The women dragged chairs over for themselves. Sitting, they crossed their legs under voluminous skirts. The movement reminded Hawes of the days when hippies roamed the earth.

"How can I help you?" he said.

"I'm first deacon at the Church of the Bornless One," Stanley said.

The Church of the Bornless One. *Devil-worship*, Kristin Lund had said. Hawes wondered if Coral and Laramie were second and third deacons respectively. He also wondered what their real names were.

"We're disciples," Laramie said, indicating the blonde with a brief sideward nod.

She had a husky voice. Hawes wondered if she sang in the church choir. He wondered if there were choirs in churches that worshipped the Devil.

"We're here about the dead priest," Stanley said.

Hawes moved a pad into place.

"No, no," Stanley said at once. "Nothing like that."

"Nothing like what?" Hawes said. His pencil was poised above the pad like a guillotine about to drop.

"We had nothing to do with his murder," Stanley said.

"That's why we're here," Coral said.

"Let's get some square handles first," Hawes said.

They looked at him blankly.

"Your real names," he said.

"Coral *is* my real name," the blonde said, offended.

Hawes figured she was lying; *nobody's* real name was Coral.

Nor Laramie, either, for that matter.

"How about you?" he asked the other woman.

"I was born there," she said.

"Where's there?"

"Laramie, Texas," she said. Note of challenge in her husky voice. Dark eyes flashing.

"Does that make it your real name?" Hawes asked.

"How'd *you* like to be Henrietta all your life?"

Hawes thought Cotton was bad enough. The legacy of a religious father who'd believed that Cotton Mather was the greatest of the Puritan priests. He shrugged, wrote "Henrietta Forbes" on the pad, studied it briefly, nodded in agreement, and then immediately asked the blonde, "How do you spell Anderson?"

"With an 'O,'" she said.

"Where are you from originally, Coral?"

"Indiana."

"Lots of Corals out there, I'll bet."

She hesitated, seemed about to flare, and then smiled instead, showing a little gap between her two upper front teeth. "Well, it was Cora Lucille, I guess," she said, still smiling, looking very much like a Cora Lucille in that moment. Hawes imagined pigtails tied with polka-dot rags. He nodded, wrote "Cora Lucille Anderson" on the pad, and then said, "And you, Stanley?"

"Stanley," Stanley said. "But in Spanish."

"Which is?"

"Estaneslao."

"Thanks," Hawes said. "Now what about the priest?"

"We're here about the gate, actually," Coral said, uncrossing her legs and leaning forward earnestly, skirt tented, hands clasped, elbows resting on her thighs, the Sixties again. Hawes was swept with a sudden wave of nostalgia.

"What gate?" he said.

"The churchyard gate."

"What about it?"

"What's painted on the gate," Coral said. "The pentagram."

"The star," Stanley said.

"Inverted," Laramie said.

"Uh-huh," Hawes said.

Let them run with it, he thought.

"We know what you must be thinking," Stanley said. His accent sounded more pronounced now. Hawes wondered if he was getting nervous. He said nothing.

"Because of the star," Laramie said.

"And its association to Satanism," Coral said.

"Uh-huh," Hawes said.

"Which many people misunderstand, of course," Coral said, and smiled her gap-toothed smile again.

"In what way?" Hawes asked.

"Is the pentagram misunderstood?"

"Yes."

"In that it's upside down," Stanley said.

"Inverted," Laramie said.

"May I borrow your pencil?" Coral said.

"Sure," he said, and handed it to her.

"And I'll need a piece of paper."

He tore a page from the back of the pad and handed it to her.

"Thanks," she said.

He noticed that she was holding the pencil in her left hand. He wondered if left-handedness had anything to do with Devil worship. He wondered if they were *all* left-handed.

"This is what a star looks like," she said, and began drawing. "The star we see on the American flag, a sheriff's star, they all look like this."

Hawes watched as the star took shape.

"There," she said.

"Uh-huh," he said.

"And this is what a star looks like when you turn it upside down," she said.

"When you invert it," Laramie said.

"Yes," Coral said, her head bent over the sheet of paper, her left hand moving. "There," she said again, and showed the page to Hawes again. Side by side, the stars looked like a pair of acrobats turning cartwheels:

"Uh-huh," Hawes said.

"Do you see the difference?"

"Yes, of course."

"What's the difference?" Coral asked.

"The difference is that the one on the left . . ."

"Yes, the so-called *pure* pentagram . . ."

"Whatever, has only *one* point on top, whereas the other has *two*."

"Yes," Coral said. "And whereas the pure pentagram stands on *two* points, the symbol of Baphomet . . ."

"The *inverted* star . . ."

". . . stands on only one point."

"Indicating the direction to Hell," Laramie said.

"I see," Hawes said. Though he didn't really.

"If you look at the *pure* pentagram . . ." Coral said.

"The one on the left," Stanley said.

"Yes," Hawes said.

"You can imagine, can't you," Coral said, "a man standing with his legs widespread . . . those are the two lower points of the star . . . and his arms outstretched . . . those are the two middle points. His head would be the uppermost point."

"I see," Hawes said again, trying hard to visualize a man inside the upright star.

"In ancient times . . ." Coral said.

"Oh, centuries ago," Stanley said.

"The *white* magicians . . ."

"This has nothing to do with their *color*," Laramie said.

"No, only with the kind of magic they performed," Coral said. "*White* magic."

"Yes," Hawes said.

"As opposed to *black* magic," Stanley said.

"Yes."

"These *white* magicians," Coral said, "used the pentagram to symbolize the goodness of man . . ."

". . . because it showed him standing upright," Laramie said.

"But in the church of the *opposite* . . ." Coral said.

"Where good is evil and evil is good . . ."

"In the church of the *contrary* . . ." Coral said.

"Where to lust is to aspire . . ."

"And to achieve is to satisfy all things carnal . . ."

"The pentagram has been turned upside down . . ." Coral said.

"Inverted," Laramie said.

"So that the horns of the goat . . ."

". . . the Satanic symbol of lust . . ."

". . . fit exactly into the two upper points . . ."

". . . which represent Good and Evil . . ."

". . . the universal duality in eternal conflict . . ."

"And the three *other* points," Coral said, "represent in their inverted form a *denial* of the trinity . . ."

". . . the Father, the Son and the Holy Ghost," Stanley said.

". . . doomed to burn eternally in the flames of Hell . . ." Laramie said.

". . . as indicated by the single point jutting directly downward," Stanley said.

"An upside-down star," Coral said.

"Inverted," Laramie said, and all three fell silent.

"What about it?" Hawes asked.

"Detective Hawes," Coral said, "we are aware . . ."

He wondered how she knew his name.

". . . that the star painted on St. Catherine's gate might link us in the minds of the police . . ."

Sergeant Murchison had probably given it to her downstairs.

". . . to the murder of the priest there."

"*But*," Laramie said.

"*But*," Coral said, "we want you to know that we plan to question our congregation tonight and find out whether somebody if anybody painted that star on the churchyard gate."

"And if they did . . ." Stanley said.

". . . we'll make damn sure that person comes right over here to tell you about it his own self. So you can question them and see we had nothing to do with it. The murder. Even if someone, if anyone, *is* guilty of painting that gate."

"Guilt is innocence," Laramie said.

"We'll let you know," Stanley said, and all three rose in many-splendored radiance and disappeared into the sunlight and through the gate at which they had originally materialized.

Hawes wondered how Carella was doing out there on the street.

On a bright spring morning, it was difficult to think of the street as a slum. There seemed no visible evidence of poverty here. The people walking by at a leisurely pace were not dressed in tatters. There were flowerpots with blooms in them on fire escapes and windowsills. The window curtains flapping in the early morning breeze seemed clean and fresh as did the laundry hanging on backyard clotheslines. The sanitation trucks had been through early, and the garbage cans were lined up empty along wrought-iron railings that flanked recently swept front stoops. As Carella came up the street, a water truck was sprinkling the gutters, giving the black asphalt a sheen of rain-washed freshness. This could not be a slum.

But it was.

The endless crush of winter had departed, and in its place there was now the false hope of spring. But the people living in these tenements—true, the red brick did seem brighter in sunshine than it did beneath a grey and leaden sky—knew that hope was the thing with feathers, as elusive and as rare as happiness. This stretch of 87th Precinct territory was almost exclusively black. And here, despite the illusion of spring, there was indeed grinding poverty, and illiteracy, and drug addiction and malnutrition and desperation. The black man in America knew where it was at. And where it was at was not here, not in these mean streets. Where it was at was uptown someplace, so far uptown that the black man had never been there, could not even visualize it there, knew only that uptown was a shining city somewhere high on a hill, a promised land where everyone went to Choate and Yale and a thousand points of light glistened in every cereal bowl.

Read my lips, Carella thought.

Nathan Hooper lived in a tenement two blocks south of The Stem.

At eight-thirty that Saturday morning, Carella found him asleep in a back bedroom he shared with his older brother and his thirteen-year-old sister. Hooper was sixteen. The brother, dressed and out of the house already, was eighteen. The sister was wearing a white cotton slip. Hooper was wearing white Jockey undershorts and a white tank top undershirt. He was annoyed that his mother had let the police in while he was still asleep. He told his sister to cover up, couldn't she see there was somebody here? The sister shrugged into a robe and padded out to the kitchen, where Hooper's mother was having her morning coffee. She had already told Carella that she had to be at work at nine; on Saturdays and Sundays, she cleaned offices downtown. Rest of the week, she cleaned white people's houses uptown.

Hooper pulled on a pair of jeans and went out into the narrow hallway barefooted, Carella following. The bathroom was a six-by-eight rectangle containing a sink, an ancient yellowing claw-footed bathtub with a jerry-built shower over it, and an incessantly gurgling toilet bowl. A plastic curtain was drawn half-closed over the tub. The remainder of the curtain rod was hung with bikini panties. Hooper stepped in, and closed the door behind him. Standing in the hallway,

Carella could hear him first urinating and then washing at the sink. When the door opened again, Hooper was drying his hands on a peach-colored towel.

Wordlessly, scowling, he went back into the bedroom again, Carella still following him. He opened the middle drawer of the only dresser in the room, took out a black T-shirt, and pulled it on over his head. He sat on the edge of the bed, pulled on a pair of white socks, and laced up a pair of black, high-topped sneakers. He was wearing his hair in what was called a High Top Fade, currently the rage among young black men in this city. The hairdo resembled a fez sitting on top of the head, with the lower part of the skull shaved almost clean, and it required very little maintenance other than an occasional bit of topiary. Hooper passed a pick comb through it, and walked out into the kitchen, still wordlessly, still scowling, Carella still patiently following. Hooper's sister was sitting at the table, a mug of coffee between her hands. She was staring through the open kitchen window at the clothes flapping on the backyard lines, watching them in fascination, as if they were brightly colored birds. Hooper's mother was just about to leave. She was a woman in her fifties, Carella guessed. Actually, he was high by about ten years.

"Offer the man some coffee," she said, and went out.

"You want some coffee?" Hooper asked grudgingly.

"I could use some," Carella said.

"You always come see people in the middle of the night?" the sister asked.

"Sorry I got here so early," Carella said, and smiled.

The girl did not smile back. Hooper was rummaging in the cupboard over the drainboard, searching for clean cups. He made a great show of exasperation, finally banged two cups down on the counter top, miraculously unscathed, and poured them three-quarters full. A container of milk was on the table. He poured from it into his own cup, and then shoved it across to where Carella had taken the chair alongside the girl's.

"Sugar?" the girl said, and offered Carella the bowl.

"Thanks," Carella said. "What's your name?"

"Why?" she said.

"Why not?" he said, and smiled.

"Seronia," she said.

"Nice to meet you."

"When you gonna lock up the shits beat up Nate?" she said.

"That's what I'd like to talk about," Carella said.

"Be the first one since it happened," Seronia said, and shrugged.

"That's not entirely true, is it?" Carella said. "The way *I* found out about it was from a report in our files. So *someone* had to . . ."

"Yeah, the blues," Hooper said. "But wasn't no detectives come around later is whut she means."

"Well, here's a detective now," Carella said.

"You don't look like no detective *I* ever seen," Seronia said. "Mama says you showed her a badge, but, man, you don't look like no detective to me."

"What do detectives look like?" he asked.

"Like pieces a shit," she said.

Carella wasn't looking for an argument here. Nor was he even certain the girl was trying to provoke one. He was here for information. A priest had been murdered. A priest who'd protected this boy on Easter Sunday.

"According to the report . . ."

"The report's full of shit," Hooper said. "The only thing they wanted to do was get out of that church *fast*, before they got lynched. They were scareder than I was. You never seen two cops writing so fast."

"They dinn even drive him to the hospital," Seronia said. "He's bleedin' like you shoulda seen him, man. Was the *priest* finely took him to the 'mergency room."

"Where was this?"

"Greer General."

"And you say Father Michael drove you there?"

"*Walked* me there, man," Hooper said. "You know like Christ walkin' with the fuckin' cross on his back and everybody jeerin' him, whatever? That was me, man. I'm bleedin' from the head from where one of them fucks hit me with a ball bat . . ."

"Start from the beginning," Carella said.

"What's the use?" Hooper said.

"What can you lose?" Seronia said, and shrugged again.

Easter this year had fallen on the fifteenth day of April, but even in its death throes winter tenaciously refused to loosen its grip and the day was howlingly windy, with what appeared to be a promise of snow on the air. A sullen roiling sky hung in angry motion over the city, giving it the look of an El Greco painting even in neighborhoods not entirely Hispanic. In this checkerboard precinct where black squares became white squares in the blink of an eye, Nathan Hooper lived in an area that was ninety-percent black, eight-percent Hispanic, and two-percent Asian. Not two blocks away was an entirely white neighborhood composed of Italians, Irish, and a sprinkling of Jews. The melting pot in this precinct has never really come to a boil. On this windy Easter Sunday, it is about to overboil.

Hooper rarely goes to church, but today he runs into a friend of his named Harold Jones, who the other guys all call Fat Harold after the Bill Cosby routine. Fat Harold isn't truly fat; he is, in fact, rather thin and spindly-looking. He is also a crack addict who is on his way to church this Easter Sunday to pray that he can kick his habit and become a rich and famous black television star like Bill Cosby. Hooper decides to go along with him. Too fuckin' cold and windy to hang out, might as well join Fat Harold.

The church they go to is on the corner of Ainsley and Third, and it is called the First Baptist Abyssinian Church of Isola. Hooper is glad it's warm inside the church, because as far as he's concerned the rest of it is all bullshit. He's already dropped out of school because he doesn't do too good reading—none of his teachers ever once realized he was dyslexic—but one thing he did learn from all those history books he struggled through was that most of the wars that ever occurred on this planet was because one religion tried to tell another religion it was the only true way to God. So what the preacher is laying down in the church here this morning—all this stuff about Jesus getting crucified by the Romans or the Jews or whoever the fuck did it, Hooper doesn't know and doesn't give a damn—is all a lot of bullshit to him. These people want to believe fairy tales about virgins getting pregnant without nobody fucking them, that was their business. All Hooper was doing here was getting warm

They're out of church by a little past noon. Fat Harold wants to go to this crack house he knows, buy himself a nickel vial, pass the time smoking some dope. But Hooper tells him what's the sense he just went to church and prayed his ass off for salvation if the next minute he's back on the pipe, does that make sense, man? He tells Fat Harold why don't he use the five bucks they go see a movie and buy some popcorn? Fat Harold thinks he rather go smoke some dope. So they part company on Ainsley—this is now maybe ten past twelve, a quarter past—and Fat Harold goes his way to the crack house where he's gonna find hope in a pipe, man, and Hooper walks crosstown and a little ways uptown on The Stem to where this movie theater is playing a new picture with Eddie Murphy in it.

Uptown.

Is where this movie theater is.

Uptown.

Where Eddie Murphy and Bill Cosby live.

Hooper knows he is walking into white turf, he wasn't born yesterday. But, man, this is Easter Sunday and all he's doing is going to a fuckin' movie where there's hundreds of white people standing on line outside, waitin' to see a black man up there on the screen. Handful of blacks on the line, too, here and there, guys all silked up, sportin' for they girls, this is Easter Sunday, it'll be cool, man, no sweat.

Hooper wishes he had a girl with him, too. But he broke up with this chick last month 'cause she was mad he dropped out of school, which was probably for the best if she didn't understand how he wasn't *getting* nowhere in that fuckin' school, what was the sense wastin' his *time* there? Learn more on a street corner in ten minutes than you did in school the whole fuckin' term. But on days like today, dudes all around him with they girls, he misses her. Always makes him feel like some kind of jerk, anyway, going to a movie alone.

Eddie Murphy takes care of that, though.

Eddie Murphy makes him feel good.

You see a handsome black man up there, smart as hell and not takin' any shit from Whitey, it makes you feel real good. Eddie Murphy probably lived in a big house on a hill overlooking the ocean. Probably had blonde girls coming in to suck his cock and wash his feet with they hair like the preacher was talking about Jesus's feet this morning. You was Eddie Murphy, you could buy anything in the world you wanted, have anything you wanted. Didn't matter you was black. You was Eddie *Murphy,* man! In the movie theater, sitting there in the dark with mostly white people, Hooper likes to wet his pants laughing every time Eddie Murphy does another one of his shrewd things. White people all around him are laughing, too. Not at any dumb *nigger* but at dumb *Charlie* who the nigger's fuckin' around. Hooper doesn't completely understand why all these white people are laughin' at they ownselves, but he knows it makes him feel *damn* good.

He is still feeling good when he comes out of the theater at two-thirty, around then. It isn't snowing yet, but it sure feels like it's gonna start any minute. Still windy as can be, great big gusts blowin' in off the River Harb and cuttin' clear to the marrow. He can walk home one of two ways. He can go down on The Stem to North Fifth, and then come crosstown the three blocks to his own building on Culver, where maybe some of the guys'll be hangin' out, or he can go directly crosstown on Eleventh where the theater is, and then walk downtown on Culver, six of one, half a dozen of the other—except that the Eleventh Street route will take him straight through an exclusively Italian neighborhood.

Hooper does not belong to any of the neighborhood street gangs. Neither does he do dope nor run dope for any of the myriad crack dealers who are what the newspapers call "a blight on the urban landscape." He is not a good student, but this does not make him a bad person. The color of his skin does not make him a bad person, either.

He is black. He knows he is black. But he has never done a criminal thing in his life. Never. (He repeats the word fervently to Carella now: "*Never!*") This is no small achievement in a neighborhood where the word "bad" is often used with pride. I'm a *baaaad* nigger, man. If Hooper's gonna be *any* kind of nigger, it's gonna be a *good* one. Like Eddie Murphy. (He tells this to Carella, too, driving the point home by rapping a clenched fist on his T-shirted chest.)

The Italian-Americans on Eleventh Street are so far removed in time, space and attitude from their heritage in Naples or Palermo that they could, if they chose to, safely drop the hyphenated form. These are *Americans*, period, born and bred on the turf they now inhabit with somewhat confused and confusing ethnic pride. These are kids whose great-*great*-grandparents came here as immigrants at the turn of the century. Kids whose *great*-grandparents were first-generation Americans. Kids whose grandparents fought against Italy in World War II, whose parents were teenagers in the Sixties, and who themselves are now teenagers who do not speak Italian and who do not care to learn, thank you. They are Americans. And it is American to cherish home and family, American to protect one's neighborhood from evil infiltration, American to cherish God and country and to make sure no niggers fuck your sisters.

Hooper is aware of them at once.

He has come perhaps a block and a half crosstown from The Stem when he sees them on the front stoop of the building. There are six of them. This is Easter Sunday and they are all silked out in their new Easter threads, hanging out and kidding around, laughing. He tells himself that's all they're doing is hanging out and kidding around, laughing, but warning hackles go up on the back of his neck, anyway. He should not be here. He should have gone down The Stem to Fifth Street instead, he was dumb to come across Eleventh where up ahead all of a sudden the horseplay stops and the laughter stops and there is a dead silence, they have spotted him.

He figures he should cross the street.

Would Eddie Murphy cross the street?

Sheee-it, man, *no*! Hooper's got as much right as these dudes to be wherever the fuck he *wants* to be, man—but his heart is pounding. He knows there is going to be trouble. He can smell it on the air, he can feel it coming his way on the wind, blowin' on the wind, man, touching his black skin like somebody usin' a cattle prod on him . . . trouble . . . danger . . . *run*!

But would Eddie Murphy run?

He does not run.

He does not cross the street.

He keeps walking toward where the six of them have now come off the stoop and are standing on the sidewalk in a casual phalanx, hands dangling loosely at their sides like gunslicks about to draw, narrow smiles on their faces, say somethin' smart, he thinks, say somethin' cool, be Eddie Murphy, man! But nothing smart comes. Nothing cool comes.

He smiles.

"Hey, man," he says to the closest one.

And the baseball bat comes swinging out of nowhere.

"Do you know which one used the bat?" Carella asked.

"No," Hooper said.

"They *all* had bats," Seronia said.

"That was later," Hooper said. "When they start chasin' me. All at once, they *all* got bats. Or garbage can lids. It was that first bat bust my head, though. 'Cause it took me by surprise. It musta been one of them standin' in the back had the bat hid, you know? So when I come up, I'm like a sittin' duck, you know? I give 'em my shit-eatin' grin, I say 'Hey, man' politely, and *wham* the bat comes from somewhere hid behind them, breaks my head open."

"What happened then?"

"I ran, man, whutchoo *think* happen? They six of them who all at once got ball bats, and they yellin' nigger and whatnot, man I know a lynch mob when I see one. I got the hell out of there fast as my feet could carry me. But that wasn't gonna be the end of it, far as they was concerned. They was right behind me, all six of 'em, cussin' and yellin' and chasin' me off they turf. I figured once I got to Culver I be okay, I could run downtown on Culver, get the hell off Eleventh Street . . ."

"You was crazy goin' in there in the first place," Seronia said.

"It was Easter," Hooper said in explanation, and shrugged.

"All right, they're chasing you," Carella said.

"Yeah, and I'm thinkin' I gotta get off the street, I stay here on the street, they goan kill me. I gotta be someplace where they witnesses, a restaurant, a bar, anythin' where they people can *see* what's happenin' if it goes that far. 'Cause it *sounds* like it's goan all the way, man, it sounds like they out to kill me."

"Then what?"

"All at once, I see this church up ahead. I never been inside it in my life, but there it is, and I figure there's got to be people inside a church, don't there, this is Easter Sunday. I like was losin' track of time by then, I didn't realize there wouldn't be no services two-thirty, three o'clock, whatever it was by then. But the front door was open . . ."

"Standing open?"

"No, no. Unlocked. I tried it and it was unlocked. They were right behind me, man, it's a good thing it *wasn't* locked, I'd be dead right there on the church steps. So I ran in with my head busted open and drippin' blood and them behind me yellin', and I hear *more* yellin' from someplace in the church, and the first thing I think is they got me surrounded, man, there's yellin' behind me and yellin' in front of me, I'm a dead man."

"What do you mean, yelling in front of you?"

"From like behind these columns. Two people yelling."

"Behind what columns?"

"Where they on the right side of the church, you know? They's like these columns and what I guess must be a little room back there 'cause . . ."

"Is that where the yelling was coming from? This little room behind the columns? On the right-hand side of the church?"

"I'm only *sayin'* it was a room, I was never in it. But this door opened, and a priest came out . . ."

"From the room?"

"From whatever was there behind the door. He heard all the yellin' in the church, you see. Heard them yellin' nigger and they was goan kill me, like that, and heard me yellin' Help, somebody help me! So he came out lookin' surprised and scared and first thing he sees is me spillin' blood from my head, and he goes, 'What's this, what's this?' like he can't believe it, you know, here's a nigger bleedin' on his floor and six white guys chasin' him. So I yell, 'Hey, man, *hep* me, they goan *kill* me!' and the priest sees what's happenin' now, gets it all in a flash, man, and steps between me and them and tells them get the fuck outa his church, tells them this is God's house, how dare they, all that shit. Meanwhile somebody'd called the cops, and by the time they showed up there was a big crowd outside, everybody yellin' and screamin' even if they didn't know what the fuck was happenin'. It was the priest walked me to the hospital. The cops were too scared. If you're gonna write up a report . . ."

"I am."

"You better mention them fucks was too scared to put me in the car and drive me the six blocks to Greer. I had to walk it with the priest."

"I'll mention it," Carella said.

A lot of good it'll do, he thought. The police protected their own. This was a simple, perhaps regrettable fact. But he would mention it.

"You say the priest was arguing with someone when you came into the . . ."

"Yeah."

"Who, do you know?"

"No. It was behind the door there."

"A man? A woman?"

"A man, I think. There were six fuckin' guys tryin'a *kill* me, you think I gave a shit who . . ."

"How do you know they were arguing?"

"'Cause they were yellin' at each other."

"Did you hear anything they said?"

"Just these loud voices."

"Two voices? Or more than two?"

"I don't know."

"Well . . . after it was all over . . . did you *see* anyone?"

"What do you mean?"

"Coming out of that room."

"Oh. No. We went straight to the hospital. The cops opened up a path in the crowd out there, and me and the priest went through. I didn't see nobody else inside the church."

"You know Father Michael was killed on Thursday night, don't you?"

"Sure," Hooper said. "And I know who done it, too."

Carella looked at him.

"Them wops," Hooper said. "They made a blood vow they gonna get both me *and* the priest. For what happened on Easter. So now they got the priest, so that means I'm next. And for what? For walkin' on the street mindin' my own fuckin' business."

"For bein' *black*," Seronia said.

Carella had no argument.

"It was very nice of you to come up here, Miss Lund," Hawes said. "I know it's Saturday, and I hate to intrude on your time."

"Not at all," she said. "Happy to help in any way I can."

The clock on the wall read twenty minutes past eleven. Krissie was wearing blue jeans, leather boots, a white T-shirt, and a fringed leather vest. No makeup except lipstick and eye liner. Long blonde hair pulled to the back of her head in a ponytail. She smelled of spring flowers.

"As I told you on the phone, the lab sent over this whole batch of letters and bills and whatnot, all Father Michael's stuff, you know, which I just finished going through. The point is, the lab found some very good latents on them, and we . . ."

"Latents?"

"Father Michael's, of course, but also some wild prints that may have been left by the killer. In case he'd been in the office looking through the files for something, which is still a possibility because of that open file drawer and the papers on the floor. Okay, so far?"

"Yes," Krissie said, and smiled.

"So what we're trying to do is track down the wild prints—the ones we know for sure weren't left by Father Michael—and eliminate whoever might have had a *legitimate* reason to be handling the papers. One of the logical..."

"Yes, his secretary," Krissie said, and smiled.

"Yes, would be a logical choice. Typing them, filing them, and so on."

"Yes."

"You look very pretty this morning," he said.

The words startled her. They startled him, too. He hadn't expected to say them out loud. A second earlier, he'd only been *thinking* them.

"Well, thank you," Krissie said.

"Sorry," he said.

"No, no."

"But you do."

"Well, thanks."

There was an awkward silence. They stood side by side in a shaft of sunlight streaming through the window. The squadroom was unusually silent this morning. Somewhere down the hall, a telephone rang. Outside on the street, a horn honked.

"The thing is," he said, and cleared his throat, "if the killer *did* touch any of the papers—and chances are he at least had his hands on that stuff he threw all over the floor—then by eliminating as many of the latents as we can, we might have a shot at identification later on. If we come up with anybody. Which so far we haven't. But if we do."

"Yes."

"Which is why I asked you to stop by to have your prints taken, if it's no bother."

"No bother at all," she said.

"It'll take ten, fifteen minutes at the most."

"I've always wondered what it'd be like to have my fingerprints taken."

"Really? Well, here's your chance to find out."

"Yes," she said.

"Yes," he said, and cleared his throat again.

"Are you catching a cold?" she asked.

"No, I don't think so."

"Because you keep clearing your throat, you know . . ."

"No, that's . . ."

"So I thought maybe . . ."

"No, that's a nervous reaction," Hawes said.

"Oh," she said.

"Yes."

"Oh."

They looked at each other.

"Well, how do we do this?" she asked.

"Well . . . if you'll step over to this table . . ."

"Just like in the movies, huh?"

"Sort of."

"I've never had my fingerprints taken before," she said.

"Yes, I know."

"Did I tell you?"

"Yes."

"Oh. Then it must be true," she said.

"Yes."

"The first thing I have to do," he said, "is lock my pistol in the desk drawer there because what happened once—I don't know how long ago this was—a police officer somewhere in the city was fingerprinting a felon and the guy grabbed the gun and shot him dead."

"Oh my!" Krissie said.

"Yeah," Hawes said. "So now it's a rule that whenever we're fingerprinting anyone, we have to take off the gun."

He walked over to his desk, dropped his pistol into one of the deep drawers on the right-hand side, locked the drawer, and then came back to the fingerprinting table. Krissie watched apprehensively as he began squirting black ink from a tube onto a pane of glass.

"This stuff washes right off with soap and water," he said.

"Thank God," she said.

"Oh sure, nothing to worry about."

"You must be an expert at this," she said.

"Well, it becomes second nature. Although we rarely do it any-more. This is all done at Central Booking now. Downtown. At Head-quarters."

"Mugging and printing," she said. "Is that what you call it?"

"Yes."

"Mugging and printing," she said again.

"Yes."

He was rolling the ink onto the glass now, spreading it evenly. She watched him with great interest.

"You have to spread it, huh?" she said.

"Yes."

"Like blackberry jam," she said.

"I never thought of it that way," he said, and put down the roller. "There we go. Now I'll just take one of these cards . . ."

He took a fingerprint card from the rack at the back of the table.

"And if you'll let me have your right hand first . . ."

She extended her hand to him.

"I have to . . . uh . . . sort of . . . uh . . . if you'll just let your hand hang sort of . . . uh . . . loose . . . I have to roll them on the glass first, you see, each finger . . ."

"I hope this stuff really washes off," she said.

"Oh, yes, with soap and water, I promise. There, that's better."

She was sort of standing with her right hip sort of against him somewhat, his arms sort of cradling her arm, sort of holding her hand in both his hands as he rolled her fingers one at a time on the glass, and then rolled them in turn on the fingerprint card . . .

"Now the thumb," he said.

"Am I doing this right?" she asked.

"Just let me do it," he said, "just relax, that's the way . . ."

. . . sort of standing very close to each other in the silent sunwashed squadroom, he could smell the scent of her flowery perfume . . .

"Now the other hand," he said.

. . . sort of guiding each finger onto the glass, rolling it there, lifting it, rolling it onto the card, sort of moving together with a special rhythm now, her hand in his, her hip sort of molded in against him . . .

"This is sort of fun," she said.

"Yes," he said, "can you have dinner with me tonight?"

"I'd love to," she said.

She'd finally chosen the Walther PPK, a neat little .32 caliber automatic with an eight-shot capacity. Shad Russell had showed her some guns that had five, six-shot capacities, but she figured if push came to shove she might need those few extra cartridges. Seven in the magazine, he'd told her, another in the breech. He'd also showed her some .22 caliber pistols, but she insisted on the heavier firepower. Shad told her the caliber didn't mean a thing. You could sometimes do more damage with a .22 than with a .45. She didn't believe him. If you had to bring down a giant, you didn't go after him with a pea shooter.

She wasn't even sure *this* gun would do the job. But all of his bigger caliber guns seemed either too bulky or too heavy. The Walther had a short three-inch barrel, with an overall length of only five and a half inches, and the lightweight model she chose weighed only a bit more than twelve ounces. It fit snugly in her handbag, alongside of— and not very much bulkier than—her wallet. Shad had charged her six hundred dollars for the gun. She figured that his profit on this deal alone would pay for a vacation at Lake Como.

She had discovered that a person did not jaywalk when she was carrying an unlicensed pistol. She suspected that not many such gun-toters exceeded the speed limit, either. Or spit on the sidewalk. Or even raised their voices in public places. She was breaking the law. And would break it further if she had to. Break it to the limit if she had to. Her bag felt heavier with the gun in it. The weight was reassuring.

She had spent this Saturday morning shopping in the midtown area, and had boarded an uptown-bound, graffiti-covered subway train at twenty past two. She was not in the habit of taking expensive taxi rides all over the city, and she did not plan on changing her habits now. Moreover, she sensed that there would be safety in crowded places; they had spooked yesterday when she'd led them directly to a cop.

The train rattled along in the underground dark.

Marilyn wondered if there were such things as passionate, poetic men who looked like lions and made their homes in subway caves. She wondered if there were alligators in the city's sewers. She wondered if there was such a thing as happily ever after.

The train pulled into a station stop.

The doors hissed open.

She watched the passengers coming on. She did not expect anyone even remotely resembling her two Hispanics to board. The doors hissed shut again. The train was in motion.

It was two-thirty-five when she got off the train uptown on The Stem and began walking northward toward the river. She was certain that they knew where she lived, had undoubtedly followed her from there to the school. As she approached Silvermine Oval now, her eyes swept both sides of the street ahead. Her handbag was slung on her left shoulder. Her right hand rested on its open top, hovering over the butt of the Walther.

Nothing.

She kept walking.

Entered the Oval, came around it. Nanny pushing a baby carriage in the bright sunshine. Such a lovely day. The weight of the gun in her bag. Around the Oval and onto Harborside. The small park across the street from her house. Potential danger there. A man approaching on the park side of the street. Short man wearing a tan sports jacket. Little mustache under his nose. Charlie Chaplin lookalike. Went on by, buried in his own thoughts. She scanned the park entrance.

Nothing.

1211 Harborside was just ahead, on her left. No one on either side of the street, not a sign of activity in the park. A pigeon fluttered overhead, glided over the park fence, settled on the walk inside the gate. She approached the building and fished into her bag for her keys, the back of her hand brushing up against the Walther. Found the keys, unlocked both locks on the door, came into the entryway, and secured the locks behind her. She was wearing a Chanel ripoff, blue skirt and blue jacket with a blue ruff. Unbuttoning the jacket, she went to the answering machine, saw that she'd had three messages, and pressed the playback button.

"Honey, it's me."

Willis's voice.

"Did you make dinner reservations for tonight? Because *I* didn't, and it's Saturday night, and we'll have a hell of a time this late. I kind of feel like Italian, don't you? Do you think you could try Mangia Bene? I'm at the lab, I should be home around four-thirty, see you then, love ya."

She looked at her watch.

Ten minutes to three.

"Hello, Miss Willis, this is Sylvia Bourne, I'm the real estate person you were talking to Thursday night, at the open house? Oliphant Realty? The co-op? I wonder if you and Mr. Hollis have had a chance to think about that penthouse apartment? I'm sure the sponsor would entertain a bid lower than the three-fifty, if you'd care to make an offer. Let me know what you think, won't you? It's negotiable. I know I gave you my card, but here's the number again."

As she reeled off the number—twice, no less—Marilyn wondered why no one could ever get their names straight. It would be worth getting married just so they'd have only *one* name to worry about.

"Hello, Marilyn?"

A woman's voice.

"It's Eileen."

Eileen?

"Burke. If you've got a minute, can you give me a call? At home, please. Few things I'd like to discuss with you. Here's the number."

Marilyn listened to the number, writing, thinking this had to be mental telepathy. Yesterday she'd thought of calling Eileen about a gun, and today Eileen was calling *her*. The difference was that today she already *had* a gun. And she *still* wasn't sure Eileen liked her very much. So why call me? And, conversely, do *I* like *her* enough to call her back?

First things first, she thought.

Mangia Bene.

She found the number in her personal directory, dialed it, said she was calling for Detective Willis—why *not* a little P.D. muscle on a Saturday night?—and asked if they could take two of them at eight o'clock. Unconsciously, she looked at her watch again. Three o'clock sharp. He'd be home in an hour and a half. She waited while the maître d' consulted his reservations book, clucking his tongue all the while. Finally, he said, *"Sì, Signora* Willis, two of you at eight, we look forward to seeing you then."

Willis again.

She cradled the phone, debated calling Eileen right that minute, get it over with, decided she'd rather bathe first. Slinging her shoulder bag, she went upstairs to the third floor of the house.

They were waiting for her in the bedroom.

5

She went for the gun.

She went for it at once, not a moment's hesitation, right hand crossing her body and dipping into the open mouth of the bag, fingers curling around the grip, gun coming up and out of the bag, forefinger inside the trigger guard, thumb snapping off the safety, gun leveling to—

He was on her in an instant.

The big one.

Moving swiftly across the Persian rug on the parqueted floor, past the canopied bed and the love seat upholstered in royal-blue crushed velvet. He was an experienced street fighter, he did not grab for the gun, the gun was where the danger was. He came up on her left side instead, ducking inside the gun hand and throwing his shoulder against her chest before she could pull off a shot. She stumbled backward. He hit her full in the face, his huge fist bunched. She felt immediate pain, and brought her left hand up at once, forgetting the gun, the pain shrieking, cupping her nose, pulling her hand away covered with blood. He took the gun out of her hand as if taking a toy from a naughty child. She knew he'd broken her nose. The pain was excruciating. Blood poured onto her hand, blood dripped through her fingers, blood stained her blouse and the front of her jacket, blood spattered onto the Persian rug, she wondered abruptly if the stains would come out, the pain, where was the gun?

He was grinning.

Big fucking gorilla standing there grinning while she held back the screams that bubbled into her throat, the small gun in his huge hand, King Kong standing on the Empire State Building swatting airplanes.

"No more of that," he said in Spanish, grinning.

The other one, the handsome one, was moving into the bathroom. She kept her eyes on the ugly one, the one who had hurt her. He did not know there was also a switchblade knife in her bag. She would slit his throat the moment she had a chance. The handsome one came out of the bathroom.

"Here," he said in Spanish and handed her one of her good bath towels. White. With the initials MH monogrammed on it in curliqued lettering fit for royalty. Gold on white. She did not want to stain her good towel. But she was bleeding all over the floor. She put the towel to her nose.

"Noses bleed a lot," the ugly one said in Spanish, as if making a comment on the weather.

The other one merely nodded.

"Do you have a license for this gun?" the ugly one said in Spanish, and laughed.

She said nothing.

Held the towel to her nose, trying to stop the flow of blood. Nothing to do for the pain. The pain shrieked and shrieked. She kept her teeth clenched to keep from screaming. She would not scream. She would not reveal her terror. She would wait for the proper moment, and then go for the knife. Cut him. Hurt him the way he had hurt her. And then go after the other one, the handsome one.

"Answer him," he said.

In Spanish. They were both speaking Spanish, assuming she understood, recognizing that if she was in fact Mary Ann Hollis, then she too would speak Spanish, she had learned Spanish in that fucking Mexican hellhole and had polished it on her knees in Buenos Aires.

She pretended not to understand. Stupidity, she realized. The initials
MH were on every towel in the bathroom.

"Did you hear me?" the handsome one said. "Answer him!"

"I don't understand you," she said in English.

"She doesn't understand us," he said in Spanish, "so knock out all
her fucking teeth."

The big one moved toward her, turning the gun up in his hand,
flipping it so that the butt was in striking position. He was grinning
again.

"No," she said.

"No what?" the handsome one said.

In Spanish.

"No, don't hit me," she said.

In English.

"I don't understand you," he said in Spanish.

"No me pegues, por favor," she said.

"Muy bien," the handsome one said. "Now we will speak only
Spanish, *comprendes?"*

"Sí," she said, *"solo español."*

Until I go for the knife, she thought.

"Do you know why we're here?" he asked.

"No."

"Do you know who we are?"

"No."

"My name is Ramon Castaneda. My colleague is Carlos Ortega."

She nodded.

"Do you think it foolhardy of us? Telling you our names?"

She said nothing.

"We trust you not to tell anyone after we're gone," Ramon said.

"Or we'll come back to kill you," Carlos said, and grinned.

The gun was no longer in his hand. Had he put it in his pocket?
She should have been paying more attention, but she'd been too fucking intent on her Spanish lesson, too afraid the big one, Carlos, would
really use the gun on her teeth. She had let them frighten her. They
had won the first small battle, not even a battle, a tiny skirmish,

frightening her into revealing that she spoke Spanish fluently. But they'd known this already. Just as they knew she was Marilyn Hollis. Or, more accurately, Mary Ann Hollis. On the street yesterday, they had called her first Marianna and then Mariucha. They knew her as Mary Ann Hollis. In which case she could claim . . .

"What do you . . . ?" she started in English, and immediately switched to Spanish. "What do you want here?"

"The money," Ramon said.

Straight to the point, she thought.

"What money?"

"The money you stole from Alberto Hidalgo," Carlos said.

Even more directly to the point.

"Four hundred million Argentine australes," Ramon said.

"Two million dollars American," Carlos said.

"We want it back."

A pair of international bankers discussing high finance in Spanish.

"I don't know what you're talking about," she said.

Still speaking Spanish. This was a cozy little meeting among high-born Spanish-speaking people. This was a tea party on the duchess's lawn. The duchess had invited the two bankers here to meet the dazzling international traveler, Mary Ann Hollis, whose nose was still bleeding into a white towel.

"You must be mistaking me for someone else," she said in Spanish.

Everyone speaking Spanish. How nice to have a second language.

"No, there's no mistake," Ramon said.

"We know who you are, and we know you stole the money," Carlos said.

"And we'll kill you if you don't give it back to us," Ramon said simply, a slight shrug of his narrow shoulders, this was merely one of the rules of international banking.

"*Marilyn* Hollis?" she said. "Are you looking for someone named *Marilyn* Hollis?"

"No, we're . . ."

"Because that's my name, you see, and . . ."

"Shut up," the ugly one said.

Very softly.

The word sounding not at all menacing in Spanish, *cállate*, the word rolling mellifluously off his tongue, *cállate*, shut up.

"Your name is Mary Ann Hollis," he said.

Still softly. Explaining something to a very young and possibly quite stupid child.

"Ah, *bien*," she said, "there's the mis . . ."

"No," he said.

The word identical in English and in Spanish.

No.

Softly.

No, we've made no mistake. You are Mary Ann Hollis. And we are going to kill you if you don't give us the money you stole form Hidalgo.

All in that single word.

No.

The bag was still on her shoulder.

The knife was in the bag.

The clock on the mantel read 3:15.

I should be home around four-thirty, see you then, love ya.

No sense wishing for the cavalry. Do or die. Go for the knife, or . . .

The clock ticked into the room. Her nose had stopped bleeding. She tossed the towel aside, seeing her own reflection in the ornately framed mirror opposite the bed, her reverse image partially obscured by the backs of the two gentlemen from Buenos Aires.

"I have identification," she said. "My driver's license . . ."

The one to go for was the big one.

". . . my credit cards . . ."

Him first.

"We don't need identification," the handsome one said. Ramon. "We know exactly who you are."

"But that's just it, you see . . ."

Moving across the room toward where the big one stood with his hands dangling at his sides.

"If I can prove that I'm not who you *think* I am . . ."

Her hand dropping into the bag as she moved.

". . . then you'll realize your mistake, and you'll . . ."

"There *is* no mistake," Ramon said, shaking his head.

Fingers searching for the knife.

"But there is. Look, I'd be happy to pay you back . . ."

"Then pay us and shut up!" Ramon said.

Fingers closing on the handle of the knife.

". . . but I'm just not this person you think I am. I mean it. Truly."

"*Enough* of this shit!" Carlos said.

Verdad, she thought, and yanked the knife out of the bag.

Her mistake was going high.

She should have gone low instead, for the gut, plunge the blade in low, rip it across his belly, his hands would have had to cross in front of his body to block the thrust, a clumsy unnatural maneuver. But instead she went for the throat. Arm stiff and extended, right hand clutching the handle of the knife, blade going for his throat like a matador's sword, that was her mistake. Because his hands came up at once in a fighter's instinctive defensive stance, fists clenched for the tick of an instant, and then the hands opening when he recognized in another instant's beat exactly what was happening here, she was coming at him with a knife, this was a knife here!

His eyes said Oh, yeah?

Ah sí?

In which case I will break your fucking face.

She saw those eyes at once, read those eyes, had seen the message in those eyes many times before when she'd been repeatedly beaten and raped in that Mexican prison, and she thought No, mister, never again, and stopped the knife in mid-thrust because his hands were there and she did not want those massive fingers closing on her wrist.

She shifted her stance, stood wide-legged and fierce, the knife moving in tiny circles, waiting for his move. He was not going for the

gun in his pocket or wherever the hell he'd put it. This meant that he
respected the knife. You didn't grow up a fucking hoodlum in B.A.
without having been cut at least once. You didn't spend time in a
Mexican prison, either, without becoming an expert on reading eyes.
The big one's eyes were saying that she was the one with the knife,
and he did not want to get cut. *Her* eyes were saying If you make a
move for the gun, I'll go for your eyes. I'll blind you. Mexican
standoff.

She'd forgotten the handsome one.

He moved in as gracefully and as swiftly as a flamenco dancer.
She caught his motion almost a moment too late, spotted him from
the tail of her eye, and turned immediately to her right as he lunged
for her. She thought again, No, mister, and swung the knife out in a
wide slashing arc, backhanded. He put out his hand as if trying to
deflect the thrust, and then started to pull it back when he remembered this was cold hard steel—but he was too late. The knife caught
him. It ripped through the meaty flesh on the edge of his hand, just
below the pinky, slicing horizontally, opening a wide bloody gash. He
yelled "Aiiii," and caught the hand in his free hand, the left one,
cradling it, trying to cradle it, pulling both hands in against his body,
his face going pale, his eyes glazing over in fear, the blood covering
both hands now—she went for him again.

And cut him again.

Slashed out viciously at both hands where he held them in tight
against his belly, the blade ripping across the knuckles of the left
hand, slashing through to the bone. He began whimpering. His nose
was running. He stood there with terror in his eyes, his nose running,
his hands bleeding, whimpering like a baby. She had them both in her
line of vision now, the handsome one backing away toward the big
one, whimpering, the gun still nowhere in sight, she wondered why
the big one didn't pull the gun. And then she realized in a sudden
exhilarating rush that they could not kill her; if they killed her, they
would never get the money they'd come for. In the world they inhab-
ited, you did not kill delinquent debtors except as an example to other
debtors. If you wanted your money, you threatened and you maimed

—yes, they could hurt her very badly—but you did not kill. Not if you wanted your money. They could not *kill* her!

She felt suddenly invincible.

"Come on," she said.

Knife swinging out ahead of her.

"Come on, you cocksuckers!"

In Spanish, so they'd know exactly what she was saying.

Knife testing the air.

"You want it? Come get it! Come *on!*"

The handsome one was still whimpering.

He kept his hands tucked in against his belly. His shirt was covered with blood.

The big one's eyes had naked murder in them.

She almost burst out laughing. He wanted to kill her but he couldn't. Anger twisted his features, frustration caused his lips to quiver. His fury was monumental, a towering rage that set him trembling like a volcano about to erupt. His face was livid, teeth clenched, mouth twitching, eyes blazing.

"Sure, come on," she said.

Hoping he *would* come.

Actually *wishing* he would come.

Blind you, she thought.

Put out your eyes.

He backed away from her instead, guiding the handsome one around her, his eyes never leaving the knife, edging cautiously back and away from her, around her toward the bedroom door, Marilyn turning so that the knife was always between them, prodding the air. The handsome one could not stop whimpering. At the door, the big one whispered, *"Volveremos."*

Which meant "We'll be back."

Nobody on Eleventh Street knew anything about what had happened on Easter Sunday. This meant that *everybody* in the neighborhood knew *exactly* what had happened. But around here, there was no need to talk to cops ever. If somebody was bothering you, you went to people who could do something about it. The only thing cops could do was write parking tickets and sit around with their thumbs up their asses.

Around here, they told a story about these four black guys went in the Capri Grot one night. This was a restaurant on Ainsley, it was actually named Il Grotto di Capri, but everybody called it the Capri Grot, even the guys who owned it. So these black guys walk in on a crowded Friday night, they're all strapped with huge guns like .45's or Magnums, it depended on who was telling the story. And they shove the guns in the cashier's face and they announce this is a stickup, man, and the headwaiter just stands there with his arms folded across his chest, shaking his head. Like he can't *believe* this is *happening*, man! Four dumb fucking niggers walking into a place has Mafia written up one side and down the other, they're here pulling a job. Amazing! So they clean out the cash register and go off in the night, and the headwaiter is still there shaking his head at the wonder of it all.

Next day one of the niggers comes back to the restaurant. His arm is in a sling, and his right eye is half-closed and there's a bandage wrapped around his head from where somebody busted it for him. He's carrying a briefcase. He asks to see the owner and then he tells him some friends of his made a terrible mistake last night, coming in here the way they done, and like, man, here's all the money back, let's let bygones be bygones, man, keep the briefcase, too, it's a Mark Cross.

People around here still laughed at that story.

Which is why nobody around here went to the cops when they had any kind of problem that needed solving. They went instead to the people who knew what to do about it. Which is why on any given Friday night, the customers at the Capri Grot could park their Benzes or their Jags outside and nobody would even *dream* of touching them. And if the cars happened to be double-parked in a clearly marked No Parking zone, that was okay, too, because some of the cops on the beat here were *also* in the pockets of the people you went to whenever you had a problem. Which is why you didn't tell cops a fucking *thing* around here, even if they asked you was your mother a virgin before she got married.

Nobody on the street knew who had busted that nigger's head on Easter Sunday.

Nobody on the street even knew there'd been any trouble at all that day.

Except Angelo Di Napoli.

Di Napoli was thirty-seven years old, a cop whose family name (which translated as "of Naples") promised short and dark with curly black hair but who was in fact an even six feet tall with blond hair and blue eyes. Di Napoli was a recent transfer to the Eight-Seven from the CPEP Unit at the Five-One in Riverhead. CPEP was an acronym for Community Police Enrichment Program, a law enforcement concept rudely imitative of the foot-patrol programs in several other large American cities. Here in this city, the centralized 911 emergency response system had gone into effect some thirty years ago, bringing with it the need for quick *motorized* response, and leaving in its wake a reduction in the number of foot patrols. Then, as so often happened when speed became confused with quality, many police officers began thinking that motorized patrol was in actuality a more diverse and interesting assignment, with the attendant result that those poor souls assigned to a foot beat approached the job with less than optimum enthusiasm. All by way of saying that the foot-patrol officer was almost entirely eliminated in the city's scheme of law enforcement and crime prevention.

CPEP—pronounced Cee-Pep by the police department—had been designed to correct what was now perceived as an error. Its sole intent was to reestablish the foot-patrol cop as an essential part of the process of essential contact between police and community. Di Napoli had been a part of the highly effective NarcPoc Drive, a combined blues-and-suits operation aimed at narcotic pockets in the Fifty-First precinct and resulting in a total of some ten thousand buy-and-bust arrests. It was a measure of the man that he considered it a challenge to be transferred to the newly organized CPEP Unit at the Eight-Seven, under the command of a sergeant who'd initiated Operation Clean Sweep out of the notorious Hundred-and-First in Majesta. Di Napoli was a good cop and a dedicated cop. Like any good cop, he listened. And like any dedicated cop, he put what he heard to good use.

He would not have known that Carella was on the job if Carella hadn't introduced himself. Di Napoli couldn't recall seeing him around the station house, but then again he was new here. They exchanged the usual pleasantries...

"How's it going?"

"Little quiet."

"Well, give it time, it's Saturday."

"Yeah, I can't wait."

... and then Carella got straight to the point.

"I'm investigating the murder of that priest at St. Kate's," he said.

"Yeah, Thursday night," Di Napoli said.

"That's the one. I'm looking for whoever chased a black kid into the church on Easter Sunday."

"I wasn't here then," Di Napoli said. "I only got transferred the first of the month." He hesitated and then said, "I hear Edward-car panicked, huh?"

"Let's say they got out of there fast."

"The people around here laugh about it."

"I'll bet."

"Bad for the old image, huh?" Di Napoli said, and raised his eyebrows. "I bust my ass out here day and night and two jerks run when it gets hot."

"Have you heard anything about who it might have been?"

"That jumped the black kid?"

"Yeah."

"I'll tell you," Di Napoli said, "there's a thing happening around here where they're starting to be *proud* of it, you know what I mean? The neighborhood people. They *like* the idea these bums beat up the black kid and got away with it. That the cops cooled it, you know? For whatever reason, who the hell knows, maybe Edward-car was afraid they'd have a riot on their hands, who knows? The point is, a kid got beat up, and nobody paid for it. Nobody. So around here they're saying Yeah, it served him right, he shoulda stayed in his own neighborhood, why'd he come around here, and so on, this is a nice neighborhood, we don't need niggers coming in . . ."

Di Napoli shook his head.

"I'm Italian, you know," he said, "I guess you are, too, but I can't stand the way Italians feel about black people. It's a fuckin' *shame* the way they feel. Maybe they don't know how much prejudice there's still around about *us*, you know? Italians. Maybe they don't know you say somebody's Italian he's supposed to be a thief or a ditchdigger or a guy singing O Sole Mio in a restaurant with checked tablecloths and Chianti bottles dripping wax. I'm only a cop, I mean I know I'm not a fuckin' account executive or a bank president, but there're Italians who *are*, you realize that? So you get these dumb wops in this neighborhood—that's exactly what they are, excuse me, they're dumb fucking *wops*—they beat up this black kid and then they laugh about it later and *all* Italians suffer. All of us. I hate it. Man, I absolutely *hate* it."

"You sound like you know who did it," Carella said.

"Not completely. But I've been listening, believe me."

"And what've you heard?"

"I heard a guy in his forties, he's in the construction business, his name is Vinnie Corrente, I heard he's been bragging to people that his son Bobby was the one used the bat. I didn't hear him say this personally, otherwise his ass would be up the station house and I'd be reading him Miranda, the dumb fucking wop."

"On the other hand . . ."

"On the other hand, *you're* investigating a homicide . . ."

"Uh-huh."

"So maybe you got probable to pull him in."

"Let's say I'd like to talk to him."

"Let's say he's in apartment 41 at 304 North."

"Thanks," Carella said.

"Hey, come on," Di Napoli said, pleased.

304 North Eleventh was a five-story brick set in a row of identical buildings undoubtedly put up by the same contractor at the turn of the century, when the neighborhood was still considered desirable. At three-thirty that afternoon, several old women wearing the black mourning dresses and stockings you could see on widows all over Italy were sitting in late afternoon sunshine on the front stoop, chatting in Italian. Carella nodded good afternoon to them, and then walked through them and past them into the building foyer. He found a mailbox nameplate for V. Corrente in apartment 41, and began climbing the steps.

The building was scrupulously clean.

Mouth-watering cooking smells wafted in the hallways, suffused the stairwells. Oregano and thyme. Sweet sausage. Fresh basil. Delectable meats simmering in olive oil and garlic.

Carella kept climbing.

He found apartment 41 to the right of the staircase on the fourth-floor landing. He listened at the wood for a moment, heard nothing, and knocked on the door.

"Who is it?" a man's voice said.

"Police," Carella answered.

There was a brief silence.

"Just a minute," the man said.

Carella waited.

He heard several locks coming undone, and then the door opened some three inches or so, held by a night chain.

"Let's see your badge," the man said.

Gruff no-nonsense voice, somewhat gravelly. A smoker's voice. Or a drinker's.

Carella flipped open his leather case to show a blue-enameled, gold detective's shield and a laminated I.D. card. "Detective Carella," he said. "Eighty-seventh Squad."

"What's this about, Carella?" the man asked. He had still not taken the chain off the door. In the narrow wedge between door and jamb, Carella could dimly perceive a heavyset man with a stubble on his cheeks, dark hooded eyes.

"Want to open the door?" he asked.

"Not till I know what this is about," the man said.

"Are you Vincent Corrente?"

"Yeah?"

Surprise in his voice.

"I'd like to ask you a few questions, Mr. Corrente, if that's okay with you," Carella said.

"Like I said, what about?"

"Easter Sunday."

"What about Easter Sunday?"

"Well, I won't really know until I can ask you some questions."

There was silence behind the door. In the wedge, Carella thought he detected the eyes narrowing.

"What do you say?" he asked.

"I say tell me more," the man said.

"Mr. Corrente, I want to ask you about an incident that occurred at St. Catherine's Church on Easter Sunday."

"I don't go to church," Corrente said.

"Neither do I," Carella said. "Mr. Corrente, I'm investigating a murder."

There was another silence. And then, suddenly and unsurprisingly—the word "murder" sometimes worked magic—the night chain came off with a rattle, and the door opened wide.

Corrente was wearing a pair of brown trousers and a tank top undershirt. He was a jowly, paunchy, unkempt man with a cigar in his mouth and a smile on his face, Hey, come in, how nice to see the Law here on my doorstep, come in, come in, don't mind the way the place looks, my wife's been sick, come in, Detective, please.

Carella went in.

A modest apartment, spotlessly clean despite Corrente's protestations and apologies. Little kitchen to the right, living room dead ahead, doors opening from either side of it, presumably to the bedrooms. From behind one of the closed doors, a television set was going.

"Come on in the kitchen," Corrente said, "so we won't bother my wife. She's got the flu, I hadda get the doctor in yesterday. You want a beer or anything?"

"Thanks, no," Carella said.

They went into the kitchen and sat opposite each other at a round, Formica-topped table. The air-shaft window was open. In the backyard, four stories below, Carella could hear some kids playing Ring-a-Leevio. From the other room, he could hear the unintelligible drone of the television set. Corrente lifted an open can of beer that was sitting on the table, took a long swallow from it, and then said, "So what's this about St. Catherine's?"

"You tell me."

"All I know is I heard there was some fuss there on Easter."

"That's true."

"But I don't know what."

"A black boy was badly beaten by a gang of six white boys. We think the boys were from . . ."

"There are no gangs in this neighborhood," Corrente said.

"Anything more than two in number, *we* call a gang," Carella said. "Any idea who they might've been?"

"Why should that be important to you?" Corrente asked. His cigar had gone out. He took a matchbook from his trouser pocket, struck a match and held it to the tip of the cigar, puffing, filling the kitchen with billowing smoke. "'Cause, you know," he said, "maybe this black kid had no right comin' to this neighborhood, you understand?"

"I understand that's the prevailing attitude, yes," Carella said.

"Which may not be the *wrong* attitude, hmmm?" Corrente said. "I know what you're thinking, you're thinking this is a bunch of preju-

diced people here, they don't like the colored, is what you're thinking. But maybe the same thing woulda happened if this kid hadda
been *white*, you follow me, Detective?"

"No," Carella said, "I'm afraid I don't."

He did not like this man. He did not like the beard stubble on his
face, or the potbelly hanging over his belt, or the stench of his cigar,
or his alleged barroom boasts that his son Bobby had wielded the bat
that had broken Nathan Hooper's head. Even the way he said "Detective" rankled.

"This is a nice neighborhood," Corrente said. "A family neighborhood. Hardworking people, nice clean kids. We want to keep it
that way."

"Mr. Corrente," Carella said, "on Easter Sunday, half a dozen
nice clean kids from this neighborhood attacked a black kid with
baseball bats and garbage can lids and chased him down the street
to . . ."

"Yeah, the Hooper kid," Corrente said.

"Yes," Carella said. "The Hooper kid."

All of a sudden, Corrente seemed to know the name of the Easter
Sunday victim. All of a sudden, he seemed to know all about the fuss
that had happened at St. Catherine's, although not ten minutes ago he
hadn't known nothing from nothing.

"You familiar with this kid?" Corrente asked.

"I've talked to him."

"What'd he tell you?"

"He told me what happened to him here on Eleventh Street."

"Did he tell you what he was *doing* here on Eleventh Street?"

"He was on his way home from the . . ."

"No, no, never mind the bullshit," Corrente said, taking his cigar
from his mouth and waving it like a conductor's baton. "Did he tell
you what he was *doing* here?"

"What was he doing here, Mr. Corrente?"

"Do you know what they call him down the schoolyard? On Ninth
Street? The elementary school? You know what they call him there?"

"No," Carella said. "What do they call him there?"

"His nickname? Did he tell you his nickname?"

"No, he didn't."

"Go ask him what his nickname is down the schoolyard. Go ask him what he was doing here Easter Sunday, go ahead."

"Why don't you save me the trouble?" Carella said.

"Sure," Corrente said, and inhaled deeply on the cigar. Blowing out a cloud of smoke, he said, "Mr. Crack."

Carella looked at him.

"Is his nickname, right," Corrente said. "Mr. fucking nigger Crack."

There was a need that took him back here.

Something inexplicable that did, in fact, take him back to the scene of any murder he'd ever investigated, time and again, to stand alone in the center of a bedroom or a hallway or a kitchen or a roof or—as was the case now—a small cloistered garden suffused with the late afternoon scent of hundreds of roses in riotous bloom.

The Crime Scene signs had all been taken down, the police were through with the place so far as gathering evidence was concerned. But Carella stood alone in the center of the garden, under the spreading branches of the old maple, and tried to sense what had happened here this past Thursday evening at sunset. It was yet only a little before five, the priest had been slain some two hours later, but Carella was not here now to weigh and to evaluate, to discern and to deduce, he was here to feel this courtyard and this murder, to absorb the essence of it, breathe it deeply into his lungs, have it seep into his bloodstream to become a part of him as vital as his liver or his heart —for only then could he hope to understand it.

Mystical, yes.

A detective searching for a muse of sorts.

He recognized the absurdity of what he was doing, but bowed to it nonetheless, standing there in dappled shade, listening to the sounds of the springtime city beyond the high stone walls, trying to absorb through his very flesh whatever secrets the garden contained. Had not something of the murderer's rage and the victim's terror flown helter-skelter about this small, contained and silent space, to be claimed by stone or rose or blade of grass, and held forever in time like the image of a killer in a dead man's eye? And if so, if this was in fact a possibility, then was it not also possible that the terror and the rage of that final awful moment when knife entered flesh could now be recovered from all that had borne silent witness here in this garden?

He stood alone, scarcely daring to breathe.

He was not a religious man, but perhaps he was praying.

He stood there for what seemed a long time, some ten or fifteen minutes, head bent, waiting for . . .

He didn't know what.

And at last, he took a deep breath and nodded and went back into the rectory and into the small office angled into a nook that—judging from the replastering—had once served as something else, he could not imagine what. There were secrets here, too; perhaps there were secrets everywhere.

The report from the Fingerprint Section had informed him that any latents recovered from the open drawer of the file cabinet had been too smudged to be useful in any meaningful search. There had been latents as well on the various papers scattered on the floor and separately delivered in an evidence envelope marked CORRESPONDENCE: FLOOR and then initialed by the lab's R.L., whoever he might be. Some of the latents matched the prints lifted from the dead priest's fingers and thumbs. The rest of them were wild, with the possibility that some had been left on the correspondence by Kristin Lund.

Carella knelt beside the filing cabinet.

The bottom drawer, the one that had been found open, was labeled:

CORRESPONDENCE
G–L

He opened the drawer, no danger in doing that since the Mobile Lab had been through here with everything from a vacuum cleaner to a pair of tweezers. He felt around inside, along the back of the front panel; sometimes people Scotch-taped things to the inside of a drawer, where no one but a cop or a thief would think of looking. Nothing. Correspondence, G–L. Presumably, whoever had thrown those papers all over the place was looking for something in this drawer, something beginning with the letters of the alphabet that fell between G and L. Six letters altogether. God only knew what piece of paper the vandal had been looking for or whether or not he'd found it. Or even whether the ransacking had had anything at all to do with the murder. Carella was getting to his feet again when a voice behind him said, "Excuse me, sir."

He turned from the filing cabinets.

Two young girls were standing just inside the entrance door to the office.

They could not have been older than thirteen, fourteen at the most.

A blonde and one with hair as black as pitch.

The blonde was a classic beauty with a pale oval face, high molded cheekbones, a generous mouth, and dark brown eyes that gave her a thoughtful almost scholarly look. The other girl could have been her twin: the same delicate face, the same sculpted look, except that her hair was black and her eyes were a startling almost electric blue. Both girls wore their hair in stylists' cuts that fell straight and clean to the shoulders. Both were wearing sweaters, skirts and—in a replay of the Fifties—bobby sox and loafers. They exuded a freshness that Americans arrogantly assumed only their own healthy young girls possessed, but which was actually an asset of most teenage girls anywhere in the world.

"Sir," the black-haired one said, "are you with the church?"

Same one who'd spoken not a moment before.

"No," Carella said, "I'm not."

"We thought they might have sent someone," the blonde said. "A new priest."

"No," Carella said, and showed his shield and I.D. card. "I'm Detective Carella, Eighty-seventh Squad."

"Oh," the black-haired one said.

Both girls huddled in the doorway.

"I'm investigating Father Michael's murder," Carella said.

"How terrible," the blonde said.

The black-haired one nodded.

"Did you know Father Michael?" Carella asked.

"Oh, yes," both girls said, almost in unison.

"He was a wonderful person," the black-haired one said. "Excuse me, I'm President of the C.Y.O. My name is Gloria Keely."

"I'm Alexis O'Donnell," the blonde said. "I'm nothing."

Carella smiled.

"Nice to meet both of you," he said.

"Nice to meet you, too," Alexis said. "C.Y.O. means Catholic Youth Organization."

Thoughtful brown eyes in her delicate, serious face. I'm nothing, she had said. Meaning she was not an officer of the club. But something indeed, in that she was easily the more beautiful of the two girls, with a shy, and thoroughly appealing manner. He wondered how parents who had named their daughter Alexis could possibly have known she'd turn out to be such a beauty.

"Thank you," he said, and smiled.

"We were wondering about the funeral tomorrow," Gloria said. "About what time it'll be. So we can tell the other kids."

A grimace. A shrug. Still the little girl in the developing woman's body.

"I really don't know," Carella said. "Maybe you can call the archdiocese."

"Mm, yeah, good idea," she said. Electric blue eyes sparkling with intelligence, midnight hair cascading to her shoulders, head bobbing in agreement with a plan already forming. "You wouldn't happen to have the number, would you?"

"I'm sorry."

"Do you know what they'll be doing about mass tomorrow?" Alexis asked.

The same soft, shy voice.

"I really don't know."

"I hate to miss mass," she said.

"I guess we can go over to St. Jude's," Gloria said.

"I guess," Alexis said.

A heavy silence shouldered its way into the room, as if the priest's death had suddenly made itself irretrievably felt. Father Michael would not be here this Sunday to say mass. They guessed they could go to St. Jude's, but Father Michael would not be there, either. And then—he would never know which of the girls started it—both were suddenly in tears. And hugging each other. And holding each other close in clumsy embrace. And comforting each other with small keening female sounds.

He felt utterly excluded.

The twins were watching television in the family room at the other end of the house. Teddy Carella sat alone in the living room, waiting for her husband. He had called from the office to say he might be late, not to worry about dinner, he'd catch a hamburger or something. She wondered if he might be walking into danger again, there was so much danger out there.

There was a time when the shield meant something.

You said, "Police," and you showed the shield, and you *became* the shield, you were everything the shield represented, the force of law, the power of law, this was what the shield represented. The shield represented civilization. And civilization meant a body of law that human beings had created for themselves over centuries and centuries. To protect themselves against others, to protect themselves against themselves as well.

That's what the shield used to mean.

Law.

Civilization.

Nowadays, the shield meant nothing. Nowadays the law was overwritten with graffiti, scrawled in the blood of cops. She felt like calling the President on the telephone and telling him that the Russians weren't about to invade us tomorrow. Tell him the enemy was already here, and it wasn't the Russians. The enemy was here feeding dope to our kids and killing cops in the streets.

"Hello, Mr. President?" she would say. "This is Teddy Carella. When are you going to *do* something?"

If only she could speak.

But, of course, she couldn't.

So she sat waiting for Carella to come home, and when at last she saw the knob turning on the front door, she leaped to her feet and was there when the door opened, relief thrusting her into his arms and almost knocking him off his feet.

They kissed.

Gently, lingeringly.

They had known each other such a long time.

She asked him if he'd like a drink . . .

Fingers flashing in the sign language he knew so well . . .

. . . and he said he'd love a martini, and then went down the hall to say hello to the kids.

When he came back into the living room, she handed him the drink she'd mixed, and they went to sit on the sofa framed in the three arched windows at the far end of the room. The house was the sort Stephen King might have admired, a big Victorian white elephant in a section of Riverhead that had once boasted many similar houses, each on its own three or four acres of land, all dead and gone now, all gone. The Carella house was a reminder of an era long past, a more gracious, graceful time in America, the gabled white building with the wrought-iron fence all around it, a large tree-shaded corner plot, no longer all those acres, of course, those days of land and luxury were a thing of the dim, distant past.

He sat drinking his gin martini.

She sat drinking an after-dinner cognac.

She asked him where he'd eaten—putting the snifter down for a moment so that she could have free use of her hands—and he watched her flying fingers and answered in a combination of voice and sign, said he'd gone to a little Chinese joint on Culver, and then he fell silent, sipping at his drink, his head bent. He looked so tired. She knew him so well. She loved him so much.

He told her then how troubled he was by the murder of the priest.

It wasn't that he was religious or anything . . .

"I mean, you know that, Teddy, I haven't been inside a church since my sister got married, I just don't *believe* in any of that stuff anymore . . ."

. . . but somehow, the murder of a man of God . . .

"I don't even believe in *that,* people devoting themselves to religion, devoting their lives to spreading religion, *any* religion, I just don't believe in any of that anymore, Teddy, I'm sorry. I know you're religious. I know you pray. Forgive me. I'm sorry."

She took his hands in her own.

"I wish I *could* pray," he said.

And was silent again.

And then said, "But I've seen too much."

She squeezed his hands.

"Teddy . . . this is really getting to me," he said.

She flashed the single word *Why?*

"Because . . . he was a priest."

She looked at him, puzzled.

"I know. That sounds contradictory. Why should the death of a *priest* bother me? I haven't even *spoken* to a priest since . . . when did she get married? Angela? When was her wedding?"

Teddy's fingers moved:

The day the twins were born.

"Almost eleven years ago," he said, and nodded. "That's the last time I had anything to do with a priest. Eleven years ago."

He looked at his wife. A great many things had happened in those eleven years. Sometimes time seemed elastic to him, a concept that could be bent at will, twisted to fit ever-changing needs. Who was to say the twins were not now *thirty* years old, rather than eleven? Who was to say that he and Teddy were not still the young marrieds they'd been back then? Time. A concept as confusing to Carella as was that of . . . well, God.

He shook his head.

"Leave God out of it," he said, almost as if he'd spoken his earlier thoughts aloud. "Forget that Father Michael was a man of God, whatever that means. Maybe there *are* no men of God anymore. Maybe the whole world . . ."

He shook his head again.

"Figure him only for someone who was . . . okay, not *pure*, nobody's pure, but at least *innocent*."

He saw the puzzlement on her face, and realized she had misread either his lips or his sloppy signing. He signed the word letter by letter, and she nodded and signed it back, and he said, "Yeah, think of him that way. Innocent. And, yes, pure, why *not*? Pure of *heart*, anyway. A man who'd never harmed another human being in his entire life. Would never have *dreamt* of harming anyone. And all at once, out of the night, out of the sunset, into his peaceful garden, there comes an assassin with a knife."

He drained his glass.

"That's what's getting to me, Teddy. On New Year's Eve, I caught a baby smothered in her crib, that was only five months ago, what's today, Teddy, the twenty-sixth of May, not *even* five full months. And now another innocent. If people like . . . like . . . if people like *that* are getting killed . . . if the . . . if even the . . . if nobody *gives* a damn anymore . . . if you can kill a baby, kill a priest, kill a ninety-year-old grandmother, kill a pregnant woman . . ."

And suddenly he buried his face in his hands.

"There's too much of it," he said.

And she realized he was weeping.

"Too much," he said.

She took him in her arms.

And she thought Dear God, get him out of this job before it kills him.

*　*　*

Seronia and her brother were eating pizza in a joint on The Stem. They had ordered and devoured one large pizza with extra cheese and pepperoni, and were now working on the smaller pizza they'd ordered next. Seronia was leaning forward over the table, a long string of mozzarella cheese trailing from her lips to the folded wedge of pizza in her hand, eating her way up the string toward the slice of pizza. Hooper watched her as if she were walking a tightrope a hundred feet above the ground.

She bit off the cheese together with a piece of the pizza, chewed, swallowed and washed it down with Diet Coke. She was very much aware that the white guy throwing pizzas behind the counter was watching her. She was wearing an exceptionally short mini made to look like black leather. Red silk blouse with a scoop neck. Dangling red earrings. Black patent pumps. Thirteen years old and being eyed up and down by a white man shoveling pizza in an oven.

"You shoonta lied to him," she told her brother. "He fine out *why* you was on 'Leventh Street, he be back."

"You the one say they was nothin' to lose," Hooper said.

"That dinn give you no cause to lie."

"I tole him basely d'troof," Hooper said.

"No, you lied about Fat Harol'."

"So whut? Who gives a shit about that skinny li'l fuck?"

"Sayin' as how he do crack. Sheee-it, man, he a momma's boy doan know crack fum his *own* crack."

Hooper laughed.

"Sayin' as how he wenn to a crack house, bought hisself a nickel vial. An' paintin' yourself like a . . ."

"It was true we wenn t'church t'gether, though, me an' Harol'," Hooper said.

"I doan do no dope," Seronia said, imitating her brother talking to Carella, "an' I doan run dope for none a'these mis'able dealers comes aroun' here tryin' a'spoil d'chirren."

"This was the *Man* we talkin' to," Hooper said. "Whutchoo 'spec me to tell him?"

"I never done no crim'nal thing in my life," Seronia said, still doing a pretty fair imitation of her brother's deeper voice. "Never!" she said, and clenched her fist and rapped it against her small budding breast.

"Is 'zackly whut I tole the Man," Hooper said, and grinned.

"I like to wet my pants when I heerd that," Seronia said, and shook her head in admiration and pride. "I goan be *any* kine a'nigger, it's goan be a *good* one," she mimicked. "Like Eddie Murphy." And again shook her head and rolled her big brown eyes heavenward.

"Eddie Murphy, right," Hooper said.

"You goan wish you *was* Eddie Murphy when he comes roun' again," Seronia said. "'Cause he look to me like the kine a'fuzz doan let go, bro. An' he goan *talk* to the people 'long 'Leventh Street, an' somebody gonna tell him sumpin' you *dinn* tell him. An' then he goan fine out whut happen 'tween you an' the pries', an' then you goan be in deep shit, bro."

"Ain' nothin' happen 'tween me an' the pries'."

"'Sep' you hid yo' stash in the church," Seronia said, and bit into another slice of pizza.

6

Willis did not get back to the house on Harborside Lane until almost eight o'clock that Saturday night. He called her name the moment he stepped into the entry foyer.

There was no answer.

"Honey?" he called. "I'm home."

And again there was no answer.

He was a policeman, trained to expect the unexpected. He was, moreover, a policeman who had lived on the thin edge of anticipation from the moment he'd committed himself to Marilyn Hollis. The words he'd heard on the telephone this past Thursday night suddenly popped into his mind— *Perdóneme, señor*—and just as suddenly he was alarmed.

"Marilyn!" he shouted, and went tearing up the stairs two at a time, made a sharp right turn on the second-floor landing and was starting up the steps to the third floor when he heard her voice coming from somewhere down the corridor.

"In here, Hal."

She was in the kitchen. Sitting at the butcher block table, the stainless steel ovens, refrigerator and range forming a grey metallic curtain behind her. She was holding a dish towel to her nose. The towel bulged with angles. There was an empty ice cube tray on the table.

"I fell," she said.

Hand holding the dish towel to her nose, eyes wide above it and flanking it, flesh under the eyes already discolored.

"Down the stairs," she said. "I think I broke my nose."

"Well, Jesus, did you call the . . . ?"

"It just happened a few minutes ago," she said.

"I'll call him," he said, and went immediately to the phone.

"I don't think they can do anything for a broken nose," she said. "I think it has to heal by itself."

"They can set it," he said, and began searching through their personal directory on the counter under the wall phone. Rubenstein, the doctor's name was Rubenstein. Willis realized all at once that he was irrationally irritated; the way a parent might become irritated when a child did something that threatened its own well-being. He was relieved that Marilyn had not hurt herself more badly, but annoyed that she had hurt herself at all.

"How'd you manage to fall down the goddamn *stairs*?" he said, shaking his head.

"I tripped," she said.

"Isn't his number in this thing?" he asked impatiently.

"Try D," she said. "For doctor."

More annoyed now, he turned to the D section of the directory, and scanned through a dozen names and numbers in Marilyn's handwriting before he found a listing for Rubenstein, Marvin, Dr. He dialed the number. It rang four times and then a woman picked up. The doctor's answering service. She advised Willis that the doctor was out of town for several days and asked if she should notify his standby, a Dr. Gerald Peters. Somewhat curtly, Willis said, "Never mind," and hung the phone back on the wall cradle.

"Come on," he said, "we're going to the hospital."

"I really don't think . . ."

"Marilyn, *please*," he said.

He hurried her out of the house and into the car. He debated hitting the hammer, decided against it. Use the siren on a personal matter, the Department would take a fit. The nearest hospital was Morehouse General on Culver and North Third, just inside the precinct's western boundary. He drove there as if he were responding to a 10-13, foot heavy on the accelerator, ignoring traffic signals unless a changing light posed a danger to another vehicle, and then made a sharp right turn on Third, and wheeled the car squealing up the driveway to the Emergency Room.

This was Saturday night.

Only eighteen minutes past eight, in fact, but the weekend had already begun in earnest, and the E.R. resembled an army field station. Two black cops with identifying 87 insignia on their uniform collars were struggling to keep apart a pair of lookalike white goons who had done a very good job of cutting each other to ribbons. Their T-shirts, once white, now clung in tatters to bloody streamers of flesh. One of the men had opened the other's face from his right temple down to his jaw. The other man had slashed through the first guy's bulging biceps and forearm all the way down to the wrist. The men were still screaming at each other, their hands cuffed behind their backs, shoulder-butting the cops trying to keep them separated.

A resident physician who looked Indian and undoubtedly was — in this city, there were more Indian interns than in the entire state of Rajasthan — kept saying over and over again, quite patiently, "Do you wish medical treatment, or do you wish to behave foolishly?" The two goons ignored this running commentary because they had *already* behaved foolishly, had probably been behaving foolishly all their lives, and weren't about to *stop* behaving foolishly now, just because a foreigner was sounding reasonable. So they kept bleeding all over the E.R. while the two sweating black cops struggled with a pair of enraged men twice their size and tried to keep their uniforms clean, and a saintly nurse patiently stood by with cotton swabs, a bottle of antiseptic, and a roll of bandages and tried to keep *her* uniform clean, and an excitable orderly circled warily, trying to mop the goddamn floor as blood spattered everywhere on the air.

Elsewhere in the room, sitting on the bench, or crowding the nurse's station, or standing about in various stages of distress and discomfort, Willis saw and registered with dismay:

A twelve-year-old Hispanic girl whose blouse was torn open to reveal a training bra and tiny budding breasts. Blood was streaming down the inside of her right leg. Willis figured she'd been raped.

A forty-year-old white man being supported by yet another police officer and yet another Indian resident, who were maneuvering him toward one of the cubicles so that the doctor could examine what looked to Willis like a gunshot wound through the left shoulder.

A black teenager sitting on the bench with one high-topped sneaker off and in his hands. His right foot was swollen to the size of a melon. Willis figured him for a non-crime victim, but in this precinct you never could tell.

There were also . . .

There was *Marilyn,* period.

"Excuse me, doctor," Willis said, and a redheaded resident standing at the nurse's station studying a chart glanced up as though wondering who had had the unspeakable audacity to raise his voice here in the temple. On his face, there was the haughtily scornful, one-eyebrow-raised look of a person who knew without question that his calling was godly. It was a look that managed to mingle distaste with dismissal, as though its wearer had already singled out and was now ready to punish whoever had dared fart in his immediate presence.

But Willis's woman had a broken nose.

Unintimidated, he flashed the tin, announced his own godly calling—"Detective Harold Willis"—and then slapped the leather case shut as though he were throwing down a glove. "I'm investigating a homicide, this woman needs immediate medical attention."

What a homicide had to do with this woman's broken nose—in a single glance, he was able to make this diagnosis—the redheaded resident couldn't possibly imagine. But the look on the detective's face said that the matter was extremely urgent, the matter was in fact positively critical, and there would be hell to pay if this woman's broken nose resulted in a bungled homicide investigation. So the resi-

dent ignored all the other people clamoring for attention in that Saturday night purgatory and immediately tended to the blonde woman's
needs, determining (as he'd known at once, anyway) that the nose
was in fact broken, and giving her an immediate shot for the pain, and
then setting the nose, and dressing it with plaster (such a beautiful
face, too) and writing a prescription for a pain-killer should she have
difficulty getting through the night. Only then did he ask her how this
had happened, and Marilyn told him unhesitatingly that she'd tripped
and fallen down a flight of stairs.

This was when Willis fully realized something he had only partially known from the moment he'd found her in the kitchen with the
ice pack to her nose.

Marilyn was lying.

"But why did you lie to them?" Sally Farnes asked.

This was eight-thirty P.M. The two of them were sitting on the
little balcony outside their living room, looking out at the lights of the
Saturday night city and the splendor of the sky overhead. Sunset had
stained the western horizon an hour and a half ago. They had eaten an
early dinner and then had carried their coffee out here onto the balcony, anticipating the brilliant show of color that had been their special treat these past several weeks. Tonight's spectacle had not been at
all disappointing, a kaleidoscopic display of reds and oranges and
purples and deeper blues culminating in a dazzle of stars wheeling
across an intensely black sky.

"I didn't lie," he said.

"I would say that allowing them to think you and the priest had
settled all your differences . . ."

"Which we did," Farnes said.

Sally rolled her eyes heavenward.

She was a big woman with brown hair, full-breasted and wide
across the hips, a woman who had ironically chosen to remain child-
less while equipped with a body seemingly designed for childbearing.
In a nation where being thin and staying young were the twin aspira-

tions of every woman past the age of puberty, Sally Farnes at the age of forty-three thumbed her nose at all the models in *Vogue* and called herself voluptuous, even though she was really twenty pounds overweight according to all the charts.

She had always been a trifle overweight, even when she was a teenager, but she'd never looked fat, she'd merely looked *zaftig*—a term she understood even then to mean voluptuous because a Jewish boy who later became class valedictorian told her so while he was feeling her up in the back seat of his father's Oldsmobile. Actually, the boy had been thinking of the word *wollüstig,* which indeed did mean voluptuous, whereas *zaftig* merely meant juicy. In any case, Sally had looked both voluptuous *and* juicy, and pleasantly plump besides, with a glint in her blue eyes that promised a sexiness wanton enough to arouse the desires of a great many pimply-faced young men.

She still looked supremely desirable. Even sitting alone here in the dark on her own balcony with her own husband, her legs were crossed in a provocative manner, and the three top buttons of her blouse were undone. There was a thin sheen of perspiration over her upper lip. She was wondering if her husband had killed Father Michael.

"You know you had a fight with him," she said.

"No, no," he said.

"Yes, yes. You went there on Easter Sunday..."

"Yes, and we shook hands and made up."

"Arthur, that is *not* what you told me. You told me..."

"Never mind what I told you," Farnes said. "We shook hands and made up is what I'm telling you now."

"Why are you lying?" she asked.

"Let me explain something to you," he said. "Those detectives..."

"You shouldn't have lied to them. You shouldn't be lying to me now."

"If you don't mind," he said, "you asked me a question."

"All right," she said.

"Do you want an answer, or do you want to keep interrupting?"

"I *said* all right."

"Those detectives came to see me because a priest was killed, do you understand that? A priest. Do you know who runs the police department in this city?"

"Who?"

"The Catholic Church. And if the church tells the cops to find whoever killed that priest, the cops are going to find him."

"That still doesn't . . ."

"That's right, interrupt again," Farnes said.

In the light spilling onto the balcony from the living room inside, his eyes met hers. There was something fierce and unyielding in those eyes. She could remember the last time she'd challenged him. She wondered again if he'd killed Father Michael.

"Catching the *real* killer isn't important to them," he said. "The only thing that matters is catching *a* killer, *any* killer. They came to the store trying to make a big deal out of my differences with Father Michael. Was I supposed to tell them we'd had an argument on Easter Sunday? No way. We shook hands and made up."

"But that's *not* what you did."

"That is what we did. Period."

From the street far below, the sounds of traffic filtered up. Distant, unreal somehow, the honking horns and ambulance sirens sounding like canned background sweetening for a daytime soap. They sat listening to the murmur of the city. The wingtip lights of an airplane blinked across the sky. She wondered if she should push this further. She did not want him to lose his temper. She knew what could happen if he lost his temper.

"You see," she said, as gently as she could, "I just think it was stupid to lie about something so insignificant."

"You must stop saying that, Sally. That I lied."

"Because certainly," she said, still gently, still calmly, "the police weren't about to think that a silly *argument* . . ."

"But that's exactly what they *were* thinking. That's exactly why they came to the store. Waving that damn letter I'd written! Finding something threatening in every paragraph! So what was I supposed to say? What did you want me to say, Sally? That the letter was only the beginning? That we had a violent argument shortly after I'd written it? Is that what you wanted me to say?"

"All I know is that policemen can tell when someone is lying."

"Nonsense."

"It's true. They have a sixth sense. And if they think you were lying about Father Michael . . ."

She let the sentence trail.

"Yes?" he said.

"Nothing."

"No, tell me. If they think I was lying about Father Michael, then what?"

"Then they may start looking for other things."

"What other things?"

"You know what things," she said.

Hawes was learning a few things about Krissie Lund.

He learned, to begin with, that she'd come to this city from a little town in Minnesota . . .

"I love it here," she said. "Do you love it here?"

"Sometimes."

"Have you ever been to Minnesota?"

"Never," he said.

"Cold," she said.

"I'll bet."

"Everybody runs inside during the winter. You can freeze to death out there in the snow and ice, you know. So they all run to the bunkers and lock up behind them and wait till springtime before they show their faces again. It's a sort of siege mentality."

It seemed odd to be talking about the dead of winter when everywhere around them springtime was very much in evidence. They had come out of the restaurant at a little after ten, and it was now almost ten-thirty and they were walking idly up Hall Avenue toward the

Tower Building on Midway. On nights like tonight, it was impossible to believe that anyone ever got mugged in this city. Men and women strolled together hand in hand, glancing into brightly lighted store windows, buying pretzels or hot dogs or ice cream or yogurt or souvlaki or sausages from the bazaar of peddlers' carts on almost every corner, browsing the several bookstores that would be open till midnight, checking out the sidewalk wares of the nighttime street merchants, stopping to listen to a black tenor saxophonist playing a soulful rendition of *Birth of the Blues,* the fat mellow notes floating out of the bell of his golden horn and soaring upward on the balmy air. It was a night for lovers.

They were not yet lovers, Hawes and Krissie, and perhaps they'd never be. But they were learning each other. This was the difficult time. You met someone, and you liked what you saw, and then you hoped that what you learned about him or her would make sense, would mysteriously jibe with whatever person you happened to be at this particular stage of your life. The way Hawes figured it, everything depended on where you were and who you were at any given time. If he'd met Krissie a year ago, he'd have been too occupied with Annie Rawles to have initiated and pursued any other relationship. Five years ago, ten years ago, he found it difficult to remember which women had figured largely in his life at any given time. Once there had been another Krissie—well, Christine, actually, close but no cigar. Christine Maxwell. Who'd owned a bookshop. Hadn't she? May was the month for remembering. Or forgetting.

"How'd you happen to start working uptown?" he asked.

"There was an ad in the paper," she said. "I was looking for something part time and the job at the church sounded better than waitressing."

"Why part time?"

"Well, because I have classes, you know, and also I have to make rounds . . ."

Oh, Jesus, he thought, an actress.

"What kind of classes?" he asked hopefully.

"Acting, voice, dance . . ."

Of course, he thought.

"And I work out three times a week at the gym..."

Certainly, he thought.

"So the job at the church is just to keep me going, you know..."

"Uh-huh," he said out loud.

"Till I get a part in something..."

"Right, a part," he said.

Every actress he'd ever met in his life had been a totally egotistical, thoroughly self-centered airhead looking for a *part* in something.

"Which is why I *came* here, of course," she said. "I mean, we've got the Guthrie out there and all, but that's still regional theater, isn't it?"

"I guess you could call it that," Hawes said.

"Yes, well, it is, actually," Krissie said.

He had once dated an actress who was working in a little theater downtown in a musical revue called *Goofballs* written by a man who reviewed books while he was learning to become Stephen Sondheim. If he reviewed books as well as he wrote musical revues, the writers of the world were in serious trouble. The actress's name was Holly Tree, and she swore this was her real name even though her driver's license (which Hawes—big detective that he was—happened to peek at while she was still asleep naked in his apartment the morning after they'd met) read Marie Trenotte, which he later learned meant Three Nights, the Trenotte not the Marie. Three nights was the exact amount of time she spent with him before moving on to bigger and better things, like the reviewer who had composed the show.

He had known another actress who'd been living with a heroin dealer he'd arrested—this was before cocaine and then crack became the drugs of choice—and who told him she was up for the part of a lady cop on *Hill Street* and would he mind very much if she moved in with him while her man was away so she could do some firsthand research, who she didn't know was dealing drugs anyway. Her name was Alyce (with a y) Chambers and she was a beautiful redhead who mentioned that if they had any children their hair would be red since both their parents had red hair, did he ever notice that a lot of actresses and especially strippers had boyfriends who were cops? He had never noticed. She did not get the part on *Hill Street*. Nor any other part she ever tried out for, it was that son of a bitch in prison, she informed Hawes, pulling strings from all the way upstate. In all the while she lived with him, she never once talked about anything but herself. He began to feel like a mirror.

Then one day she met a man with a Santa Claus beard and twinkling blue eyes and a diamond pinky ring the size of Antigua and he told her he was producing a little show out in Los Angeles and if she cared to accompany him out there she could stay with him temporarily at a little house he owned on the beach at Malibu . . . not the *Colony*, but close to it . . . just south of it, in fact . . . closer to Santa Monica, in fact . . . if that's what she would like to do. She moved out the very next day. She still sent Hawes a card every Christmas, but somehow she seemed to think his name was *Corry* Hawes.

And he'd known another actress who washed out her panties in . . .

"Penny for your thoughts," Krissie said.

"I was just thinking how nice, an actress," Hawes said.

"Actually," she said, "it's not very nice at all."

He braced himself for an Actress Atrocity Story. Producer asking her to strip for a nude scene in a film that turns out to be a porn flick. Actor soul-kissing her while they're auditioning together for a theaterful of potential back . . .

"In fact," she said, and her voice caught, "I'm beginning to think I'm not so hot, you know what I mean?"

He looked at her, surprised.

"No," he said. "What do you mean?"

"Not such a good actress, you know?" she said, and smiled somewhat pallidly. "No talent, you know?"

He kept looking at her.

"But I don't want to spend the rest of the night talking about me," she said, and took his hand. "Tell me how you got into police work."

* * *

She had tried to get the blood stains out of the carpet, but Willis was a cop and he could spot a worked-over stain from a mile away. She had similarly tried to soak the blood out of the monogrammed hand towel from the master bedroom, a much more difficult job in that it was white whereas the carpet was a Persian with lots of red in it. She'd used Clorox on the towel and then had taken it downstairs to the washing machine off the kitchen on the second floor, thrown it in with a lot of other towels, but the stain was still just barely visible, blood was tough. He'd known murderers who'd worked for days trying to get blood stains out of a wooden knife handle or even the blade of a hatchet, witness Lizzie Borden, whom he had not known personally. Blood was blood. Blood told.

And now, so did Marilyn.

It was five minutes past eleven.

Saturday night was still with them.

Across town and downtown, Cotton Hawes was about to ask Krissie if she'd care to stop by his place for a nightcap.

Closer to home, at the Church of the Bornless One on Ninth and North End, Schuyler Lutherson was fastening a black silk cord about the waist of his black cotton robe, rehearsing aloud the words of the Introit which he would say at the beginning of the midnight mass.

She told Willis about the first approach the two men had made.

Ramon Castaneda and Carlos Ortega.

"They gave you their names?" he said.

"Not then," she said. "This afternoon."

She told him everything that had happened here in this bedroom this afternoon. Everything. He had found the window they'd jimmied on the third floor, and now he listened intently, his heart beating wildly, she could have been killed. But no, he agreed with her, they could not kill her if they expected to get money from her, you can't collect from someone who's dead.

"Give them what they want," he said at once. "Get rid of them."

"How?" she said.

"Sell the house, I don't *care* how. Get the money and give it to them, send them back to Argentina."

"In a minute, right? Put a house worth seven-fifty on the market, and hope to sell it in a minute."

"Then borrow against it. Mortgage it to the hilt. Liquidate whatever other assets you have, call your broker . . ."

"There isn't that much, Hal."

"You left Buenos Aires with two million dollars!"

"I put five hundred of that down on the house, and spent another three hundred furnishing it. I made some bad investments, a gold-mining operation in Papua New Guinea, an electronics firm in Dallas, some big loans to friends who never paid me back . . ."

"All right, how much *can* you raise?"

"If I sold off all the stock I have, let's say four, five hundred. Plus whatever I can get on a second mortgage. Unless somebody buys the house tomorrow. Even so . . ."

"Maybe they'll settle for that," Willis said.

"I don't think so."

"Because if not . . ."

She looked at him.

"I can't let anything happen to you," he said. "I love you too much."

The worshippers had been informed that the meeting before tonight's mass would begin at eleven-thirty, and so they had begun assembling in the old stone church at twenty past the hour. It was written in the sacred Black Book that all church business must perforce be concluded before the hour of midnight when it was further ordained that the Introit should be said and the mass begun. On most occasions, there was scant church business to discuss. Tonight there was the matter of who, if anyone, in the congregation had painted the sign of Baphomet on the murdered priest's gate.

The assemblage numbered some fifty-one people . . .

If divisible by two, impure . . .

. . . among whom were the nine who would preside over and participate in the ritual of the mass . . .

If divisible by three, sublime.

The remaining forty-two were worshippers who had been told that the mass tonight would be more expressive of the *joys* of Satanism than had the more solemn Mass of the Expulsion earlier this week. But in contradiction to the announced purpose of the celebration tonight, the clothing they wore appeared conservative if not austere, the hues black or grey or dun for an overall appearance of unrelieved drabness, the cut angular and restrictive for an almost uniform look of severity.

It was only when one looked more closely...

A man standing at the rear of the church seemed to be wearing a long leather blacksmith's apron over black leather trousers. But when he turned in profile to greet a newcomer, it became evident that the trousers were in fact high boots and that between the tops of those boots and the hem of the apron there was naked flesh and nascent tumescence.

Through surmise, surprise.

A redheaded woman sat with her legs crossed on the aisle some three rows back from the altar, her auburn tresses caught and contained in a heavy black snood that added to them the seeming weight of mourning. She was wearing as well a black silk blouse, tailored grey slacks, and high-topped, laced, black leather shoes. But when she uncrossed her legs to lean forward and whisper something to a man on the row ahead of her, it became apparent that the slacks were crotchless and that beneath them she wore nothing. The revealed thatch of her fiery red pubic hair and lipstick-tinted nether lips were in direct contrast to the trapped hair on her head and the plainness of her unpainted mouth.

Throughout that vaulted holy place, then, there were unexpected...

Through ignorance, knowledge...

...glimpses of the flesh these celebrants were here tonight to honor. In Satan's name, they exposed discreetly and posed ingenuously. Speaking in whispers as befitted the sanctity of the Lord's meeting place, candid eyes met and held, glances neither roamed nor wavered, expressions never once indicated that a promised later offering to Satan was now being shown in fleeting preview:

A woman's severe black gown, cut high on the neck and low on the ankle with a cutout circle the size of a quarter exposing the nipple of her left breast painted a red as deep as blood . . .

A black man's grey homespun trousers, worn with a long-sleeved black shirt and a hangman's hood, his penis thrusting through an opening in the trousers and held in an upright position by the silken white ribbons wrapped around it and tied about his waist . . .

An exquisitely beautiful Chinese woman wearing a loosely crocheted black dress, pale diamonds of flesh showing everywhere except where tightly woven patches of black covered her Venus mound and breasts . . .

Through concealment, revealment.

In many respects, this socializing before the mass began was not too very different in tone or appearance from the little parties and gatherings occuring all over the city tonight. Except that here in this group, among these people openly worshipping the Devil, there was in the reverse order of their beliefs an honesty of intent that Schuyler Lutherson considered less hypocritical. Coming through the black curtains at the rear of the church now, he reflected solemnly upon the fervor of those who spoke most righteously for any God they claimed to admire—be it Jesus, Muhammed, Buddha or Zeus—and wondered if these people might not find a better home here at the Church of the Bornless One. Because it seemed to him that those who most vehemently denounced the sinful actions of unbelievers were those who most vigorously and secretly *pursued* those actions. And those who defended their religions against the imagined onslaughts of infidels were those who, in the very name of whichever god they professed to serve, most often vilified the sacred teachings of that god.

Come to Satan, Schuyler thought, and made the sign of the goat in greeting, and then went directly to the living altar and faced her, and passed his tongue over the forefinger and middle finger of his left hand, the Devil's hand, wetting his fingers, and then ran both fingers slick and wet over the lips of Coral's vagina, from my lips to thy lips, and said in Latin, "By your leave, most beloved Lord, I beseech thee," which was a plea upon Satan's own altar for the Unborn One to please remain patient yet a moment longer while this tiresome church business was attended to.

The worshippers fell silent as Schuyler stepped forward. Immediately behind him was the living altar, Coral, with her legs spread and bent at the knees, bare feet flat on the velvet-covered trapezoid, arms at her sides, clutching in each hand a phallic-shaped candelabra in which was an as-yet-unlighted black candle. The beginning of the mass would be signaled by the lighting of these candles, followed by the recitation of first the Introit and then the Invocation. For now, the deacon and sub-deacons stood ranked behind the altar in readiness.

The four acolytes (four tonight rather than the customary two, in that this was a special mass following the high holy Feast of the Expulsion) stood seriously and solemnly in boy-girl pairs on either side of the altar. Two eight-year-old girls, one of whom was tall for her age, a boy who was also eight, and another who was nine, all of them barefooted and wearing silken black tunics beneath which they were naked. Coral's long blonde hair cascaded over the pointed end of the trapezoid, almost touching the cold stone floor.

Without preamble, Schuyler said, "The death of this priest is troublesome. It may bring unwanted, unneeded visitors to the church. It may lead to suspicion of our order, and possible harassment, see, from the police. Or perhaps even more serious measures from them, I don't know, I don't care. What I'm asking tonight is for anyone here among us, if he or she is responsible for painting an inverted pentagram on the gate of St. Catherine's church, to come up here and say you did it. If you did it, then you know who you are, and I want you to come forward and explain *why* you did it. So we can straighten this out."

There was silence out there in the congregation.

Hesitation.

And then a blond giant of a man rose and stepped out into the aisle. He was in his early twenties, weathered and suntanned and muscular and lean, wearing a pair of faded grey jeans and a T-shirt tie-dyed in varying swirls of black, black headband and black leather sandals. In further keeping with the tone and stated purpose of the mass tonight, a black leather thong was tied tightly around his left thigh some three inches below his crotch. No one so much as glanced at the thong, no one seemed to notice that it held fastened against the man's leg . . .

Through bondage, freedom . . .

. . . a penis enormous by any standards, hidden of course by the fabric of his jeans . . .

Through disguise, discovery . . .

. . . but clearly discernible in massive outline.

"I did it," he said. "I painted the priest's gate."

"Come on up," Schuyler said in a friendly manner, but he was scowling. Perhaps because he himself was blond and considerably handsome and so was the young man, and he may have felt this constituted a threat to his leadership. Or perhaps he sensed, even before the young man reached the front of the church, and even though he'd only heard him speak eight short words, that here in the Church of the Bornless One was yet another of Dorothy's friends, too damn *many* of whom had been attracted to the services here in recent weeks.

"Tell us your name," Schuyler said, still pleasantly. But something seemed coiled within him.

"Andrew Hobbs," the young man said. "I started coming here in March."

Something Southern in his speech. The lilt. The intonation. Something else as well. A more familiar lilt.

"Jeremy Sachs introduced me here."

Sachs. Jeremy Sachs. Schuyler searched his memory for an image to connect with the name. A face. A character trait. A verbal tic. Nothing came.

"Yes?" he said.

"Yes."

"And the gate?"

"I did it," he said.

Through confession, condemnation.

"Why?"

"Because of her."

"Who?"

Was it possible, then, that he was *not* one of Dorothy's friends? And yet the *look* of him, and the cleverness of the thong, the understatement of it. But he hadn't yet said "her" name. And among those who roamed Oz, the female pronoun was often substituted for the . . .

"Her," Hobbs said. "My mother."

Ah, then. Were we still on the yellow brick road?

"What about her?" Schuyler asked.

They often nursed long-term grievances against Mama.

"She went to him."

"Went to who?"

"The priest. And told him."

"Told him what?"

If only this wasn't so much like pulling *teeth*.

"That I've been coming here. That Jeremy took me here. That we've been doing . . . things here."

Jeremy. Sachs. And now the name took on visual dimensions, Jeremy Sachs, a squat, rather simian-looking young white homosexual—without doubt one of Dorothy's friends, a longtime traveler among the Munchkins—who'd declared fealty to the Devil by reversing his own natural preferences and going down helter-skelter and willy-nilly on every naked snatch offered to Satan within these sacrosanct walls.

Schuyler could not recall seeing his young blond friend at any of the masses before tonight, but often there was wholesale confusion and resultant obscurity. In any case, here he was now, the young friend of a friend of Dorothy, perhaps homosexual himself, who had just now confessed defiling the dead priest's gate because of his goddamn *mother*. All mothers should be forced to suck a horse's cock, Schuyler thought. Including my own.

"But why did you paint the gate?" he asked.

"As a statement," Hobbs said.

Schuyler nodded. So what this was, it was merely a case of someone telling his Mama to keep out of his life. Completely understandable. This was not someone with any hard feelings for the priest. No bad intentions here at all. Just somebody making a personal family statement. But nonetheless . . .

"The statement you have to make *now*," Schuyler said, "is to the police. To let them know you didn't paint that pentagram as any kind of warning or anything. This priest was killed, see, and we don't want his murder connected to this church in any way. So what I suggest you do is leave here right this minute, see, and go home and change your clothes . . ."

"What's wrong with my clothes?" Hobbs asked.

"Nothing," Schuyler said. "In fact, what you're wearing is well-suited . . ."

He didn't know he was making a pun.

". . . to the ceremony tonight. But it might be misunderstood by the police, see, so go put on something that'll make 'em think you work in a bank."

"I *do* work in a bank," Hobbs said.

There was laughter in the assemblage. Laughter of relief, perhaps. This wasn't going to be as bad as it had appeared at first. Young homosexual here had argued with his mother, had gone off in a snit, and in defiance had painted the sign of his religious belief on the enemy's gate. He'd explain all this to the police and they'd understand, and send him on his way, and everyone could go right on practicing his chosen religion in freedom again, this was a wonderful country, the U.S. of A.

It was four minutes to midnight.

Hobbs asked where the nearest police station was, and from where he was standing behind the living altar, Stanley Garcia—who had been there early yesterday morning—gave him directions to the 87th Precinct. Hobbs asked if he could come back here for the mass *after* he'd talked to the police, but Schuyler pointed out that the doors would be locked at the stroke of midnight, which in fact was now only three minutes away, so perhaps Hobbs had better get moving.

Hobbs appeared to be sulking as he left the church. One of the worshippers closed and bolted the door behind him, and then dropped the heavy wooden crossbar into place, in effect double-locking the doors.

It was a minute to midnight.

The church was expectantly silent.

The redhead in the grey slacks sat with her knees pressed closely together, her head bent.

"It is the hour," Schuyler said, and signaled to his sub-deacons to come forward and light the candles. The sub-deacons tonight were two nineteen-year-old girls who looked like sisters but who weren't even cousins. Both brunettes with brown eyes, they were wearing the customary black robes of the church, naked beneath them, for it was ritual that following consecration of the altar by the minister, his sub-deacons (traditionally female) would then in turn and in sequence be consecrated by the deacon.

Solemnly and silently, the girls—whose names were Heather and Patrice—went to the altar, knelt in reverence before her, and then parted, one going to the left, the other to the right, where Coral's hands clutched the thick phallic candelabra. Tapers sputtering, they lighted both black candles, and then went behind the altar to where Stanley Garcia stood with an oxidized and blackened brass censer in each hand. The girls lighted the incense, and then accepted the thuribles from Stanley. Swinging them on the ends of their short black chains, they sweetened with incense first the altar and the surrounding apsidal chapters and then went up the center aisle to spread the cloying scent throughout the entire church. They returned then to stand flanking their deacon.

It was time for the Introit.

The word itself derived from the Middle English word for "entrance," from the Old French *introït* from the Latin *introitus*. It was pronounced not in the French manner but rather to rhyme with "Sin-Show-It," as many in the congregation were fond of explaining. In Christian churches, the introit was in fact an *entrance*, the begining as such of the proper, and it consisted either of a psalm verse, an antiphon, or the Gloria Patri. In the true church of the Devil, however, the introit was a short and personal opening dialogue intended as a despoliation of innocence and an introduction to the Devil, who would be invoked more seriously later tonight. The ritual blasphemy that Schuyler and the four child acolytes were about to perform was, in essence, a rude dismissal of Jesus and an acknowledgment of Satan—*Daemon est Deus Inversus:* The Devil is the other side of God.

Schuyler nodded to his deacon.

Stanley rang the heavy bell nine times, three times facing south and the altar, and then kept turning counterclockwise to ring the bell twice at each remaining cardinal point of the compass.

The air now purified, Schuyler went to stand in the open angle formed by the naked legs of the altar. Facing the assemblage, he lifted both arms, and formed the sign of the goat with the fingers of both hands. At this signal the four acolytes came to face him, a boy and a girl on each side.

In Latin, Schuyler said, *"In nomine magni dei nostri Satanas . . ."*

In the name of our great god Satan . . .

". . . we stand before thy living altar."

And in their piping voices, the acolytes responded in unison and in Latin, "We beseech assistance, oh Lord, save us from the wicked."

"To our Lord who created the earth and the heavens, the night and the day, the darkness and the light," Schuyler intoned, "to our Infernal Lord who causes us to exult . . ."

"Oh Lord, deliver us from unjustness," the children chanted.

"Lord Satan, hearken to our voices," Schuyler said. "Demonstrate to us thy terrible power . . ."

"And give to us of thy immeasurable largess."

"Dominus Infernus vobiscum," Schuyler said. "The Infernal Lord be with you."

And the children responded, *"Et tecum.* And also with you."

And the assemblage rose to its feet and shouted tumultuously and victoriously, "All hail Satan, all hail Satan!"

* * *

Detective Meyer Meyer was in the squadroom only by chance—
trying to catch up on half a dozen reports that were already weeks
late—when a blond young man wearing a dark pencil-stripe suit materialized on the other side of the wooden rail divider to the squadroom.

"Excuse me," he said.

"Yes?" Meyer said, looking up from his typewriter.

"I'm looking for whoever's investigating the priest murder. Sergeant downstairs told me there might be somebody in the squadroom."

"Not on the priest case," Meyer said, and thought Never turn
away a volunteer. "Come in, please," he said, "I'm Detective Meyer.
Maybe I can help you."

Hobbs opened the gate and walked into the room. Judging
from the way he looked it over, he'd never before been inside a
police station. He shook hands with Meyer, accepted the chair he
offered, introduced himself, and then said, "I'm the one who painted
that garden gate."

Which, as it turned out, was the opening gun in a salvo aimed
at Hobbs's mother, who—to hear him tell it—was the cause
of all his miseries. Not only was she responsible for his homo-
sexuality...

"I'm gay, you know," he said.

"Wouldn't have guessed," Meyer said.

"Yes," he said, "Which of course is *Abby's* fault, dressing me up
in little girl's dresses and forcing me to wear my hair in a long blonde
pageboy..."

At which point Meyer, while still wondering about the garden
gate, was treated to the recitation of a childhood atrocity story no
more horrifying then most atrocity stories he'd heard except that it
had resulted in what Hobbs described as a human being "not moving
left, not moving right"—a great many homosexuals knew Sondheim
lyrics by heart.

Hobbs kept referring to his beloved mother as "Abby," sarcasti-
cally spitting out the word as though they were great good buddies

whereas he hadn't seen her since she'd moved to Calm's Point six months ago, and neither knew nor cared to know her present address or telephone number. It was clear that he despised her and blamed her exclusively for his current life-style, which incidentally included worshipping the Devil. So, naturally, he had painted an inverted pentagram on St. Catherine's garden gate.

". . . to let her know I'd worship wherever I damn well please," he said. "It had nothing to do with the priest."

"Then why'd you pick *his* gate?" Meyer asked.

"To make a point," Hobbs said.

"What was the point?" Meyer asked. "I seem to be missing it."

"The point was she went to this priest and complained about me going to Bornless . . ."

"Bornless?"

"The Church of the Bornless One, when she had no right to do so. And incidentally, *he* had no right, either, preaching about our church to his congregation. No one was telling *his* congregation which church *they* should go to. Nobody at Bornless was running around saying Jesus is a menace, which by the way, he is, but we keep that to ourselves."

"But Father Michael wasn't keeping *his* beliefs to himself, is that what you're saying?"

"Only in passing, don't get me wrong. I had nothing at all against Father Michael. Though I must tell you, after *Abby* went *bleating* to him, he gave a few hot little sermons denouncing the Devil-worshippers up the block . . . well, *four* blocks away, actually, but close enough if you're wetting your pants worried that Satan's going to come burn down your shitty little church."

"So what you did," Meyer said, "was paint the Devil's sign . . ."

"Yes."

"On the priest's garden gate . . ."

"Yes."

"But not as a warning to the priest."

"No."

"Then why?"

"To let *Abby* know she should keep her big mouth shut."

"I see. And now you want us to understand you didn't paint that gate in malice."

"Correct. And I didn't kill that priest, either."

"Who said you did?"

"Nobody."

"Then why are you here?"

"Because Schuyler doesn't want you guys harassing us over this thing. He thought it'd be a good . . ."

"Schuyler?"

"Schuyler Lutherson, who runs Bornless."

"I see," Meyer said.

He was thinking he'd have to tell either Carella or Hawes about this pleasant early morning chat, because perhaps one or the other of them might wish to ask Schuyler Lutherson why he was so worried about police harassment.

"Thanks for stopping by," he said. "We appreciate your candor."

Hobbs wondered if he meant it.

Sitting on the third row of benches, the redhead in the grey tailored slacks watched the children as they rushed to escort Stanley to the altar, hurrying along on each side of him as he approached with a sword cushioned on a black velvet pillow. Schuyler grasped the sword by its silk-tasseled handle. The redhead's legs parted slightly. The children were back at the altar again. Schuyler raised the sword over his head, turned suddenly to point it at the hanging sign of Baphomet, and shouted in a voice hoarse with emotion, "Bornless One, I invoke thee!"

"Thou who didst create the universe," the assemblage chanted.

"Thou who didst create the earth and the heavens . . ."

"The darkness and the light . . ."

"Thou who didst create the seed and the fruit," Schuyler said, and on cue two of the acolytes—the tall eight-year-old girl and the shorter eight-year-old boy—stepped forward and faced each other. Holding the handle of the sword in one hand and the tip in the other, Schuyler lowered it horizontally over their heads. The redhead in the tailored grey slacks leaned forward expectantly.

In a high piping voice, the little boy said, "Behold! My staff is erect!" and lifted his tunic to show his limp little penis.

And the little girl responded, "Behold! My fruit drips nectar!" and raised her tunic to show her small hairless pudendum.

"My poison shall erupt and engulf!" the little boy said.

"My venom shall enclose and erode!" the little girl said.

"My lust is insatiable!" the little boy said.

"My thirst is unquenchable!" the little girl said.

"Behold the children of Satan," Schuyler said softly and reverentially.

Symbolically, he gently touched the tip of the sword first to the boy's genitals and then to the girl's. He returned the sword to the pillow. Stanley carried it back to where the two nineteen-year-old sub-deacons were waiting for him, the hems of their robes fastened above their waists, their hands resting on their naked flanks, palms turned outward toward the congregation.

The redhead on the third row placed her hands on her thighs and opened her legs a trifle wider.

Schuyler approached the altar.

"In thy name, oh Bornless One," he said, "I offer myself unto the altar of thy power and thy will."

He threw up his robe.

"Glory to God," he said, "may all hail Satan. Glory to Satan," he said, "whom we love and cherish. All hail Satan," he said, "we sing glory to thy name. All praise Satan," he said, "we sing honor to thy name. All bless Satan," he said, and positioned himself at the joining of the altar, "we adore thee, Great Lord, we thank thee, Infernal Lord, we cry unto thee, all hail Satan, all hail Satan, all hail Satan."

As he thrust himself onto and into the altar, the gong sounded three times and the assemblage chanted in unison and in Latin, *"Ave Satanas, ave Satanas, ave Satanas!"*

The redhead on the third row spread her legs wide.

The mass was beginning in earnest.

7

At eleven o'clock that Sunday morning, the twenty-seventh day of May, they buried Father Michael Birney in the Cemetery of the Blessed Virgin Mary of Mt. Carmel, all the way uptown in Riverhead, where there was still a little ground left in which to put dead people. The priest who delivered the funeral oratory was a man named Father Frank Oriella, who had been appointed by the archdiocese of Isola East as temporary pastor of St. Catherine's Roman Catholic Church. Among the mourners was Detective Steve Carella of the 87th Precinct. Father Oriella chose to read his elegy from the first letter of the apostle Paul to the Corinthians.

"The first man was of earth," he read, "formed from dust. The second is from heaven. Earthly men are like the man of earth, heavenly men are like the man of heaven. Just as we resemble the man from earth . . ."

Carella studied the small group of assembled mourners.

Father Michael's sister, Irene Brogan—who had made the arduous trip from Japan via Los Angeles in order to be here for the funeral today—stood by the graveside now, listening intently to Father Oriella's carefully chosen text. Martha Hennessy, the priest's housekeeper, had introduced her to Carella when he'd arrived. A petite

woman with travel-weary eyes, she told him she'd be happy to help
with the investigation in any way possible. Carella said he was eager
to talk to her, and asked if he could have a moment of her time after
the service.

". . . to tell you a mystery. Not all of us shall fall asleep, but all of
us are to be changed—in an instant, in the twinkling of an eye, at the
sound of the last trumpet . . ."

The forecasters had promised continuing good weather for the entire Memorial Day weekend. A blazing sun shone down mercilessly
on the shining black top of the coffin poised above the grave. A dozen
or more young people stood beside the open grave, listening to Father
Oriella. Carella recognized in the group of teenagers the two young
girls he'd spoken to yesterday. They were dressed more sedately
today, not in black—this was a largely alien color in a young person's
wardrobe—but in dark shades of blue that seemed appropriate to the
day's burden. They stood side by side, the one with the black hair
(Gloria, was that her name?) and the blonde girl, Alexis. Both girls
were crying. For that matter, so was the entire group of young people
with them. He had been a well-loved man, this priest.

". . . then will the saying of Scripture be fulfilled: 'Death is swallowed up in victory. Oh, death where is thy victory? Oh, death, where
is thy sting?' The sting of death is sin, and sin gets its power from the
law. But thanks be to God who has given us the victory through our
Lord Jesus Christ . . ."

Poking about the fringes of the crowd like scavenger birds were
half a dozen reporters and their photographers, but there were no
television crews in evidence, and this surprised Carella. The priest
story had received extensive coverage, especially on television, ever
since it broke last Thursday. Carella was aware that this was already
Sunday. The clock was ticking—and the older a case got, the wider
became the murderer's edge.

"Lord, hear our prayers," Father Oriella said. "By raising your
Son from the dead, you have given us faith. Strengthen our hope that
Michael, our brother, will share in His resurrection."

Here in the sunshine, the assembled priests paid honor to one of their own, standing in solemn black at the edge of the grave, listening to Father Oriella's final words. High-ranking police officers were here, too, in blue and in braid, a show of color and support to let the citizens of this fair city know—via the newspaper people—that the police were still on the job, if only to weep huge crocodile tears at graveside.

"Lord God, you are the glory of believers and the life of the just. Your Son redeemed us by dying and rising to life again. Our brother Michael was faithful and believed in our own resurrection. Give to him the joys and blessings of the life to come. We ask this, oh Lord, amen."

"Amen," the mourners murmured.

A hush fell over the grave site.

There must have been a signal, someone must have pressed a button because the coffin on its straps began lowering hydraulically, a photo opportunity that could not and would not be missed by the paparazzi, who moved forward as the coffin hung between heaven and earth, silhouetted blackly against the piercing blue sky. Another signal perhaps, because the lift stopped, and the coffin hung suspended now some several inches below the lip of the grave, and Father Oriella said another prayer, almost a private communication between him and his slain brother in Christ, whispering, his lips moving, and then he made the sign of the cross over the grave and knelt to scoop up a handful of moist spring earth and sprinkled it onto the coffin lid gleaming in sunshine.

The mourners came now with baby roses distributed by the funeral home, came in a last orchestrated effort to lend dignity to death, came in staged and solemn farewell, each passing this way for the last time, pausing at the grave with its shiny black coffin waiting to descend, tossing the roses onto the coffin, the priests from churches all over the city, the brass from Headquarters downtown, the priest's sister Irene Brogan, and some forty parishioners from St. Catherine's, and the dozen or more teenagers from the church's Catholic Youth Organization, all filing past to toss their roses in farewell, and now the pair from yesterday, Gloria, yes, and Alexis.

And then it was over.

As they moved past the grave and away from it, starkly illuminated in a clear sharp light the photographers must have loved, there was another unseen signal, and the hydraulic lift began humming again, and the coffin dropped slowly into the grave, deeper, deeper, until it was completely out of sight. Two gravediggers freed the canvas straps from beneath the coffin. They were beginning to shovel earth onto the coffin and into the grave when Carella walked over to where Irene Brogan was standing with Father Oriella, telling him what a beautiful service it had been.

He stood by awkwardly.

At last, she turned from the priest who had replaced her brother, and said, "I'm sorry to have kept you waiting. Please forgive me."

Tear-streaked face. Blue eyes shining with tears. Close up, in this harsh light, she looked to be in her early forties. A woman who just missed being pretty, her separate parts somehow not adding up to a completely satisfying whole. They walked together to where the funeral home limousines were waiting in line, shining in the sun. Standing beside the fender of the closest limousine, Carella watched the mourners moving past behind Irene, heading for their cars or the closest public transportation. Riverhead was a long way from home.

"Mrs. Brogan," he said, "I don't mean to intrude on your family privacy..."

She looked at him, puzzled.

"But in the course of the investigation...early on, as a matter of fact...I read a letter you wrote to your brother. Which was when I started calling you in San Diego."

"I think I know the letter you mean," she said.

"The one referring to *his* letter of the twelfth."

"Yes."

"In which he told you...I'm just putting all this together from what you wrote, Mrs. Brogan. But it seemed he was deeply troubled about something."

"He was."

"What would that have been?"

Irene sighed heavily.

"My brother was wholly devoted to God," she said.

"I've no doubt," Carella said.

And waited.

"But even Christ was sorely tempted in the wilderness," she said.

And still Carella waited.

"Let's . . . can we get in the car?" she asked.

He opened the back door of the limousine for her and then followed her into an interior as secluded as a confessional. The door closed behind him with a snug, solid click. And now, here in this dim and secret space with its tinted windows and its black leather seats, Irene Brogan seemed to find the privacy she needed to tell her brother's story. She described first the receipt of his letter . . .

"It was postmarked the twelfth, but I didn't get it on the Coast till the following Thursday, the seventeenth. My husband and I were leaving for Japan that Saturday. He sells heavy machinery, this was a business trip, he's still there, in fact. I . . . I called my brother that Friday. And when . . . when he told me what was *really* troubling him . . . the letter . . . you see, the letter had only hinted at it . . . but when I called him that Friday . . ."

At first, he is reluctant to speak about it, The Priest.

He tells her it's nothing, really, he shouldn't have written the letter at all, everything's fine now, she must be very excited about the trip to Japan, hm?

But Irene knows him too well. She was thirteen when he was born, which puts her at forty-five now, and she raised him almost as if he were her own child, her mother being a businesswoman who ran off to work every day and then complained of utter exhaustion all weekend long. She knows her brother all too well, and she knows he is hiding something now, excited about the trip to Japan indeed; she has accompanied her husband to Japan on every business trip he's made in the past six years! So she bides her time, and listens patiently to him telling her about someone in the congregation who took umbrage over his sermons about the tithe . . .

"He mentioned Arthur Farnes, did he?"

"I don't remember the man's name. But, yes, this was *one* of the things troubling him . . ."

. . . and someone's mother coming to seek solace and advice about her homosexual son's involvement with, of all things, *devil* worship . . . and something about . . .

"He was beginning to rattle on by then," Irene said, "do you know the way people sometimes do? When they're trying to avoid what's *really* troubling them? I'm not saying these things weren't actually bothering him . . . the tithe . . . and the drugs . . . and the . . ."

"The *what*?" Carella said.

"Well . . . drugs, yes. My brother seemed to think someone was using the church as a sort of storehouse. For drugs. He tore the whole place apart one weekend, looking for where they were hidden, but . . ."

"Are you saying illegal *drugs*? Controlled substances?"

"Well, yes, I'm sure that's what he meant."

"He found *drugs* inside the church?"

"Well, no, he didn't. But he certainly *looked* for them. At least, that's what he told me. As I said, he was starting to get a bit hysterical by then. Because he was coming to what the *real* problem was, and it didn't have a damn thing to do with any of the *little* things he was talking about. It had to do with . . ."

A woman.

Her brother is involved with a woman.

He does not tell Irene how this started or even how long it has been going on, but it is tormenting him that he has violated his vows of chastity and trapped himself in a situation from which there is no honorable escape. He loves Jesus Christ and he loves this woman and the two loves are incompatible and irreconcilable. He mentions that he has considered suicide . . .

"He told you this?"

"Yes. On the telephone."

"Had he considered a way of *doing* it?"

"What?"

"Did he tell you *how* he planned to kill himself?"

"Well, no. I mean, what difference would that make?"

"A lot," Carella said.

"It frightened me, I can tell you that," Irene said. "I almost canceled the trip. I thought I'd come east instead, be with my brother, see him through this . . ."

But he tells her that taking his own life would be an even greater sin than breaking his solemn vows. He swears to her and to the good Lord Jesus that he will not even *think* such thoughts again, swears this on the telephone. At Irene's urging, he swears as well that he will tell this woman he cannot go on with a relationship that is tearing him apart, cannot continue deceiving God in this way, destroying what is dearest to him. He will once again renounce the flesh, as he'd sworn to do so long ago, and pray for God's help in living forevermore a chaste and spiritual life.

He promises this to his sister.

"And then . . . when I got the call from Bishop Quentin . . . we'd just come upstairs from dinner . . . it was a lovely night there in Tokyo, the cherry blossoms still in bloom, the air so sweet . . . and he . . . he told me my brother was dead. And . . . and . . . the first thing I thought was that he'd killed himself. He'd done it. He'd broken his promise to me."

The limo went still.

"But this is worse, isn't it?" Irene asked. "Someone killing him that way."

Yes, Carella thought. This is worse.

Not to kill him, no. To *talk* to him. To ask him about her. Because you can't condemn a person without first hearing his side of the story, isn't that true? You can't just begin *hating* a person until you prove for sure that there's really a *reason* to hate him. Because this is a man of God, don't forget, this is not just someone like you or me, this is a man who's dedicated his life to God. And if he's going to break the rules that way, then he shouldn't be saying one thing and doing another thing. The rules should apply to everybody. That's the way rules work. Everybody knows you have to stop when a traffic light turns red. If you don't stop when it's red, then nobody is obeying the rules, and there'll be an accident, and someone might get killed. Of *all* people, he should be the one obeying rules, especially the promises he made to God. If you make a promise to God, you have to keep it or God will strike you dead. That's in the Bible, vengeance is mine, I will repay, says the Lord. Kissing her. But maybe there was some explanation. On the lips. Maybe he had some explanation for why he was doing that. Maybe there was something in church custom or church law that you had to kiss a woman on the lips in order to whatever. Bless her maybe. Greet one another with a holy kiss, that's in the Bible. It was all right to kiss in Scriptures, it was common practice. The one I shall kiss is the man and he came up to Jesus at once and said Hail, Master, and he kissed him. Or when he's sitting at table in the Pharisee's house and the sinner brings an alabaster flask of ointment and wets his feet with her tears and kisses his feet, this was Jesus getting his feet kissed. It was common in the Bible, look at Solomon, O that you would kiss me with the kisses of your mouth for your love is better than wine, your anointing oils are fragrant, your name is oil poured out, therefore the maidens love you. So maybe there was an explanation, and if you go to the person and ask him what the reason is, if there *is* a reason, then maybe he can tell you, explain that he was only greeting with a holy kiss, you shouldn't judge a book by its cover, ask and it shall be delivered unto you. Was the intention. To ask. To inquire. To discover. To hear from his own lips that this this *kiss* was not what it appeared to be, was not a *man* kissing a *woman,* a beautiful woman, in fact, but was instead a *priest,* a holy priest, performing some kind of of of ceremony to do whatever it was he was doing. A holy kiss, it's in the Bible, there are holy kisses, what's in the Bible is true, every word of it. Not to kill him, no. To *talk* to him. To ask him about her. But how could he explain his hands under her skirt, her panties down around her ankles, this was not a holy kiss, this could not have been a holy kiss, not with her blouse open and her naked breasts showing, Oh, may your breasts be like clusters of the vine, and the scent of your breath like apples, and your kisses like the best wine that goes down smoothly, gliding over lips and teeth, goes down smoothly, goes down no this was not a holy kiss it was not that no.

The call came at twenty minutes to one that afternoon, not five minutes after Willis had gone out for the Sunday papers. The moment she heard the voice, Marilyn realized they'd been watching the house, waiting for him to leave before they placed the call.

In Spanish, the voice said, "Good afternoon."

Buenas tardes.

She recognized the voice at once. The handsome one. The one she had cut.

In Spanish, she answered, "I've been waiting for your call."

"Ah, did you know we would call?"

Politely. In Spanish. No sense playing games now. They knew who she was. If they were to do business, it would be simpler to do it in their native tongue. From now on, nothing but Spanish.

"Yes, in fact, I was *hoping* you'd call," she said. "We have business to discuss."

"Ah."

A note of sarcastic skepticism in that single word. The Spanish were wonderful at conveying shades of meaning by inflection of the voice alone.

"Yes. I want to pay you. But I'll need time."

"Time, yes."

"But I'm not sure I'll be able to raise the entire two million."

"Ah, what a pity."

"Because even if I sell everything I own . . ."

"Yes, that is surely what you must do."

". . . I'll still be short."

"Then perhaps you should sell yourself as well."

A smile in his voice. A nod to the former hooker. Sell yourself as well. We understand you were very good at selling yourself.

"Look," she said, "I think I can raise half a million, but that's all. More or less."

Más o menos.

There was a silence on the line. Then:

"You owe us a great deal more than half a million. More or less."

"To begin with, I don't owe you or your big friend *anything*. If that money belongs to *anyone,* it belongs to . . ."

"It belongs to whoever will kill you if you don't pay it."

"Let's talk straight here, please," she said. "You're not going to kill me."

"You're mistaken."

"No, I'm not mistaken. You kill me, you don't get *any* of the money. If I were you, I'd settle for the five hun . . ."

"If I were you," he said, slowly and silkenly, "I would recognize that there are worse things than being dead."

"Yes, I know that," she said.

"We thought you might know that."

"I do. But I've only got so many arms and legs . . ."

"Y tu cara," he said.

And paused meaningfully.

"Y tus pechos," he said.

And paused again.

"Y así sucesivamente," he said.

Her face . . .

Her breasts . . .

And so on.

The last three words, though spoken softly and casually—*Y así sucesivamenta*—implied unspeakable acts.

She was suddenly very frightened again.

"Look, you're right," she said, "it's true, I don't want anything to happen to me. But . . ."

"Then you should learn not to cut people."

"If you're saying you're going to hurt me even if I *do* come up with the money . . ."

"I'm saying we'll *surely* hurt you if you *don't* come up with the money. Is what I'm saying.

"I understand that."

"I hope so."

"But what *I'm* saying is that it's impossible to come up with *all* of the money. Is what I'm saying."

"Then that's too bad."

"Look, wait a minute."

"I'm still here."

"How much time do I have here?"

"How much time do you need?"

"Even to raise the five hundred, I'd need a week, ten days."

"That is out of the question."

"Then how *much* time? Name a fucking amount of time!"

"Ah," he said.

Chastisingly. Scolding her for the language she'd used. Tsk, tsk, tsk.

She said nothing for several seconds. Regaining control. Calming herself. Then she said, "I need to talk to people who can turn assets into money. That takes time. I have to know exactly how much time I have."

"Wednesday," he said, and she had the feeling he'd picked a deadline out of the air.

"I don't think I can manage that," she said. "That's not enough time."

"It will have to be enough time."

"I don't think you understand."

"We understand completely."

"No. Look, can you listen to me a minute? Please? I want to pay you back, you have to understand that, I want this thing to be over and done with. But . . ."

"So do we."

"But you can't show up on someone's doorstep and expect them to raise two million dollars in . . ."

"You tell me," he said.

"How much time I'll need?"

"Yes. Tell me."

"You understand I can only raise half a million. It would be im-poss . . ."

"No, the full two million. How much time?"

"I . . ."

"Say."

"Can I get back to you?"

"We'll call you. Tell us when."

"This is Sunday . . ."

"Yes, a day of rest."

Sarcasm in his voice, the son of a bitch.

"I'll have to make some calls tomorrow, find out how long it'll take."

"Good. What time?"

"Can you call me at three-thirty? No later than that."

"Why? Will your boyfriend be coming home?"

"Three-thirty," she said. "Please. But, you know, I really think you should prepare yourself for . . ."

And hesitated.

Silence.

He was waiting.

The silence lengthened.

"Because you know . . . I really meant it when I said . . ."

And again she hesitated.

Because she knew what he would say if she told him again that it was impossible to raise much more than half a million. He would threaten her with punishment, raise fears of acid or steel, promise her mutilation. But the facts had to be stated.

"Listen," she said, "I'm being completely honest with you. I don't want to get hurt, but there's no way I can possibly raise more than half a million. Well, maybe a *little* more, I'm being honest with you, I hope you realize that, but two million is absolutely out of the question, I just can't do it, there's no way I can turn half a million into *two* million overnight."

There was another long silence.

And then he surprised her.

He did not threaten her again.

Instead, he offered a solution.

"There *is* a way," he said.

"No, there . . ."

"*Sí,*" he said. "*La cocaína.*"

And hung up.

Carella did not get back to the squadroom until almost two that Sunday afternoon, after extracting from Irene Brogan a promise that she would call her housekeeper in San Diego as soon as she returned to the hotel. He had previously asked her if she still had her brother's May twelfth letter. Irene said she thought it might be somewhere on her desk. The call to the housekeeper was to ask her to look for that letter. If she found it, she was to Fed Ex it to Carella at once. Irene seemed to understand why he wanted to read the letter himself: a fresh eye, an emotional uninvolvement, a mind trained to search for nuance of meaning. But she assured him once again that her brother —neither in his letter nor when she'd spoken to him on the telephone —had revealed the name of the woman with whom he was involved.

Meyer's note was waiting on Carella's desk.

It was typed on a D.D. form, but it was really a lengthy memo and not a report as such. Informal and chatty, it detailed Andrew Hobbs's visit to the squadroom late last night (early this morning, actually) to confess that he'd painted the pentagram on the church gate and to explain that "it was not the Devil who made him do it, but his mother Abby." Meyer's words. Touch of humor here at the old Eight-Seven. The report ended with the suggestion that either Carella or Hawes talk to Schuyler Lutherson at the Church of the Bornless One.

Carella carried the memo to the filing cabinet, found the file for the Birney case, and dropped it into the manila folder. He remembered again that this was Sunday. Even the hottest of cases got cold after a few days without a lead. This case had been cold from the beginning. Nothing solid to pursue until this morning, when suddenly there was a woman in the priest's life. Solid enough, Carella suspected. But cause for murder? In this precinct, where looking cock-eyed at another man's wife could result in a pair of broken legs, a *priest* fucking around could very well provoke murder, yes. Perhaps even those words—a priest fucking around—could incite riot.

He suspected that back in the good old days—when jolly friars were tossing up the skirts of giggling peasant girls and tickling their fancies on haystacks—religion wasn't taken quite as seriously as it was today. Perhaps something had been lost over the centuries. Maybe priests weren't supposed to be gods, maybe only God was supposed to be God. But didn't God ever smile? Wouldn't He perhaps find it comical that in a parish only four blocks from a congregation that openly worshipped the Devil, one of His faithful servants was—well, you find another way to describe it, Carella thought. To me, he was fucking around.

He suddenly realized that Father Michael's indiscretion—which was perhaps a better way of putting it—made him enormously angry.

Cherchez la femme, he thought.

But first let's go find Bobby Corrente and ask him what *he* knows about the events that took place on Easter Sunday.

Bobby Corrente was an even six feet tall and he weighed at least a hundred and ninety pounds, every bit of it lean, hard muscle. He had sand-colored hair and hazel-colored eyes, and he bore no more resemblance to his father than a beanpole did to a fire hydrant. Carella figured his mother must have been a prom queen. All clean good looks and friendly charm, he rose from the stoop where he'd been sitting with two girls who appeared to be a year or so younger than he was, fifteen, sixteen, in there.

"Nice to meet you, Detective Carella," he said, and extended his hand.

They shook hands. The girls seemed more in awe of Bobby than they did of the visiting cop. Open-mouthed, wide-eyed, they looked up admiringly at this handsome young man who could talk so easily and naturally to a detective, even shake *hands* with him. When Bobby said, "Excuse us, won't you, girls?" signaling that he wanted the girls to depart as graciously as they could, Carella thought they would wet their pants in gratitude. Smiling, fumbling to their feet, bowing and scraping like handservants in a movie about ancient China, they managed to back away without tripping all over themselves, and then hurried off up the street, glancing back frequently at the radiant boy-emperor who had granted an audience with the local constabulary. Bobby gave a sort of embarrassed shrug coupled with a boyish grin that said, What're you gonna do when you're so handsome? Carella nodded in sympathetic understanding, even though he'd never had such a problem.

"I'm glad I found you," he said. "Few things I'd like to ask you about."

"Sure, anything," Bobby said.

"From what your father told me, Nathan Hooper was here trying to sell dope on Easter Sunday, is that right?"

"Mr. Crack," Bobby said, and nodded.

"That's his street name, huh?"

"That's what they call him at the school."

"Mr. Crack."

"Yeah, the kids at the elementary school. Which is why we didn't want him in the neighborhood. It's bad enough he's at the school, am I right? We warned him, we told him stay away from the school and stay away from where we live. But he came here, anyway."

"Why do you suppose he did that?" Carella asked.

"I still can't figure it," Bobby said, shaking his head. "I think he was just looking for trouble."

"Tell me what happened," Carella said.

What happened was it's two-thirty, three o'clock in the afternoon on Easter Sunday, and all the guys and girls are hanging around outside where Danny Peretti lives. This is 275 North Eleventh, near the Italian deli. It wasn't such a good day, Easter, do you remember? A lot of wind, very grey, in fact it looked like it might snow. We'd all gone to church that morning, well, the twelve o'clock mass, actually, this was Easter, we went to St. Kate's where Father Michael later chased us away. But you can't blame him, he didn't know what was happening. All he knew was a bunch of kids yelling and hollering inside his church.

So we were, I don't know, showing off for the girls, clowning around. I remember Allie was doing his imitation of what was supposed to be Tony Bennett singing I Lost My Heart in San Francisco, but he sounded more like Jerry Lewis, did you ever hear Jerry Lewis sing? Man. Anyway, we were making our own fun, you know what I mean? Because the weather was so terrible, and Easter's supposed to be spring, supposed to be sunshine—*Easter,* you know? So we were making the best of it.

And all at once, there he was.

I couldn't believe my eyes.

None of us could.

I mean, here's Mr. Crack in person, who we told at least a hundred times to keep his shit out of our neighborhood and out of the elementary school, and he comes strutting up the street like he owns it. Man. Allie stopped doing Tony Bennett, and all of us just sat there watching him come closer and closer. He wears his hair the way they're all wearing it now, shaved close all over and then what looks like an upside down flowerpot on top. He's all dressed up, it's Easter Sunday. He keeps coming. We're all watching him do his shuffle up the street. Sitting there dumbfounded. Trying to figure out is he crazy or what? He's got a big grin on his face. Big watermelon-eating grin. Here's Mr. Crack, boys and girls, here to dispense his goodies. Break out your five-dollar bills, here's the man's going to chase all your cares away.

Afternoon, ladies, he says, and nods to the girls.

As if he's Eddie Murphy, you know?

Instead of some nigger here to sell crack.

Boys, he says, how we doin'?

One of the guys, this is Jimmy Gottardi, he knew Hooper person-

ally from when they were doing this Operation Clean-Up on Fifth.
What it was, the neighborhood people were cleaning out this lot that
was full of garbage and junk and whatnot. Jimmy and some of the
other guys on the block, but who weren't there that Sunday, volun-
teered to go over and lend a hand. So you see right off it isn't true
what they say happened on Easter. I mean, these were *white* guys
going over to a black neighborhood to help clean up an empty lot.
They weren't getting paid for it, they were doing it as a community
service. So whoever says this thing on Easter Sunday was racist is out
of his mind.

Anyway, Jimmy knew Hooper from the Clean-Up thing, so he
says Hey, Nate—Hooper's first name is Nathan, he calls himself Nate
when he ain't Mr. Crack—Hey, Nate, how you doing, and so on, like
he's giving him the benefit of the doubt, he's giving him an opportunity to say he ain't here selling crack. And Hooper stands there grinning, telling Jimmy Oh so-so, man, ever'thin' cool, man—you know
how they go—and Jimmy says What brings you here to Eleventh
Street, Nate, and Hooper slides his eyes up the street, checking it out,
you know, and his eyes come back all serious and hard and there's no
smile on his face anymore, and he says Anybody needin'?

What he means, of course, is does anybody need some crack.
Because if we need it, he's here to sell it. He turns to one of the
girls . . .

"This is only what you *figured*, right?" Carella said. "That he
meant he was selling crack."

"Figured, what do you mean *figured*? He came right out and
said it."

"I thought he only asked if . . ."

"No, no, that was at *first*. But then he turned to one of the girls,
and he goes, 'Honey? You lookin' for some choice crack?'"

This is a fifteen-year-old girl he's talking to, Laurel Perucci, she
lives in my building. Fifteen years old, I don't think she even knows
what crack *is*, he's asking her is she looking for some choice crack.
Man. But we still didn't do anything, I mean it. He was here, he was
selling dope, but nobody got excited, nobody flew off the handle. In

fact, Jimmy who worked with him on the Clean-Up, looks at him and says Come on, Nate, this ain't that kind of neighborhood, something like that, letting him know this is where we live, we don't want no dope here, okay, cool it. And Hooper goes Oh, that right, man? This ain't that kind of neighborhood, that right? And he turns to Laurel again and he goes, Honey, how you like some of this sweet stuff, huh, baby? and he's holding the vial of crack like right where his cock is, you understand what I'm saying? There's like a double meaning. He's like spitting in our eye. He's saying not only is he gonna sell crack here, he's also gonna insult this innocent fifteen-year-old girl. So it happened.

"What happened?" Carella asked.

"A fight started, what do you *think* happened?"

"Someone hit him with a baseball bat, isn't that right?"

"No, what baseball bat? There was no baseball bat. It was a fist fight. This was Easter Sunday, who was playing baseball? Where was a baseball bat gonna come from?"

"Hooper says he got hit with a ball bat."

"Hooper's a lying bastard."

"He says he got chased up the street with baseball bats and garbage can lids."

"Sure. Because *he* was the one with the fucking *knife*."

"He had a knife?"

"A switchblade knife. He pulled it the minute the first punch was thrown."

"Who threw the first punch?"

"Me. I admit it," Bobby said, and grinned.

"And you say he pulled a knife?"

"First thing he did."

"Then what?"

"One of the guys hit him from behind, the back of the head. And he must've figured the knife wasn't going to help him here, he'd better get the hell out of here fast. So he began running. And we ran right after him."

"To the church."

"Yeah, he ran inside St. Kate's. We chased him inside, too. And then Father Michael started yelling we were hoodlums and all that, and get out of his church, and we tried to tell him this was a crack-dealer here, he was trying to sell dope in our neighborhood, he insulted one of our girls, he had a *knife,* for Christ's sake . . . I admit I said that in church, I admit I took the name of the Lord in vain. Father Michael had a fit. What? What did you say? How dare you? Get out of here, this is God's house, all that. So we left. Some things you walk away from, you know what I mean? Some things are a no-win situation."

"Then what?"

"Then *what* what? We went home. That was it."

"Did you see anyone else in the church? While you were there?"

"No. Just Father Michael."

"Hear anyone else?"

"No."

"You didn't hear two people arguing?"

"No. What two people?"

"Is it true that you made a blood vow to get both Hooper *and* Father Michael? For what happp . . ."

"What are you talking about? What blood vow?"

"For what happened on Easter Sunday."

"I don't even know what a blood vow is. What's a blood vow?"

"You didn't swear to get them, is that right?"

"For what? Did Hooper come back to the neighborhood since then? He didn't. Has he been hanging around the school peddling dope? He hasn't. So what's there to get him for? We got him good enough on Easter."

"And the priest? Father Michael?"

"He only did what he thought was right. He figured he was helping a poor innocent kid getting beat up by a gang of hoodlums. I'da done the same thing, believe me. If I thought somebody was in the right? The very same thing. So why would we hold anything against him? In fact, I've been to church every Sunday since. The other guys, too. Church is like a meeting place for us. We go to ten o'clock mass every Sunday. We go to the C.Y.O. dances on Friday nights. We had nothing against Father Michael. In fact, he was like one of the guys until what happened on Easter. This was a terrible thing that happened to him. A terrible thing."

"When you say he was like one of the guys . . ."

"He was always kidding around with us, you know, telling jokes, asking us about our problems, a real nice guy, I mean it, you sometimes forgot he was a priest. I still think he did what he did on Easter because he misunderstood the situation. He didn't know the kind of person Hooper really is. In fact, I wouldn't be surprised . . ."

Bobby stopped, shook his head.

"Yes, what?" Carella asked.

"I wouldn't be surprised if it turned out Hooper had something to do with his murder."

"Why do you say that?"

"A feeling, that's all."

"But what gives you that feeling?"

"I don't know. I just know that when a guy's selling dope, *any-thing* can happen. Including killing somebody. That's all I know," Bobby said, and nodded in utter certainty. "That's all I know."

Willis made the call from the squadroom at a little before three that afternoon. With late afternoon sunlight streaming through the windows, he sat at his desk and direct-dialed first 0–1–1 and then 5–4–1, and then the number listed in his international police directory. He waited. The foreign ringing sounded somehow urgent. Across the room, Andy Parker was typing up a report, pecking at the keys with the forefingers of both hands. The squadroom was otherwise empty. The phone kept ringing. He wondered what he could possibly say if the lieutenant asked why he'd called Buenos . . .

"*Central de Policía,*" a woman's voice said.

"Hello," he said, "do you speak English?"

"Perdóneme?"

"I'm calling from the United States," he said, careful not to say *America*, they were very touchy about that down there. *"Los Estados Unidos,"* he said, "I'm a policeman, *un policía,"* trying his half-assed Spanish, *"un detective,"* giving it what he thought to be the proper Spanish pronunciation, day-tec-tee-vay, "is there anyone there who speaks English, please, *por favor*?"

"Juss a mom'enn, please," the woman said.

He waited.

One moment, two moments, three moments, a full *six* American moments which probably added up to one Argentinian moment, and then a man's voice came on the line.

"Teniente Vidoz, how can I be of assistance, please?"

"My name is Harold Willis," Willis said, "I'm a Detective/Third Grade with the 87th Squad here . . ."

"Sí, señor?"

"We're investigating a case you might be able to help us with."

"Oh?"

Warily.

There was not a cop in the world who wanted a foreign investigation added to his own already topheavy case load. Foreign meant anything outside the cop's own precinct. It could be the precinct right next door, this was still foreign. Bahía Blanca, some three hundred and more miles south of Buenos Aires, was very definitely foreign. Río Gallegos, all the way down near Chile, was practically *in* a foreign country. And the United States? All the way up *there*? Don't even ask.

But here was a person who'd identified himself as a third-grade detective, which Lieutenant Vidoz assumed was some sort of inferior in the police department, and he was investigating a case, and he needed help. Help. From the police in Buenos Aires. *Norteamericanos* were a nervy bunch.

"What kind of help?" Vidoz asked, hoping his voice conveyed the unmistakable impression that he desired not to help in any way, manner, or form. What he desired was to go to see his mistress before he went home. It was already a quarter to six in Argentina. This was what he desired.

"I have two names," Willis said. "I was hoping you'd be able to run them through for me."

"Run them through *what*?" Vidoz asked.

"Your computer. I think they may have criminal records. If so, perhaps you can fax me the . . ."

"What sort of case *is* this?" Vidoz asked.

"Homicide," Willis said at once.

The secret password.

Homicide.

No cop in the world wanted to be burdened with a foreign case, but neither would any cop in the world turn his back on a homicide. Willis knew this. Vidoz knew it. Both cops sighed heavily. Willis in mock weariness after days and nights of working a murder he'd just invented, Vidoz because satisfying this request was a supreme pain in the ass but an obligation nonetheless.

"What are the names?" he said.

"Ramon Castaneda and Carlos Oretga," Willis said.

"Give me your fax number," Vidoz said.

Willis gave it to him.

The information from Buenos Aires came through on the fax at a little past seven that night, which made it a bit past eight down there in Argentina, where Lieutenant Francisco Ricardo Vidoz was feeding the photocopied records into the machine and cursing over having missed his evening *cita* with one Carla de Font-Alba. In the Clerical Office at the 87th Precinct, Sergeant Alfred Benjamin Miscolo pulled the pages as they inched their way out of the fax machine, remarked to his assistant Juan Luis Portoles that they were in Spanish, and then noticed that they were earmarked for "Det/3 Harlow Wallace" who he guessed was Hal Willis. Glancing at the pages—there were eight altogether—Portoles whistled and said, "These are *some* bad hombres, Sarge."

He was probably referring to several words that had caught his eye, words such as . . .

Robo . . .

Asalto con Lesiones . . .

Violación . . .

. . . and especially *Homicidio*.

8

The call from Kristin Lund came as something of a surprise that Monday morning. On her doorstep Saturday night, when she'd pointedly held out her hand for a good-night handshake, Hawes figured that was the end of that. But here she was now, bubbly and bright, asking if he'd had lunch yet.

"Well, no," he said.

"Because I'm cleaning out some things here at the church, and I thought since I'm in the neighborhood anyway..."

"I'd love to," he said. "Shall I pick you up there?"

"Why don't I come by the station house?" she said. "Maybe you can take my fingerprints again."

"Maybe," he said, and wondered why the handshake Saturday night. Actresses, he thought, and shook his head.

"Half an hour okay?"

"Fine," he said.

"I wasn't even sure you'd be working today," she said.

"How come?"

"Memorial Day."

"Oh. Yeah."

For cops, holidays came and went like any other day.

"But I'm glad you are," she said. "See you later."

And hung up.

He put up the receiver, and glanced at the clock. It was now a quarter past eleven. He sat for several seconds staring blankly at the sunshine streaming in through the grilled windows, still wondering.

A uniformed cop handed the Federal Express envelope to Carella some ten minutes after Hawes left the office. He explained that it had been buried under some other shit on the muster desk downstairs, and Sergeant Murchison had just now discovered it. When he apologized for any delay this may have caused, he sounded slightly sarcastic.

The red-and-blue package contained the letter Father Michael had written to his sister on the twelfth of May. It was written on church stationery, *St. Catherine's Roman Catholic Church* printed in raised black letters across the top of the page, the address just below that. Father Michael had written the letter by hand, but there was nothing in his handwriting to reveal the obvious emotional distress that had caused him to open his heart to his older sister. Instead, the hand was small and precise, the words marching evenly across the page as if to the steady cadence of a secret drummer:

> *My dear sister,*
>
> *It's been a long time since you and I have talked meaningfully about anything, and I suppose much of this has to do with the disparate—and distant—lives we lead. Whatever the cause, I strongly miss the intensely personal and private talks we used to have when I was growing up, and the good advice you gave on more than one occasion. Not the least of which, by the way, was your advice to follow my heart about the call and to enter into the service of our Lord, Jesus Christ.*
>
> *I write this letter in the hope that I may still reveal to you my deepest feelings.*

Irene, I'm very troubled.

I have for the past little while now, since shortly before Easter as a matter of fact, been entertaining the most serious doubts about my ability to love God and to serve Him as devoutly as I've vowed to do. I now have reached the point where I feel incapable of facing a congregation on Sunday, of hearing confessions, of leading the young people in our youth organization, of counseling those in need of spiritual guidance — in short, of fulfilling the duties and obligations of the priesthood.

My self-loathing reached its highest peak on Easter Sunday, when I failed to extricate myself from a situation that had become all-consuming and debilitating. I realized then that I was caught in the Devil's own snare and had become a threat not only to myself and the lambs of my flock, but also to God.

I don't know what to do, Irene. Help me. Please.

> *Your loving brother,*
> *Michael*

Carella read the letter yet another time, and then he looked at the opening paragraph of Irene's return letter to him:

My dearest brother,

I am now in receipt of yours of May 12th, and I cannot tell you with what a saddened heart I hasten to respond. Michael, how have you managed to construct such a tower of doubt for yourself? And don't you feel you should relate your fears to the bishop of your diocese? I just don't know how to counsel or advise you.

This from a sister who, in the days of Michael Birney's youth, had given him "good advice on more than one occasion." To Carella, her letter read like a brush-off. Don't tell me your troubles, I'm on my way to Japan. I'll call you before I leave, we'll have a nice chat. By then, it'll be blue skies again, anyway. Besides, I know you'll be able to pray your way to enlightenment and salvation. Poor tormented son of a bitch is having an affair with someone, as it later turns out, but she can't be bothered. Eyes all full of tears at the funeral yesterday. Carella shook his head.

And then he went to the Clerical Office, and made a copy of Father Michael's letter, and used a yellow highlighter to mark those words or sentences that he thought might prove helpful to the case:

I have for the past little while now, since shortly before Easter as a matter of fact . . .

The affair, then, had started "shortly before Easter." "Shortly" being a relative term, it could have begun two *days* before Easter or two *weeks* or even two *months*. In any case, he hadn't said "For a long time now." His exact words were "For the past little while." Go pinpoint that.

My self-loathing reached its highest peak on Easter Sunday . . .

Here was Easter Sunday again. The day Nathan Hooper had sought sanctuary in the church. The day he'd heard Father Michael arguing with an unseen man. The day the priest had heatedly thrown out Bobby Corrente and his friends.

. . . when I failed to extricate myself from a situation that had become all-consuming and debilitating.

Was he referring here to the argument he'd had with this unseen, unknown man? Had they been arguing about the affair . . .

. . . that had become all-consuming and debilitating?

What had this man been telling him when Hooper burst into the church, dripping blood and chased by an angry mob?

I realized then that I was caught in the Devil's own snare...

The Devil's own snare, Carella thought, and wondered what the priest had meant.

"What were you cleaning out at the church?" Hawes asked.

"Oh, just some things in my desk. The priest who's replacing Father Michael is bringing his own secretary with him."

"Father Oriella? I thought he was only temporary."

"Well, apparently not," Krissie said, and tossed her hair the way actresses did. Hawes guessed there were acting classes where they taught you how to toss your hair. "I'll be looking for something else tomorrow. Unless a part comes along," she said, and shrugged.

On Saturday night, she had told him honestly and sincerely that sometimes she doubted a part would *ever* come along. But apparently hope sprang eternal. Here it was Monday, and she was singing the actress's same sad song again. A part will come along. And when it comes along, I'll be *up* for it. And if I lose it, it was because they were looking for someone who was taller. Or shorter. Or blonder. Or darker. Actresses, he thought, and wondered what the hell he was doing here.

They were eating in a new Italian restaurant on Culver. In this city restaurants sprang up like mushrooms (or, in some cases, toadstools) and most of the new ones were Italian, the American craze for pasta seemingly knowing no limits. Some of the restaurants survived. Most of them went under after struggling for two or three months. Krissie had ordered the veal piccata. Hawes had ordered the cannelloni. Judging from the taste of the sauce, he gave this joint two or three *weeks*.

"Would it bother you if I talked about the case?" he asked.

This morning, Carella had filled him in on what he'd learned at the cemetery yesterday. The priest having an affair. Hawes had listened silently. He guessed the news bothered him, but he didn't know quite why.

"Go right ahead," Krissie said.

"I was wondering . . . did Father Michael ever discuss personal matters with you?"

"Like what?"

"Well . . . personal matters."

"Like which dentist he should go to? Or whether or not he could afford a new car?"

"No, I was thinking more of . . . doubts . . . fears."

"No. Never."

"Did you ever open his mail? Or answer his telephone?"

"Yes, of course. All the time."

"Were there ever any letters or calls from . . . ?" He hesitated and then thought Go ahead, bite the bullet. "Were there ever any letters or calls from women?"

"Yes, of course," she said.

"Any women in particular?"

"I don't know what you mean," she said.

"Any women who wrote or called more often than . . . well . . . might have seemed appropriate."

"I still don't know what you're saying."

"Well . . ." he said, and hesitated. "We have reason to believe that Father Michael may have been involved in something he didn't know how to handle. Something that was causing him distress. If you know of anything like that, you'd be helping us a lot by . . ."

"No, I don't know of anything that was troubling him," she said.

"Never mentioned any problems or . . ."

"Never."

"And these women who called or wrote . . ."

"Different women. Women in the parish mostly," she said.

"Would you remember their names?"

"Not offhand. But any letters would be in the file..."

"Yes, I saw them."

"...and I kept a log of all telephone calls—unless the new secretary's already thrown it out."

"Where would it have been?"

"On my desk. To the right of the phone."

"A book, a pad...?"

"One of those printed message pads. Pink. While You Were Out, and so on. And then a space for the message and the caller's name and number."

"These women who called...did any of them ever *visit* Father Michael?"

"Visit him?"

"Yes. Come to the church. To see him. To talk to him."

"There were women who came to the office, yes," Krissie said, and looked at him. "You know," she said, "I get the feeling you're ...well...never mind, I'm sure I'm wrong."

"Maybe you're right," he said. "What are you thinking?"

"That...well...from the questions you're asking...well, you seem to be suggesting that Father Michael was...well..."

"Yes?"

"Well, was having an *affair* or something."

"Do you think that might have been the case?"

"No."

"You sound very positive."

"I think Father Michael was wholly devoted to God and to the Catholic Church. I doubt if he even *noticed* women as such. Or thought of them in that way."

"In what way?"

"A sexual way. He was very good-looking, you know...well, you saw him..."

Hawes had seen a corpse.

Someone repeatedly stabbed and slashed.

". . . all the little parish girls were crazy about him, those classic black-Irish looks, that Gene Kelly smile . . ."

The body on the stone floor of the garden had not been smiling.

They had caught a homicide, period.

The victim was a white male in his early thirties, dark hair, dark eyes.

Good-looking?

Hawes could not remember.

". . . is what I'm saying. He was sensitive and marvelously understanding, and these are traits that women naturally find appealing. But he was a priest, don't you see? And as such, he couldn't dwell on . . . well . . . matters of the flesh. He couldn't think of himself as being attractive to women. And he certainly couldn't allow himself to be attracted to them."

"His sister thinks otherwise," Hawes said.

"Oh?" Krissie said.

"She seems positive her brother was having an affair with someone."

"Someone in the parish?"

"He didn't say, and she doesn't know."

"I'm surprised," Krissie said. "Really."

"You never saw any indication that he might have . . ."

"Not the slightest."

"Even though there were calls and letters . . ."

"Well, from *men,* too."

"And visits . . ."

"Yes, from both men *and* women. St. Catherine's is a busy parish and he was a responsive pastor. I remember how surprised I was when I first began working there, the number of people he found time to see. His energy was . . . well . . . amazing. I don't think the man ever slept, really."

"This was when?"

"When I started the job? The beginning of March, it was snowing

I remember. I walked from the subway stop to the church . . ."

. . . and had trouble finding the entrance. You come in on the Culver Avenue side, you know, well, you've been there. The church is laid out like a cross, *all* churches are, with the central portal opposite the altar. The rectory at St. Catherine's is on the western side of the church, you come through this little arched door, and you go through the sacristy and then into a wood-paneled corridor and into the rectory. Father Michael's office is in a corner that once was a part of the kitchen. In fact, there used to be a wood-burning stove where the filing cabinets now are, against the southern wall.

It's funny, but Krissie feels as if she's there auditioning for a part.

Maybe because there's another girl in the office when she arrives. You go to a theater to try out for something, there're always a hundred other girls there. In the theater, of course, you call anyone under the age of thirty a girl, but the girl in Father Michael's office on that blustery March morning really *is* a girl, thirteen years old if that, wearing jeans and a grey sweatshirt, and yellow rubber rain boots, her long dark hair spilling down over her face as she leans over the desk. He is saying, "You didn't put in the ticket price, Gloria," it turns out they're discussing a big church dance that won't take place till the beginning of June, and the beautiful little dark girl has designed the poster for it, and brought it here for Father Michael to look at. "What do you think of it?" he says to Krissie, lifting the poster off the desk and showing it to her.

She hasn't even told him who she is yet, hasn't even said she's here about the part-time secretarial job, but immediately he's getting her involved in church matters. She looks at the poster, which shows a lot of young girls and boys dancing, and features big fat black music notes floating on the air over their heads, and balloon-type lettering that announces The June Hop, to take place at St. Catherine's Hall on Friday night, the first of June. This is only the beginning of March, but Father Michael likes to get his young people involved long in advance of any planned event. "So?" he says, and grins at her . . .

"He really did have a Gene Kelly smile . . ."

. . . and waits for her answer as if the entire future of the Catholic Church depends upon it. The little girl—she's not truly *little,* she is in fact five feet six inches tall, but to Krissie she's only a little girl, twelve, thirteen, whatever—is also waiting for her decision, critics, critics everywhere. This is a first-night opening up here on North Eleventh Street, and they're waiting for the reviewer from Channel 4 to express an opinion. Gloria, he'd called her Gloria, is a beautiful little girl, with a pale oval face and high cheekbones, long black hair falling clean and straight to her shoulders, lips slightly parted, electric blue eyes opened wide in anticipation.

Krissie feels a sudden empathy for the girl, who obviously drew the poster and who is now yearning desperately for the priest's approval, which may or may not hinge upon what Krissie has to say about her effort. Krissie knows what it's like to be thirteen, however, and she also knows what a "sell" review can mean to a show, and so she expresses the opinion that the poster really makes a person want to come here and dance, at which point Gloria yells "Yippee!" or something equally adolescent and throws her arms around Krissie and gives her a great big hug.

Krissie is here for a job, remember. And she's beginning to think this isn't such a dignified first impression, a teenager jumping up and down in her arms and yelling when she hasn't even yet introduced herself. So she listens to Father Michael telling the girl that the poster is terrific except for the price she forgot to put in, and the girl is still so excited by Krissie's rave review and the priest's terrific Gene Kelly grin of approval and his gung-ho Let's Put On A Show contagion that she's almost wetting her pants there in the office. But finally she scoops up the poster and thanks Krissie again and leaves the office all adolescent happiness and smiles. The handsome young priest shakes his head when she's gone and says something about the wonderful kids in this parish, and *finally,* Krissie gets to introduce herself and to tell him she's here about the job. And do you know what he says?

"He says, 'Can you start today?' Just like that," Krissie said, and shook her head. "I guess he liked what happened there with Gloria, the way I handled myself with Gloria—who, by the way, is a terrific kid, president of the C.Y.O., bright as can be, and beautiful besides."

"I know," Hawes said, "Carella told me."

"The point is . . . well . . . he was a fine, decent man, and . . . look, I don't know his sister, I can't say whether she's telling the truth or not. But if she told you he was . . . involved with some woman . . . I mean, I find that hard to believe. That he was having an *affair* with some woman . . . I mean, I guess she said they were sexually involved, didn't she?"

"Yes, he told her he'd violated his vows of chastity."

"With some woman."

"Yes. A woman he said he loved."

Krissie shook her head sadly.

"What a pity," she said. "That he couldn't work it out. If it was true. That he loved this woman, and couldn't work it out."

"Yes," Hawes said.

Memorial day.

Just what Marilyn needed.

A national holiday.

The banks closed, her stockbroker's office closed, and two hoods from Argentina expecting answers at three-thirty this afternoon. She looked at her watch. Five minutes past two. And ticking.

One of the men she'd known before she started seeing Willis was an attorney named Charles Ingersol Endicott, Jr., a man in his late fifties who carried as a holdover from his prep school days the nickname "Chip"—as if life did not have enough burdens. She dialed his number now and hoped he wasn't out on a boat for the weekend; sailing was Chip's passion. The phone rang four times, five, six. She was about to hang up when—

"Hello?"

"Chip?" she said. "It's me. Marilyn."

She had not spoken to him in months. She wondered suddenly, and with an odd sense of panic, whether he would even remember her. And then his voice boomed onto the line, deep and resonant and welcoming—"Marilyn, my God, how *are* you?"—and she visualized at once the good friend with whom she'd shared so many wonderful hours in a city where good friends and good men were scarce.

"I'm fine, Chip, how are you, I hope I'm not interrupting anything," remembering his kind handsome face and intelligent brown eyes, a man thirty-one years older than she was, the father she'd never known perhaps—

"Is something wrong?" he asked at once.

"No, no," she said, "I was just thinking about you and . . ."

She could not lie to him. He'd been too good a friend, and she hoped he was still a friend now. But either way, she could not lie to someone who'd once meant so much to her.

"I need advice," she said.

"Legal advice?"

"Not quite."

"Okay," he said, but now he sounded puzzled.

"Chip . . . what do you think I could get for a second mortgage on my house?"

"Why? What's the trouble?"

"No trouble. I need some money, is all."

"How much money?"

"A lot. I wouldn't be bothering you with this, but the banks are closed today, and this is somewhat urgent."

"You're alarming me, Marilyn."

"I don't mean to. I'm simply trying to get an estimate . . ."

"How much did the house cost?"

All business now.

"Seven-fifty."

"How much is the present mortgage?"

"Five hundred."

"You could expect something like a hundred and thirty-five thousand. That would be about eighty percent of the value."

"How long would it take to get it?" she asked.

"Usually a full month. How soon do you need it?"

"Yesterday," she said.

"Marilyn, I don't want to know what this is, truly. But if you need money, you don't have to go to a bank. I can lend you however much you want."

"Thank you, Chip, but . . ."

"I'm serious."

"Have you got two million bucks lying around?" she asked, and thought it amazing that she could still smile.

There was a silence on the line.

"What is it?" he said.

"An old debt came up."

"Gambling?"

"No."

"Then what?"

"A former time, a former life."

"Something you'd like to talk about?"

"No, Chip, I don't think so."

"I can go to five hundred thousand," he said. "Pay me back whenever you can."

"Chip . . ."

"No interest, no strings."

"I couldn't."

"You'll never know how much you meant to me," he said. "Come to my office tomorrow, I'll arrange a transfer of funds."

"I can't, Chip. But thank you, anyway."

"If you change your mind . . ."

"I don't think I will."

"We were such good friends," he said suddenly, his voice catching.

"Yes," she said.

"I miss you, Marilyn."

"I miss you, too," she said, and realized that she meant it.

"Marilyn, I'm serious," he said. "If you want the money, call me. It's here. And so am I. Call me, won't you? I'd like to talk to you every now and then. That's permitted, isn't it?"

"It is, Chip."

"Good," he said. "Stay well, darling," and hung up.

She lowered the receiver gently onto its cradle.

Her stockbroker was a man named Hadley Fields, but there was no sense calling him at the office today, and she did not have his home number. She went to the file cabinets in the study on the second floor of the house, and from the file marked STOCKS (she believed in generic labeling) she dug out the most recent statements. A glance at the last figure in the Market Value column showed that as of the last quarterly statement on March 31, the assets in her account totaled $496,394. Of this total, $443,036 was invested in equities, and the remainder was a cash equivalent of a bit more than $50,000 invested in what was called a short term income fund paying 8.6% interest. She began going down the list of stocks she owned:

500 Abbott Laboratories, bought in June two years ago at $45.125 per share for a total cost of $22,793. Now worth $54.75 per share or $27,435 — up almost $5000 . . .

300 Walt Disney Co, bought at $57.00 a share in April two years ago, now worth $78.50 a share for a total increase of $6,270 . . .

500 Morton Thiokol Inc, bought in February of last year at $40.625 per share, now selling for $44.375 for a total gain of $1,657 . . .

There were losers, too:

1,000 Republic New York Corp purchased for $46,058 a year and a half ago, now worth $44,750, for a loss of $1,308 . . .

500 Sprague Technologies Inc. Purchased for $7872, now worth $5812 for a loss of a bit more than $2000 . . .

. . . but overall, the investments she'd made since coming to this city had increased in value by more than $60,000. Hadley Fields had been doing a good job for her; she would not be selling at a loss. Not that it made any difference. The proceeds would not be going to her. They would be going back to Argentina.

Tomorrow morning, she would call Hadley and advise him to sell everything she owned and to make a wire transfer of the proceeds to her bank account.

Meanwhile, she had to place another call to Shad Russell.

The man Willis spoke to at the Identification Section office that Memorial Day afternoon was fluent in Spanish, having been born of parents who'd made their way to the city from Puerto Rico back in the days when newcomers from that island were still called Marine Tigers. This was because the ship that had carried them to mainland America was called the *Marine Tiger,* Harold. Sergeant Miguel Florentino Morente was called Mike by the rest of the staff. He asked Willis to call him Mike now. This was nice of him in that sergeants in this city outranked even first-grade detectives. Willis was but a mere third.

Morente looked over the records that had been faxed by Vidoz, remarked as how the one named Carlos Ortega was perhaps the ugliest human being he'd ever seen in his life (but perhaps it was a bad fax) and then reeled off for Willis all the crimes Ortega and Castaneda had committed in tandem over the past twelve years. Willis, who'd already been filled in by Portoles, listened politely but impatiently. The list of crimes—Assault and Battery, Armed Robbery, Rape, Homicide and such—only raised his anxiety level. These were the people Marilyn was dealing with. These were the ones who wanted money from her.

"What I'm really interested in, Mike," he said politely, "is whether or not we've got anything on them *here*."

"In this city, do you mean?"

"Or even in this *country*," Willis said.

"These are common names," Morente said. "In Spanish. Very common. Castaneda? Ortega? Very common. If you'd of given me something like Hoyas de Carranza, or Palomar de las Heras, or. . ."

"Yes, but these are their names," Willis said.

"Oh, sure. I'm only saying. The computer's gonna have a ball

with these names. You're gonna have four thousand Ortegas the first
time around, you wait and see."

There were in fact only eighty-three listings for Ortega, Carlos, in
the citywide Felony Offenders file, and forty-seven for Castaneda,
Ramon. Armed with the records from Buenos Aires, however, Morente knew the birth dates of both men, and he also had information
concerning height, weight, color of hair, color of eyes, scars, tattoos
and so on, which he punched into the computer as well, and amaz-
ingly—the odds had to be *what,* ten million to one?—he came up
with records for two men named Carlos Ortega who had been born on
the very same day and who seemed to be just as ugly as the Carlos
Ortega who'd presumably followed Marilyn up from Argentina.
There were no Ramon Castanedas whose pedigrees matched the
handsome one in the pair.

"You better call B.A., ask them to Fed Ex you a good set of
prints," Morente said. "'Cause I can tell you right off, we're not
gonna get a match from this fax, no way."

"Any other way we can zero in?"

"Well, unless you're looking in prisons, you can count *this* one
out," Morente said. "He's doing a five-and-dime at Castleview."

"How about the other one?"

"Carlos Ortega," Morente read out loud from the computer
screen, and then turned to the faxed record and said, "Carlos Ortega,"
and then kept turning his head from screen to paper, like a spectator
watching a tennis match, comparing records, speaking the facts out
loud, "forty-two years old, born October fifteenth," and said in an
aside to Willis "Birth date of great men" but did not amplify, "six feet
three inches tall, two hundred and sixty-five pounds, brown eyes,
bald with black sideburns, this is some kind of miracle, broken nose,
knife scar over the right eye, they sound like twins except *your* guy
was born in Argentina and *this* guy in El Salvador."

"How do their prison records match?"

"The only time *your* guy was out of jail, *this* guy was in."

"So they *could* be one and the same."

"If you conveniently forget El Salvador."

"That could be a clerical error."

"Sure, anything could be a clerical error."

"How long has your guy been in America?" Willis asked.

"Two years," Morente said, looking at the screen, and then turned to study the faxed record. "Just about when *your* guy got out of jail."

"Why was *your* guy put away?"

"Dope."

"Where is he now?"

"Out. Naturally."

"Anything in *my* guy's record about dope?"

"Nothing. But here's his whole family history. His uncle was a pimp, a guy named Alberto Hidalgo, got him started picking pockets when he was still a little . . ."

"A guy named *what*?" Willis said, and reached for the fax.

"Don't *tear* the fuckin' thing," Morente said.

"Where does it say that?"

"Right here. That's what this means in Spanish, Living Off the Proceeds. And take a look at *this*. He's dead."

"Ortega?"

"No, the uncle."

Willis caught his breath.

"Hidalgo. Got himself killed a few years back. Cyanide."

"Do they . . . do they know who did it?" Willis asked.

"Doesn't say. This is *Ortega's* record, not his uncle's."

"His uncle," Willis said softly.

"Yeah. Is exactly what I said."

Willis was silent for several moments. Then he said, "When did *your* guy get out of jail?"

"October."

"Then it's at least possible."

"That they're one and the same person? Oh, sure," Morente said. "But I wouldn't wanna bet the farm on it."

"Have you got an address for him?" Willis asked.

* * *

It was the ugly one who called her at three-thirty sharp.

Like the handsome one, he spoke only in Spanish. There was in his voice a scarcely contained rage; he was forcing himself to be civilized. She knew that he would never forget the humiliation she had caused him to suffer. She knew that once she turned over the money they wanted, he would seek revenge, he would kill her. She did not yet know quite how she would deal with that. One step at a time, she told herself. But his voice was chilling.

"Do you have the money yet?" he asked.

"I forgot that today was a holiday," she said. "Everything's closed."

"When will you have it?" he asked.

"I'm sure I can get the five hundred tomorrow," she said. "Then I'll have to see what . . ."

"That is not two million," he said.

His voice was low. She felt he'd wanted to shout the words, but instead they came out softly, and were all the more terrifying: That is not two million. Almost a whisper. That is not two million.

"I realize that," she said. "But you know, you're the ones who suggested cocaine . . ."

"Ustedes fueron los que sugerieron la cocaína . . ."

"Sí."

"So I was wondering . . . I'm sure you have contacts . . ."

"No."

"Because it would be so much simpler if I turned . . ."

"No."

". . . over the five hundred . . ."

"No, that is not satisfactory."

". . . and then *you* could handle the business of . . ."

"No. Five hundred is not two million."

"Of course not. But I'm sure you understand . . ."

Trying to appeal to his sense of fairness and justice . . .

". . . how difficult it is for a woman to handle such a trans . . ."

"You should have thought of that before you killed my uncle."

"What?" she said.

"*Nada,*" he said.

"No, what did you . . . ?"

"When will you have the two million?" he asked.

Had he said his *uncle*? Was that son of a bitch his uncle? Was *that* what this was all about? A little family vendetta here? We'd like the two mill, honey, sure, but there's also this matter of My Uncle the Famous Pimp Hidalgo.

"I'm still trying to make contact with someone," she said, "I told you, this is a *holiday*. But this is what I'm suggesting. Once I set the deal up, why don't you and your friend . . . ?"

"Are you dense?"

The word in Spanish was *pesada*. Meaning "thickheaded" or "obstinate." *Qué pesada eres.*

"We suggested cocaine as a way out of your problem. But the problem is *yours,* not ours. We don't want to become involved in anything illegal."

She almost burst out laughing.

"Do you understand what I'm telling you?" he said.

She understood perfectly. He didn't want to run any risks. She was the debtor, let *her* come up with the scratch.

"What if five hundred is all I can raise?" she said.

"You said you've already made contact with . . ."

"No, I said I'm *trying* to . . ."

"Then do what you have to do, and do it quickly!"

"I'm not in the habit of buying and selling dope. I'm . . ."

"Miss?"

Only the single word.

Señorita?

Loaded. About to explode.

"When will you have the money?"

Back to the point. No more bullshit. We're not interested in taking the five hundred and investing it in dope or in hogbellies. The only negotiable aspect of this deal is *time*. When will you have the money?

"I don't know yet. *If* I can buy the stuff . . . look, I simply don't know. I've been trying to reach this man . . ."

"When *will* you know?"

"That's just it. Until I . . ."

"When?"

"If you could let me have till the end of the week . . ."

"No."

"Please. I'm trying to work this out, I really am. If I could have till Friday. . ."

"Tomorrow."

"I can't promise anything by tomorr . . ."

"Then Wednesday."

"Can you make it Thursday?" she asked. "Please?" Groveling to the son of a bitch. "Thursday, okay?"

"No later," he said, and hung up.

Today, citizens all over America had lined the sidewalks of cities and towns, large and small, and watched the parades honoring their dead in foreign wars. Today, veterans of all ages had reminisced about their infantry platoons or their bomber squadrons or their minesweepers or their parachute drops. This was Memorial Day. A day set aside to pay tribute to the dead. A day, also, that signaled the beginning of summer. The swimming pools and outdoor tennis courts had been opened all over America today, and all over America today the promise of summer loomed large. For this was the twenty-eighth of May, and June was only four days off and ready to bust out, summer was on the way, summer was in essence *here*—this was Memorial Day.

The town was full of tourists.

This was Memorial Day, this was the symbolic beginning of summer, this was a time when most Americans dredged up memories not of warfare and bloodshed, but of summers past . . . the summer of a first kiss, the summer of a lost love, the summer all the lights went out, the summer of distant music, the summer of girls in yellow dresses, summer after summer floating past in hot recall, this was Memorial Day. The tourists came to the city not to remember either dead soldiers or dead summers. They came to celebrate the *start* of a season of corn on the cob and boiled lobsters, gin and tonic, beer frothing with foam. Summertime. High cotton and good-looking women.

Carella had read over his own reports on the Hooper and Corrente interviews, and there was no question but that the two were in absolute contradiction. It seemed to him that a *third* perspective might be valuable, and he had gone to the Hooper apartment specifically to talk to Seronia. Her mother told him where he could find her. Her mother cleaned white people's houses and offices for a living. Got down on her hands and knees to scrub floors. Her daughter got down on her hands and knees to perform quite a different service. Carella had not realized the girl was a hooker. That was the first shock.

"Arrest her," Mrs. Hooper told him. "On'y way she goan learn."

The second shock was actually seeing her.

He found her all the way downtown, standing under the marquee of a movie theater playing a pair of triple-X-rated porn flicks. She was wearing a purple satin mini and a lavender satin blouse. Amber beads on her neck. Yellow flower in her hair. High-heeled purple leather pumps to match the skirt and blouse. One hand on her hip, the other clutching a small purple leather purse. Lips pursed to kiss the air as strange men turned to look her over, whispered words. She looked twenty-seven. She was thirteen.

"Want a date?" she asked Carella, and kissed the air as he approached, and then recognized him, and started to turn away, and realized it was too late to go anyplace, and stopped dead still, one hand on her hip. "Whut's this?" she said.

"Few questions," he said.

"You goan bust me?"

"Should I?"

"No crime to stan' outside a movie show," she said.

"I agree," he said. "Can I buy you a cup of coffee?"

"I'd p'fer some ice cream," she said.

They found an ice cream shop with tables in the back. At the counter, fresh-faced black girls in red-and-blue uniforms served up double-scoops on sugar cones and earned seven bucks an hour. At a table near the window, Carella watched Seronia Hooper eating a banana split with chocolate fudge sauce, whipped cream, and a maraschino cherry, and listened to her telling him that the girls behind the counter were assholes.

"They cud make two *hunn'id* an hour," she said, "they was to get lucky."

He figured she was talking fifty dollars a trick.

"I want to know what happened on Easter Sunday," he said.

"Nate tole you whut happen," Seronia said.

"I want to hear what he told *you*."

"Same as he tole you."

"I don't think so."

"Look, man, whutchoo *want* fum me? Nate tole you the story, why'n't you go 'rest them cocksuckers busted his head?"

"Did your brother have a knife?"

"No. Who tole you he had a knife?"

"Did he go to Eleventh Street to sell crack?"

"Oh, man, doan make me laugh."

"Is his street name Mr. Crack?"

"Where you hear all this shit, man?"

"Somebody's lying, Seronia. Either your brother or a kid named Bobby Corrente, who . . ."

"Oh, *that* sum'bitch."

"You know him?"

"I know him, all right. Was him swung the fust bat, you ass me."

"Is that what your brother told you?"

"He tole me same as he tole you."

"He didn't tell me it was Bobby Corrente who swung the first bat. From the way he told it, the boys who attacked him were strangers."

"Then they was."

"But *you* know Corrente, huh?"

Silence.

"Seronia? How come *you* know Bobby Corrente?"

"I seen him aroun' is all."

"Where?"

"Aroun'."

"What are you hiding?"

"Nuthin'. You know Corren'ee, you go 'rest him. He the one broke Nate's head."

"How do you know that?"

"Jus' a guess is all."

"Is that what your brother told you? That Corrente swung the first bat?"

"You go ass Nate."

"I'm asking you."

"I got no more time to waste here," Seronia said, and wiped her mouth on the paper napkin and was preparing to get up from the table when Carella asked, "How'd you like to waste some time uptown?"

He felt no guilt whatever throwing muscle on a thirteen-year-old hooker.

"Waiting for the wagon to take you to Central Booking," he said, nailing the point home.

"Oh whut charge?" Seronia asked, supremely confident. "Anyway, my man get me out in half an hour."

"Good. Let's go then. I'm sure he'll love making bail."

"You think you bluffin' me?"

"Nope, I think I'm running you in on a Two-Thirty."

"Nobody offered you no sexual conduct, man."

"That's your word against mine," he said, and stood up. "Let's go."

"Sit down," she said, "you makin' a fuss here."

"Are we gonna talk about Easter Sunday or not?"

"They *both* lyin'," she said.

This is not *Rashomon,* not quite.

The movie *Rashomon,* as Carella remembers it, was not about people *lying.* It was about people sharing a single event but perceiving it separately and differently, so that each time the event was related, it had changed significantly. Listening to Seronia now, sitting with a thirteen-year-old hooker in an ice cream shop while she dug into her second banana split, aware that men thirty and forty years older than she is are eyeing her through the plate-glass window fronting the street, Carella begins wondering whether this version of the story, *Seronia's* version as related to her by Nate shortly after the incident occurred, is in fact the *true* version. Or is *she* lying as well?

In the game of Murder, only the murderer is allowed to lie; all the other players must tell the truth. But this is not the *game* of Murder, this is the death of a human being who also happened to be a priest, and it appears now as if *everyone* is lying, if only about what happened on Easter Sunday. And yet, there are areas where all three stories coincide, so that it becomes increasingly more difficult to tell who exactly was lying—or *is* lying—about which aspect of the Eleventh Street happening.

Seronia admits, for example, that her brother's street name is, in fact, Mr. Crack, and that he has been known to hang around the elementary school on Ninth Street enticing the little kiddies to try a bit of crack, a nickel a blow, this is not big money for kids who are ten, eleven years old. In this city, perhaps in every American city, kids are more and more often indulging in acts once exclusively reserved for adults. Seronia tells Carella—and presumably her line of work makes her an expert on the subject—that in the past three years, sex crimes committed by boys in the twelve-to-seventeen-year-old age bracket went up only twenty-eight percent, whereas sex crimes committed by boys *under* the age of twelve increased by two hundred percent. Moreover, since the rapist usually picks on someone *weaker* than he is, the female victims of these new-age sex criminals ranged in age from three years old to seven. In fact, Seronia feels she is doing a public service by engaging in sex with would-be rapists who might otherwise be chasing teeny little girls in the park.

But that is neither here nor there.

The point is that her brother, yes, is a dealer, yes. But this does not make him a bad person. This makes him a businessman filling a need in the community, much as she is a businesswoman—at thirteen, she thinks of herself as a woman, and why not, considering her occupation—filling a similar need in a different but possibly related community. All of this communicated to Carella in English that is not quite Black English, but neither is it the Queen's Own.

And on Easter Sunday, as happened on *every* Sunday, rain or shine, Christmas, Yom Kippur or Ramadān, Nathan Hooper goes uptown to Eleventh Street not to *sell* crack to the young wops gathered on their front stoops and freezing their asses off in their Easter finery, but instead to *buy* crack from his supplier, young Bobby Corrente . . .

"Are you making this up?" Carella asked.

"Do I *soun'* like I'm makin' it up, man?"

She did not sound like she was making it up.

"Bobby discounts it 'cause of the volume," she said. "Figure . . ."

. . . you can buy a vial of crack for five bucks, but you've got to go hustling customers and that takes time and energy. Bobby sells it to Nate for four bucks a vial, but he does a hundred vials in a single shot and goes home with four bills *without* having to run all over town. Nate makes a buck on each vial he sells, so on the initial investment of the four, he comes away with an *additional* hundred, which is a twenty-five percent return on the dollar, much better than you can do on Wall Street.

On this particular Sunday in question, which happens to be Easter Sunday, Nate goes uptown with three big ones in his pocket plus another hundred in twenties, intending to buy his usual hundred vials of crack from his usual dealer, Mr. Robert Victor Corrente, in case you didn't know his full name. But something happens that changes the entire complexion of the deal. What happens is that Nate hands over the money, and is reaching for the plastic bag with the vials of crack in it, same way they do business each and every time—

"An' by the way, this *wun't* on the front stoop in broad daylight, with all them silly wop girls sittin' an' watchin'. This is in the *hallway* . . ."

—where Nate is reaching for the plastic bag when Bobby tells him to disappear, vanish, get lost, nigger, words to that effect. Nate knows what it is at once, of course, but he pretends ignorance and so Bobby spells it out for him. What it is (Oh, man, you got to be kiddin' me, Nate goes) is that *last* Sunday, when Nate made his usual buy, he paid for the dope with funny money (No, man, you makin' a mistake, man, I mean it) and so *this* Sunday, Bobby is keeping the four bills, but he ain't giving Nate no dope for it, he's telling Nate instead to go shove his business up his ass, he doesn't like doing business with somebody who pays for merchandise with money printed in the cellar.

Hey, no, man, come on, man, Nate is going, but he knows Bobby's got him dead to rights, and he figures this is the end of this relationship here, he'll have to look for a suplier somewhere else. But you can't buy dope without cash, and Bobby has the four bills in his pocket already, and the only thing faintly resembling convertible cash around here is the plastic bag full of crack. A hundred vials of it. So, since the relationship is over and done with, anyway, and since Nate is a very fast runner with a good sense of rhythm . . .

"He grabs for the bag," Carella said.

"Is jus' whut he done," Seronia said.

. . . and starts running like hell, planning to get off Eleventh Street and stay off it till things cool down. Bobby Corrente wants to find him, let him come onto black turf, where *everybody* got rhythm, man, and where your life ain't worth a nickel if you start up with a brother. Which is just about when Bobby hits him on the back of the head with a baseball bat.

The blow sends Nate flying forward, he almost loses his grip on the bag of crack, but he keeps running, knowing he ain't gonna make it back home now, knowing he's bleeding too bad to make it back home, but not wanting to quit now, not with these hundred vials of crack in his hands. And all of a sudden he spots the church up ahead.

He tries the door, and it's unlocked. He runs into the church, and locks the door behind him, twists this big brass key that's sticking out of the heavy lock, and he hears the wops outside, charging up the steps, and he figures first thing he has to do is stash the dope because the dope is what this is all about, the reason he has a broken head is the dope. And now they're pounding on the door with their bats, and throwing themselves against the door, and maybe they've even got something they're using as a battering ram, Nate doesn't know. All he knows is that the door's going to give, and he's got to hide the dope.

And then he hears somebody arguing someplace in the church, and he knows his time is running out, he's got to hide that dope before whoever's arguing comes out and finds him, or before that door smashes in, which it does about three seconds after he stashes the hundred vials.

"Where?" Carella said.

"I got no idea," Seronia said.

"But in the church someplace."

"In the church someplace," she said. "Doan y'think that's funny? Nate turnin' the church into a stash pad?"

"Yes, very funny," Carella said. "What's the rest of the story?"

"The rest is like he tole you. The pries' comes out yellin' an' hollerin' an' somebody calls the cops an' then ever'body goes home an' the pries' takes Nate to the hospital where they wrap his head in ban'ages. End of story."

Not quite, Carella thought.

"You mine if I go now?" Seronia said. "I got a livin' to make."

9

Father Frank Oriella was a man in his early sixties, who'd been born into the Catholic Church when masses were still said in Latin, fish was eaten every Friday, and it was mandatory to go to confession before taking holy communion. Nowadays, he was often bewildered by the ecumenical changes that had taken place since he'd become a priest. He had only last week, for example, attended a funeral service in a church in Calm's Point, where—presumably to speed the deceased on his way to Heaven—the pastor had played a guitar and had sung what sounded like a pop song. This was in a Catholic church! This was not some little church down south with a tin roof. This was a big, substantial Catholic church! With a priest who played the guitar and sang! Father Oriella still shook his head in wonder at the memory.

That Tuesday afternoon, when Carella and Hawes arrived at the church, he was shaking his head and trying to put together a new office in the space that had once been occupied by Father Michael. This was a small church in a poor neighborhood. The rectory here at St. Catherine's was more a cottage than a true house. Fashioned of stone that echoed the floor of the adjoining garden, it consisted of two bedrooms, a small kitchen, and an even smaller office, the official church terminology for which was "chancellery." A long hall connected the rectory to the church, via the sacristy. Uptown Father Michael had enjoyed the use of a rather more opulent house.

His secretary of thirty years, a woman named Marcella Palumbo, to whom he spoke alternately in English and in Italian, was busily unpacking cardboard cartons of files which Father Oriella then transferred to the open drawers of green metal cabinets. Both Oriella and Marcella had white hair, and they were both wearing black. Looking very much like citified penguins, they bobbed busily about the small office, the priest complaining that it was inhuman to transfer a man from a parish he'd served for more than forty years, his secretary clucking her tongue in sympathy while she unloaded box after box of files. It occurred to Carella that the files they were unloading pertained to Oriella's previous parish and would be of little worth here. But perhaps he'd carted them along for sentimental reasons.

"I can understand the bishop's thinking," he said, "but this does not make his decision any more bearable for me."

His accent was not *basso profundo buffone;* he did not sound like a recent immigrant. Rather, the intonations and cadences of his speech made it sound careful, studied, somewhat formal. In contrast, Marcella spoke with a thick Neapolitan accent that belied her presence on these shores for the past fifty-odd years.

"The bishop surmises," Oriella said, "that after a tragedy such as this one, it will take an older, more experienced priest to pull the parish together again. Not mine to question. But have they given any consideration to the shambles my *old* parish will become? There are people at St. John the Martyr who've been worshipping there since I first became a priest. That was forty-two years ago. Some of these people are eighty, ninety years old. How will *they* react to such a change? To a new priest?"

"*Vergogna, vergogna,*" Marcella said, shaking her head and tackling yet another carton.

"It might have been wiser," Oriella said, "to send the newly appointed priest *here,* instead of to St. John's. This parish has *already* weathered a shock. Now there will be *two* shocks to overcome, one here and another one there."

"Sure, what do they know?" Marcella said.

It sounded like "Shoo, wottaday nose?"

"Marcella Bella here," he said, pleased when she waved away his playfully flattering nickname, "started working for me when the subways were still clean and it wasn't worth your life to travel on them after ten o'clock. I had a difficult time convincing her to accompany me here. She lives in Riverhead, just a few blocks from St. John's. The commute is a difficult one for a woman getting on in years. And the neighborhood, with all due respect for what you people do, is not the best in the world, is it?"

"No, not the very best," Hawes admitted.

"But complaining about the pasture isn't going to mend the fences, is it?" he said. "These files are the accumulation of a lifetime, my sermons, letters from priests all over the world, articles on Jesus and the Catholic Church, reviews of inspirational books, anything pertaining to the spiritual life. To have left them behind at St. John's would have been like leaving my own children there."

"Vergogna, vergogna," Marcella said again.

Hawes did not know what she was saying, but he gathered from the clucking of her tongue and the shaking of her head that she was not happy about Father Oriella's transfer here. Carella knew that she was saying, "Shame, shame," referring to the stupidity of the diocese in transferring the priest, the secretary, the files, the whole damn-a ting. She was not going to like this place. She knew that from the minute they'd walked into a rectory half the size of the one at St. John's. And what kind of housekeeper could an Irish be? Martha What*ever*, eh? This was a person to take care of an Italian priest? Or so Carella read it. *Vergogna, vergogna.*

"Actually, we'll have some more files for you in a little while," he said.

"Oh?" Oriella said.

"Cosa?" Marcella asked.

"More files," the priest said, and then, in Italian, *"Delle altre pratiche,"* and in English again, "What files?"

"Father Michael's. We're almost finished with them."

"They'll be useful to you," Hawes said. "For the receipts, records of payments . . ."

"Remind me to call the bishop," Oriella said, snapping his fingers, and turning to Marcella. "I have to ask him whether I should close out the St. John's account and start a new one here, or whether Father Daniel and I can simply use the old accounts." He turned back to the detectives and said, "They sent a young man straight out of the seminary, he's twenty-four years old, Daniel Robles, a Puerto Rican. He's going to be dealing with octogenarian Italians, young Daniel, he's going to be stepping into a lion's den."

Marcella burst out laughing.

"I should have left you there to help him out," Oriella said, teasing her.

"Hey, sure," Marcella said.

It sounded like "Ay, shoo."

"The reason we came by," Carella said, "is we'd like to do a search of the church, if that's all right with you."

"A search?"

"*Cosa?*" Marcella asked.

"*Una perquizione,*" Oriella said. "But a search for what?"

"Narcotics," Hawes said.

"Here?" Oriella said.

It was unthinkable that there would be narcotics here inside the church. This was like saying the Devil would be preaching next Sunday's mass. The single word "Here?" expressed not only surprise and disbelief but revulsion as well. Here? Narcotics? Dope? *Here?*

"If the story we have is reliable," Hawes said.

Marcella, who had apparently understood the word, was already shaking her head again.

"So we'd like to look around," Carella said, "see if we come up with anything. If there *is* dope here in the church, if dope *is* somehow involved in this . . . well . . . let's say that might change things."

"Of course," Oriella said, and shrugged as if to say This is entirely preposterous, dope inside a church, but if you wish to look for it, by all means go ahead, I am but a mere devoted servant of God transferred from my beloved parish uptown to an insufferable part of the city.

"We'll try not to get in your way," Hawes said.

"Is Mrs. Hennessy here?" Carella asked. "We thought she might show us around."

"She's in the kitchen," Marcella said.

It sounded like "She's inna kitch."

"I'll buzz her," Oriella said, and went to his desk. Pressing a button on the base of his phone, he waited, and then said, "Mrs. Hennessy, could you come in, please?" Marcella scowled. "Thank you," Oriella said, and put the phone back on the cradle. "She'll be right here," he said, and just then Alexis—the beautiful little blonde girl with the serious brown eyes and the solemn air—appeared in the doorway to the office, said, "Excuse me," and then recognized Carella.

"Hello, Mr. Carella," she said, "I'm Alexis O'Donnell, we met last Saturday."

"Yes, I remember," Carella said. "How are you?"

"Fine, thanks," she said, and hesitated, and then asked, "Have you learned anything yet?"

"Few things," he said.

Alexis nodded, her brown eyes thoughtful, her face bearing the same sorrowful expression that had preceded tears last Saturday. She was wearing a blue blazer with a gold embroidered school crest on the left breast pocket, pleated green plaid skirt, blue knee-high socks, brown walking shoes; Carella figured she had come here directly from school. She turned to Oriella and said, "I hope I'm not interrupting anything, Father..."

"Not at all," Oriella said.

"But we're not sure...the kids in the C.Y.O....we're not sure what we should do about Friday night's dance." She turned to Carella and said, "This is the big dance we have every year at the beginning of June. We've been planning it for a long time," and then, to Father Oriella again, "We canceled last Friday's *regular* dance, but we don't know what we're supposed to do now. We don't want to do anything disrespectful to Father Michael's memory. But Gloria has the check Father Michael gave her, and she doesn't know whether to give it to Kenny or not. For the band Friday night."

"Kenny?" Father Oriella said.

"Kenny Walsh," she said. "He's leader of The Wanderers, the band that's supposed to play. He asked for a hundred-dollar deposit, and Father Michael gave Gloria the check, but now we don't know."

Oriella said, "Mmm," and thought about the problem for what seemed a long time. Then he asked, "Was Father Michael involved in the planning of this dance?"

"Oh, yes," Alexis said. "In fact, he was the one who *started* them. The First of June dances."

"For what purpose?" Oriella asked. "How are the proceeds used?"

Straight to the point, Carella thought, and wondered what Arthur L. Farnes—who'd taken a fit about the money-changers in the temple—would think of the new parish priest.

"We buy baskets for the poor," Alexis said.

"Baskets?"

"Food baskets, yes, Father. To take around on Christmas morning."

"Ah," Oriella said, and nodded in satisfaction to Marcella, who nodded in return.

"Last year, we made around two thousand dollars," Alexis said.

"And you say these dances on the first day of June were Father Michael's idea?"

"Oh, yes, Father. He started them three years ago."

"Then I think it would be a fitting memorial to hold the dance as scheduled. In honor of Father Michael's devotion to the needy of this parish. You may give Kenny his check," Oriella said. "And I will attend the dance myself, and give my blessing to everyone there."

"Thank you, Father," she said. "I'll tell Gloria."

She was starting out when Martha Hennessy appeared in the door-frame behind her. The tiny office was about to get crowded. Hawes had been on too many small crafts during his tour of duty in the Navy; he was beginning to feel claustrophobic. "Mrs. Hennessy," he said, "we'd like to look through the church, we were hoping you'd show us around."

"I'd be happy to," she said, and then, to Alexis, "Hello, darlin', how are you?"

"Fine, thanks, Mrs. Hennessy," Alexis said, "thanks, again, Father, we'll look for you on Friday night," and stepped out into the small entry that separated the chancellery from the remainder of the rectory. As Hawes and Carella said their goodbyes to Father Oriella, she began chatting with Mrs. Hennessy, and was still talking to her when they came out a moment later. She turned to Carella at once, giving him the impression that she'd been waiting for him.

"There's something I want to tell you," she said.

"Sure," he said.

"Could we talk privately?"

Something in her dark eyes signaled immediacy.

"I'll meet you in the church," he said to Hawes and then led Alexis outside, to the garden where the priest had been slain. The roses were still in bloom, their aroma overpowering. Where once there had been the chalked outline of the priest on the uneven floor of the garden, there was now only the grey and weathered stone itself. They walked to the maple and sat on the low stone bench that circled it. There was moss on the tree behind them. Ivy climbed the stone walls of the cottage. This could have been a courtyard in an English village.

"I don't want to get anyone in trouble," Alexis said.

He waited.

"But . . ."

The essential word.

Still, he waited.

"This was Easter Sunday," she said. "I was going crosstown to meet my friend Gloria outside the movie theater on Eleventh and The Stem. This must have been around two-thirty, a very windy day, I remember . . ."

. . . skirts flapping about her legs, long blonde hair blowing in the wind. She is supposed to meet Gloria outside the theater at three, an

Eddie Murphy picture is playing. Gloria and Alexis are both freshmen at a private school on Seventh and Culver. The Graham School. One of the few good schools in the precinct, it is only half a block away from a public school where an assistant principal recently was stabbed trying to break up a fistfight. She still has almost half an hour before she's supposed to meet her, though, she still has plenty of time. And although she's already been to mass early this morning, she is passing St. Catherine's again now, coming up the Tenth Street side where someone has painted a peculiar red star on the green gate leading to the garden and the rectory, planning to continue north to The Stem, where the theater is, but instead making a right on Culver, and impulsively going into the church through the big entrance doors, which are closed but unlocked...

"I thought I'd say a few extra prayers, this was, like, you know, Easter Sunday..."

...coming through the narthex, and walking up the center aisle under the nave, the church empty, her heels clicking on the polished wooden floors—this is Easter Sunday and she is wearing patent leather shoes with medium-high heels—clicking as she approaches the crossing, the transept on her left, the sacristy on her right, the brass chancel rail immediately ahead of her, and behind it the altar and the huge cross with Jesus hanging on it and bleeding from a dozen wounds in his side and his chest and...

"...all at once there were voices, Father Michael's voice and someone else's..."

...coming from the paneled corridor that leads from the sacristy into the priest's small stone cottage, his rectory, the voices startling her because this is the first time she has ever heard Father Michael shouting in anger. She stops dead in the center of the crossing, here where the middle of Jesus's chest would be were this a true cross rather than the traditional stone-and-timber architectural representation of one, stands shocked and silent as the priest's voice comes down the corridor as if from the neck of a funnel into its open cup, rushing into the church, echoing into its vaulted ceiling, This is blackmail, he is shouting, *blackmail*!

She does not know quite what do do. She feels the sudden guilt of a child—she is wearing heels, but she is only thirteen—eavesdropping on an adult, fearful she will be discovered in the next instant and punished for her transgression, either by the priest or by the woman he is . . .

"A woman?" Carella said at once. "Not a man? He was with a *woman*?"

"Yes."

"And you heard him use the word blackmail?"

"Yes. And she said, 'I'm doing this for your own good.'"

"And then what?"

Alexis stands there at the middle of the stone-and-timber cross that is St. Catherine's Church, looking up at the huge plaster figure of Christ hanging on a genuine oaken cross behind the altar, the priest's voice coming again from her right, she is afraid to turn her head to locate the voice, she is afraid she will discover Father Michael lunging at her in a rage, shouting at her as he now shouts at the woman, Get out of my sight, how dare you, how dare you, and the woman is suddenly laughing, the laughter echoing, echoing, and there is the sound of a slap, flesh hitting flesh. Alexis turns and runs, terrified, they are *both* shouting behind her now, she runs for the entrance doors, heels strafing the wooden floor, slipping, almost losing her balance, grasping for the back of the nearest bench, righting herself, running again, running, running, she is not used to heels, throwing open the central portal doors and coming face to face with a black man, blood streaming down his . . .

"Nathan Hooper," Carella said.

"I screamed, I shoved myself past him, there were other men chasing him, I ran away from there as fast as I could."

She had called them men. And to her terrified eyes those husky young teenagers indeed must have appeared to be men. But hadn't she . . . ?

"Doesn't that name mean anything to you?" he asked. "Nathan Hooper?"

"Yes, of course, *now* it does, I saw his picture in the newspaper, I even saw him in person on television. But at the time, he was just this . . . this big black man with blood running down his face, and all I wanted to do was get out of there. I think in my mind I made some crazy kind of connection between Father Michael yelling and the woman yelling and all the yelling outside the church. I've never been so scared in my life. All that blood. All that anger."

"Did you *see* who the woman was?" Carella asked.

"I don't want to get anyone in trouble," Alexis said, and looked away.

He waited.

"But . . ." she said.

And still he waited.

"If she had anything to do with Father Michael's murder, then . . ."

Her eyes met his.

"Who was she?" he said. "Was she anyone you know?"

"I only saw her from the back," Alexis said.

"What'd she look like?"

"She was a tall woman with straight blonde hair," Alexis said. "Like mine."

And like Kristin Lund's, Carella thought.

"So what'd you do?" Shad Russell asked. "Rob a bank?"

"Not quite," Marilyn said.

"Then what? Saturday you're here haggling over the price of a gun—which, by the way, was a very good bargain—and Tuesday you're back with, *how* much did you say?"

"Five hundred thousand."

"You got that much change in your pocketbook there?"

"Sure," Marilyn said.

"I'll bet," Russell said knowingly. "So how'd you come into all this money?"

"Liquidation," she said.

"Of *who*? Who'd you dust, honey?"

"I understand that the normal return on a drug investment is eight to one," she said, straight for the jugular. "I need two million dollars. I'm assuming if I invest half a million . . ."

"Is *that* what we're talking here?" Russell said, surprised. "Dope?"

"I told you on the phone I was looking to make an investment."

"I thought you meant an investment of *time*. I thought you were all at once interested in one of my major situations."

"I am. The Colombian merchant."

"But not in the same way I *hoped* you'd be interested."

"No, not in that way," Marilyn said, and wondered if she'd have to go through the whole damn ex-hooker routine yet another time before they could settle down to the business at hand. They were in a little bar off St. Sebastian Avenue, three blocks from Russell's hotel. There were enough working girls in it, even at this early hour, to satisfy the needs of every major Colombian merchant in town. But they were all either black or Hispanic, and maybe Colombian gentlemen preferred blondes.

Smiling like a crocodile, Russell leaned over the table and said, "Maybe you could mix a little pleasure in with the business, what do you think?"

"I think no, and let's cut the crap, please. How many keys of cocaine can I get for the five hundred?"

"That kind of bread, that's peanuts nowadays," Russell said, immediately getting down to brass tacks. "There's no chance of a discount, you'd have to pay the going rate, which is very high these days because of all the pressure. Forty, fifty grand a key, depending on the quality. So what does that come to? Divide five hundred by fifty, what do you get?"

"Ten," she said, and wondered where he'd gone to school.

"Okay, that's if we're paying fifty, we get ten keys. If we're paying forty, what do we get?"

"Twelve and a half."

"So average it out, let's say you pay forty-five, let's say you get eleven keys for the five hundred, that'd be doing good these days."

"And how much would those eleven keys be worth on the street?"

"You're talking high, eight to one, that's high."

"Then what?"

"You step on a kilo even once, you come away with ten thousand bags of crack. Nowadays, a bag is selling for twenty-five bucks. That's a quarter of a mill you come away with, for the one key. That you paid forty-five for. That's around five and a half to one you'd be getting. So figure you can turn the five hundred into like two million seven, something in there. Exactly the amount you need," Russell said, and smiled his crocodile smile.

"No, all I need is two."

"Plus my commission," he said, still smiling.

"That seems very steep."

"Seven hundred thou is *steep*?" Russell said, looking offended. "You know somebody cheaper? In fact, you know anybody at *all*?"

"I can always call Houston again. I'm sure Sam can find me . . ."

"Sure, call him. Meanwhile, I got the feeling you were in some kinda hurry."

"Even so, that's steep," she said, shaking her head. "Seven hundred thousand? That's very steep."

Bargaining. When her fucking life was at stake.

Settle with the man, she thought.

"So is that it?" Russell said. "Are we finished talking here?"

"For that kind of money I'd expect you to handle the entire transaction," she said.

Still bargaining.

"Meaning what?"

"Setting it up, making the buy, turning the dope a . . ."

"I can tell you right now nobody's going to sell eleven keys to somebody invisible."

"Oh? Did you suddenly get invisible?"

"I'm talking about they smell I'm making the buy for somebody else, the Uzis come out. They like to know who they're doing business with."

"I can't get involved in this," she said.

Not bargaining this time. Merely thinking of Willis. Thinking that if something went wrong during the transaction, if the police came down, it might hurt Willis somehow. Thinking . . .

"Then don't get involved in moving dope," Russell said. "If you want to make a deal, I'll set up the buy for you. You show with the money, you make the buy yourself. Then I'll see about turning it around."

"I have to be *positive* you can turn it around."

"Tell you what. If I can't turn it around, you don't owe me a nickel. Is that fair?"

"Then what do I do with the eleven keys?"

"Snort it," Russell said, and smiled his crocodile smile. "When do you need this money?"

"How about tomorrow afternoon?"

"Impossible."

"Then when?"

"I can't set up the buy before Thursday night, soonest. Have you got your hands on this money already?"

"I have a cashier's check."

"Honey, please don't make me laugh. In this business? A check?"

"A cashier's check is as good as cash."

"Then cash it."

"All right."

"You know anything about high-grade coke?"

"A little."

"Enough to know whether they're selling you powdered sugar instead?"

"No."

"I'll teach you. They'll expect you to test the stuff. Everything's a fuckin' ritual with them. You test it, you taste it, you give them the cash, they give you the shit, and you go your separate ways. You deviate from the ritual, they think you're undercover and they blow you away. It ain't without its certain risks, this business," he said drily.

"When will you know for sure?"

"Tomorrow."

"I'll call you," she said.

"No, let me call you."

"No," she said.

"Why not?"

"Just no."

"Okay, you know where to reach me," Russell said, and shook his head as if to say there was no understanding the ways of beautiful broads who once earned a living on their backs. "Give me a call around this time tomorrow. If everything goes the way I figure, you better cash that check on Thursday and I'll let you know where they wanna meet you."

"No," she said. "Specify one-on-one. And I'll pick the place."

"They may not go for that."

"I'm paying top dollar. If they don't like the terms, tell them to go fuck themselves and we'll find somebody else."

"Tough lady," he said, and smiled. "You still got that gun I sold you?"

"No."

"You want my advice? Buy another one. From me or somebody else, it don't matter. A bigger one this time."

"What kind of gun did you have in mind?" she asked.

"We done this before, you know," Mrs. Hennessy said. "Father Michael and me. Went over the church top to bottom searching for the dope."

"Yes," Carella said. "His sister told me."

"Nice lady, ain't she? The sister."

"Yes," Carella said. "Very nice."

"I thought so first time I met her," Mrs. Hennessy said, smiling at the memory.

"When was that?"

"Shortly before Easter," she said. "Around St. Paddy's Day."

Which fell each year on the seventeenth of March. Which certainly would have qualified as "shortly before Easter" in that Easter this year had fallen on the fifteenth of April. Carella wondered if by then Father Michael had been involved with his mysterious lady. In which case, why hadn't he mentioned her to his sister while she was visiting here?

"...a search for dope?" Hawes was saying.

"Well, we got a phone call," Mrs. Hennessy said.

"What phone call?"

"Krissie took a phone call one afternoon, I was in the office when it..."

"When was this?"

"Last month sometime."

"When last month?"

"About a week after that black boy got beat up," Mrs. Hennessy said. "The call was for Father Michael. He took it, listened for a few minutes, said, 'I don't know what you're talking about,' and hung up."

"Who was it?"

"Who was who?"

"On the phone."

"Oh. I don't know. But Father Michael turned to Krissie and said, 'Kris, this guy says...'"

"Is that what he called her?" Hawes asked. "Kris?"

"Yes. Or sometimes Krissie."

Hawes nodded and said nothing. But Carella saw the look that crossed his face.

"'Kris, this guy says there's dope hidden in the church here and he wants it back,'" Mrs. Hennessy said, and nodded.

"So it was a *man* on the phone," Hawes said.

"I guess so."

"Did Father Michael say who it was?" Carella asked.

"No, sir."

"He didn't say it was Nathan Hooper, did he?"

"No, sir."

"Did he say it sounded like a black person?"

"No, sir. He didn't say nothin' but what I just told you he said.

'This guy says there's dope hidden in the church here and he wants it back.' Is what Father Michael said. So we begun looking for it."

"Where'd you look?"

"Everywhere."

"Meaning?'

"Meaning *everywhere*. Places hadn't been cleaned or disturbed since the church was built, dust a hundred years thick. Nooks and crannies I didn't know existed. Secret passageways..."

"Secret *passage*ways?" Hawes said.

"This church used to be part of the underground railway," Mrs. Hennessy said. "Slaves escaping from the south used to come hide in the church here."

"What goes around comes around," Hawes said, and nodded.

Carella, deep in thought, missed Hawes's reference to history's little repetitions. He was remembering back to when Marilyn Hollis was a suspect in a poisoning, and Willis had fallen hopelessly in love with her. It had made things difficult—even though the ending turned out to be a happy one. Carella was all in favor of happy endings. But judging from the look that had crossed Hawes's face when he'd heard that the priest called his secretary either Kris or Krissie rather than Kristin or Miss Lund or Whatever the Hell, Carella suspected that his partner *this* time around had been similarly stricken, and he hoped with all his might that Krissie Lund turned out to be similarly clean.

Because *if* she was the woman who'd tried to blackmail Father Michael on Easter Sunday...

Or, worse, *if* she was the woman who'd been intimately involved with the priest...

Or, worse yet, *if* she was both adulteress *and* blackmailer at one and the same time...

"Show us the easy places first," Hawes told Mrs. Hennessy.

She always became apprehensive when he started drinking heavily before dinner. All the other times had happened when he'd come directly home from the store and started the evening by pouring him-

self a stiff drink. It was only a little past six now, and he'd already
consumed two healthy gins-over-ice, and was pouring himself a third
one at the counter near the kitchen sink. Ice-cube tray open on the
counter. Tanqueray gin, he drank only the best. Tanqueray or Beef-
eater. Wouldn't allow a cheaper gin in the house. Asked her once if
she knew that gin was made from juniper berries? And did she know
that juniper berries were poisonous? She hadn't known whether he
was kidding or not. He sometimes said things just to confuse her. He
could be cruel that way.

She never knew whether one of his drunken...spells, she
guessed you could call them...was triggered by something that had
happened at the store that day, or whether they had something to do
with the calendar, or the phases of the moon, or the tides—like a
woman's period. She suspected there was something sexual about
these spells of his, that what happened was some kind of substitute
for sex, that he got off on first getting drunk and then...

"You disapprove, right?" he said.

"I'm making a nice dinner for us," she said.

"Which means you disapprove, right?"

Pouring the gin liberally over the ice cubes in the short fat tumbler. Fingers curled around the glass. Outside, there was thunder in
the east. It had been days now since they'd had any rain. Rain would
be welcome.

"I asked you a question, Sally."

She wondered if he was already drunk. Usually it took more than
two of them, however heavily he'd poured them. She didn't want
anything to start. And yet, whenever he got this way, no matter how
carefully she tiptoed around him, there didn't seem to be anything she
could do to prevent what came next. It was like a button inside him
got pushed, and then all the gears started turning and meshing, and
there was nothing you could do to stop the machine. Except maybe
get out of here. Get *away* from the machine. Far away from it. She
thought maybe she should get out of here right this minute, before the
machine started again.

"Sally?"

"Yes, Art," she said, and realized this was a mistake the moment it left her mouth. His name was Arthur, he liked to be called by his full name. Arthur. Not Art, not Artie, but Arthur. Said Arthur sounded majestic, Arthur the King, whereas Art or Artie sounded like garage mechanics. "I'm sorry," she said at once.

"You still haven't answered my question," he said.

Good. He was ignoring the fact that she'd called him Art rather than Arthur. Maybe this wasn't going to be a bad one, after all, maybe tonight the machine would merely grind to a halt before it . . .

"Did you hear my question, Sally?"

"I'm sorry, Arthur . . ."

Making certain she called him Arthur this time.

". . . what was the question?"

"Do you disapprove of my drinking?"

"Not when you do it in moderation. Because I'm making us a nice dinner tonight, Arthur . . ."

"What nice dinner are you making us tonight?" he asked mockingly, and lifted the short fat tumbler to his lips, and drained it.

Outside, lightning flashed and thunder followed.

"Salmon steak," she said quickly. "With some lovely asparagus I got fresh at the Koreans'."

"I hate asparagus," he said.

"I thought you liked asparagus," she said. "I thought it was broccoli you hated."

"I hate asparagus *and* broccoli," he said, and went to the counter again and lifted two ice cubes from the tray and dropped them into the tumbler. She hoped he would not pour himself another drink.

He poured himself another drink.

"Asparagus and broccoli and cauliflower and all the *other* shitty vegetables you make that I *hate*," he said. "Brussels sprouts . . ."

"I thought you liked . . ."

". . . and cabbage and *all* of them," he said, and lifted the glass to his lips. "A man gets to be forty-nine years old, he's been married to the same woman for twenty-five years, you think she'd *know* what he likes to eat and what he *doesn't* like to eat. But oh no, not Fat Sally..."

The Fat Sally hurt.

He was going to hurt her tonight.

"...Fat Sally goes her merry fat way, cooking whatever the fuck she *wishes* to cook, with never a thought as to what her husband might..."

"I give a lot of thought to..."

"Shut up!" he said.

I have to get out of here, she thought. The last time I waited too long, I waited until it got out of hand, and then there was no getting away. I don't care if the dinner burns to a crisp, she thought, I don't care if a *fire* starts in the stove, I have to get out of here. Now.

But she waited.

Giving him the benefit of the doubt.

Because after the last time, when she'd gone to Father Michael to tell him what had happened, things seemed to get a little better, this was what... almost two months ago, the beginning of April, shortly before Easter, right after he'd written that terrible letter. She'd asked him not to write the letter, she'd told him he'd be making a fool of himself before the entire congregation, but he'd insisted on typing it here in the apartment and then taking it to the bank to Xerox however many copies he'd needed, said he resented the way the priest was turning the church into a *financial* institution, his exact words. And, of course, the congregation *did* think he was a fool for writing that dumb letter, and the very next Sunday Father Michael made another sermon about money, this time mentioning the letter he'd received, the letter Arthur had sent... yes, that's right, this was exactly a week before Easter Sunday, this was the second Sunday in April. He'd got drunk that night. And the very next day, she'd gone to see Father Michael, her eyes puffy, her lip split...

"The very bad habit you have, Sally, is interrupting," he said.

"Oh, I *know*," she said pleasantly, still giving him the benefit of the doubt, still hoping that her going to the priest had changed the situation here at home, that now that Arthur *realized* someone else knew what was going on here . . .

But the priest was dead.

Someone had killed the priest.

". . . even when I was a young girl," she said, her voice trailing, "I used to . . ."

And fell silent.

Interrupt, she thought.

All the time, she thought.

He was standing at the counter, putting more ice cubes into the glass. She had lost count of how many drinks he'd had already. Outside, there was more lightning, and then thunder, and then the rain came down in sheets, driven by a fierce wind. She kept staring at his back. He stood stock still at the counter, his hand wrapped around the lever that pried open the ice-cube tray. Little egg-crate compartments in the tray, the lever fastened to them. The tray empty now. The ice cubes all gone. The rain coming down in sheets outside.

"Miss Zaftig," he said. "Isn't that what your little Jewboy used to call you?"

"Actually, he *did* refer to me as *zaftig*, yes," she said, "but he never called me *Miss* Zaftig as such."

Don't contradict him, she thought. Agree with everything he says!

"Little Miss Zaftig," he said, "running to the fucking priest!"

"Well, if you hadn't . . ."

"Washing our dirty laundry in public!"

"There wouldn't have *been* any dirty . . ."

"Taking our dirty laundry to church and washing it for the priest!"

"Next time, don't . . ."

His arm came lashing out at her in a backhanded swipe. His hand was still curled around the lever of the egg-crate divider, the metal outlining twelve empty squares now, the metal edges hitting her face but only barely scratching it because this was truly an ineffectual weapon, a silly weapon really, this aluminum tray divider dangling limply at the end of a lever, hardly a weapon at all.

The gin bottle was quite another thing.

The gin bottle was green and stout, and it had a little red seal on it that identified it as the genuine article, the Tanqueray, the good stuff. As quickly as he had swung the tray divider, he now dropped it clattering to the tiled kitchen floor, and immediately grasped the bottle by its neck and yanked it off the counter, and pulled it back as though preparing for a forehand tennis shot, the bottle coming around as if it were a racket level with a ball coming in about shoulder high, swinging it, eye on the ball, shoulder high was where her head was.

A red circle of blood splashed onto the bottle alongside the red seal. Gin sloshed from the open neck of the bottle onto his wrist, onto the floor, blood spurted now from the gash the bottle had opened alongside her left eye. The blood startled him. He seemed to realize all at once that he was attacking her with a lethal weapon, that this heavy bottle fashioned of thick green glass could very easily *kill* her if he were not terribly careful. He said, "Oh, *really?*" as if blaming her for his own stupidity in picking up the bottle, in using the bottle on her, "Oh, *really?*" and threw the bottle into the sink, deliberately smashing it, shards of green glass exploding up onto the air, caught for a moment against a dazzling backdrop of yellow-white light as lightning flashed again beyond the window.

Thunder rolled.

Oddly, he seemed more dangerous now.

Bereft of any weapons but his hands, miscalculating how powerful or how dangerous those hands could be (but she knew), he closed in on her where she stood cowering against the refrigerator door, blood gushing from the wound on her head, her bloody left hand clenched to her temple, her right hand held out like a traffic cop's, the fingers widespread, "Don't, Arthur," she said, "please, don't," but he just kept repeating over and over again, quite senselessly now, "Oh, *really?*" as if he were contradicting something she had just said, or perhaps asking for further explanation of what she'd said, "Oh, *really*?" while he slapped her over and again, methodically, his huge hands punishing her for whatever sin in his drunkenness he imagined she'd committed.

She reached for the knife on the drainboard.

And quite calmly stabbed him.

10

The Q and A took place in Lieutenant Byrnes's office at the 87th Precinct, not half an hour after Arthur Llewelyn Farnes was released from Greer General. He had been treated there for a knife wound in the left shoulder and had been charged immediately with Assault 1st Degree: "With intent to cause serious physical injury to another, causing such injury to such person or to a third person by means of a deadly weapon or a dangerous instrument," a Class-C Felony punishable by a minimum of three and a max of fifteen.

To sweeten the pudding, he had also been charged with Attempted Murder, a Class-B Felony punishable by a minimum of three and a max of twenty-five. His wife, Sally Louise Farnes, had been charged with the identical crimes, but opinion around the old station house was that she would easily beat both raps by pleading self-defense. The gathered detectives and an assistant district attorney named Nellie Brand were here this Wednesday morning at ten o'clock not so much to make certain their case against Farnes would stick—they knew they had real meat here—but to find out what he knew about the murder of Father Michael Birney.

Carella had called Nellie the moment he realized they had here a violent man whose wife had earlier gone to Father Michael to report previous abuses. This same man had written the priest a letter that in itself seemed to imply a threat, however veiled. And, by his own admission, he had gone to the church sometime during the afternoon of Easter Sunday, where at least one witness—Nathan Hooper—had reported hearing the priest in violent argument with a man.

Nellie was thirty-two years old, with alert blue eyes and sand-colored hair cut in a flying wedge that seemed appropriate to her breezy style. She was wearing this morning a dark blue skirt with a grey jacket, a pink man-tailored shirt with a narrow red-and-blue silk rep tie, and blue pumps with moderate heels. Carella liked her a lot; she reminded him somehow of his sister Angela, though she didn't resemble her in the slightest.

Sitting on the edge of the lieutenant's desk, she once again informed Farnes of his rights, and then asked him if he was certain he did not wish an attorney present. Like most amateurs who suddenly find themselves involved with the law, Farnes told her he didn't need a lawyer because he hadn't *done* anything, it was his *wife* who'd committed the goddamn crime here! Carella was thinking that every little cheap thief on the street asked for an attorney the moment he was clapped in cuffs.

Nellie dutifully informed Farnes that he could nonetheless stop the questioning at any time he chose to, or even request a lawyer whenever he felt he needed one, even though he'd declined one now, and asked him again if he understood all this, and Farnes rather testily said, "Of *course* I understand, do I look like an idiot? My wife tried to *kill* me!"

Miranda-Escobedo safely out of the way, Nellie switched on the tape recorder, nodded to the stenographer who was taking standby shorthand notes, said for the tape that this was 10:07 on the morning of May 30, identified the location and everyone in it, and then began the questioning:

Q: May I have your full name, please?
A: Arthur Llewellyn Farnes.

Q: And your address?

A: 157 Grover Park South.

Q: In what apartment, please?

A: 12C.

Q: Do you live in that apartment, at that address, with your wife, Sally Louise Farnes?

A: I do. Who tried to kill me last night.

Q: Mr. Farnes, were you treated at six-forty-five last night in the Emergency Room at Greer General for a knife wound in the left shoulder?

A: Damn *right* I was.

Q: And were you held for overnight observation at Greer General, and . . .

A: I was.

Q: . . . and released at nine-thirty-two this morning in custody of Detectives Hawes and Carella . . .

A: I was.

Q: . . . who transported you here to the 87th Precinct for questioning, is that correct?

A: That's correct.

Q: You've been informed, have you not, that you've been charged with First Degree Assault, a Class-C felony . . .

A: I have.

Q: And with Attempted Murder as well, which is a Class-B felony.

A: It was my *wife* who tried to kill *me*!

Q: But were you informed of these charges against you?

A: I was.

Q: And, of course, you were read your rights in accordance with the Supreme Court decisions in Miranda and Escobedo, and you said you understood those rights, did you not?

A: You read them to me, and I said I understood them.

Q: And declined your right to an attorney, is that also correct?

A: Yes.

Q: Very well, Mr. Farnes . . .

Leaning in closer to him now, conveying the impression that now that all the bullshit was out of the way, she was ready to take off the gloves.

Q: ... can you tell me how you happened to get that knife wound in your shoulder?

A: She went crazy.

Q: Who do you mean, please?

A: Sally.

Q: Your wife, Sally Louise Farnes?

A: Yes.

Q: Went crazy, you say?

A: Yes.

Q: Can you tell me what you mean by that?

A: She went crazy, what do you *think* that means? We were sitting in the kitchen, and all at once she picked up the knife and stabbed me. Nuts! Totally nuts!

Q: Sitting where in the kitchen?

A: At the table.

Q: Doing what?

A: Talking.

Q: About what?

A: I don't remember.

Q: Try to remember.

A: How am I supposed to remember what we were talking about? She *stabbed* me, goddamn it!

Q: Do you remember telling your wife that she had a bad habit of interrupting you while you were ... ?

A: No.

Q: The way you just interrupted me.

A: I'm sorry if I interrupted you. I thought you were finished with what you were saying.

Q: No, I wasn't.

A: Then I'm sorry.

Q: But isn't that what you told your wife? That she had a bad habit of interrupting?

A: I may have said that, I don't remember. It *is* a bad habit. You said so yourself.

Q: I don't believe I said that.

A: Well, you seemed to get upset when I interrupted *you* just now.

Q: Did you get upset when your wife interrupted you?

A: People shouldn't interrupt other people.

Q: Does that upset you? When your wife interrupts?

A: It would upset anyone. Getting interrupted. I suppose you realize, don't you, that she stabbed me, don't you? I mean, I really don't see the point of did she interrupt me, did I interrupt her, it was *me* who got stabbed, there are hospital records to prove I got stabbed, you said yourself there's a knife wound in my left shoulder, it didn't get there by *magic*; my wife *stabbed* me, goddamn it!

Q: Do you also remember telling your wife . . . ?

A: Did you hear what I just said?

Q: Yes, Mr. Farnes, I heard you.

A: I mean, did you hear a *word* of what I just said?

Q: I heard all of it, yes.

A: Then do you understand that my wife *stabbed* me?

Q: Yes, sir, I understand that. She has, in fact, admitted stabbing you.

A: Well, good, at least she had the decency to do *that*!

Q: Do you remember telling her that she also had a bad habit of washing your dirty linen in public?

A: No, I don't remember that.

Q: Of taking your dirty linen to the church and washing it for the priest?

A: No, why would I say anything like that?

Q: Washing it for Father Michael Birney.

A: No. No.

Q: Telling him about certain personal problems you were having.

A: We weren't having any personal problems.

Q: Mr. Farnes, did you strike your wife with the divider from an ice-cube tray?

A: No.

Q: Mr. Farnes, I show you this tray-divider which was recovered from apartment 12C at 157 Grover Park South and tagged as evidence by Detectives Carella and Hawes of the 87th Precinct. Do you recognize it?

A: I do not.

Q: Mr. Farnes, you are aware, are you not, that your fingerprints were taken when you arrived here at the station house?

A: I am.

Q: And you are aware, of course, that the Police Department's Fingerprint Section can recover latent prints from inanimate objects and compare those prints with, for example, your fingerprints taken here at the station house?

A: I am aware of that.

Q: Do you still say you do not recognize this tray-divider?

A: I never saw it in my life.

Q: Mr. Farnes, I show you the broken neck of a bottle recovered from the sink in apartment 12C at 157 Grover Park South and tagged as evidence by Detectives Carella and Hawes of the 87th Precinct. Keeping in mind what I just told you about fingerprints, I ask you now did you strike your wife with the bottle this neck was once a part of?

A: I did not.

Q: That is to say, a bottle containing what remained of a fifth of Tanqueray gin?

A: I did not.

Q: Mr. Farnes, where were you on Easter Sunday?

A: What?

Q: I asked you where you were on Easter Sunday.

A: Home, where do you think I was? Easter? Of *course* I was home.

Q: All day?

A: All day.

Q: Didn't you tell Detectives Hawes and Carella that you went to St. Catherine's Church sometime that afternoon?

A: Oh. Yes. I'd forgotten that.

Q: *Did* you go to the church that afternoon?

A: Yes.

Q: Why?

A: To talk to Father Michael.

Q: What about?

A: A letter I'd written to him. We'd had a misunderstanding about the letter. I wanted to clear it up with him.

Q: What time did you get to the church?

A: I don't remember.

Q: Would it have been between two-thirty and three?

A: I really don't know. There was a police car outside.

Oh, Jesus, Carella thought, there it goes, straight up the chimney! Both Nathan Hooper and Alexis O'Donnell claimed to have heard the priest arguing—with either a man *or* a woman, depending on whose story you believed—sometime between two-thirty and three. But if Edward-car was already there when Farnes came to the church, this had to be sometime *after* the argument had taken place. So unless Farnes was lying . . .

Q: Can you describe that car for me?

Trying to make certain the car had actually been there when he arrived. She'd been briefed before the questioning began, she knew that the half hour between two-thirty and three was critical. If Farnes had come to the church *after* that time, then he could not have been the person arguing with Father Michael.

A: It was a *police* car. What's there to describe about a police car?

Q: Do you remember the markings on it?

A: No. A blue-and-white car, like any other police car in this city.

Q: Mr. Farnes, where were you between seven and seven-thirty on the night of May twenty-fourth?

The night of the murder. She was going for the gold. Never mind beating around the bush. Farnes could either account for his time while the priest was being murdered—or he could not.

A: When was that? May twenty-fourth?

Q: Last Thursday. Do you remember where you were?

A: Last Thursday.

Q: Yes.

A: I'm trying to remember. I think I worked late last Thursday. I think I was at the store taking inventory.

Q: What do you mean by the store?

A: My store. I sell men's clothing.

Q: Where is this store, Mr. Farnes?

A: On The Stem. Between Carson and Coles. It's called C&C Men's Furnishings. Because of the cross streets. Carson and Coles. Up past Twentieth. Across the street from the new McDonald's.

Q: And you say you were there taking inventory on the night of May twenty-fourth.

A: Yes. I'm pretty certain that's where I was.

Q: Were you there at seven P.M.?

A: If I was there, then yes, I was there at seven P.M.

Q: And if you were there, were you also there at seven-thirty P.M.?

A: Yes, if I was there, I would have been there at that time, too.

Q: And at eight P.M.?

A: Yes.

Q: And at nine?

A: Yes. All night.

Q: *If* you were there.

A: Yes. But I'm fairly certain I was there.

Q: But you're not positive.

A: No, I'm not positive.

Q: Was anyone with you?

A: No.

Q: You were alone.

A: Yes.

Q: Do you normally take inventory alone?

A: Yes.

Q: So *if* you were at the store that night, you were there alone.

A: Yes.

Q: Which means we have only your word for your whereabouts on the night of May twenty-fourth.

A: Well, if I was there, there'd be a record.

Q: Oh? What kind of record, Mr. Farnes?

A: My inventory sheets would have a date on them. An inventory is worthless, you see, unless it's dated. The whole purpose of an inventory is to keep you up to date on what you have in stock. That's the whole purpose.

Q: Yes. And where would you have indicated this date?

A: In the inventory log. The date, and the quantity and size and color of any particular item. So I'll know when to reorder. That's the purpose of an inventory.

Q: Yes. Do you still have this inventory log?

A: I'm sure I do.

Q: Where is it?

A: At the store, most likely. I usually keep it at the store.

Q: And can you lay your hands on it at any time? To check the date? So that you can positively say you were in the store taking inventory all night long on May twenty-fourth?

A: Unless it's missing for one reason or another.

Q: Missing? Why would it be missing?

A: Well, you know this city. Things get stolen all the time.

Q: Are you saying that someone may have *stolen* your inventory log?

A: It's possible.

Q: Why would anyone want to steal an inventory log?

A: This city, who knows?

Q: So what you're saying, actually, Mr. Farnes, is that if the inventory log has been stolen, you have no way of verifying when this inventory-taking happened.

A: Or lost. The inventory log.

Q: Stolen or lost or misplaced, you would have no way of verifying where you were on the night of May twenty-fourth.

A: What has this got to do with my wife stabbing me?

Q: It has to do with someone stabbing a *priest,* Mr. Farnes.

A: Is that supposed to be a surprise?

Q: I beg your pardon?

A: I mean, you're oh-so-very *smart* here, aren't you, with your trick questions and your beating all around the mulberry bush, do you think you're dealing with a fool here? I have a very successful business, I've been at the same location for fifteen years, I'm not a fool.

Q: No one said you were, Mr. Farnes.

A: Oh, no, you didn't come right out and *say* it, of course not. With the tape going? And this man taking notes? Of course not. But don't you think I realize what you're trying to do here? You're trying to make a mountain out of a molehill. You're trying to say that because I had an argument with Father Michael, that means . . .

Q: Did you have an argument with him?

A: I *told* you we had a misunderstanding.

Q: Yes, but you didn't say you'd had an argument.

A: A misunderstanding, I said, a misunder*stand*ing. Over a letter I sent to the entire . . .

Q: Yes, but just now you said you'd had an argument. When did you have this argument, Mr. Farnes?

A: A misunder*stand*ing. Listen, I want to make this clear . . . is that tape still going? I want it made perfectly clear on the tape that I *meant* to say misunderstanding, not argument. Misunderstanding. Your detectives came to *see* me about that damn letter, I *told* them the misunderstanding had been cleared up, Father Michael and I settled the whole thing on Easter Sunday. There was *no* damn *ar*gument, is that clear?

Q: On Easter Sunday, do you mean?

A: On Easter Sunday or any *other* time. We did not argue. Period.

Q: Ever?

A: Never.

Q: Mr. Farnes, I can ask for a search warrant to locate the inventory log you mentioned, but I feel certain you would want to help us find it. I wonder if you could accompany these detectives to your store . . .

A: No. I want a lawyer.

Nellie looked at Carella. Carella looked at Hawes. The stenographer looked up from his pad. Lieutenant Byrnes shrugged. The only sound in the room was the whirring of the tape recorder.

"Mr. Farnes," Nellie said at last, "am I to understand . . . ?"

"You've got it, sister."

"Am I to understand that you will *not* help us locate that log?"

"Not unless a lawyer tells me you can do this."

"What is it you think we're doing?"

"Taking me to the store against my will."

"Very well, Mr. Farnes, we'll request a search warrant. Am I to understand further that you wish the questioning to stop at this time?"

"You've got it, sister," Farnes said again.

Nellie snapped off the tape recorder.

"We're off the air," she said. "You ever call me sister again, I'll kick you in the balls, *got* it?"

"I'll mention that to my attorney," Farnes said.

"Please do," Nellie said, and walked out of the room.

* * *

It was not until one o'clock that afternoon that Carella and Hawes obtained both a search warrant from a Superior Court judge and a key to C&C Men's Furnishings from Sally Farnes. Sally said she hoped it turned out that her husband *had,* in fact, killed Father Michael, and she hoped further that he would be sent to prison for the rest of his natural life. She also mentioned that he usually kept his inventory log in the lower right-hand drawer of the desk in his office at the back of the store.

They found the office, they found the desk, and they found the log in the lower right-hand drawer.

The log indicated that Farnes had indeed taken inventory of his stock on the twenty-fourth of May.

"Nellie'll be disappointed," Carella said. "She was hoping we'd catch him in a lie."

"This could *still* be a lie," Hawes said. "Just 'cause he wrote the twenty-fourth doesn't mean he actually *did* it on that date. He could have done it a week earlier, three days earlier, whenever."

"Say he killed the priest," Carella said. "What do you see for his motive?"

"He's a nutcase," Hawes said. "He doesn't *need* a motive."

"Even a nutcase has what he *thinks* is a motive."

"Okay, he was annoyed that his wife ratted on him."

"Then why not kill *her*? Why the priest?"

"Because he had a *further* grievance with the priest."

"The whole business with the letter, huh?"

"Yeah, and being made to look foolish in the eyes of the congregation. Nutcases take themselves seriously, Steve."

"Yeah," Carella said.

Both men were silent for several moments.

Then Carella said, "Do *you* think he did it?"

"No," Hawes said.

"Neither do I," Carella said.

* * *

The way Martha Hennessy later described it, this was just another teenage wolf pack. You read about them all the time now, these gangs going totally crazy and doing unspeakable things. This was maybe a dozen strapping young men, all of them white—Mrs. Hennessy could have understood it if they'd been black or Hispanic, but *white*? Came storming into the church around three o'clock it must've been, she was in the rectory, heard a lot of noise in the church itself, ran through the paneled corridor leading to the sacristy where three of them were already there, knocking over things, tearing the place apart. Inside the church itself, Father Oriella was yelling in English and in Italian, and his secretary, this old Italian woman whose English was atrocious, was screaming for them to stop. Mrs. Hennessy ran back into the rectory and dialed 911 from the office telephone. A police car arrived in about three minutes flat.

The responding car was Edward-car, because the church was in the precinct's Edward Sector, and the two officers driving the car were the same man and woman who'd responded to the fracas here on Easter Sunday. The difference this afternoon, and the reason their response-time was so rapid, was that after the priest's murder, they'd been called downtown to Headquarters and asked a lot of questions about their behavior on Easter Sunday, which Inspector Brian McIntyre from Internal Affairs had found somewhat less than exemplary in a community rife with white-black tensions. Mindful of the inspector's diatribe and reprimand, the moment Officers Joseph Esposito and Anna Maria Lopez caught the 10–39—a Crime In Progress, specified by the dispatcher as a "rampage at St. Catherine's Church" —they hit the hammer and screeched over to the church, where if this wasn't a rampage it sure as hell looked like one. Officer Lopez got on her walkie-talkie and called in an Assist Police Officer, and within another three minutes, cars from the adjoining David and Frank sectors, and half a dozen foot-patrol officers assigned to CPEP were responding to the 10–13 and swarming all over the church and the church garden and the rectory, rounding up what eventually turned out to be six teenagers, all of them white, all of them with Italian names, least of whom was Robert Victor Corrente.

Bobby and his pals all seemed to be rather high on an unidentified substance of a controlled nature. He seemed not to care that he was now in handcuffs, in a police squadroom, being charged with an assortment of crimes, among which was an assault upon Father Frank Oriella with a brass candlestick Bobby had seized from the main altar while his friends were knocking over the altar, and ripping the altar cloths from it, and otherwise ransacking the church. Bobby was screaming that he wanted a lawyer. His assorted friends, some handcuffed to desk legs in various parts of the squadroom, some already in the detention cage in the corner of the room, parroted every word he said. Bobby wanted a lawyer, *they* wanted a lawyer. He yelled for his father, they yelled for *their* fathers. It was an opera here in the squadroom, with everyone in fine voice. Carella wished he had ear plugs.

When Vincent Corrente arrived at the squadroom at four P.M. that afternoon, he looked much as he had the day Carella talked to him, except that he was not wearing a tank top undershirt. Or, if he was, it was not visible under the Hawaiian print, short-sleeved sports shirt he wore hanging outside his tan slacks. Otherwise, he was still jowly and paunchy and unkempt and he was still smoking an El Ropo cigar that lent a distinctive olfactory dimension to the auditory squadroom medley of yelling teenagers, clacking typewriters, ringing telephones, and cops telling everyone to shut the fuck up. Corrente was furious. It was difficult to tell, however, whether he was angrier with his son or with the people who'd arrested him.

"You dumb bastard," he told Bobby, "wha'd you do to the church, hah?" and belted him upside the head. To Carella, he shouted, "You! Take these cuffs offa my son or you're in deep shit!"

Carella looked at him calmly.

"You hear me? I know people!" Corrente shouted.

"Mr. Corrente," Carella said, "your son has been charged with . . ."

"I don't care *what* he's been charged with, he's a juvenile!"

"He's been charged as an adult."

"He's only seventeen!"

"That's an adult, Mr. Corrente. And he's been charged with . . ."

"I want a lawyer!" Bobby shouted.

"Shut up, you dumb bastard!" Corrente said. To Carella, he said, "He don't say anything till my lawyer gets here."

"Fine," Carella said calmly.

He was wondering when Bobby would come down off his high.

The lawyer Corrente called was a man named Dominick Abruzzi.

This was getting to be a regular reunion of WOPS, the World Order for the Prevention of Subterfuge, a watchdog society dedicated to the proposition that any American born with an Italian name must keep that name forever, neither changing it completely, nor even Anglicizing it, lest he be mercilessly and eternally hounded to his grave with reminders that he is merely an ignorant peasant with hoity-toity pretensions. Abruzzi looked as Italian as Richard Nixon. Carella guessed his teeth were capped.

Thirty-five, thirty-six years old, wearing a tailored suit, a button-down shirt, and a somber tie, he breezed into the squadroom as if he'd been in it (or one similar to it) a thousand times before. He said hello to Corrente, waved to Bobby who seemed to be sinking lower and lower into a depressive mire, and then asked, pleasantly enough, "What seems to be the trouble here?"

Carella told him what the trouble seemed to be. The trouble seemed to be First-Degree Assault, Second-Degree Burglary, First-Degree Criminal Mischief, and Reckless Endangerment of Property.

"That's what the trouble seems to be," he said.

"Well, that's *your* contention, Detective," Abruzzi said.

Carella was aware of the sense in which Abruzzi was using the word "Detective." His intonation made it sound like "Pig."

"No, that's not *my* contention, Counselor," he said, "that's what Robert Corrente's been charged with."

He did not like attorneys who defended criminals. He especially did not like Italian-American Attorneys who defended criminals, especially when they looked like Richard Nixon and smelled of snake oil, and especially when the criminal was himself an Italian-American.

Abruzzi was aware of the sense in which Carella was using the word "Counselor." His intonation made it sound like "Shyster." Abruzzi hated high and mighty Italian-American Law Enforcement Officers who thought their calling was as pure and exalted as a priest's. In a democracy, everyone was entitled to counsel and everyone was innocent until he was proved guilty, and Abruzzi was here to make certain that no American citizen would ever be deprived of his rights, God bless America.

"If you don't mind, Detective," he said, "I'd like to talk to my client and his father privately."

"Sure," Carella said. "Go right ahead. Counselor."

A uniformed cop escorted Abruzzi and the Correntes down the hall to the Interrogation Room. Carella went to the cage, threw back the slip bolt, opened the door, and said, "One at a time, you first, son. Want to step outside, please?" The kid was eighteen and looked fifteen. Dark hair, wide brown eyes, a pretty mouth. Like Bobby, he had come down from the high induced by whatever the hell they'd ingested and now looked as if he'd been run over by a railroad locomotive. Carella took him over to his desk. Hawes was coming from the Clerical Office with a cup of tea; he liked his afternoon tea.

"What's your name, son?" Carella asked the kid.

"Rudy Perucci," the kid said.

"Rudy, you're in trouble," Carella said, and read him his rights. Rudy listened gravely. Carella asked him if he'd understood everything he'd heard. Rudy said he had. Carella asked him if he wanted an attorney.

"Do I need one?" Rudy asked.

"I'm not permitted to advise you on that," Carella said. "You can have one or not, it's entirely up to you. Either way, it won't reflect upon your guilt or innocence."

"It wasn't me who hit the priest," Rudy said.

"Rudy, before you say anything else, I have to know whether you want an attorney. If you want one, you can have one. Either your own, or we're required by law to get one for you if you don't have one. So please tell me now if you want an attorney."

"What else do they say I done?" Rudy asked.

Carella read off the list of charges.

"That's serious, huh?" Rudy said.

Carella started to tell him exactly how serious it was. The assault charge was punishable by a max of fifteen. The burglary charge . . .

"We didn't steal anything," Rudy said.

"Rudy, please don't say anything else, okay?" Carella said. "Let me tell you what these charges mean, and then you can decide about a lawyer. You can get up to fifteen years for the assault, fifteen for the burglary, twenty-five for the reckless endangerment, and seven for the criminal mischief."

"I only went along," Rudy said. "I didn't do anything."

"Do you want a lawyer, Rudy?"

"If I didn't do anything, why do I need a lawyer?"

"Yes or no, Rudy?"

"No, I don't need a lawyer."

"Are you willing to answer questions without a lawyer present?"

"Yes. I don't need a lawyer, I didn't do anything."

"Can you tell me what happened?"

"I only went along," Rudy said.

"How did it start?"

"We were trying some stuff Bobby got hold of."

"What stuff? What'd you take, Rudy?"

"I don't even know the name of it. We just said yes."

He grinned. He had just made a joke about Nancy Reagan's famous and foolish slogan. Anybody who'd ever smoked only so much as a joint knew exactly how stupid the Just Say No campaign had been. Rudy was testing Carella now. To see if *he* knew how dumb it had been. Carella smiled back. Two old buddies familiar with the ways of drug abuse. But only one of them had gone berserk inside a church.

"It was real good, man," Rudy said, still grinning.

Carella was willing to bet it had been real good.

"So what happened?" he asked pleasantly.

"Bobby wanted to go get his stuff back."

"What stuff?"

"The stuff the nigger ripped off."

"Ripped off?"

"Yeah, you know."

"No, I don't know. Tell me."

This is the fifth episode of *Rashomon*. After this, there will be no more installments. This is the final chapter. At least Carella *hopes* it is the final chapter. They are back to Easter Sunday again, the same windy, shitty day, everyone seems to agree on the weather. And it is still two-thirty, three o'clock in the afternoon, everyone agrees on the time as well. And the star player, or at least *one* of the star players in this tedious and interminable little melodrama, is once again coming up Eleventh Street, doing what Rudy calls his Nigger Shuffle, and grinning into the wind like he owns the world. Alexis has not said anything about *this* part of the saga because she was not witness to it, but so far Hooper's, Bobby's, and Seronia's versions are all in agreement. But they are coming to the dope part again, which dope Hooper was first there to *sell*, and next there to *buy*, and next ran off with after Bobby accused him of using funny money the last time they traded. And, sure enough, they are going into the hallway again, and another dope transaction is about to go down, these two—Bobby and Hooper—are in the *habit* of exchanging money for dope, you see, and vice versa, Mrs. Reagan, which is why little girls in red hoods should not go wandering off into the woods where evil and corruption lurk, hmmm?

So there in the hallway, out comes the crack. A hundred vials, identical to the tiny glass tubes perfume samples come in, except that *these* vials don't contain *Eau du Printemps*. These vials contain little crystals that look like exaggerated grains of salt but which are actually cocaine base, which is made by heating a mixture of baking soda,

cocaine hydrochloride and water, and then letting it cool. *These* little
vials are deadly.

Out comes the crack . . .

"And out comes the piece," Rudy said.

"The what?"

"The piece."

"A gun?"

"A gun."

"Bobby pulled a gun?"

"No, no. The *nigger* pulled the gun."

. . . because what he has in mind, you see, is taking these hundred
vials worth four hundred bucks and not giving Bobby a red cent for
them. That is what the piece is for. Which upon closer examination
looks like a .38 caliber Smith & Wesson Regulation Police Model 33,
capable of putting very large holes in anyone's head who is stupid
enough to try grabbing that plastic bag of crack away from Hooper.
Unless the someone is standing a little to the side of and slightly
behind the nigger, and unless there's a baseball bat (and also a softball
and a mitt, but it is only the bat that is of importance) in the corner of
the hallway, where one of the kids left it when his mother called him
upstairs to Easter dinner. The bat is propped against the wall, and the
mitt and the softball are on the floor, the ball in the pocket of the mitt
(although this is an insignificant detail) and the kid standing slightly
behind and to the left of Hooper is not Bobby Corrente but his kid
brother Frankie Corrente, who is rapidly learning the ways of the
street, and especially how to seize the opportunity.

Not to mention the handle of a ball bat.

Which he does, in fact, seize.

And swings the bat with practiced ease at the target that is Nathan
Hooper's head. From the corner of his eye, Hooper sees the bat coming, and he kind of raises his left shoulder, sort of hunkering down
into it, turning at the same time, trying to deflect the blow, which he
partially succeeds in doing in that the bat hits his shoulder first and
only then bounces off to graze his head. This is not enough to prevent

a serious wound, but it is enough to prevent concussion and possible coma. It is also enough to cause his grip on the gun to loosen before he can fire a shot. And as the gun clatters to the floor and young Frankie pulls back the bat for yet another swing at the fences, Hooper recognizes it is time to get the hell out of here, but not without the dope for which he has now paid with a broken head. So off he goes with the bag of dope in his left hand and the pack in full cry behind him, and the rest of the story ends in church—not once, but twice.

"The second time is today," Rudy said. "When we went back to look for the stuff."

Because, yes, Virginia, it *is* true that Hooper stashed the dope someplace inside the church. Bobby and his pals know this is so. Not because when he came out with the priest on the way to the hospital, they couldn't see the bag of crack nowhere in sight; he could've had it in his pocket, right? But because pretty soon after the incident on Easter, Hooper began bragging around Fifth Street that as soon as it was safe to go back to St. Kate's he was gonna be one rich nigger. And also, this must've been three, four days before the priest got killed, they were fooling around with a pussy kid named Fat Harold, kidding around with him, you know, giving him knucks and the burn, this was near the school, and he told them he was with Hooper when he called the church and warned the priest he wanted his dope back.

So the dope is there inside the church, right?

Someplace inside the church.

Four hundred *dollars* worth of crack.

And there hasn't been a single black guy snooping around looking for it because first of all there aren't any blacks go to St. Catherine's, and second of all, they know what happened to Hooper on Easter, and they don't want a taste of the same medicine.

This doesn't mean Bobby and the guys haven't been in there tip-toeing around half a dozen times looking for it, but they can't *find* the fucking stuff, the nigger hid it too good. So it's beginning to look like four hundred bucks is going straight down the toilet.

Until today.

Today, Bobby gets sore.

And he tells them they're going to that church and they're gonna turn it upside down till they find that fuckin' dope.

Which is what they done.

"But not me," Rudy said. "I just went along. I didn't hit the priest, I didn't knock over any of the things, the candlesticks, the altars, the thing with the incense, I didn't do any of those things. And, also, how is it burglary if nobody stole nothing?"

Carella explained that it was burglary if someone knowingly entered or remained unlawfully in a building with intent to commit a crime.

"But we *didn't* go there to commit a crime," Rudy said. "We went there looking for dope rightfully belongs to Bobby."

Carella explained that criminal mischief was a crime. And so was assault. And so was reckless endangerment.

Rudy shook his head over the inequity of the law.

"Good thing I didn't do none of those things," he said.

"Who *did*?" Carella asked.

The entire reason for this little exercise. Get one of them talking, get him to nail one of the others. Then get another one talking to save his own skin, and have him nail yet another one. The Domino Theory of law enforcement and criminal investigation.

"I just went along," Rudy said.

"Too bad you've been charged," Carella said sympathetically. "But you get a thing like this, a bunch of guys acting in concert . . ." He shook his own head over the inequity of the law.

"I don't see why I should take the rap for something I didn't do," Rudy said, beginning to sound a bit indignant.

"Yeah, it's too bad," Carella said. "But if you didn't 'see who knocked over the altar, for example, or who hit the priest . . ."

"Bobby hit the priest."

"Bobby Corrente?"

"Yeah. I saw him grab the candlestick and hit him with it. And Jimmy Fava knocked over the altar, the big one. And . . ."

And that was the beginning.

When Dominick Abruzzi came back into the squadroom after

having talked to his client, he said, "May I have a word with you, Detective Carella?"

No more sneering of the word "Detective."

"Sure," Carella said.

"My client went into the church because he was having an allergy attack," Abruzzi said.

Carella looked at him.

"Lots of pollen in the air this time of year. The church is relatively pollen free. It was a haven for him."

"I'm sure," Carella said. "Dust free, too, probably."

Abruzzi looked at him.

"The wagon gets here at six," Carella said. "After that, you can talk to your client downtown. Good night, Mr. Abruzzi," he said, and went to the lieutenant's door and knocked on it.

"Come!" Byrnes shouted.

11

Here in this church, here in this hallowed place, *Our father who art in Heaven, hallowed be Thy name,* searching now behind a life-sized plaster statue of the Virgin Mary holding the crucified Christ in her arms, here in this place, on his hands and knees but not praying, lifting altar cloths instead and looking under them, groping along stone walls inch by inch, inspecting niches in which there were statues of saints he did not recognize or could not remember, Carella was transported back to a time when a young boy who looked somewhat like the man he'd grown into, sat in a church not too far away from this one—the family had not yet moved uptown to Riverhead— sat Sunday after Sunday listening to the drone of ritual, barely able to keep his eyes open.

Sunday after Sunday.

He was inside a church again today, seeking not salvation but dope. Because Lieutenant Byrnes had told him to find that dope. Because if there was dope inside the church, then the black girl was telling the truth about her brother stashing it there and Mrs. Hennessy was telling the truth about somebody calling up and wanting it back, and the possibility existed that Corrente or somebody else had come back for it sometime *before* this afternoon. And if that was the case, then maybe the somebody'd who'd come looking for it had run into the priest instead. And such a chance encounter called up a great many possibilities, least of which was violence. Where there was dope, the possibility of murder always existed. So find the goddamn dope and at least maybe you had your goddamn motive!

Sunday after Sunday.

Sundays with sunshine blazing through the long high windows on either side of the church, illuminating stained glass that had been fashioned by a local artisan here in this Italian section of the city (which was no Firenze, that was certain), dust motes climbing to the ceiling while from the organ loft soft fat notes floated out onto the scintillated air, and a boy with slanting eyes and unruly hair listened to the priest and wondered what it was all about.

On the day of his first holy communion when he was ten or eleven, somewhere in there—a spiritual life was so alien to him now that he could no longer remember the exact dates of the most important events in a young Catholic's life—his mother slicked down the cowlick at the back of his head, and he walked to the church with her and his father and his Uncle Lou, all so long ago.

Carella—he was called Stevie back then, a name he'd always sort of liked until a girl a few years later dubbed him Stevie-Wee-vie in an attempt to make him feel childish; he was twelve and she was fourteen, a vast difference at that age, he'd gone home in tears. But on the day of his first holy communion Stevie Carella accepted the wafer on his tongue, allowed it to melt there, careful not to bite it because this was the flesh and the blood of Jesus Christ, and the wafer would bleed in his mouth, Christ's blood would flow in his mouth, or so he'd been given to understand by one of the nuns who'd taught him his catechism every Monday and Wednesday afternoons after school.

He'd felt a deep and reverent attachment to God that day. He did not know exactly what it was he believed, it was all mumbo-jumbo of a sort to him, but he knew that he felt an inner glow when that wafer dissolved in his mouth, and he knelt there at the altar railing with his head bent and his cowlick plastered down, and he felt somehow enriched by what had happened this day, so very long ago. Enriched. And somehow joyous. He'd gone to his first confession the day before, nothing to confess at that age, he truly was without sin, an innocent . . . well . . . I lied, Father, and I ate meat on Friday, and I talked back to my mother. Sins. A boy's sins. Forgiven, absolved with a handful of Hail Marys, a couple of Our Fathers, and an Act of Contrition, pure again, the lamb again, joyous in the presence of God on the following day, the Sunday of his first holy communion.

A year or so later, two years, so difficult to remember now, he was confirmed in that very same church, wearing the same blue suit, which he was beginning to outgrow, red arm ribbon on his sleeve, his Uncle Lou looking tall and handsome in a blue suit that matched his own, neatly trimmed little mustache, his father gave him a gold signet ring with his new initial on it, L for Louis, in honor of his godfather, SLC for Stephen Louis Carella, today I am a man. Sunday after Sunday in that church and then in the smaller church in Riverhead, three blocks from the house his parents were renting, Carella had his own bedroom, he was a man now, he no longer shared a bedroom with his sister Angela. No one called him Stevie anymore. He was Steve now. Sunday after Sunday.

Rainy Sundays in the new church, rainsnakes slithering down the windows, plain glass here in Riverhead, he missed the stained glass they'd had in Isola, the priest's sonorous voice floating out over the heads of the worshippers, the scent of incense wafting from thuribles, a lightning flash, the boom of thunder, the scent of something else now, imagined or real, the perfume of young girls, its scent much headier than the incense, he was beginning to notice, his mind wandered, he thought of panties when he should have been thinking of God.

Years later, on the Saturday before Easter—he must have been fifteen or sixteen, he could hardly remember anymore—he was infused with the same sort of spiritual fervor he'd felt on that day of his first communion, and he'd got on his bicycle, a black and white Schwinn with a battery-powered horn, and he'd pedaled over to the church, and locked the bike to the wrought-iron fence outside . . .

His father used to tell stories about the days when you didn't even have to lock your front door, but that was when there were chariots in the streets . . .

. . . and he took off his hat . . .

He used to wear this shabby blue baseball cap that had seen better days, but it was the good luck hat he'd worn when he pitched a no-hitter . . .

. . . and he went into the church and dipped his hand into the font of holy water and made the sign of the cross, and then sat down and waited his turn to enter the confession box. And he knelt on the padded kneeling bar, and the little door slid open and he could vaguely see the priest's face behind the screen partition, and he crossed himself and said, "Bless me, Father, for I have sinned, this is six months since my last confession."

There was a silence behind the screen.

Carella waited.

And then the priest said, "And you pick the busiest time of the year to come?"

Carella confessed his sins. He had done a lot of bad things that had kept him away from the church for six months because he'd been afraid of telling all those things to a priest, evil things like feeling up an Irish girl named Marge Gannon, and masturbating a little . . . well, a lot . . . and saying Fuck you, and You dirty bastard. The priest told him what he had to say as penance, and Carella said, "Thank you, Father," and left the confession box, and was starting down the center aisle toward the altar, fully intending to say the penance so that tomorrow he could receive communion and feel the same glow he'd felt that first time, when all at once he stopped dead in the middle of the aisle, and he thought What do you *mean*, the busiest time of the year? Does God have busiest times of the year? I was feeling *good* when I came in here, I wanted to be near *God*! So what the hell do you mean—he actually thought those words, what the hell, here in the church, standing in the middle of the aisle halfway to the altar—what the hell do you *mean*, the busiest time of the year?

And he turned his back to the altar, and walked up the aisle, and out of the church, and he slammed his lucky baseball cap down on his head, and he unchained his bike, and rode away from the church without looking back at it. He had not been inside a church again until his sister's wedding eleven years ago.

He was in one today.

Looking for dope.

Father Michael had searched the church thoroughly, and undoubtedly he'd known its nooks and crannies more completely than any outsider could have. And Carella had searched it again with Hawes, and Bobby Corrente and his friends had done another more reckless search, and no one had come up with the hundred vials of crack. So maybe the crack wasn't here, after all, maybe *all* the versions of *Rashomon* were false. And even if the crack *was* here, what were we talking about? Five hundred dollars? That was the street value of the crack Nathan Hooper allegedly had stashed inside St. Catherine's. A lousy five hundred dollars. Was that enough to kill someone for? In this city, yes. In this city five hundred *pistachio* nuts was enough to kill someone for. And if someone had come to this church to retrieve that dope . . .

And had been intercepted by Father Michael . . .

Perhaps challenged by him . . .

Yes, it was possible. The lieutenant was right. Where there was dope, there was often murder.

Sighing heavily, he started the search one more time.

From the top.

Playing his own *Rashomon* tune.

Imagining himself as Nathan Hooper entering this church on Easter Sunday with the pack in full cry behind him.

Through the massive center doors. Urn of holy water on the left. Stainless steel, sitting on a black wrought-iron stand. Little upright brass cross fastened to the top of its lid. Little brass spigot on the container below. He pressed the button on the spigot. A drop of water fell onto the fingers of his right hand. He could remember back to a time when all the fonts of holy water in a church were filled to the brim every day of the week. Now, they were empty except on Sundays. The urn was simpler. It held . . . what, three gallons of water? You didn't have to run all around the church filling all those little basins all the time.

To the right of the entrance doors was a rack containing religious reading matter. Newspapers titled *National Catholic Register* and *Our Sunday Visitor* and *Catholic Twin Circles*. Pamphlets with titles like *Serving God's People with a Bequest in Your Will* and *Students Pursue the Infinite Wisdom of God* and *Proclamation: Aids for Interpreting the Lessons of the Church Year,* this particular issue subtitled *Lent.* The rack was fashioned of wood, with troughlike partitions holding the printed matter. He had felt inside those troughs, searching behind the newspapers, when he'd gone through the church with Hawes. He did it again now. Nothing.

The offerings box stood alongside the newspaper rack; one was expected to make donations for the reading material. There were twenty-two of these boxes scattered throughout the church; he had counted them on his earlier search. Each box resembled nothing so much as a black iron chest with a black iron tower growing out of it. The box was a foot square, with a heavy padlock fastened to its front, where the box opened. The tower sprang from the center of the box, rising to about Carella's belt buckle. It was a three-inch-square chute with a slit in the top of it. The slit was perhaps three inches long and half an inch wide. Big enough to accept even a wadded bill.

Or a vial of crack.

But wouldn't Father Michael have emptied all the boxes in the church since Easter Sunday? And even if Hooper had dropped a dozen vials here and there in offerings boxes around the church . . .

But this would have taken time.

He was being chased by an angry mob.

But, hold it. *Rashomon*, okay?

He comes running into the church, carrying his plastic bag with his precious hundred vials in it. The vials are identical to the ones perfume samples come in. In fact, most crack dealers get their vials from wholesale specialty houses. The sale of these tiny containers has skyrocketed since crack came into vogue. If you checked the books of these houses, you'd think half the population of this city had suddenly gone into the perfume business. Little perfume tubes containing the crack crystals, most of them white, some of them with a yellowish tint, little clear crystals looking as if they've been chipped from a larger rock, it is sometimes *called* rock because of its appearance. White or yellow, when you smoke the shit, when you melt it and inhale the vapors, it produces an immediate high that knocks the top of your head off. So he's carrying his hundred vials of crack in a small plastic bag . . .

They'd have fit in a small bag.

They're what, those vials? An inch long? Quarter of an inch in diameter? Little plastic cap sealing the top of the vial, well, just like the perfume sample vials, those are what these deadly little containers *are*. So yes, they were small enough to fit inside the smallest of the commercial plastic bags, one of those sandwich-sized things and yes, practically the first thing he'd have seen when he came running into the church would have been the offerings box with its black conning tower. It wouldn't have taken him more than a few minutes to dump those vials into the slot on top of the tower, turn over the bag maybe, sort of funnel them in, using the edge of his free hand as a shovel, it was possible. Two, three minutes at most. If he *had* two, three minutes. With all of them roaring up behind him?

But suppose he'd been too frightened to pause there in the entrance narthex, suppose he'd run into the church instead . . .

Carella stepped through the doors into the nave . . .

. . . and was suddenly confronted with a veritable *feast* of offerings boxes. There were shrines to his right and to his left . . . *Dedicated to the very Reverend* . . . there were more statues of saints, there were marble altars with goldleaf screens above them, there were standing racks holding votive candles and there were racks fastened to the wall and holding yet more votive candles, and everywhere the candles flickered, there was an offerings box. Nathan Hooper had to have seen what Carella was seeing now. Candles everywhere. Candles and flowers. The stations of the cross starting on the north wall of the church, to the right of the altar . . . *Jesus is condemned to death* . . .

Jesus is made to bear His cross . . . Jesus is nailed to the cross . . .

Carella walking up the side aisle now . . .

. . . a stained glass window with an air-conditioner under it.

He passed his fingers over the evaporating fins. About an inch of
space between each fin. Had Hooper dropped his vials into one of the
air-conditioners set under windows everywhere around the church?
But he was being *chased*! He didn't have time to look, to find, to . . .

More candles against the wall.

And another offerings box.

Maybe Farnes had been right about the good priest's obsession
with the tithe.

Jesus falls the first time under His cross . . .

And more candles.

And an offerings box.

And a shrine with a statue of Jesus with his open heart revealed in
his chest, radiating gold-leaf rays, fresh flowers under the statue. And
votive candles. And an offerings box.

Jesus meets His afflicted Mother . . .

A candle rack fastened to the stone wall had a metal lip at its
topmost edge, forming a troughlike angle with the wall. He felt behind the lip. Nothing.

Double rows of candles flickering.

Where? he thought.

There were niches all over the church, rounded little insets in the
stone, all of them containing statues.

He felt behind each statue for the third time, fingers widespread,
searching. Nothing.

Niches everywhere.

He passed a font designed for bearing holy water, little steel basin
sitting in a stone cavity. He lifted the empty basin. It fit the cavity
exactly, there was not a millimeter of an inch to spare. No place to
hide crack here, and besides it would have contained water on Easter
Sunday, Hooper was being *chased*, he wouldn't have had time to . . .

Hey.

Hey, *wait* a minute.

Wait a holy goddamn minute!

He came running up the right-hand side of the church, passing the stations of the cross in reverse order...

Jesus is placed in the sepulchre ...

... running past the arched doorway that led to the sacristy and the rectory beyond ...

Jesus is taken down from the cross ...

... passed another little shrine with a statue of yet another saint, flowers at his feet ...

Jesus dies on the cross ...

... opened the center inner doors, and stepped into the entrance lobby, and turned instantly to his right.

Because if the offerings box with its black tower was one of the first things Hooper had seen immediately upon entering the church, then the *next* thing he'd have seen, *had* to have seen, was the urn of holy water.

Stainless steel, sitting on a black wrought-iron stand. Little upright brass cross fastened to the top of its lid. Little brass spigot on the container below. He did not know how often this urn was refilled. But it looked too heavy to be carried to a water tap, and he was willing to bet it was regularly filled right here on the spot. Which, if true, meant that someone would simply lift the lid and pour water into the urn. He took off his jacket, unbuttoned the right-hand sleeve of his shirt, shoved the sleeve up to his elbow, and with his left hand, reached out for the brass cross fastened to the urn's lid. Virtually holding his breath, he lifted the lid and reached into the water with his free hand. Felt around. And...

There.

He lifted the plastic bag dripping out of the water.

It was sealed with one of those little yellow plastic ties.

He loosened it.

Kneeling, he shook the contents of the bag onto the stone floor. The bag wasn't waterproof, and so the first thing that spilled out onto the floor was a small amount of water. The vials came spilling out next. He could tell at once that water had seeped into some of them as well, partially dissolving many of the crystals, melting others entirely. But what remained looked a hell of a lot like crack.

It occurred to him that if the urn had been refilled since Easter Sunday. . .

And if Father Michael had blessed the water between then and the time of his death . . .

Then the *crack* was holy, too.

Which, in a way, in America today, it probably was.

It began raining again later that evening, just as Willis was heading crosstown to a shop called *El Castillo de Palacios*. He was going there because nobody at 1147 Hillsdale knew anyone named Carlos Ortega. This was the address Ortega had given his Parole Board when he was released from prison in October of last year. If there was now a new address, the Department of Corrections was unaware of it. Trying to find a Carlos Ortega in a city that had locked up eighty-three of them in the last little while was akin to finding a pork roast in the state of Israel.

El Castillo de Palacios would have been ungrammatical in Spanish if the *Palacios* hadn't been a person's name, which in this case it happened to be. *Palacio* meant "palace" in Spanish, and *palacios* meant "palaces" and when you had a plural noun, the article and noun were supposed to correspond, unlike English where everything was so sloppily put together. *El Castillo de* los *Palacios* would have been the proper Spanish for "The Castle of the Palaces," but since Francisco Palacios was a person, *El Castillo* de *Palacios* was, in fact, correct even though it translated as "Palacios's Castle," a play on words however you sliced it, English *or* Spanish.

Francisco Palacios was a good-looking man with clean-living habits (now that he'd served three upstate on a burglary rap) who owned and operated this pleasant little store that sold medicinal herbs, dream books, religious statues, numbers books, tarot cards, and the like. His silent partners were named Gaucho Palacios and Cowboy Palacios, and they ran a store *behind* the other store, and *this* one offered for sale such medically approved "marital aids" as dildos, French ticklers, open crotch panties (*bragas sin entrepierna*), plastic vibrators (eight-inch and ten-inch in the white, twelve-inch in the black) leather executioner's masks, chastity belts, whips with leather thongs, leather anklets studded with chrome, penis extenders, aphrodisiacs, inflatable life-sized female dolls, condoms in every color of the rainbow including puce, books on how to hypnotize and otherwise overcome reluctant women, ben-wa balls in both plastic and gold plate, and a highly popular mechanical device guaranteed to bring satisfaction and imaginatively called Suc-u-lator.

Selling these things in this city was not illegal; the Gaucho and the Cowboy were breaking no laws. This was not why they ran their store *behind* the store owned and operated by Francisco. Rather, they did so out of a sense of responsibility to the Puerto Rican community of which they were a part. They did not, for example, want a little old lady in a black shawl to wander into their backstore shop and faint dead away at the sight of playing cards featuring men, women, police dogs and midgets in fifty-two marital-aid positions, fifty-*four* if you counted the jokers. Both the Gaucho and the Cowboy had community pride to match that of Francisco himself. Francisco, the Gaucho, and the Cowboy were, in fact, all one and the same person, and they were collectively a police informer.

Naturally, the police had something on Palacios in any one of his incarnations; nobody — well, hardly anybody — becomes a snitch merely because he believes he will be performing a community service while simultaneously enjoying a life of romantic adventure. What they had on Palacios was a small tax-fraud violation that would have sent him to a federal prison for a good many years had they chosen to exercise their option to arrest him. Palacios cheerfully accepted the grip the police held over him, and tried to lead an exemplary life. If every now and then he did a little something illegal — like moving hot CD players along with his dildos and doodads — he figured there wasn't much more he could lose. With a federal rap hanging over his head, all else seemed minor.

Willis went to him not because he was a better informer than Fats

Donner—actually Donner had a slight edge when it came to providing quality information—but only because over the years Donner's penchant for young girls had become more and more unbearable; being in the same room with him was like inhaling a mix of baby powder and spermicidal gel. The Cowboy was actually pleasant to be with. Moreover, Carlos Ortega was of Hispanic origin, and so was the Cowboy, whose shop was in a section of the Eight-Seven known as *El Infierno,* which until the recent influx of Jamaicans, Koreans and Vietnamese had been almost exclusively Puerto Rican.

He was combing his hair when Willis, soaking wet after a two-block run from the bus stop, came into the back of the shop. High pompadour, the way kids used to wear it back in the Fifties. Dark brown eyes. Matinee idol teeth. It was rumored in The Inferno that Palacios had three wives, which was also against the law, but they already had him on the tax fraud. One of the wives was supposed to have been a movie star in Cuba before Castro took over. That had to put her in her fifties or sixties, Willis guessed. He got straight to the point.

"Carlos Ortega," he said.

"Gimme a break," Palacios said. "You guys come in here with Spanish names that all sound alike."

"Forty-two years old, ugly as homemade sin."

"What'd he do?"

"Nothing that we know of right now, except he's not where he's supposed to be."

"Where's that?"

"1147 Hillsdale."

"Tough neighborhood," Palacios said, which was sort of comical in that he lived in a neighborhood that had racked up three dozen corpses since the beginning of the year.

"He was busted on a drug charge," Willis said. "Did good time, got paroled in October. He's really *very* ugly, Cowboy, that might be where you start."

"If I had a nickel for everybody's ugly in this city. . ."

"Big bald guy, knife scar over his right eye, partially closing. . ."

"Popeye Ortega," Palacios said.

Which is the way it went sometimes.

The one thing Palacios forgot to tell him was that this was a crack house.

"Here's where you'll find him," he said, and gave him an address and an apartment number. If Willis had known where he was going, he might have realized that the twelve-year-old kid standing outside the building was a lookout. As it was, he walked past him as innocent as the day is long, which is maybe why the kid didn't challenge him. Or maybe it was because he didn't look at all like a cop. Five-eight, slender and slight, wearing a sports shirt open at the throat, sleeves rolled up to his elbows, blue slacks, and scuffed loafers, he could have been anyone who lived here in a housing development where blacks, whites, Hispanics and Asians lived side by side in a volatile mix. The twelve-year-old scarcely gave him a passing glance.

Still all unaware, Willis went into the lobby and took the elevator up to the third floor. Apartment 37, Palacios had told him. Ask for Popeye. A kid of about sixteen or seventeen was lounging against the wall opposite the elevator doors. The moment Willis stepped out into the third floor corridor, he said, "You looking for something?" Big husky white kid wearing a T-shirt and jeans. The shirt had the call letters of a rock radio station on it. You looking for something? And all at once, the twelve-year-old downstairs registered and Willis realized that the Cowboy had sent him to a crack house.

"I'm supposed to meet Popeye Ortega," he said.

The kid nodded.

"You know the apartment number?"

"Yes," Willis said. "Thirty-seven."

"End of the hall," the kid said, and stepped out of his way.

He did not want to go in here as a cop. If he flashed the tin, the roof would come down around his ears. But passing the scrutiny of a twelve-year-old outside and a sixteen-year-old here in the hallway was not quite the same thing as slipping undetected through enemy lines. He thought at once that he should split, put the joint under surveillance, come back another time with a hit team. But he wanted Popeye Ortega.

He went to the door of apartment 37, knocked on it.

A peephole opened.

"I'm supposed to meet Popeye Ortega," he said.

If it worked once, he figured it might work again. It did. The door opened. The man standing just inside was a big, good-looking black man who could've got a job playing the sidekick cop on a police show. The first thing he said was, "Have I seen you here before?"

"No," Willis said.

"I didn't think so."

"Popeye told me to meet him here."

"He's upstairs. What can I get you?"

"Nothing right now," Willis said.

The man looked at him.

"I'll just go talk to him," Willis said, and walked past him into the apartment. Kitchen on the left. Dead ahead, in what would have been the living room, three young men sat at a table. One black, one white, one Hispanic. Crack pipes on the table. Butane torch. Butane fuel. Crack vials. Three cream-colored rocks in a vial, cost you five bucks here and in L.A., fifteen in D.C., the nation's capital. Three rocks. Good for an instant high that lasted about thirty minutes. Then you were back in the toilet again till your next hit.

On the Coast, they called it rock. In D.C., they called it Piece of the Mountain. In this city, there were a dozen different names for it. You made the stuff in your own kitchen. You mixed cocaine powder in a pot with baking soda and you stirred it till you had a thick paste. Then you cooked the paste on your stove and you let it dry out until it resembled a round bar of soap. You broke it into chips. Another name for it. Chip. If you were a roller, you packaged it and sold it under your own brand name. If you used crack made from coke powder that had already been cut with some deadly shit like ephedrine or amphetamine, you could end up in the morgue. Users liked to know what they were smoking. They looked for brand names they could count on. Lucky Eleven. Or Mister J. Or Royal Flush. Or Paradise. Or Tease Me.

Actually, you didn't *smoke* the stuff, you *inhaled* it.

Although you *could* crunch up the rocks, and sprinkle them inside a marijuana cigarette. You called this "whoolie," the pot laced with crack, and it was one way you *could* actually smoke the product.

But you didn't normally burn it the way you burned tobacco or pot. Normally, you *melted* it.

The three young men at the table were ready to go.

They were each holding a glass pipe. This did not resemble a *real* pipe the way a glass slipper resembled a *real* slipper. This "pipe" was fashioned of a clear glass bowl with two glass tubes protruding from it on opposite sides at right angles to each other, one vertical, one horizontal. It looked more like a laboratory instrument than a smoking apparatus. You expected to see it over a Bunsen burner, with some mad scientist's evil brew boiling in it. The bowl was about the size of a tennis ball, and it had a hole in it through which water could be poured. Each glass tube was about five inches long, with a diameter of half an inch or so. You wedged your rocks—each rock weighed about a hundred milligrams—into the top of the vertical glass tube, which after very few uses became blackened, and you put the horizontal glass tube in your mouth, and you picked up the butane torch . . .

"Beam me up, Scotty," one of the young men said.

Intent on what they were doing now. Sucking flame into the tube. The rocks beginning to melt. Sucking the vapors through the water in the bowl of the pipe. Up through the other glass tube, lips tight around it, inhale the vapors, a five-second journey from the lungs to the brain, and *whammo*!

The equivalent of an orgasm, most addicts said.

Rapture.

Euphoria.

In laboratory tests, rats ignored electric shocks to get at their cocaine doses, chose cocaine over food, chose it over sex, allowed it to dictate the very course of their lives. By the end of a month, nine out of ten of them were dead.

Willis watched the young men sucking up death.

The crack house was in actuality three separate apartments on the second, third and fourth floors of the building. The floor and ceiling of the third-floor apartment had been broken through and ladders set up to allow access to the second floor below and the fourth floor above. There were entrance doors on each floor, of course, but anyone wanting to come in and smoke away the time had to come in on the third floor, where he paid his money for his vial and his pipe. The three-level arrangement also served a more practical purpose. In the event of a raid, the second and fourth floors could be emptied in a flash while the cops milled about on the entrance floor of the dope sandwich.

He found Popeye Ortega on the fourth floor.

He was sitting at a table in the far corner of the second bedroom, looking through a rain-lashed window, at least a dozen empty vials of crack spread on the table top before him. Willis did not know how long he'd been here. He looked as if he had not changed his clothes or shaved in days, and he smelled of the stench of his own urine. He kept staring through the window at the rain outside, as if viewing somewhere in the streaked greyness colors and images mere mortals could not see.

"Ortega?" Willis said.

"Scotty got dee chip, man," he said.

He was, in truth, as ugly as Marilyn had described him, as ugly as his picture and/or his description in the Buenos Aires documents and the I.S. printouts. But there was something missing here.

Willis stepped out of the room, opened a window in the hallway, and allowed the cool, clean scent of fresh rain to sweep into the apartment. He would wait until Ortega came down from his high, and then he would question him. But he already knew for certain that the man sitting in there, staring out the window and stinking of his own piss, could not be the same man who was threatening Marilyn's life.

What was missing in this man was the vitality Marilyn had described. The huge ugly man in there had long ago lost all sense of direction, ambition or drive. Crack had stolen his life force. He was, in effect, already dead.

Willis took a cigarette from the package in his pocket, lighted it, and stood by the window puffing on it, looking out at the rain, wondering how long it would be before Ortega surfaced. He could hear voices from downstairs welling up in the hole that had been cut in the ceiling. The good-looking black man greeting a customer. Willis figured that while he was here, and just so it shouldn't be a total loss, he might as well ruffle a few feathers. He went down the ladder again to the third floor. He walked past the three young men sitting at the table. They had been joined by a fourth man, who was at that very moment firing up. This has to be China in the 1800's, Willis thought. This has to be a nation of drug addicts. This has to be the disgrace of the planet. This has to be an America that makes you ashamed.

The good-looking black man was sitting at a table in the kitchen.

Willis walked in with his gun in one hand and his shield in the other.

"What's this?" the black man said.

"What do you think it is?" Willis asked.

"Hey, come on, man."

"Meaning what?"

"Meaning you know."

"No, I *don't* know. Tell me."

"Come on, man."

Meaning, of course, that the fix was in. As simple as that. Hey, come on, man, this has been taken care of, huh? Go talk to your people, man, they tell you let it slide, huh, man? With the numbers involved in the drug trade, there would always be somebody letting it slide, somebody looking the other way.

"What's your name?" Willis asked.

"Come on, man."

"What's your fucking *name*?"

"Warren Jackson."

"Mind if I use your phone, Warren?"

"You steppin' in deep shit, man."

"Wait'll you see what *you're* steppin' in," Willis said, and yanked the phone from the wall hook, and dialed the precinct number. Charlie-car showed up in five minutes. The driver looked surprised. So did the man riding shotgun. Both of them knew Willis.

"Gee, Hal," one of them said, "when did *this* joint spring up?"

"Surprises every day of the week," Willis said.

Warren Jackson was scowling at both of the Charlie-car cops. Willis figured they were both in on the deal. Partners. Helping Young America smoke its fucking brains out.

"More detectives on the way," he said conversationally.

"Good," the shotgun cop said.

"You know Detective Meyer? He's on the way."

"Oh, sure," the driver said. "Meyer Meyer. The bald guy, right?"

"Right. He's got young kids."

Both cops looked at him.

"He has a thing about crack," Willis said, smiling pleasantly.

So far Warren Jackson wasn't saying anything. He was possibly waiting for somebody to tell Willis to fuck off. But nobody was doing it. Not yet. The young crack addicts sitting around the table knew something was going on, but they were so far out of it, so high up on the third moon of the planet Belix in the galaxy Romitar that they figured maybe those guys in blue uniforms were the palace guard, standing there with the big black eunuch and the short curly-haired jester, all of them guarding the Emperor Pleth's harem, this was a good movie.

"Where's your sergeant?" Warren said at last.

This was Charlie Sector, the Patrol Sergeant's name was Mickey Harrigan, a big redheaded red-faced hairbag who'd been on the force since Hector was a pup. It was entirely possible that Harrigan was in on it, too. Maybe every cop in the *sector* was in on it, including the CPEP cops on the beat.

"Call your fuckin' sergeant," Warren said, "tell him we got a misunderstandin' here."

The Charlie-car cops looked at each other. They were trying to figure what the protocol was here. They knew their Patrol Sergeant outranked Willis, but if it came to a matter for Internal Affairs, rank didn't mean a goddamn thing. Unless Willis himself was in on the deal. In which case . . .

"Sure, call him," Willis said.

They figured he wasn't in on the deal.

"Go ahead," Willis said.

The shotgun cop's name was Larry Fitzhenry. He raised Harrigan on the walkie-talkie and asked him could he please, Sarge, stop by this apartment here on Ainsley and Fifth, apartment 37, Sarge, where there seems to be some sort of misunderstanding here? Harrigan said he'd be right over. His voice sounded noncommital. Over the years, Willis had learned that you should never trust anyone named Mickey unless his last name was Mouse.

Meyer got there before Harrigan did.

He did not like what he saw. Willis took him aside and told him he thought the proprietor was ready to blow the whistle. He figured some uniforms were about to hit the fan, at least one of them decorated with a gold shield. Meyer looked even more annoyed. The Charlie-car cops looked extremely nervous. Warren Jackson was getting angrier and angrier over the untrustworthiness of the police department.

When Harrigan showed up, he said, "What is this? What is this?"

Warren Jackson told him to get his men in line, this wasn't what three grand a week was supposed to buy.

Harrigan told the detectives he didn't know what the fuck Jackson was talking about.

Meyer said, "You're full of shit, Mickey."

Willis went upstairs to talk to Ortega.

Shad Russell refused to discuss it on the telephone.

When they met later that night, at a delicatessen on The Stem, he told her why.

"It occurs to me that perhaps you're setting me up," he said.

This was already nine o'clock. The dinner-hour rush had peaked, but neighborhood people were still straggling in and taking seats at tables near the window, where they could watch the springtime rain drilling the sidewalk outside. There were still things in this city that were nice.

"You still think I'm a cop, huh?" she said.

"Or *working* for the cops, yes," he said.

"Setting you up for *what*?"

"First for dealing guns and next for dealing dope."

"Don't be ridiculous," she said.

"Maybe I *am* being ridiculous," he said, and shrugged. "But maybe I'm not."

"I thought you called Houston."

"I did."

"I thought you talked to Sam Seward, how could I be a cop?"

"Maybe *he's* in their pocket, too, the Houston cops. And maybe they got you sewed up here, the cops here. All I know is first you come around looking to buy a gun, and next thing I know you've got five hundred K, and you wanna buy dope. To me, that sounds like a setup."

"Well, it isn't."

"For all I know you're wired. For all I know, you got a mike hung between your knockers. I set up a drug buy for you, I end up in a holding cell."

"I'm not wired."

"Prove it."

"How?"

"Strip," he said.

She looked at him.

She sighed heavily.

"So we're back to that again, huh?" she said.

"No, we're *not* back to *that* again," he said, mimicking her, "get your fuckin' mind out of the gutter. I call up this lady friend of mine, we go to her place, you strip for *her*, not me. She tells me you're clean, we talk."

"Did you find a deal for me?"

"No strippee, no talkee," he said.

"I cashed that check today," she said.

Shad looked at her and said nothing.

"I've got five hundred thousand in hundred-dollar bills."

Still he said nothing.

"Come on, don't be a jackass," she said.

"Lady," he said, and stood up, "it was nice meeting you."

"Sit down," she said.

"My friend lives on Darrow," he said. "Near the old Franklin Trust building. Yes or no?"

Marilyn was shaking her head in amazement.

"Yes or no?" Shad said.

Russell's lady friend was a hooker, for sure, but her apartment was tidy and well-furnished, and Marilyn guessed she worked solo. Her name—or at least the name by which she introduced herself—was Joanne. This was a common hooker name. Like Kim or Tracy or Julie or Deborah. She looked to be in her mid-thirties, but Marilyn guessed she was at least a decade younger. She told Marilyn she could undress in the bathroom.

The bathroom was spotlessly clean. Through force of habit, Marilyn checked out the medicine cabinet and found several bottles of mouthwash, three boxes of condoms, and a bottle of Johnson's Baby Oil. She took off her clothes and folded them neatly on the small wooden table opposite the sink. There were two robes hanging on the back of the door. Marilyn put on one of them. Silk. The aroma of perfume clinging to it. Something she recognized but could not for the life of her name. Not a cheap scent. She fastened the sash at her waist and came out into the bedroom wearing only the robe and her own high-heeled pumps.

Joanne looked at the robe and said, "Make yourself at home, why don't you?"

"Sorry, I thought . . ."

"You mind taking it off, please?"

Shad was sitting on the edge of the bed.

Marilyn looked at him.

"This is a *search*," Joanne said, "take off the fuckin' robe."

Shad got up, and went into the other room. Marilyn took off the robe. Joanne looked her up and down.

"Nice," she said.

"Thanks."

"Your own?"

"Yes."

"Nice," she said again. "Turn around."

Marilyn turned.

"Nice," Joanne said again. "You gay?"

"No."

"Bi?"

"No."

"That's a shame. Take off the shoes, okay?"

Marilyn slipped out of the pumps. Joanne picked them up, felt inside each of them, tested each heel to see if she could slide it away from the body of the shoe, and then handed the shoes back.

"I'll check your clothes," she said, and went into the bathroom.

Marilyn put the robe on again, and sat on the edge of the bed, her legs crossed. She desperately wanted a cigarette. In the bathroom, Joanne picked up each article of clothing—the skirt, the blouse, the bra, the slip, the pantyhose—and patted them down. She opened Marilyn's handbag, then, and whistled when she found the .38.

"Shad sold that to me," Marilyn said.

"I don't want to know," Joanne said, and continued rummaging through the bag. At last, she snapped the bag shut, said, "I'll tell him you're clean, you can dress now," and went out into the living room. Marilyn went into the bathroom, looked for her package of cigarettes, immediately lighted one, and then closed and locked the door. In the living room, she could hear their muffled voices. Alternately puffing on the cigarette and resting it on the edge of the sink, she dressed silently, and then flushed the cigarette down the toilet. When she walked out into the living room, Joanne was gone.

"She said we can talk here," Shad said.

"Fine."

"Sit down."

"Thanks."

He was sitting on a sofa covered with a pale blue fabric. Behind him was a Van Gogh poster, all yellows and oranges and bolder blues. She took a chair opposite his, crossed her legs. At the far end of the room, rain lashed the window.

"What'd you think of her?" he asked.

"Nice lady," she said.

"She told me she'd like to go down on you."

"Sorry, I'm not interested."

"You're a difficult person," he said, and sighed.

"Shad, can we talk business? Please?"

"That *is* her business," he said, and smiled the crocodile smile. "I'm glad you were clean. It really bothered me to think that maybe you were fuzz."

"Good, now let's get on with it. Have you found . . . ?"

"Did you really cash that check?"

"Yes."

"Half a mill in hundreds, huh?"

"Yes."

"What'd they say?"

"What do you mean?"

"What'd you *tell* them? Why you wanted the C-notes."

"They didn't ask."

"But didn't you feel funny? Getting all that bread in hundred-dollar bills?"

"I told them I was buying an antique vase, and the man wouldn't accept anything but cash."

"An antique vase, huh?"

"Yes. Ming Dynasty."

"Ming Dynasty, huh?"

"Museum quality."

"And they bought that, huh?"

"I'm a regular customer at the bank, they never asked me why I wanted . . ."

"But you told them, anyway, huh?"

"Yes."

"Because you felt funny, right?"

"No, because it was an unusual transaction."

"And because you used to be a hooker, right?"

Marilyn looked at him.

The rain beat a steady tattoo on the window.

"I can understand why you walked easy," he said.

"I wasn't walking *easy*," she said. "The bank *knows* me. But I felt my request *was* a bit . . ."

"But they don't know you used to be a hooker, I'll bet."

Big smile on his face. Little man with a big smile and a big secret. She wished he'd get off this tack, but he kept coming back to it, the blonde used to be a hooker, what do you know?

"So did you find a deal for me?" she asked.

"Yes," he said, "I found a deal for you."

"Good. Who?"

"A man up from Colombia, I done deals with him before."

"When will it be?"

"He'll have the eleven keys by tomorrow night."

"Good. Did you tell him I wanted to pick the place?"

"I told him. He didn't like it *but* . . ."

Shad shrugged and smiled again.

"Did you tell him one-on-one?"

"I told him. He agreed to it."

"Where'd you leave it?"

"He'll call me tomorrow night, when he's got the stuff together. I call you, you tell me where you want him to come, he'll be there in ten minutes, provided it ain't in Siam."

"What's his name?"

"Why do you need to know that?"

"I guess I don't."

"You guess right, you don't. All you need is the money."

"After I've got the stuff . . ."

"Yeah, well, first you gotta get it."

"Yes. But *after* I have it, how long do you think it'll take to turn it around?"

"Depends on who I can find. Two days maybe. Somebody to step on it—it'll cost, you know . . ."

"Yes."

"And then somebody else'll take it off your hands. All in time. Two, three days."

"Because the thing is, I haven't *got* much time, you see."

"I figured."

"I'm getting a lot of pressure, you see."

"Mmm."

"So the sooner we can turn it around, the happier I'll be."

"Oh, sure," he said. "But first you gotta make the buy, don't you?"

"Yes. But that's tomorrow night."

"Provided," Shad said.

"What do you mean *provided*? You *said* tomorrow night, didn't you?"

"Yeah, to meet him."

"Yes."

"Test the stuff, taste it . . ."

"Yes."

"Which you don't know how to do, right?"

"Well . . . that shouldn't be a problem. You said you'd . . ."

"Yeah, I said I'd teach you."

"Yes."

"To taste it," he said, and smiled.

She looked at him.

A fresh wind swept torrents of rain against the window.

"You really want me to put you in touch with this guy, don't you?" he said.

Smiling.

She kept looking at him.

"Well, don't you?" he said.

"You know I do."

"Because this deal is very important to you, right?"

"Yes," she said.

"Very important," he said.

"Yes."

"Sure."

Smiling.

"Well, don't worry about it," he said. "Everything'll be all right."

"I hope so," she said.

"Oh, sure," he said. "Provided."

His eyes met hers.

The rain and the wind rattled the window.

"Come here, baby," he said, and began unzipping his fly.

She went immediately to the door.

It was locked.

A dead bolt.

The key gone.

In prison that first time, the door had been locked from the outside. The warden—*El Alcaide,* a squat little man wearing jodhpurs and high, brown-leather boots, a riding crop in his hand—had asked her to raise her gown for him. She'd run to the door, but it was locked. She'd twisted the unresponsive doorknob again and again, shouting "Help!" in English and then *"Socorro!"* in Spanish, the warden coming up behind her, the riding crop raised . . .

Never again, she thought.

She took the .38 from her handbag.

"Unlock the door," she said.

He looked at the gun in her fist.

"Now," she said.

"You're a hooker," he said. "What's another blowjob more or . . . ?"

She almost shot him dead on the spot that very minute. Her finger almost tightened that last millimeter on the trigger, she almost spat-

tered his brains on the wall. Instead, she turned to the door and leveled the gun at it, and fired repeatedly at the wood, splintering the
area around the lock. Shad sat bolt upright on the sofa, his words cut
off by the explosions, his eyes saucer wide, his fly open. Marilyn
twisted the knob, and pulled open the door, tearing the latch assembly
from the tattered wood, its bolt still engaged in the doorframe's striker
plate.

"Now there'll be cops," he said, almost petulantly.

"Good," she said. "*You* explain it to them."

Doors were opening all up and down the hallway. Curious tenants
who knew that a hooker lived in 6C, and who were expecting trouble
sooner or later, and here it was on a rainy spring night. She walked
swiftly past them, and went down the steps and out into the street.
People who had heard the shots were gathering near the front stoop.
She could hear a police siren in the distance. She walked away
swiftly, through the rain.

She was thinking that now she'd have to kill the two men from
Argentina.

12

The two detectives stood before Lieutenant Byrnes's desk like a pair of apprehensive schoolboys about to be birched by the headmaster. The fact that it was still raining that Thursday did little to help the pervasive feeling of impending doom. This was the last day of May. It was now two in the afternoon. In just five hours, the priest would have been dead for a full week.

Silvery rainsnakes slithered down each of the lieutenant's corner windows, the grey beyond much duller than the grey of his hair, which was still short-cropped but growing increasingly whiter over the years. Frowning, he sat behind his desk, hands folded in front of him. The knuckles were oversized, a legacy from his youthful days as a street fighter. His shaggy white brows were lowered over flinty blue eyes. The rain oozed on either side of him.

"Let me hear it," he said.

"I went to see Bobby Corrente late last night," Carella said. "He's already out on bail . . ."

"Naturally."

". . . I found him at home with his parents. I figured since we've already got him for tearing a church apart and assaulting a priest . . ."

"Yes, yes," Byrnes said impatiently.

"But he's got an alibi for the night of the murder."

"A reliable witness?"

"His father."

"Worthless," Byrnes said.

"Hooper's got an alibi, too," Hawes said. "I talked to him this morning."

"Who's *his* witness?"

"His sister."

"Also worthless," Byrnes said.

"But they both knew there was crack hidden inside . . ."

"Where was it, by the way?"

"In the holy water urn."

"Jesus," Byrnes said, and shook his head. "How about the weapon? Have you found that yet?"

"Not anywhere in the church. And we've searched it a hundred times already. The point is, if either Hooper *or* Corrente went back for that dope . . ."

"Except you're just telling me they've both got alibis."

"Which *you're* telling me are worthless," Carella said.

"Which they are," Byrnes said. "What about this Farnes character, is that his name?"

"Farnes, yes."

"What's *his* alibi."

"His inventory log," Carella said.

"Which he himself dated," Hawes said.

"So far you're giving me nothing but alibis that aren't alibis at all," Byrnes said. "What else have you got?"

"Only *more* alibis that aren't alibis," Carella said. "This gay guy who painted the star . . ."

"His name again?"

"Hobbs. Andrew Hobbs. He claims he was in bed with a man named Jeremy Sachs on the night of the murder."

"Terrific."

"We haven't been able to locate his mother . . ."

"Her name?"

"Abigail. I guess. He calls her Abby, I guess it's Abigail."

"Okay, Abigail Hobbs, what about her?"

"She went to Father Michael for help. We want to ask her just how angry this made him."

"The son?"

"Yeah. Meyer says he was *still* pissed about it. The priest was stabbed seventeen times, Pete. That's anger."

"Agreed. So find her."

"We're trying."

"What about the secretary?" Byrnes asked.

"What about her?" Hawes said.

Defensively, it seemed to Carella.

"Could she have been the one the priest was diddling?"

"I don't think so," Hawes said.

"On what do you base that?"

"Well . . . she just doesn't seem like the sort of person who'd get involved in something like that."

Byrnes looked at him.

"She just doesn't," Hawes said, and shrugged.

"The Class Valedictorian, right?" Byrnes said.

"What?" Hawes said.

"Brightest kid in the class, handsome as can be, witty, ambitious, kills his mother, his father, both his sisters and his pet goldfish. But he didn't *seem* like that sort of person. Right?"

"Well . . ."

"Don't give me *seems,*" Byrnes said. "And don't tell me there aren't any secretaries who fool around with their bosses. Find out where she was and what she was doing on the night of the murder."

"Yes, sir," Hawes said.

"And locate this gay guy's mother, Hobbs, find out what the hell *that's* all about."

"Yes, sir," Carella said.

"So do it," Byrnes said.

* * *

A good time to visit a church devoted to worshipping the Devil was on a rainy day, Carella guessed. As he came up the street, he saw through the falling rain the old soot-stained stones of what had first and very long ago been a Catholic church, and then a storehouse for grain during the Civil War, and briefly a Baptist church, and then a warehouse for sewing machines, and then a convenient location for antiques shows and crafts shows until the neighborhood began crumbling everywhere around it. Now it was The Church of the Bornless One, though nothing advised the casual observer of this fact.

He saw only wet, sootened stones against a gunmetal sky, the outline of a building that seemed to squat on its haunches ready to pounce, tethered to the earth by flying buttresses. He climbed the low flat steps to the entrance and tried the knobs on both doors. Both were locked. He went around the side to what he guessed was the rectory door. A bell button was set into the stone. A tarnished brass escutcheon over it read *Ring for Service*. He rang for service. And waited in the rain.

The woman who answered the door had long blonde hair, a button nose dusted with freckles, and eyes the color of cobalt. She was wearing blue jeans and a white T-shirt with a tiny red devil's head as a discreet logo over the left breast. Carella figured he'd come to the right place.

"Yes?" she said.

"I'm looking for Mr. Lutherson," he said, and showed her his shield and his I.D. card.

"You're not the one we spoke to," she said.

"No, I'm not," Carella admitted. "May I come in, please? It's a little wet out here."

"Oh, *yes*," she said, "*excuse* me, come in, come in, please."

She stepped back and away from him. She was barefoot, he noticed. They were standing in what was a small oval entrance foyer fashioned of stone and lined with niches similar to the ones at St. Catherine's, except that these were devoid of statues.

"Didn't Andrew Hobbs come talk to you?" she asked at once.

"Not to me personally," Carella said. "But, yes, he did speak to us."

"Then you know he's the one who . . ."

"Yes, painted the star."

"The pentagram, yes."

"Yes."

"Let me tell Sky you're here," she said. "What was your name again?"

"Carella. Detective Carella."

"I'll tell him," she said, and turned and went padding off into the gloom.

He waited in the foyer. Outside a water spout splashed noisily. He wondered what they did here. He wondered if they were breaking any laws here. You read stories about all these sensational ritual murders, people killing people for the Devil, you began to think the whole *world* was worshipping Satan. Slitting the throats of little babes, dripping their blood into sacrificial basins. Most of these cults sacrificed chickens or goats, hardly any of them were foolish enough or reckless enough to dabble in human sacrifice. In this city, there were no laws as such against sacrificing animals. Who was to say that tossing a lobster into a pot of boiling water wasn't sacrifice of a sort? There were, however, laws against inhumane methods of slaughtering, and if you were in a mood to bust a cult that practiced animal sacrifice, you could always nail them on a bullshit violation. He was not here to bust a cult. He was here to learn a bit more about . . .

"Mr. Carella?"

He turned.

A tall blond man had materialized in the foyer, stepping from the darkness beyond one of the arched portals. Like the woman who'd answered the door, he too was wearing jeans and the white T-shirt with the devil's-head logo. He, too, was barefoot. The body of a weight lifter, lean and clean, Carella was willing to bet next month's salary that this cat had done time. A bend in the otherwise perfect nose, where it had once been broken. A Mick Jagger mouth. Pearly white teeth. Eyes as blue as the woman's had been, were they brother and sister?

"I'm Schuyler Lutherson," he said, smiling, "welcome to The Church of the Bornless One."

He extended his hand. Carella took it, and they shook hands briefly. Lutherson's grip was firm and dry. Carella had read someplace that a firm, dry grip was a sign of character. As opposed to a limp, wet one, he guessed. He was willing to bet another month's salary that a great many murderers in this world had firm, dry grips.

"Come on inside," Lutherson said, and led him through an arched portal opposite the one through which he'd entered, and down a stone corridor, more empty niches in the walls, and then opened a heavy oaken door that led into a wood-paneled room that had once been a library, but which was now lined only with empty shelves. A thrift-shop desk was in the center of the room. There was a chair behind it and two chairs in front of it. A standing floor lamp with a cream-colored shade was in one corner of the room. Lutherson sat behind the desk. Carella sat opposite him.

"So," Lutherson said. "I hope you're making progress with your case."

Hands tented, fingers and thumbs gently touching. Looking at Carella over his hands. Smiling pleasantly.

"Not very much," Carella said.

"I'm sorry to hear that. I thought when we offered our cooperation, this would at least, see, clear up any doubts along *those* lines. That anyone here at Bornless might be involved, see. In the murder of the priest."

"Uh-huh," Carella said.

"Which is why we asked him to go to the police. Hobbs. The minute we found out he was the one who'd defaced that gate."

"As a matter of fact, he's the reason I'm here today."

"Oh?"

Blue eyes opening wide.

"Yes. We've been trying to locate his mother, but we can't find a telephone listing for her, and we . . ."

"Why don't you ask Hobbs?"

"We did. He doesn't know."

"He doesn't know his own mother's *telephone* number?"

"They don't get along. She moved six months ago, and neither of them has made any attempt to contact each other since."

"Well, I wish I could help you, but . . ."

"Did Hobbs ever mention her to you?"

"No. In fact, the first time I ever *spoke* to Hobbs was last Saturday night."

"I thought he was a regular member of your congregation. According to Jeremy Sachs . . ."

"Yes, I know Jer . . ."

". . . he introduced Hobbs to your church in March sometime."

"I do know Jeremy, and that may be true. But people come and go, see, it's a transient group. A lot of people are attracted by the novelty of it, and then they realize that this is a serious *religion* here, see, we're serious *worshippers* here, and they drop out."

"But you'd never talked to Hobbs before last Saturday."

"Correct."

"You'd seen him here, though, hadn't you?"

"Not that I can recall. But I'm sure if Jeremy says he's been coming here since March, then I have no reason to doubt his word. It's just that I wasn't familiar with him personally."

"And so you wouldn't have any information about his mother."

"No."

"Abigail Hobbs."

"No. I'm sorry."

"You wouldn't have met her . . ."

"How would I have met her?"

"Well, she could have come here in an attempt to . . ."

"No, I've never met anyone named Abigail Hobbs."

"I guess you'd remember if she came here."

"Yes, I'm sure I'd remember."

"Before going to see Father Michael. To ask you to talk to her

son, convince him to leave the church, whatever. You don't remember anything like that, is that right?"

"Nothing like that, no. I can say very definitely that I don't know
anyone named Abigail Hobbs."

"Well, thank you, Mr. Lutherson," Carella said, and sighed. "I
appreciate your time."

"Not at all. Feel free to stop in whenever you like," Lutherson
said, and rose from behind the desk and extended his hand again.

The men shook hands. Firm and dry, the grip of the Devil's
disciple.

"I'll show you out," Lutherson said, which Carella thought happened only in movies.

She'd told him she was going to a cattle-call audition that afternoon and that he could meet her outside the Alice Weiss Theater
downtown at about five o'clock, by which time she hoped she'd be
through. Hawes waited under the theater marquee now, watching the
falling rain, watching the pedestrians rushing past on their way to the
subways and home. He wanted to be going home, too. Instead, he
stood here waiting for Krissie Lund.

Right after their meeting in the lieutenant's office, Carella had told
him that Alexis O'Donnell had seen a blonde woman with Father
Michael on Easter Sunday. Whether or not the blonde had been Krissie was yet another matter; there were a great many blondes in this
world, including Alexis herself. But it bothered Hawes that she might
have been. Because *whoever* the blonde was, Father Michael had
accused her of blackmail. And blackmail, otherwise known as extortion, was defined in Section 850 of the state's Penal Law as "the
obtaining of property from another induced by a wrongful use of force
or fear." And listed under the threats that constituted extortion was: *To
expose any secret affecting him.*

If, for example, the blonde arguing with Father Michael on Easter
Sunday had threatened to expose his love affair unless he paid her a
substantial sum of money or gave her property *worth* money—a

house in the country, a diamond bracelet, an Arabian show horse—this would have been blackmail.

This is blackmail, the priest had shouted.

According to Alexis O'Donnell.

Who had seen a blonde.

Blackmail, or extortion, was punishable by a max of fifteen years.

A long stretch up the river if you threatened to tattle unless someone paid you off. Which potential stay in the country often provided a good reason for murder. Most often, of course, it was the intended victim who murdered his blackmailer. Better murder than exposure. But what if the victim threw all caution to the winds and threatened to *report* the blackmail attempt? Oh, yeah? Take this, you dirty rotten rat!

Not so funny when it happened in real life.

If Alexis O'Donnell had heard and seen correctly, a blonde had been with Father Michael on Easter Sunday, and she had threatened him with what he'd considered blackmail. If that blonde was Krissie Lund . . .

"Hi, have you been waiting long?" she said, and took his arm.

Carella was waiting outside the First Fidelity Savings and Trust when Andrew Hobbs came out of the bank at a quarter past five that afternoon. Hatless and without an umbrella, he pulled up the collar of his raincoat, ducked his head, and plunged bravely into the teeming rain.

"Mr. Hobbs?" Carella said, and fell into step beside him. "I'm sorry to bother you again . . ."

"Yes, well, you *are*," Hobbs said.

"But we've been unable to reach your mother . . ."

"I don't want to hear another word about that bitch."

The rain was relentless. Both men virtually galloped through it, Hobbs obviously intent on reaching the subway kiosk on the corner, Carella merely trying to keep up. When at last they'd reached the sanctuary of the underground station, Carella grabbed Hobbs's arm, turned him around, and somewhat angrily said, "Hold *up* a minute, will you?"

Hobbs was reaching into his trouser pocket for a subway token. His blond hair was plastered to his forehead, his raincoat, trouser legs, and shoes were thoroughly soaked. He shook off Carella's hand impatiently, found his token, glanced toward the platform to see if a train was coming in, and then impatiently said, "What is it you want from me?"

"Your mother's phone number."

Sodden, homeward-bound commuters rushed past on their way to the token booth and the turnstiles. Standing against the graffiti-sprayed tile wall some four or five yards away were two young men, one of them playing acoustic guitar very badly, the other sitting against the wall with a cardboard sign hanging around his neck. The sign read: WE ARE HOMELESS, THANK YOU FOR YOUR HELP. Hobbs glanced again toward the platform, and then turned back to Carella and said in the same impatient voice, "I don't *have* her number, I already *told* you that. Why don't you look it up in the damn phone book?"

"We have, she's not listed."

"Don't be ridiculous. Abby not listed? Abby taking the risk of missing a phone call from a *man*? Really."

"Mr. Hobbs," Carella said, "your mother was one of the people who'd had contact with Father Michael in the several weeks before his death. We'd like to talk to her."

"You don't think *she* killed him, do you?"

"We don't know *who* killed him, Mr. Hobbs. We're merely exploring every possibility."

"Wouldn't *that* be a hoot! Abby killing the asshole who was supposed to save me from the Devil!"

"The point is . . ."

And here Carella launched into a somewhat creative improvisation, in that the *real* reason he wanted to talk to Abigail Hobbs was to explore further her son's anger and his potential for violence . . .

" . . . whatever Father Michael may have said to her, however unimportant it might have seemed at the time, could possibly be of enormous value to us now, in retrospect, if it sheds light on events in the past that could conceivably relate to the murder, though at the time it may have appeared insignificant."

Hobbs tried to digest this.

Then he said, "You're not suggesting he might have *confided* in Abby, are you? Because quite frankly, Mr. Carella, that would be tantamount to confiding in a boa constrictor."

"We won't know until we talk to her, will we?" Carella said.

"Don't you people have ways of getting unlisted numbers?"

"We do. And we tried them. The phone company doesn't have a listing anywhere in the city for anyone named Abigail Hobbs."

"Small wonder," Hobbs said, and smiled.

Carella looked at him.

"Her name isn't Abigail Hobbs."

"Your mother's name . . ."

"She divorced my father ten years ago," Hobbs said. "She's been using her maiden name ever since."

The hotel had a French name but its staff was strictly American and when the maître d' in what was called the *Café du Bois* said, "Bonn swarr, mess-yoor, will there be two for drinks?" Hawes didn't feel particularly transported to Gay Paree. The maître showed him through a glade of real birch trees under a glass canopy, usually nourished by sunshine but not today when the rain was beating steadily overhead. At the far end of the lounge a man was playing French-sounding songs on the piano. Krissie slung her shoulder bag over the back of the chair, sat, tossed her hair, and said, "I have to call my agent when I get a minute. She'll want to know how it went."

On the way here in the rain, she'd told Hawes that they'd asked her to read *two* scenes rather than the one scene they'd asked all the other actresses to read. She considered this a good sign. Hawes said he hoped she'd get the part. He ordered drinks for both of them now—the gin and tonic Krissie requested, and a Diet Pepsi for himself since he was still on duty—and then he said, "There are some questions I have to ask you, Krissie, I hope you don't mind."

"Don't look so serious," she said.

"I want you to tell me, first of all, where you were between six-thirty and seven-thirty on the night of May twenty-fourth."

"Oh, my," she said, and rolled her eyes. "This *is* serious, isn't it?"

"Yes."

"That's when Father Michael was killed, isn't it?"

"Yes."

"And you want to know where I . . ."

"Where you were while he was being killed, yes."

"My, my."

"Yes," he said.

"What are you going to ask next? Was I having an affair with him?"

"Were you?"

"As for where I was that night," she said, "I can tell you in a minute."

"Please do," he said.

"Because I write down everything in my appointment calendar," she said, and swung the shoulder bag around so that she could reach into it, and pulled out a binder book with black plastic covers. "Although I can't say I appreciate your inviting me for a drink under false pretenses."

"Krissie," he said wearily, "I'm investigating a murder."

"Then you should have told me on the phone that this was a *business* meeting."

"I told you I . . ."

"You said you wanted to see me," she said, angrily flipping pages, "not that you wanted to see me to *question* me. Here," she said, "May," she said, "let's see what I was doing on the twenty-fourth, okay?"

The waiter came back to the table.

"The gin and tonic?" he asked.

"The lady," Hawes said.

It occurred to him that she had not yet said whether or not she was having an affair with Father Michael.

The waiter put down her drink, and then turned to Hawes and said, "And a Diet Pepsi," giving him a look that indicated *real* men drank *booze*. "Enjoy your drinks, folks," he said, and smiled pleasantly, and walked off. At the other end of the room, the piano player was playing a song about going away. Krissie took a sip of her drink and turned immediately to her calendar again.

"May twenty-fourth," she said.

Hawes waited.

"To begin with, the twenty-fourth was a Thursday, so I was *working* that day, I worked at the church on Tuesdays and Thursdays, remember?"

"Yes."

"Which meant I was there from nine to five, so my first appointment was at five-thirty, do you see it here?" she said, "with Ellie, here's her name," turning the book so Hawes could see it. "That's my agent, Ellie Weinberger Associates, I met her at The Red Balloon at five-thirty."

"Okay," Hawes said. He was already reading ahead in the calendar space for Thursday, the twenty-fourth of May. On that day, Krissie's next appointment was . . .

"At eight o'clock, I met this man for dinner, he was putting together an off-Broadway revue of famous vaudeville skits, and he wanted to talk to me about directing one of them. I've never directed before, this would have been a wonderful opportunity for me. His name is Harry Grundle, I met him at a restaurant called . . . do you see it here? Eight P.M., Harry Grundle, Turner's? That's where I was."

"What time did you leave your agent?"

"Around six-thirty."

"Where's The Red Balloon?"

"On the Circle."

"Where'd you go when you left her?"

"Home to bathe and change for my dinner date."

"And where's Turner's?"

"In the Quarter. Near my apartment, actually."

"Do you drive a car?"

"No."

"How'd you get from one place to the other?"

"By subway from the church to The Red Balloon. I took a taxi home, and walked from my apartment to Turner's."

"Do you remember what you were wearing?"

"I wore a cotton dress to work and to meet Ellie. Then I changed into something dressier."

"Like what?"

"A blue suit, I think. Also cotton. It was a very hot day."

"What color was the dress you wore to work?"

"Blue."

"Both blue, is that it?"

"It's my favorite color," she said, and closed the book.

He was thinking that it would not have taken more than twenty minutes by subway from the church to Grover Park Circle. If she'd left her agent at six-thirty, as she said she had, she could have been back uptown again by ten minutes to seven. The priest was killed sometime after seven. And she'd still have had time to taxi downtown to meet Grundle.

He was also thinking that he would have to check with Mrs. Hennessy to get a description of the dress Krissie had been wearing to work that day, and he would have to look up Harry Grundle to ask him what she'd been wearing that night. Because if she *hadn't* gone home to bathe and change her clothes . . .

"How about Easter Sunday?" he said. "Does your calendar have anything for Easter Sunday?"

"I don't like you when you're this way," she said.

"What way?"

"Like every shitty cop I've ever met in my life."

"Sorry," he said, "but I *am* a cop."

"You don't have to be a shitty one."

"Where were you on Easter Sunday between two-thirty and three P.M.?"

"You know, it occurs to me that maybe I ought to have a lawyer here."

"Shall I read you your rights?" he asked, and tried a smile. But there was something that truly bothered him here. Not that she had no real alibi for the hour and a half between six-thirty and eight on the twenty-fourth of May, but because her attitude had become so very defensive the moment he began asking questions. Maybe his technique was rotten, maybe that was it. Or maybe . . .

"I really don't think you need a lawyer," he said. "Do you *know* where you were on Easter Sunday?"

"Yes, of *course* I know where I was," she said, and flipped the book open again, and said, "When the hell was Easter Sunday?"

"The fifteenth, I think. Of April."

"I'm pretty sure I was in the country. My friends have a house in the country, I'm pretty sure I spent Easter with them."

She kept flipping pages until she came to April.

"The fifteenth," she said, almost to herself.

"Yes," he said.

"I have nothing for that day," she said, and looked up. "That's odd. Because I could swear I went to the country. I can't imagine being alone on Easter Sunday. Unless I was in rehearsal for something. In which case . . ." She looked at the book again. "Well, sure, here it is. I did a showcase on the twenty-first, a Saturday night. I was probably learning lines the Sunday before because—here, do you see it?—rehearsals began the next day, Monday the sixteenth, here."

She was tapping the calendar box with her forefinger.

Rehearsal, the entry read.

YMCA.

7:00 P.M.

"Was anyone with you?" he asked.

"Oh, yes. We were rehearsing a scene from a new play, there were at least . . ."

"On Easter. While you were learning your lines."

"I believe I was alone."

"No one to cue you?"

"No, I believe I was alone."

"You didn't go up to St. Catherine's that day, did you?"

"Why would I do that?"

"I have no idea. Did you?"

"No."

"What was your relationship with Father Michael?"

"I *wasn't* having an affair with him, if we're back to that."

"Was there ever anything between you that went beyond a strictly business relationship?"

"Yes," she said, surprising him.

"In what way?" he asked.

"I found him extremely attractive. And I suppose . . . if I'm to be perfectly honest with myself . . . I suppose I flirted with him on occasion."

"Flirted how?"

"Well, the walk . . . you know."

"What walk?"

"Well, you know how women walk when they want to attract attention."

"Uh-huh."

"And eye contact, I guess. And an occasional show of leg, like that. Well, you know how women flirt."

"Are you Catholic?" he asked.

"No."

"So you found it perfectly okay, I guess, to flirt with a priest."

"You sound angry," she said, and smiled at him.

"No, I'm not angry, I'm simply trying to . . ."

"But you sound angry."

"It was okay to flirt with a priest, is that right? The walk, the eye contact, the occasional show of leg, isn't that what you called it, all that? That was all perfectly okay."

"Oh, come on, we've all had that fantasy, haven't we? Nuns? Priests? What do you think *The Thorn Birds* was all about, if not wanting to go to bed with a priest? Didn't you read *The Thorn Birds*?"

"No," he said.

"Or see the mini-series?"

"No."

"Only everybody in the entire *world* saw the mini-series."

"But not me. Was that *your* fantasy? Wanting to go to bed with Father Michael?"

"I thought about it, yes."

"And apparently acted on it."

"Acting's a pretty good word for it, actually. Because in many ways it was almost like playing Meggie in *The Thorn Birds*. Or Sadie Thompson in *Rain,* do you know *Rain*? I did it in class last year. You have to try *all* sorts of parts, you know, if you want to stretch your natural talent. These women involved with priests are very interesting. Or the Bette Davis character in *Of Human Bondage,* do you know that one? He's not a priest, of course, he's a cripple, but that's sort of the same thing, isn't it? Not that I'm suggesting a priest is a cripple, but only that he's a person handicapped by his vows, who can't give vent to his natural instincts or desires, his urges really, because he's bound by these vows he's made, he's handicapped in *that* way . . . well, he *is* sort of crippled, actually. So it was . . . well, very interesting. To be playing this sort of part, and to . . . well . . . observe his reactions. It made the job more interesting. I mean, the job was *very* boring, you know. This made it interesting."

"Sure," Hawes said.

Actresses, he thought.

"But it never went beyond that," he said.

"Never."

"You never . . ."

"Well," she said, and hesitated.

He waited.

"I could see he was interested, you know."

"Uh-huh."

"I mean . . . he was *aware* of me, let's put it that way."

"Uh-huh."

"Watching me, you know."

"Uh-huh."

"Aware of me."

She sipped at her drink, and then looked thoughtfully into her glass, as if searching for truth under the lime and the ice cubes.

"I have to admit," she said, and again hesitated. "If he'd made the slightest move . . . if he'd taken it that single step beyond . . . you know . . . *looking* . . . I might have gone all the way. Because, I'll tell you the truth, I'm being perfectly honest with you, I'm scared to death of sex these days. Because of AIDS. I haven't been to bed with anyone in the past year, I'm telling you the absolute truth. And I thought . . . and maybe this is why I started it, the flirting, you know . . . I thought at least *this* would be safe. Sex with a priest would be completely safe."

She looked up into his face.

Her eyes met his.

"I don't know," she said, "do you think I'm terrible?"

"Yes," he said.

But that didn't mean she'd killed him.

"I'll just get the check," he said.

Abigail Finch was a beautiful blonde woman wearing yellow tights, a black leotard top, and high-heeled black leather pumps that added a good three inches to her already substantial height. When she let Carella into her Calm's Point apartment at seven o'clock that evening, she explained that she'd just come in from exercise class when he called, and hadn't had time to change. Except for your shoes, he thought, but did not say.

Miss Finch . . .

"Please call me Abby," she said at once . . .

. . . had to have been at least forty (her son was, after all, in his twenties) but she looked no older than thirty-two or -three. Proud of her carefully honed appearance, she walked ahead of him into the living room, offered him a seat, asked if he'd like something to drink, and then turned to face him on the sofa, her knees touching his briefly before she repositioned herself, folding her long legs under her, placing her hands demurely in her lap. There was incense burning somewhere in the room, and Miss Finch herself—*Abby*—was wearing a perfume thick with insinuation. Carella felt as if he'd inadvertently dropped into a whorehouse in Singapore. He decided he'd better get to the point fast and get the hell out of here. That was exactly how threatened he felt.

"It was good of you to see me, Miss Finch," he said. "I'll try not to . . ."

"Abby," she said. "Please."

"I'll try not to take up too much of your time," he said. "It's our understanding . . ."

"Are you sure you wouldn't like a drink?"

Leaning toward him, placing one hand lightly on his arm.

A toucher, he thought.

"Thank you, no," he said, "I'm still officially on duty."

"Would you mind if I had one?"

"Not at all," he said.

She swiveled off the sofa, moved like a dancer to a bar with a dropleaf front, opened it, looked back over her shoulder like Betty Grable in the famous World War II poster, smiled, and said, "Something soft?"

"Nothing, thank you," he said.

She poured something dark into a short glass, dropped several ice cubes into it, and came back to the sofa.

"To the good life," she said, and smiled mysteriously, as if she'd made a joke he could never hope to understand.

"Miss Finch," he said, "it's our . . ."

"Abby," she said, and raised her eyebrows in reprimand.

"Abby, yes," he said. "It's our understanding that you went to see Father Michael to ask for his assistance in . . ."

"Yes, in March sometime. Toward the end of March. Because I'd learned that my son was fooling around with witchcraft . . ."

"Well, not witchcraft, certainly . . ."

"The same thing, isn't it? Devil worship? Worse, in fact."

And smiled again, mysteriously.

"And you wanted his help, you wanted him to talk to your son..."

"Well, yes, would you want *your* son involved in such stuff? I went to see Father Michael because Bornless was so *close* to St. Catherine's. And I thought if Andrew got a call from a priest...he was raised as a Catholic, you know...it might carry some weight."

"How'd you find out your son was attending services...if that's what they're called..."

"Masses," she said. "I guess. I forget who told me. It was some-one I ran into, she said did I know my son was involved in Satanism? A woman who knew both me *and* Andrew."

"But why did you care?"

"I'm sorry?"

"You and your son are estranged, why'd you care *what* he was doing?"

"My son worshipping the *Devil*?" she said, looking astonished. "How would you like to have *that* going around town? That your faggot son is also involved in *Satanism*?"

"You mean...well, I'm not sure what you mean. Were you afraid this would reflect upon you in some way?"

"Of course it would. God knows I'm not a good Catholic any-more, but a person can't just forget her upbringing *entirely,* can she?"

And smiled mysteriously again, as if mocking her own words.

"So you went to see Father Michael..." Carella said.

"Yes. That was the church I used to attend. Before my fall from grace," she said, and lowered her eyes like a nun, and again he had the feeling that she was mocking him, but he could not for the life of him imagine why.

"I see," he said. "And you told him..."

"I told him my son was worshipping the Devil. Three, four blocks from his own church! And I asked him to get in touch with An-drew..."

"Which he did."

"Yes."

"Which made your son very angry."

"Well, I really don't care how *angry* it made him. I just wanted him to stop going to that damn church."

"And this was toward the end of March? When you went to see him."

"Yes, the first time."

"Oh? Were there other times?"

"Well, I . . ."

Her blondeness suddenly registered on him.

That and her blatant sexuality.

"How often *did* you see him?" he asked.

"Once or twice."

"Including your initial visit toward the end of March?"

"Yes."

"Then it was only twice."

"Well, yes. Well, maybe three times."

"Which?"

"Three times. I guess."

"Starting sometime toward the end of March."

"Yes."

"*When* in March?"

"Would you mind telling me . . . ?"

"Do you remember when?"

"Why is this important to you?"

"Because he was killed," Carella said flatly.

Her look, accompanied by an almost indiscernible shrug, said *What's that got to do with* me?

"When in March?" he asked again.

"It was a Friday," she said. "I don't remember exactly when."

Carella took out his notebook, and turned to the calendar page at the back of the book. "The last Friday in March was the thirtieth. Was that it?"

"No. Before then."

"The twenty-third?"

"Possibly."

"And the next time?"

"In April sometime."

"Can you remember the date?"

"I'm sorry, no. Look, I know the man was killed, but . . ."

"Were you with him on Easter Sunday?" Carella asked.

Sometimes, when you zeroed in that way, they figured you were already in possession of the facts. You had them. They didn't know how, but they knew you already knew, and there was no sense lying.

"As a matter of fact, I was," she said.

Rashomon never ends.

Carella has already heard five tellings, count 'em, *five,* of the Easter Sunday Saga, as it is now known to the entire literate world, but there is yet another version to come and this one will be Abigail Finch's, Her Story, and she is going to tell it full out, no holds barred, a premise—and a promise—that is evident in her first eight words: "I went there to make love to him."

By that time . . .

This is now the fifteenth day of April, and a blustery day at that, perfect for making love in the cozy stone corners of a rectory. . .

By that time, they've been doing *exactly* that—here and there, on and off, so to speak—for a good two weeks, ever since the first of April, when she went to see the priest for the *second* time. As she reports it now, it was there in the rectory on that April Fool's Day that she was mischievously prompted, in the spirit of the occasion, to seduce the good father. Attracted at their first meeting to his Gene Kelly smile and his breezy unpriestlike manner, she had begun wondering what he *wore* under that silly cassock of his, and she was now determined to find out. She was astonished to learn, however . . .

For whereas she *knows* she's an enormously desirable woman who takes very good care of herself, after all, not only the exercise classes, but also bicycling in the park, and milk baths for her skin, she's been told by people who should know that she possibly ranks among the city's great beauties, of which there are many, well, she doesn't wish to sound immodest . . .

. . . but she was nonetheless enormously surprised, on that first day of April, by his extreme state of *readiness*. It was almost as if some designing woman had been *preparing* him for her—working him over, softening the ground, so to speak—because as it turned out, the good father was an absolute pushover, Little Mr. Roundheels himself, head over cassock, a flash of eye, a show of leg, and he was on her in a minute, fumbling for the buttons of her blouse and confessing that once upon a time, before he joined the ministry, he'd done it on a rooftop for the first and last time with a fourteen-year-old girl named Felicia Randall.

Abby admits to Carella now that there was something deliciously sinful about doing it with a priest, something that kept her coming . . .

"You should pardon the expression . . ." she said.

. . . back to the church again and again, three, four times a week, morning, noon and night . . .

"I lied about only having seen him a few times . . ."

. . . something that took her back there on Easter Sunday as well. Which, after all, is a time for celebration, isn't it, Easter? The Resurrection of Christ, and all that? So why not celebrate? Which she is there to do on this Holy Day of the Sixth Telling of Rashomon, Easter Sunday, the fifteenth day of April in the Year of Our Lord, Amen.

She is wearing for the occasion of the priest's twelfth despoiling —she has counted the number of times they've done it since April Fool's Day—a simple woolen suit appropriate to the chill of the season, beneath which are a garter belt and silk tap pants she bought at Victoria's Secret, and seamed silk stockings and nothing else, the priest having told her on more than one occasion that he loves watching her naked breasts spill free each time he unbuttons her blouse, perhaps recalling his similar experience with the young but bountiful Felicia on the rooftop. But all to her surprise, he tells Abby that he wants to end it, that their relationship is filling him with guilt and remorse, that he feels a traitor to his church, his God, and his sacred vows, and that he has even contemplated suicide . . .

"A lot of men have told me that," she said.

. . . so please, Ab, we must end it, this is driving me crazy, Ab . . .

"He used to call me Ab, it was a pet name . . ."

. . . please, have mercy on me, let me end it, please, my dearest.

"He also called me his dearest . . ."

. . . which Ab, his dearest, has no intention of doing. Ending it, that is. She is enjoying this too much, this sinful expedition into the darkest heart of religiosity, this corruption of a priest, this sticking it to God, so to speak, in his own house, oh no, she is not about to end it now. Not now when her pleasure is so fulfilling, not now when she is at the peak of her ardor and he is at the peak of his delirium. So she tells him . . .

"I told him if he ended it now, I'd let the whole world know about it."

She smiled at Carella, mysteriously.

"Which is when he started . . ."

"Which is when he started yelling blackmail," Carella said.

"Oh?" Abby said.

"You were heard and you were seen," Carella said, lying only a little bit, in that Alexis hadn't seen her face.

"Well, yes, that's exactly what he started yelling. Blackmail. This is blackmail, this is blackmail, how dare you . . . how *silly*, really! I told him it was for his own good. Because, really, I *was* incredibly good for him."

"What happened then?" Carella asked.

"*Everything*," Abby said. "A black kid came running into the church, bleeding, and there was pounding on the doors, and the doors caved in, and a bunch of white kids came running in after him, and mister, I have to tell you, I was out the back door as fast as my feet would carry me."

"When did you see him again?"

"Who?"

"Father Michael."

"Never. I figured if he wanted out, fuck him."

She looked up at Carella and smiled.

"Would *you* have wanted out?" she asked.

He ignored the question.

"Where were you on May twenty-fourth between six-thirty and seven-thirty?" he asked.

"I wasn't out killing a priest, that's for sure."

"Okay, now we know where you weren't," he said. "Can you tell me where you *were*?"

"Not without getting personal," she said, and smiled that same infuriating, mysterious smile.

"Miss Finch . . ." he said.

"I was right here," she said. "All night long. With a man named Dwight Colby. Check it," she said, "he's in the phone book."

"Thank you," he said. "I will."

"He's black," she said.

The ugly one again.

"Qué tal?"

His first words. Signaling that they would speak only in Spanish, *his* language. She went along with it. Tomorrow it would be over and done with. Forever.

In Spanish, she said, *"Yo tengo el dinero."*

I have the money.

"Oh?" he said, surprised. "That was very fast."

"I met with my contact last night. The deal is too complicated to explain, but . . ."

"No. Explain it."

"Not on the telephone. You can understand that. Let me say only that it turned out to be simpler than I thought it would."

"Well, that's very nice, isn't it?"

Forced joviality in his voice.

Pero, eso está muy bien, no?

"Yes," she said. "Can you come here tomorrow afternoon?"

"I'm not sure we *want* to come there," he said. "You live in a dangerous place. A person can get hurt in that place."

Reminding her that there was still an *additional* debt she owed.

For the cutting of the handsome one. The two million would pay for the killing of Alberto Hidalgo . . . maybe. But she knew the ugly one would not be content until the cutting was paid for as well. *Machismo* was invented by Spanish-speaking people. So was *venganza*.

"Well, I'm sorry," she said, "but I'm not about to go out on the street carrying two million dollars in cash."

Show them the green.

"You have the full amount, eh?"

"All of it."

"In what denominations?"

"Hundreds."

"How many hundreds?"

He almost trapped her. She surely would have counted that much money, she surely would have known how many hundred-dollar bills there were in two million dollars. Her mind clicked like a calculator. Drop two zeros, you come up with . . .

"Twenty thousand," she said at once, and then embroidered the lie. "Two hundred banded stacks, a hundred bills in each stack."

"Good," he said.

"Can you be here at three tomorrow?"

Willis would be working the day watch again. He'd leave here at a quarter past eight, and he wouldn't be home till four-fifteen, four-thirty. By that time it would be finished.

"Three-thirty," he said.

"No, that's too . . ."

"Three-thirty," he repeated.

"All right," she said, sighing. "You'll have fifteen minutes to count the money and get out."

"I hope there won't be any tricks this time," he said.

The word *trucos* meant only that in Spanish. Tricks. It did not have the secondary or tertiary meanings it had in English, where a trick was either a prostitute's client or the service she performed for him. He was not making veiled reference to either her own or his uncle's former occupations. Too much the gentleman for that. No Shad Russell here, this man's mind wasn't in the gutter. He was simply warning her not to come up with any surprises.

"No guns," he said, "no knives, eh?"

Reminder of the debt again.

The cutting of the handsome one.

"No tricks," she said. "I just want this over and done with."

"Yes, so do we."

The something in his voice again. The promise. Running deep and dark and icy cold beneath the surface of his words.

"I'll see you at three-thirty tomorrow," she said, and hung up.

And realized all at once that she was trembling.

13

He went back to the church again at noon that Friday, the first day of June. He had called ahead to ask if he could look through the dead priest's files again, and Father Oriella had told him it would be no bother at all, he himself had a meeting at the archdiocese downtown, and would be out of the office most of the day. "If you need any assistance," he'd added, "just ask Marcella Bella."

Marcella Palumbo, as it happened, was out to lunch when Carella got there. It was Mrs. Hennessy who let him into the rectory and then took him back to the small office. Where there had been papers scattered all over the floor on the night of the murder, and cartons stacked everywhere when the new priest was moving in, there was now order and a sure sense of control.

"What is it you're looking for?" Mrs. Hennessy asked.

"I'm not sure," Carella said.

"Then how will you know where to look?"

Good question.

He was here, he guessed, to do paperwork again. To some people, Hell was eternal flames, and to others it was getting caught in mid-town traffic, but to Carella it was paperwork. He was being punished now for having walked out of church without having said his penance all those years ago. A vengeful God was heaping more paperwork on him.

He asked Mrs. Hennessy if she knew where Father Oriella had put the calendar, checkbooks, and canceled checks that had been returned to him by the police. She said she thought Mrs. Palumbo had filed them in the M–Z file drawer, though she had no idea why the woman had put them there since checks and calendars both started with a C, so why hadn't she put them in the A–C drawer? Carella had no idea, either. But sure enough, there they were, at the front of the M–Z drawer. He thanked Mrs. Hennessy, declined her offer of a cup of coffee, sat down at the desk and began going through the material yet another time.

As earlier, the priest's appointment calendar told him nothing of importance. On the day of his murder, he had celebrated masses at eight A.M. and twelve noon, and then had done the Miraculous Medal Novena following the noon mass. He had met with the Altar Society Auxiliary at two, and the Rosary Society at four. He was scheduled to meet with the Parish Council at eight that night, presumably after dinner, an appointment he never kept. That was it for the twenty-fourth day of May. Carella skimmed back through the pages for the preceding week. Again, there was nothing that seemed significant.

He put the appointment calendar aside, took the St. Catherine's Roman Catholic Church Corporation checkbook from the drawer, and began looking through the stubs for checks the priest had written during the month of May. Here again were the checks for photocopying and garage, mortgage and maintenance, medical insurance, flowers, missalettes, and so on. Carella turned to the check stubs for May 24.

The first stub on the page was numbered 5699. In a hand that was not Father Michael's, and which Carella assumed to be Kristin Lund's, the stub recorded that a check had been written to Bruce Macauley Tree Care, Inc. for spraying done on 5/19 in the amount of $37.50. As he'd done last Friday in the squadroom, Carella now went down the stubs one after the other, all of them dated May 24, each numbered sequentially:

5700

To: US Sprint
For: Service thru 5/17

$176.80

5701

To: Isola Bank and Trust
For: June mortgage

$1480.75

5702

To: Alfred Hart Insurance Co.
For: Honda Accord LX, Policy
      # HR 9872724

$580.00

5703

To: Orkin Exterminating Co.
      Inc.
For: May services

$36.50

5704

To: The Wanderers
For: Band deposit

$100.00

That was the last check Father Michael had written on the day of his murder.

Carella closed the checkbook.

Nothing.

Paperwork, he thought. That's why he was here. Punishment. The ransacked G–L file. The eighth circle of Hell would be going through that file yet another time, and trying to discern what was *missing* from it. Because no one zeros in on a single file, pulls that file drawer out, searches through that file in haste, tosses papers recklessly into the room and onto the floor, unless that someone is *looking* for something. And if the something had in fact been found and taken from the priest's office, then the something may have been the *reason* for the priest's murder. So perhaps if he studied the papers in order, as they'd been filed, he might discover a break in the continuity, a lapse, a gap, a hole in the records. And then, by studying the *surrounding* papers, and by using his admittedly weak powers of deductive reasoning, he hoped he might be able to figure out what the purloined something had been. In short, he planned to study the doughnut in order to define the hole.

It occurred to him that Father Oriella might have replaced the dead priest's G–L file with a G–L file of his own. But no, the fastidious Marcella had refiled the dead priest's papers exactly where they'd been on the night of the murder, there to be consulted whenever or if ever his successor had need to look up something concerning the church. Carella opened the drawer—the bottom one on the left—took out the first hanging folder in line, made himself comfortable at the desk again, and began going through the folders one by one.

He thought, at one point, that he'd found a meaningful absence in a file labeled GUTTERS. Last autumn, Father Michael had been in correspondence with a man named Henry Norton, Jr., at a firm called Norton Brothers Seamless Gutter Company, regarding the repair and possible replacement of the church's leaders and gutters. He had written a letter on September 28, making an appointment with Mr. Norton to visit the site and give an estimate, and then he'd written another letter on October 11, stating that he would like to see a *written* estimate in addition to the verbal estimate Mr. Norton had given him after his visit, and then a further letter on October 16, stating that he was now in receipt of the written estimate and that this would serve as agreement to the terms. It closed saying he would be looking forward to word as to when the actual work would commence. The missing document was the written estimate Father Michael said he'd received. It turned out, however, that the estimate had been misfiled. Carella ran across it later, in a folder labeled HOLY NAME SOCIETY. There it was. On a Norton Brothers Seamless Gutter Company letterhead. An estimate of $1,036 to repair the leaders and gutters at St. Catherine's Church. Filed between the minutes of the Holy Name Society meetings for January and February of this year.

The last folder in the file was a hefty one labeled LENT.

Carella read every last document in that folder.

There was nothing else in the G–L drawer.

Sighing heavily, he replaced the folder in the bottom file drawer, and pushed the drawer back into the cabinet. It did not close all the way. He pulled it open again. Eased it shut. It still would not close completely. An inch or more of the drawer jutted out from the cabinet frame. He opened the drawer again and checked the slide mechanism. The drawer was seated firmly on its rollers, nothing seemed to be snagging. So what the hell . . . ?

He tried closing it again. It slid back into the cabinet and then abruptly stopped. Something at the back of the drawer, or perhaps behind the drawer, was preventing it from sliding all the way into the cabinet. He opened the drawer again, got down on his hands and knees, leaned in over the drawer, and reached in behind it. Something was stuck down there. He couldn't see what it was, but . . .

He yanked back his hand in sudden searing pain.

A thin line of blood ran across his fingertips.

The something back there was a knife.

He had found the murder weapon.

* * *

The defense attorney, a man named Oscar Loring, leaned in closer to Willis and said, "And what time was this, exactly, Detective?"

He had a bristly mustache and the breath of a lion who'd just eaten a warthog. It was now a quarter to three. Willis had been on the stand for an hour and a half this morning, and had been on again since two o'clock, when court had reconvened. Trying to explain, first, why he'd requested a no-knock warrant, and next why he'd shot a man who'd tried to kill him with an AR-15. This had been in October of last year, during a raid on a stash pad. The case had just come to trial. Loring was attempting to show that Willis had lied on his affidavit making application for the search warrant, that he'd had no reasonable cause to believe there'd be either weapons *or* contraband material in the suspect apartment, and that in fact he'd *planted* both the weapons and the contraband after he'd kicked in the door!

He now wanted to know *exactly* what time it was that Willis—*and* Bob O'Brien *and* four uniformed cops from CPEP—had kicked in the door to the apartment.

"It was nine o'clock in the morning," Willis said.

"*Exactly* nine o'clock?" Loring asked.

"I don't know if it was *exactly.* We had the raid scheduled for nine o'clock, it's my belief we were assembled by nine and went in at nine."

"But you don't know if it was *exactly*. . ."

"Excuse me," the judge said, "but where are you going with this?"

His name was Morris Weinberg, and he had a bald head fringed with sparse white sideburns, and he was fond of telling people that he'd lost all his hair the moment he'd been appointed to the bench.

"Your Honor," Loring said, "it's essential to my client's case that we know at *exactly* what time illegal entry was . . ."

"Objection!"

The prosecuting attorney. Bright young guy from the D.A.'s office, hadn't let Loring get away with so much as an inch of bullshit.

"Sustained. What difference will it make, Mr. Loring, if the police went in at a minute before nine or a minute after nine? What possible . . . ?"

"If Your Honor will permit me . . ."

"No, I'm not sure I will. You've kept this officer on the stand for almost two and a half hours now, picking at every detail of a raid he and other policemen made under protection of a no-knock warrant duly signed by a justice of the Superior Court. You've questioned his integrity, his motives, his methods, and everything but the legitimacy of his birth, which I'm sure you'll get around to before the . . ."

"Your Honor, there *is* a jury pres . . ."

"Yes, I'm aware of the jury. I'm also aware of the fact that we're wasting a great deal of time here, and that unless you can tell me *why* it's so important to pinpoint the time of entry, then I will have to ask you to leave off this line of questioning."

"Your Honor," Loring said, "my client was awake and eating his breakfast at nine o'clock."

"So?"

"Your Honor, this witness claims they kicked in the door at nine o'clock and found my client in bed. Asleep, Your Honor."

"So?"

"I'm merely suggesting, Your Honor, that if the detective is willing to perjure himself on . . ."

"Objection!"

"Sustained. Now cut that out, Mr. Loring. You know better than that."

"If the detective is *mistaken* about what actually happened on the morning of the raid, then perhaps he made a similar mistake regarding cause."

"Are you referring to probable cause for the search warrant?"

"Yes, Your Honor."

"Detective Willis," Weinberg said, "why did you believe there were weapons and contraband materials in that apartment?"

"An undercover police officer had made several buys there, Your Honor, in advance of the raid. Of a controlled substance, namely cocaine. And he reported seeing weapons there. Of a type, I might add, that was fired at us the moment we entered the apartment."

"What's his name? This undercover officer?"

"Officer Charles Seaver, Your Honor."

"His precinct?"

"Same as mine, Your Honor. The Eight-Seven."

"Does that satisfy you as to probable cause, Mr. Loring?"

"I'm just hearing of this, Your Honor. This was not stated on Detective Willis's petition for a . . ."

"I said information based on my personal knowledge and be . . ."

"You didn't mention a police officer . . ."

"What difference does it make? The warrant was *granted,* wasn't it? I went into that damn apartment with a . . ."

"Just a minute now, just a minute," Weinberg said.

"Sorry, Your Honor," Willis said.

"Can we get Officer Seaver here this afternoon?" Weinberg asked.

"I'd need time to prepare, Your Honor," Loring said.

"Tomorrow morning, then. Be ready to call him at nine A.M."

"Your Honor . . ."

"This court is adjourned until nine A.M. tomorrow morning," Weinberg said, and banged his gavel, and abruptly stood up.

"All rise!" the Clerk of the Court shouted, and everyone in the courtroom stood up as Weinberg swept out like a bald Batman, trailing his black robes behind him.

The clock on the wall read 2:55 P.M.

They were due at three-thirty.

When they announced themselves over the speaker at the front door, she would tell them the door was open. When they stepped into the entrance foyer, she would call, "I'm in here." And as they walked into the living room . . .

The entire house was already in disarray.

She had spent the past hour yanking out dresser drawers and strewing their contents onto the floor, unplugging television sets and stereo equipment, gathering up silverware, jewelry and fur coats, carrying all of this down to the living room where it would appear they had assembled it after ransacking the house. Her story to the police would be that she had walked in on two armed men . . .

She hoped they'd be armed. If not, she would change her story. . .

. . . two armed men whom she'd shot dead in self-defense. Two armed intruders shot to death while burglarizing a house they thought was empty. Criminal records a mile long on both of them, Willis had shown her copies. Open and shut, don't cry for me, Argentina.

She did not have a permit for the gun she'd bought from Shad Russell, but she was willing to look that charge in the eye when the time came, even if it meant going to prison again. The important thing was to make certain none of this rubbed off on Willis. She did not see how it could. The day watch was relieved at a quarter to four. He would not be home until four-fifteen, four-thirty. It would be over by then. All of it.

She looked at the mantel clock now.

Seven minutes to three.

She picked up the gun Russell had sold her.

A .38 caliber Colt Detective Special. Six-shot capacity. Three for each of them. She had better shoot fast and she had better shoot straight.

She rolled out the cylinder, checked that the gun was fully loaded, and then snapped it back into the barrel.

The clock read five minutes to three.

The two girls came down the front steps of the Graham School on Seventh and Culver, both wearing pleated green skirts, white blouses, blue knee-high socks, brown walking shoes, and blue blazers with the school crest over the left breast pocket. They were both giggling at something another girl had said. Books held against their budding bosoms, girlish laughter spilling onto the springtime air, sparkling and clear now that the rain had stopped. One of them was a killer.

"Hello, girls," Carella said.

"Hi, Mr. Carella," Gloria said. Blue eyes still twinkling with laughter, long black hair dancing in sunshine as she came down the steps.

"Hi," Alexis said. She wore the solemn look even in the aftermath of laughter, her brown eyes thoughtful, her face serious. I'm nothing, she had told him. Blonde hair falling to her shoulders, bobbing as she came down the steps. They could have been twins, these two, except for their coloring. But one of them was a killer.

"See you guys," the other girl said, and waved as she went off.

They stood in the sunlight, the detective and the two schoolgirls. It was three o'clock sharp. Students kept spilling out of the school. There was the sound of young voices everywhere around them. Neither of the girls seemed particularly apprehensive. But one of them was a killer.

"Alexis," he said, "I'd like to talk to you, please."

She looked first at him, and then at Gloria. The serious brown eyes looked suddenly troubled.

"Okay," she said.

He took her aside. They chatted quietly, Alexis's eyes intent on his face, concentrating on everything he said, nodding, listening, occasionally murmuring a few words. A girl wearing the Graham School's uniform and a senior hat that looked like a Greek fisherman's cap, except that it was in the orange-and-blue colors of the school, came skipping down the front steps, said, "Hi, Lex," and then walked off toward the subway kiosk on the corner.

Some little distance away, Gloria watched them in conversation, her books pressed against her narrow chest, her eyes squinted against the sun.

Carella walked back to her.

"Few questions," he said.

"Sure," Gloria said. "Is something wrong?"

Books still clutched to her chest.

Behind them and off to the left, Alexis sat on the school steps and tucked her skirt under her, watching them, puzzled.

"I spoke to Kristin Lund before coming here," Carella said. "I asked her if she'd seen you at the church on the day of the murder. She said she hadn't. Is that correct?"

"I'm sorry, but I don't understand the question."

"Did you go to the church at anytime before five o'clock on the day of the murder?"

"No, I didn't."

"I also spoke to Mrs. Hennessy. She told me *she* hadn't seen you, either."

"That's because I wasn't there, Mr. Carella."

Blue eyes wide and innocent. But clicking with intelligence.

"Gloria," he said.

Those eyes intent on his face now.

"When I talked to Alexis last week—and I just now verified this with her, to make sure I wasn't mistaken—she told me you had the check for the band deposit and wanted to know whether the dance was still on. This was on Tuesday afternoon, the twenty-ninth of May. Is that right? Were you in possession of the deposit check at that time?"

"Yes?"

Wariness in those eyes now.

"When did Father Michael give you that check?"

"I don't remember."

"Try to remember, Gloria."

"It must have been on Wednesday. Yes, I think I stopped by after school and he gave me the check then."

"Are you talking about Wednesday, the twenty-third of May?"

"Yes."

"The day before the murder?"

"Yes."

"What time on Wednesday, would you remember?"

"After school. Three, four o'clock, something like that."

"And that was when Father Michael gave you the deposit check made out to The Wanderers, is that correct? For a hundred dollars."

"Yes."

"Gloria, when I spoke to Kristin Lund, I asked her if she was the person who'd written that check. She told me she was. She wrote that check and then asked Father Michael to sign it."

Eyes steady on his face.

"She wrote it on the twenty-fourth of May, Gloria."

Watching him, knowing where he was going now.

"You couldn't have picked it up on the twenty-third," he said.

"That's right," she said at once. "It was the twenty-fourth, I remember now."

"*When* on the twenty-fourth?"

"After school. I told you. I went to the church right after school."

"No, you told me you didn't go to the church at *all* on the day of the murder."

"That was when I couldn't remember."

"Are you telling me now that you *were* at the church?"

"Yes."

"Before five o'clock?"

"I'm not sure."

"Kristin left at five. She says you . . ."

"Then it must have been *after* five."

"What time, Gloria?"

"I don't remember exactly, but it was long before seven."

He looked at her.

They had not released to the media the estimated time of the priest's death. Only the killer knew that. He saw realization in her eyes. So blue, so intelligent, darting now, on the edge of panic. He did not want to do this to a thirteen-year-old, but he went straight for the jugular.

"We have the knife," he said.

The blue eyes hardened.

"I don't know what you're talking about," she said.

Which words he had heard many times before, from murderers much older and wiser than young Gloria here.

"I'd like you to come with me," he said.

And in deference to her youth, he added, "Please."

Maybe she's scared them off, he thought.

They hadn't heard from the two Argentinians since the day she'd cut the handsome one. That was on Saturday afternoon. A week tomorrow. And no word from them. Every night this past week, when he'd come home from work, his eyes had met hers expectantly. And every night she'd shaken her head, no. No word. So maybe they'd given her up as a lost cause. Maybe they'd bandaged the handsome one's hands and packed up and gone home, no sense trying to ride a tigress.

Maybe.

He came down the steps from the street outside the Criminal Courts Building, into the tiled subway passageway, and was walking toward the turnstiles when he saw the roses. Lavender roses. A man selling long-stemmed lavender roses, just to the left of the token booth. A dollar a rose. In the Mexican prison, there'd been a woman from Veracruz who'd wistfully told Marilyn that all the days were golden there, all the nights were purple. Lovely in Spanish. Lovely the way Marilyn repeated it. *En Veracruz, todos los días eran dorados, y todas las noches violetas.*

The roses weren't quite purple, but lavender would do.

Maybe it *was* time to celebrate, who the hell knew?

Maybe they were really gone for good.

"I'll take a dozen," he told the vendor.

The clock on the wall of the token booth read ten minutes past three.

In this city, the Afghani cab drivers had a private radio network. You got into the taxi, you told them where you wanted to go, they threw the flag, and that was the last you heard from them. For the rest of the trip, they ignored the passenger entirely and talked incessantly into their radios, babbling in a language incomprehensible to the vast majority of the city's population. Maybe they were all spies. Maybe they were plotting the overthrow of the United States government. This did not seem likely. More reasonable was the assumption that they were homesick and needed the sound of other Afghani voices to get them through the grinding day.

Carlos Ortega didn't *care* what the needs of the Afghani people might be. He knew only that someone with an impossible name printed on the Hack Bureau license affixed to the dashboard of his taxi was shrieking into the radio at the top of his lungs in an unintelligible language that was abrasive and intrusive.

"You!" he said in English.

The cabbie kept babbling.

"You!" he shouted.

The cabbie turned to him.

"Shut up!" Carlos said.

"What?" the cabbie said.

"Shut your mouth," Carlos said in heavily accented English. "You're making too much noise."

"What?" the cabbie said. "What?"

His ethnic group back home in the Wākhān Corridor was Kirghiz, although a moment ago he'd been speaking not the language of that area, but Farsi instead—which was the *lingua franca* of the city's Afghani drivers. His ancestors, nonetheless, had come from Turkey, and he tried now to muster some good old Turkish indignity, which disappeared in a flash the moment he looked at the ugly giant sitting in the back seat. He turned away at once, muttered something soft and Farsic into his radio, and then fell into an immediate and sullen silence.

Carlos merely nodded.

He was used to people shutting up when he told them to shut up.

In Spanish, now that the chattering din had subsided, he said, "I don't trust her, do you?"

"Beautiful women are never to be trusted," Ramon said.

He was still angry over the fact that she'd cut him. His hands were still bandaged and medicated and for the most part his wounds had healed. But there were some wounds that never healed. You did not cut the hands of a person as handsome as Ramon Castaneda. You did not even *touch* Ramon Castaneda unless he gave you permission to do so. For her indiscretion, the blonde whore would pay. As soon as she gave them the money.

"Why her house?" Carlos asked.

"Because she's stupid," Ramon said.

"No, she's very smart, give her that at least."

"I'll give her *this*," Ramon said, and grabbed his genitals.

"Yes," Carlos said, and smiled. "After she gives us the money."

"And then *this*," Ramon said, and took from his pocket a small bottle with glass stopper in its top. The bottle was full of a pale yellowish liquid. The liquid was nitric acid. Ramon hoped that Marilyn Hollis would live to have many children and grandchildren, so that she could tell all of them how her face had come to be scarred in such a hideous manner. You did not cut someone who looked like Ramon Castaneda, no.

"Put that away," Carlos said.

Ramon put the bottle away.

"Why her house?" Carlos asked again. "Will the police be there? Has she notified the police?"

"She murdered your uncle," Ramon reminded him.

"Still."

"If you had murdered someone, would you call the police?"

"The police in Argentina aren't looking for her."

"True. But she doesn't know that. Believe me, Carlos, she hasn't called the police."

"Then why her house?"

"I told you. She's stupid," Ramon said again. "*All* beautiful women are stupid."

"Can she be planning a trap?"

"Stupid people don't know how to plan traps."

"I think we should be careful."

"Why? We'll roll over her like a tank. Take the money, fuck her, throw the acid in her face," Ramon said, and nodded at the utter simplicity of it all.

But Carlos was still concerned.

"Why do you think she chose the house?" he asked again. "Why not a public place?"

"She *told* you why. She's afraid of carrying all that money on the street."

"A public place would be safer for her."

"Women think their own houses are the safest places in the world. They think their houses are nests."

"She'll be armed in her nest," Carlos said.

"Certainly. She was armed last time."

Both men fell silent.

Carlos looked at his watch.

The time was a quarter past three.

Suddenly, he grinned. He looked particularly ugly when he grinned.

"Do you remember how we got in last time?" he asked.

Ramon grinned, too.

She heard the key in the front door at exactly twenty-eight minutes past three. There were only two people who had keys to this house. The person opening the front door had to be . . .

"Marilyn?"

Willis's voice. Calling from the entry hall. Calling to her where she sat in the red leather armchair facing the open-arch entrance to the living room, the .38 Colt Detective Special in her fist.

Exactly what she hadn't wanted. Willis home and the other two not here yet. Willis stepping into the middle of it. The one person she wanted to keep *out* of it, *clear* of it . . .

"Hi, honey," he said, and came into the room with a bouquet of flowers wrapped in white paper, and saw the gun in her hand. The flowers made her want to weep, the incongruity of flowers when she was expecting . . .

His eyes suddenly shifted to the left, toward the stairs, and she knew even before his hand snapped up to his shoulder holster that they were already in the house. Somehow, they had got into the house again.

The spring-release on Willis's holster snapped his pistol up and out into his hand.

She came up out of the chair just as he fired.

He must have hit one of them—she heard someone yelling in pain just as she turned toward the stairway—and then there was shooting from the steps, and she stuck the .38 out in front of her the way she had seen lady cops do on television shows, holding it in both hands, leveling it. The big one was hit and was lurching toward Willis, firing as he stumbled into the living room. The handsome one was on his left, coming toward her, a gun in his hand. She fired at once. The bullet went low, she'd been aiming for his chest. But she was sure she'd hit him because she saw a dark stain appear where his jacket pocket was and at first she thought it was blood, but it wasn't dark enough for blood, and suddenly he began screaming. His screaming startled her, but there was no time to wonder what was causing it, there was time only to fire again because the hit hadn't stopped him, he was still coming at her, screaming, his handsome face distorted in anger and pain. The big one was still headed straight for Willis. Both of them still coming. The bad and the beautiful in one spectacular fireworks package.

Willis had his pistol stuck out straight in front of him, holding it in both hands the way she'd seen detectives do it on television, except that he happened to be a *real* detective and not Don Johnson. He was aiming very carefully at the ugly one's chest, taking his time, because this one was for the money. He fired in the same instant that the ugly one did. She fired, too. And saw the handsome one throw back his arms, the way extras did in movies, and then fly over backward as if he'd been hit by a football linebacker. Except that the stain on his pocket seemed to be spreading and his chest was suddenly spurting blood.

So was hers.

She didn't realize at first that she'd been hit.

And then she saw the blood, saw her white blouse turning red with blood, saw the blood spurting up out of the hole in her blouse, the hole in her chest, spreading into the fabric, turning the entire blouse red, and knew that she'd truly been hit badly, and felt the pain all at once, came down all at once off the excitement of all the shooting, felt the pain like an elephant stepping on her chest and thought, oh Jesus, he's really done me, and thought oddly and belatedly that she had not yet returned Eileen Burke's call of almost a week ago. And then she fell to the floor with her mouth open and her chest still spurting blood.

Willis stood over the big one, the gun still in both hands, the gun leveled at his fucking head, ready to blow his head off if he so much as blinked an eyelash, but nobody was blinking, they were both down, he turned immediately to Marilyn.

And saw her on the Persian carpet, all covered with blood.

Saw blood spurting up from her chest.

Her heart pumping out blood.

And thought Oh Jesus no.

And ran to her.

And fell on his knees beside her.

And said, "Marilyn?"

A whisper.

"Marilyn?"

And realized all at once that he was still holding the bouquet of lavender roses in his left hand.

In the city and state for which these men and women worked, Section 30 of the Criminal Law Statutes was titled INFANCY, and Subdivision 1 of this statute read: A person less than 16 years old is not criminally responsible for conduct.

Gloria Keely had turned thirteen in February.

Her parents insisted on an attorney. The attorney said he would apply at once for removal of the action to the Children's Court. They reminded him that the crime was murder. He reminded them that she was scarcely thirteen years old, and that children (he punched home the word *children*) of thirteen, fourteen and fifteen years of age were juvenile offenders under the laws of this state. They, in turn, reminded him that the moment she hit her thirteenth birthday, she lost infancy under the laws of this state if the crime was Murder, Subdivision One or Two. Ergo, she could no longer be considered a juvenile offender, and they were charging her as an adult.

Gloria's attorney told them that the laws of this city and this state specifically forbade the questioning of a juvenile offender in a police station. They reminded him again that the crime was murder, and that she was no longer a juvenile offender. They also mentioned that the intent of that particular restriction was to keep juveniles separate and apart from hardened criminals, and besides she was no longer a juvenile—for the *third* time. The attorney said the questioning was academic, anyway, since he would not allow his young client to answer any questions put to her by the police.

They were all walking on eggs here.

The girl was only thirteen years old.

They were saying she'd killed a priest by stabbing or slashing him seventeen times.

The police were in possession of what they were certain was the murder weapon, a knife with its handle and blade caked with dried blood almost certainly the priest's. Presumably, there were also fingerprints on that knife. And presumably, the fingerprints would match Gloria's. But her attorney argued that taking her fingerprints here in a police station would be tantamount to questioning her here, which would be in violation of not ony her basic rights under Miranda-Escobedo, but also in violation of the statute specifically forbidding the questioning of a person under the age of fifteen in a police station.

They told him yet another time that she had lost infancy when she'd turned thirteen, and that under Miranda-Escobedo they would *not* be taking incriminating testimony without permission if they fingerprinted or photographed Gloria, or asked her to submit to a blood or breathalyzer test, or examined her body, or put her in a lineup, because the difference between these actions and a statement in response to interrogation was simply the difference between *non-testimonial* and *testimonial* responses on the part of the prisoner. There was no question that Gloria was a prisoner. She was in custody. They were going to charge her with the crime of Murder, Subdivision One: With intent to cause the death of another, causing the death of such person.

But this was a tough one.

Nellie Brand, who'd been called in because of her familiarity with the case, couldn't do a Q and A because Gloria's attorney said he would not permit her to answer any questions. The attorney was now saying they'd had no cause to bring her in here in the *first* place, were they perchance familiar with the expression "false arrest"? Carella had already briefed Nellie on his reason for bringing in Gloria, and whereas she considered his deduction sound enough, she also recognized that absent a fingerprint match, they were treading shaky ground. Carella was using the girl's possession of the last check written by Father Michael as proof that she'd been to the church on the day of his murder. If her fingerprints were on that knife, all well and good. If not . . .

A fingerprint match was essential to their case.

And even though Nellie felt positive that they were permitted to take Gloria's fingerprints (and the Police Department's Legal Bureau concurred on this point) she didn't want to risk what appeared to be a good case by giving anybody reason to complain about a rights violation later on; these were trigger-happy times. Anyway, once they charged the girl and booked her—and they would do that downtown at Central Booking, as soon as they quit tap-dancing here—fingerprints and photographs would be taken as a matter of course, juvenile or not. So why push Miranda-Escobedo now?

The attorney would not let go of it. So they argued it back and forth, Mr. and Mrs. Keely putting in their two cents every now and

then with strident comments about what a good girl and excellent
student their daughter was, espousing Lieutenant Byrnes's "Class
Valedictorian" line of reasoning, the lawyers and detectives quoting
chapter and verse of the various applicable laws, and in the midst of
all this, as the shouting and gesticulating reached a heated climax,
Gloria suddenly said, "I killed him."

Her attorney immediately said, "Gloria, I must advise you..."
but she rolled over him like a steamroller flattening a fly. And since
neither the police nor the district attorney were required by Miranda-
Escobedo or any other law in the land to warn a person of her rights if
she was *volunteering* a statement, they stood by silently and let her
run with it.

I didn't mean to do it, she said.

I only went there to pick up the check. This was around six
o'clock or so, I went in through the garden, the gate was open, I left
it open because I figured maybe they wanted it that way, whoever'd
left it open. The rectory door was open, too, the wooden one, not the
screen door, that was closed. I opened the screen door and went right
in. I'd promised Kenny the check, Kenny Walsh, he's leader of The
Wanderers, he plays lead guitar and writes most of the songs, he said
he needed the deposit check right away if we expected him to play the
job. So I only went there to get the check.

I went into the rectory, and...

There's like this little bend before you come to the office, this sort
of little turn after you come out of the entry, and I heard the... the
voices... before... before I made the turn... the moaning... the
woman moaning... and Father Michael saying, Oh God oh God oh
God, and the woman saying Give it to me, *give* it to me, Michael!

And...

I'm not a child, you know. I know about such things. A lot of the
girls at Graham *do* these things, they *talk* about these things, I'm not
a child, I knew what they were doing even before I...

I should have turned back, I guess.

I should have left the minute I heard them.

But I . . .

I went around the . . . the turn there . . . the little bend there where
the . . . the bench is . . . that you sit on when you're waiting to see the
priest, and I . . .

I looked.

And he was . . . they were . . . her back was to me, her skirt was
up, she was holding her skirt up, she was naked under the skirt, her
panties down around her ankles, her legs apart, his hands were up
under her skirt, they were kissing, oh dear God, and she kept moaning and moving against him, they were, you know, they were, they
were making love there in his office, her long blonde hair trailing
down her back, twisting her head, moaning, and him saying I love
you, Ab, oh God how I love you, a priest! And then he he sort of of
of *slid* down her, his hands moving down the backs of her legs, and
he he got on his knees in front of her as if he was praying, and I
realized all at once what he was doing to her, and I covered my face
with my hands and ran through the sacristy into the church and prayed
to God for guidance.

I waited till she was gone. She came out through the church, I
guess she didn't want anyone to see her leaving on the rectory side. I
was still sitting in a pew near the altar. Praying. This was about half
an hour after I'd seen them, maybe forty minutes, I don't know, she
came clicking out of the sacristy on her high heels, tall and beautiful
and clicking by in a hurry, a smile on her face, she was smiling. I
watched her, I could see the line of her panties under the yellow skirt,
I turned to look up at Jesus hanging on the cross and I looked at his
sad eyes, do you know his sad eyes, I cry when I look at those eyes,
and it seemed to me he was saying I should *discuss* this with Father
Michael, ask him about it, find out what he what he why he he was
doing this, why he had *done* this.

I didn't mean to kill him.

I only wanted to ask him why he was betraying not only God but
also *me*, too, yes, because I'd trusted him, I'd thought we were
friends, I thought we could tell each other things we couldn't tell

anyone else, hadn't I said things in the confession box, hadn't I told him things I'd never told another human being on earth, not even Alexis? So that's what I planned to do. Just ask him how he could *do* such a thing. He was supposed to be a *priest* but instead he was behaving like a like a, I just wanted to *tell* him.

He was sitting in the rectory alone, behind his desk, this had to have been, I don't know, seven, a little before seven, ten to seven, something like that? He looked up when I came in, and he smiled, and said You're here for the check, am I right? Something like that. And I said Yes, Father Michael, and he gave me the check and I put it in my purse and I I I was waiting there because I didn't know how to start this, and he said Is there something, Gloria? And I said, Father Michael, I saw you and that woman. And he said, What woman, Gloria? And I said A blonde woman, Father Michael, the one who was here earlier. And he looked me in the eye and he said I don't know what you're talking about, Gloria. I said Father Michael, why are you doing this, it's a *sin*! And he looked me in the eye again and he said You must be mistaken, Gloria, please go now.

I went out of the office.

I don't know why I took the knife from the kitchen.

Mrs. Hennessy wasn't in there, I don't know where she was.

There were things cooking on the stove.

It smelled good in the kitchen.

I took the knife and . . .

And went back to the rectory to look for him, but he wasn't there.

This made me . . .

I don't know why, but it made me angry. I mean, I wasn't going to *hurt* him, so why was he *hiding* from me? And then I . . . I heard him out in the garden . . . walking out there in the garden, and I went to the rectory door, the sun was beginning to set, the sky was red like blood, and I realized he was praying and all at once the *hypocrisy* of it, his praying to God, the *lie* of it . . .

I guess I stabbed him.

I don't know how many times.

God forgive me.

Afterwards, I . . . I went . . . I had to get rid of the knife, you see. There wasn't any blood on my clothes or on my hands . . . isn't there supposed to be a lot of blood? The blood was all over his his back, all over the knife, but none of it was on me. I couldn't go out on the street with with . . .

I ran into the rectory again . . .

Mrs. Hennessy didn't see me, she was in the kitchen . . .

Everything was happening so fast . . .

I ducked into the office . . .

I pulled open the bottom file drawer, and threw the knife into the space at the back of the drawer, and then kept yanking things out of the drawer to make it look as if somebody had come there to rob the church and had killed . . .

Oh dear God.

Had killed the priest.

Oh dear God.

Had killed dear Father Michael.

Carella listened now to the numb recitation of how she'd made her way home through streets already dark, how her parents had found her in the living room reading a book when they'd got home from work, how she'd told her mother the roast was already in the oven.

Thirteen, he was thinking, she's only thirteen.

And he recognized with a heavy sadness that nighttime in this city he loved seemed to come too swiftly nowadays. And he wondered if it wasn't already too late to say vespers.

Nellie Brand was watching him. As if reading his mind and thinking exactly the same thing. Their eyes met. In the distance, there was the sound of an ambulance siren.

Marilyn Hollis was being taken to Morehouse General, where they would declare her dead on arrival.

* * *

Night had come.

The sky was black with roiling clouds. They were sitting in the little garden behind the church. They could hear the sound of an ambulance siren fading in the distance. Faraway lightning flashes crazed the sky.

"I haven't seen you in a long time," he said.

He was wearing a black cotton robe embroidered in richer black silk with pine cones that formed a phallic pattern, slit to the waist on either side to reveal his muscular legs and thighs.

"Well, there were problems," she said.

She was wearing a red leather skirt slit to the thigh. Black silk blouse carved low over her breasts. Red high-heeled shoes. Blood-red lipstick. Dangling red earrings.

"Tell me," he said.

She told him the story.

He listened thoughtfully.

Sipped at his drink and listened.

"There was a simpler way," he said at last.

"I didn't think so."

"I'd have kicked him out, see. Plain and simple."

"I didn't want you to know I had a twenty-two-year-old son."

"So you went to a Catholic priest instead."

"Yes."

"To ask him to intervene."

"Yes. Because how could I continue coming here if *Andrew* was here with his goddamn faggot boyfriend?"

"Andrew Hobbs."

"Yes."

"I never once suspected."

"That was my married name. Hobbs."

"A twenty-two-year-old son," he said.

"Yes."

"Abigail Finch has a twenty-two-year-old son," he said, and shook his head in wonder.

"Yes. So now you know I'm a hag," she said, and smiled.

"Oh yes, some hag," he said, and returned the smile.

"The point is," she said, "it backfired. And I'm truly penitent about that."

"Backfired how?"

"I didn't expect him to get on his pulpit about *Bornless*. I only wanted him to give Andrew a little heart-to-heart. Quit seeing the Devil, son, it's bad for your soul. That sort of thing."

"Yes."

"Sure. Instead, he made a federal case out of it."

"Yes."

He was silent for a moment, sipping thoughtfully at his drink. He looked up then, and said, "Maybe you should be punished, Ab. The church can punish you, you know."

"I know that, and that's entirely up to you and the deacons, Sky. I *am* penitent, though, I really am. And you know. . ."

"Yes?"

"I *did* get him to stop, I really did. When I realized what was happening, his sermons and all, I went to him and told him I'd tell all about us if he didn't quit harassing Bornless. He said it was blackmail. I told him it was for his own good. I was being sarcastic, you know. For his own good. Walking with Satan would be for his own good."

Schuyler began laughing.

"Yeah," she said, and laughed with him. "But that was what really ticked him off, my saying that, and then laughing in his face. He slapped me, the bastard, can you believe it? Five minutes earlier he was worshipping at the mound, and all at once he slapped me. Because I'd offended his beloved *Jesus,* you know, who he'd only been betraying since the first of April, fucking me six ways from Sunday. A priest, can you believe it! Some priest. I made him pay for that slap later. But he stopped the sermons, Sky. There weren't any more sermons after Easter, did you notice?"

"To tell the truth, Ab, I didn't notice the ones *before* Easter, either."

Both of them laughed.

And sipped at their drinks.

And looked up at the threatening black sky.

There was another flash of lightning.

"Rain coming," he said.

"There's another thing, too," she said. "If you're thinking of leniency."

"And what's that?"

"I really think I *accomplished* something for the church, Sky."

"How do you figure that?"

"I seduced a Catholic priest. I seduced a servant of Jesus Christ. I think that's something, Sky."

"You do, huh?"

"Something worth considering, yes. If you're thinking of forgiving me."

"I'll see."

There was more lightning, closer now. A faint roll of thunder.

"He told me he loved me," she said, and turned to look at him, a small pleased smile on her face.

"I can't blame him."

"Through love, lust. Right?"

"Vice versa, actually."

"I had him lusting for me, Sky. He'd have done anything for me. A Catholic priest, Sky. I had him panting for me. On his knees to me. Not to Jesus, Sky. To *me*."

She looked directly into his eyes.

Lightning flashed closer. There was a loud boom of thunder.

"We're going to win," she said earnestly. "Eventually, we're going to win, Sky."

"I think we've *already* won," he said softly.

It was going to rain any moment now.

He took her hand. They rose together and started back into the church just as the first huge drops began pelting the path.

"Would you care to serve as altar tomorrow night?" he asked.

"I'd be honored," she said.

Available in hardback from Heinemann

ED McBAIN

Widows

The latest 87th Precinct novel in which Detective Steve Carella and Hal Willis must solve the dual murder of an elderly man and his twenty-two-year-old lover. The dead man has left behind four other women: his ex-wife and their two daughters, and his present wife. Four mourners. Four suspects. It's a crime that strikes close to the heart of Carella, whose own mother has become a widow as a result of a senseless act of violence.

Widows is an incisive, enthralling story of cops and killers, victims and survivors. It's Ed McBain at his best.

"Each book should be treated as a contribution to a fictionalised history of modern urban police work, a collection that has evolved into our finest procedural series"   *People* magazine on the 87th Precinct novels

ED McBAIN

Downtown

The Big Bad Apple on Christmas Eve is no place for an orange grower from Florida. Especially when a blue-eyed blonde accuses him of stealing her diamond ring, a phoney detective rifles his wallet and a casual Good Samaritan makes off with his hire car.

For Michael Barnes, that is just the beginning of a nightmarish caper through the concrete jungle of downtown Manhattan. Not even Vietnam was this bad. Crazy killers, cops, actors, bimbos and million-dollar crack dealers are all out for his blood. Even the corpses can't be trusted.

But for an unexpected ally in the shape of Connie Kee, a beautiful and streetwise Chinese girl, Barnes stands next to no chance in these unfriendly precincts. He can guess the answers to every question but the one that might save his skin. Who the hell is Mama, and why does she so badly need him dead?

Downtown is a page-flashing Christmas cracker of a novel that sparkles with all the wit and tension that fans of Ed McBain have come to expect.

'McBain has a great approach, great attitude, terrific style, strong plots, excellent dialogue, sense of place and sense of reality. He's right where he belongs – at the top' Elmore Leonard

ED McBAIN

Fuzz

It's cold, February and tough on the 87th Precinct.

Fourteen muggings, three rapes, one knifing, thirty-six assorted burglaries. All in one busy week.

But there's worse to come. Some teenage kids have found new sport in setting light to the city's vagrants. And one lone operator is eliminating its dignitaries . . .

'Lively, inventive, convincing, suspenseful . . . wholly satisfactory' *New York Times*

'Splendid . . . engrossing . . . fast moving'
Sunday Times

ED McBAIN

Doll

'The best of today's procedural school of police stories' *New York Times*

Lovely fashion model Tinka Sachs died in a furious rain of knife slashes. Terrified, alone but for her doll, the child Anna heard it all from the room next door.

Scenting the trail of the murderer, Carella is astonished to find himself the prisoner of a girl who would kill a man as easily as she could seduce him – and sounds as though she has every intention of doing both . . .

'One of McBain's very best' *Observer*

A Selected List of Fiction Available from Mandarin

While every effort is made to keep prices low, it is sometimes necessary to increase prices at short notice. Mandarin Paperbacks reserves the right to show new retail prices on covers which may differ from those previously advertised in the text or elsewhere.

The prices shown below were correct at the time of going to press.

☐	7493 0003 5	**Mirage**	James Follett	£3.99
☐	7493 0134 1	**To Kill a Mockingbird**	Harper Lee	£2.99
☐	7493 0076 0	**The Crystal Contract**	Julian Rathbone	£3.99
☐	7493 0145 7	**Talking Oscars**	Simon Williams	£3.50
☐	7493 0118 X	**The Wire**	Nik Gowing	£3.99
☐	7493 0121 X	**Under Cover of Daylight**	James Hall	£3.50
☐	7493 0020 5	**Pratt of the Argus**	David Nobbs	£3.99
☐	7493 0097 3	**Second from Last in the Sack Race**	David Nobbs	£3.50

All these books are available at your bookshop or newsagent, or can be ordered direct from the publisher. Just tick the titles you want and fill in the form below.

Mandarin Paperbacks, Cash Sales Department, PO Box 11, Falmouth, Cornwall TR10 9EN.

Please send cheque or postal order, no currency, for purchase price quoted and allow the following for postage and packing:

UK	80p for the first book, 20p for each additional book ordered to a maximum charge of £2.00.
BFPO	80p for the first book, 20p for each additional book.
Overseas including Eire	£1.50 for the first book, £1.00 for the second and 30p for each additional book thereafter.

NAME (Block letters) ....

ADDRESS ....

....

....